Cord Way

He was the closest thing to a black sheep that the Way family had ever had. But in Montana, he discovered what it really meant to be a man—and came home to turn Waysboro upside down. . . .

Ashlynne Monroe

She was used to being called trash—and worse. But she would never let the ruling class of Waysboro destroy her spirit the way it had destroyed her sister. . . .

Kendra Monroe

She didn't want to challenge the world. She just wanted to be on top of it . . . and she'd try just about anything to make her dream come true.

Wyatt Way

His family had a plan for him—and it didn't leave room for mistakes. Wyatt was used to doing things properly. But propriety is no match for temptation. . . .

Ethan Thorpe

A land developer—and a newcomer to Waysboro—his cold, logical business decisions hid a shocking quest for vengeance.

WICKED GAMES

"MS. BOSWELL HAS MORE THAN EARNED HER LAURELS as one of series romance's most popular authors."　　　　　—*Rave Reviews*

WICKED GAMES

BARBARA BOSWELL

JOVE BOOKS, NEW YORK

WICKED GAMES

A Jove Book / published by arrangement with
the author

PRINTING HISTORY
Jove edition / November 1994

ISBN: 0-515-11487-1

A JOVE BOOK®
Jove Books are published by The Berkley Publishing Group,
200 Madison Avenue, New York, New York 10016.
JOVE and the "J" design are trademarks
belonging to Jove Publications, Inc.

PRINTED IN THE UNITED STATES OF AMERICA

10 9 8 7 6 5 4 3 2 1

PROLOGUE

SHE had to tell him tonight.

Ashlynne Monroe stood behind the trunk of one of the towering oak trees that lined the bank of the Seneca Creek River. The darkness of the night and thickness of the tree trunk kept her hidden from the patrons who were swaggering into the nearby Waterside Bar. Though it was Sunday, there was no dearth of business at Waysboro's most notorious bar. There never was. The Waterside Bar was open every single night of the year, including Christmas, and every single night, its loyal clientele arrived for an evening of drinking, fighting, and the occasional scrape with the law.

From her hiding place behind the tree, Ashlynne listened to the loud music blasting from the jukebox. She knew that the shouts, hoots, and hollers that were muffled out here constituted a roaring din inside. She couldn't believe she was really here; she'd always avoided this place as assiduously as its patrons sought it.

But here she was, and she didn't dare leave. Not until she told Cord Way what he had every right to know. Even if he didn't want to know it.

A fight spilled out of the bar into the parking lot, and Ashlynne watched the group of men pound each other with their fists and their feet as they rolled around on the ground. She supposed it was uncharitable of her to hope that they might roll down the bank, right into the swift-moving waters of the river. An abrupt cold-water dousing would certainly bring them to their senses, at least temporarily. But the fools were so drunk, they'd probably drown and then she would have to come forward as a material witness.

Ashlynne nixed that idea then and there. When it came to things like drunken fights and places like the Waterside

Bar, it was wise to remain anonymous. It was certainly the wisest course for a Monroe to take in this town.

Eventually, the fight broke up and as she'd heard no splashes, and not a single ambulance or police car had arrived on the scene, she assumed it had been merely a minor scuffle. Oh well, it was only ten o'clock.

Where was Cord? She was nervous and restless and had to resist the urge to pace along the bank of the river. She didn't dare. It wouldn't do for her to be seen by the men hanging around the Waterside Bar. They would assume that she was like the other women who patronized the Waterside, women who didn't mind being pawed or groped by the hard-drinking, brawling male customers. If she were recognized as a Monroe, they would assume she'd enjoy it.

Ashlynne shuddered and remained still behind the tree trunk. Cord had to come, *he had to*! He was practically a regular, though she couldn't understand why. He was slumming, she supposed. A spoiled rich guy getting his kicks by hanging out with the have-nots. It was insulting, but she could think of no other reasonable explanation.

Unfortunately, it also explained his secret relationship with her sister.

A surge of bile burned her throat. Fraternization between military officers and enlisted personnel would be approved before it would be considered acceptable for a Way to consort with a Monroe. It was Waysboro's strictest taboo. A Way wasn't even supposed to acknowledge a Monroe's existence, let alone—

The sound of flying gravel and screeching brakes drew her attention to the bright red Ferrari that had just pulled into the parking lot. Ashlynne's heart began to thud against her ribs. He was here.

Her knees were suddenly so shaky, she wasn't sure she could walk the short distance from her hiding place to Cord Way's Ferrari. She felt light-headed and gulped in several deep breaths of air before she dared to leave the safety of the tree.

Cord climbed out of his car and paused to light a cigarette. Ashlynne approached him stealthily, her gaze fixed on him.

Every time she saw him, she was struck by his incredible good looks. His dark eyes were alert with intelligence and intensity, a most arresting feature in a face composed of attractive masculine features. Walking toward him, Ashlynne took thorough inventory of them all.

He had a straight nose and a strong jaw; his mouth was well shaped, his lips frankly sensual. His hair was thick and poker straight and worn disreputably long for Waysboro, where conservatively clipped hair was the style of choice for males of all ages. Even the male Monroes preferred the shorn-locks look, although they carried it to the extreme, either shaving their heads or having their initials and other graffiti razored into their buzz cuts.

But Cord's hair was long enough to pull back into a small ponytail, which he'd done tonight. The color was dark brown, so dark it was almost black, and it was the same shade as his eyes. Matching eye and hair color—an unusual, intriguing gift of nature. It didn't surprise Ashlynne that Cord Way would possess such a trait; it was just one of the many gifts nature had bestowed upon him. He was smart, handsome, and rich, the third son in the powerful, aristocratic Way family. If there was a single one of life's blessings that Cord Way hadn't been given, Ashlynne couldn't think of it.

And yet here he was, at the Waterside Bar, run by those troublemaking hellions themselves, the Monroe clan. Ashlynne knew she would be counted among their number, and the realization never ceased to sting. She tried so hard to be respectable and responsible, but her efforts counted for nothing; the collective Monroe reputation had been in shreds for generations.

A surge of anger swept through her, reviving her fast-fading courage. Without it, she would've never had the nerve to deliver her bombshell to Cord Way.

"I have to talk to you." Ashlynne stood before him, her voice low and urgent. "It's very important."

Cord glanced up at her, then took a deep drag on his cigarette. "Sorry, honey, I'm not buying any beer for any high school drinking parties. Find yourself another stooge."

Ashlynne stared at him. "I'm not in high school!" she

said indignantly. "I graduated two years ago," she added. She was proud of her achievement. A diploma with the name Monroe on it wasn't commonplace in Waysboro.

Cord shrugged, unimpressed. "Well, you're still underage and I'm still not buying you any booze."

"I don't want you to! Don't you know who I am?" she blurted out. Obviously, he didn't. Ashlynne's face burned.

She had thought they were friends. They'd talked and laughed together a number of times these past few weeks while he waited for her older sister Rayleen, his current girlfriend, to show up. Cord was so different from the men Rayleen usually spent her time with; Ashlynne made it a point to keep her distance from that unsavory crew. But from the moment Rayleen had introduced her to Cord Way, Ashlynne had been drawn to him. Strictly as a friend, of course. She would never dream of trying to encroach on her sister's territory, not that she would've ever had a chance with Cord Way. Even if she'd wanted one.

Certainly, that truth had been proven tonight. He couldn't even recall their friendship! She felt foolish and more than a little hurt that he knew her only in the context of Rayleen. Otherwise, she didn't exist.

Cord peered more closely at her face, then reached over and pulled her Orioles baseball cap off her head. Her hair was French-braided and lay flat against her skull. In the darkness, the honey-blond color was indistinct.

His gaze slid over her in a lazy inspection, taking in her big wide-set blue eyes with light brown brows and lashes, stubborn little chin, and cute upturned nose. She wore no makeup at all, but she was pretty enough not to have to. Her mouth was sensuously wide and generous, though currently her lips were tightened by a frown. Taken individually feature by feature, she was not a classic beauty, but she was a girl who would definitely rate a second glance. And a third.

Still, she looked very young and very wholesome. And though he prided himself on his risk-taking, fooling around with jailbait was not his game. Why bother when there were so many women of legal age who made no secret of their desire to be with him?

"You don't remember me at all, do you?" Ashlynne accused.

Cord exhaled an impatient sigh. "So who are you?"

Ashlynne sniffed the unmistakable odor of alcohol. "You've been drinking!"

"You have a remarkable grasp of the obvious." She noticed that his voice was slightly slurred. "Now get lost, little girl. I'm going inside."

"You're on the verge of being drunk, and you intend to get even drunker, I suppose."

"You suppose right. G'night." He started toward the bar.

"Just a minute! I'm not finished talking to you, Cord Way."

He stopped in his tracks and turned to stare at her. "You know me?"

Ashlynne resisted the urge to smack him. "Yes, I know you. Unfortunately. I wish I didn't." She glared from him to his car. "Why did you drive out here when you'd been drinking? Why didn't you have one of your Way lackeys chauffeur you? What if you'd hit some poor innocent driver? Or—or a pedestrian?"

"Or what if I'd driven up on the sidewalk and crashed into a store?" Cord suggested, laughing. "I heard a Monroe kid plowed right through the window of Susie's Stationary Shoppe and kept on going till he was felled by a wall of birthday cards."

"It's not funny!" Ashlynne cringed. He was talking about her cousin Ronnie Joe, who was both stupid and alcoholic, an unfortunate combination in anyone, but a disastrous one for a Monroe. Naturally, every Monroe in town had to share the scorn of Ronnie Joe's witless nighttime ride.

Cord, however, seemed to find Ronnie Joe's adventure highly amusing. "The poor idiot wrecked the car and demolished the shop but he emerged completely unscathed. Thankfully, it was three in the morning and nobody else was around. Those Monroes have nine lives, just like cats."

Ashlynne visualized the teeming Monroe family plot at Waysboro cemetery, filled with those Monroes who definitely had but one life to live. It was a far cry from the grandly baronial Way section at the opposite end of the graveyard, which was not nearly as crowded. Death was not the great equalizer, not in Waysboro.

"Monroes don't have long life spans," she countered acidly. "Unlike you privileged Ways who live to ripe old age, we cheap white trash multiply early and then die off young. Kind of like rats, I guess."

Her derisive self-reference finally jogged his memory. She saw the recognition in his eyes as he stared at her.

"You're a Monroe." His dark eyes narrowed and he studied her intently. "You're Rayleen's sister."

"Yes, I'm Rayleen's sister," she snapped. A slow heat suffused her body, turning her cheeks a deep pink. Rayleen's eminently forgettable younger sister.

"Ashlynne." Cord moved closer, leaning toward her so their bodies were almost touching. "Pretty little Ashlynne."

Ashlynne instinctively backed away. He was about six feet two, maybe even an inch taller, and his hard muscular body, encased in faded jeans and a plain white T-shirt, looked very strong. A tall, slender but strong five feet seven herself, Ashlynne wasn't used to having men tower over her.

It felt as if Cord were doing exactly that, towering over her to intimidate her. She fought the urge to turn and run.

Cord took her arm. "C'mon, honey, let's go inside. I'll buy you a drink."

"I don't want you to buy me a drink!" Naturally, he had forgotten she'd told him that she didn't drink and that she would never set foot inside the Waterside Bar.

But this didn't seem to be the time to remind him of anything, not with that intent gleam glittering in his dark eyes. Ashlynne wrenched her arm from his grasp. "Cord, I came here because I have something important to—"

"I have something important to tell you too," Cord cut in. "I'm leaving Waysboro."

His pronouncement sent her reeling. Ashlynne stared at him in shocked silence.

"Will you miss me?" he teased.

"You're leaving town? For—for how long?"

"For good," Cord said decisively. "I'm never coming back."

"Are you really leaving?" Ashlynne demanded. "Or are you just saying that because you don't want to—" She paused to take a deep, steadying breath. "Because you've decided that it's all over between you and Rayleen."

"My reasons for leaving Waysboro have nothing to do with your sister." He seemed surprised that she would even consider such an outlandish possibility. "Anyway, how can something that never existed be over? Rayleen and I had some good times but—"

"Good times?" Ashlynne flared. So he'd trivialized Rayleen to merely a good time? Well, she should've expected it; Rayleen had even told her so.

"Damn good times." Cord grinned rakishly. "But I'm not about to make them into anything more than what they actually were. And yes, I'm really leaving Waysboro. I'm not coming back."

Her throat was dry. He was determined to leave town, and he'd made it painfully clear that Rayleen meant nothing to him. Ashlynne's shoulders drooped and she stared dispiritedly at the ground. Confronting Cord had been her only hope, and now she mocked herself for her naïveté. She had been a fool to think that Cord Way was the kind of man who wouldn't turn his back on a woman carrying his child.

"So what did you want to tell me?" Cord asked amiably.

And why wouldn't he be amiable? Ashlynne thought bitterly. He was doing exactly what he wanted to do, as usual. There was no one or nothing to stand in his way.

"Good-bye." She said the word with a cold finality. "I'm here to tell you good-bye."

He didn't question her, didn't seem to realize that since she hadn't learned of his plans to leave until this moment, she was lying.

"I should've left a long time ago," Cord was saying. "I realize that now. I'm not sure where I'm going or what I'll do, but I have to get away from Waysboro."

"I've been saying the same thing for years," Ashlynne said flatly.

But thanks to Cord Way, her departure would be post-poned once again. He could leave a pregnant Rayleen, but Ashlynne knew she never could—or would. Anxiety surged through her. Maybe she never would leave! She would die here and be dumped in the Monroe family plot with all the others who'd never made it out.

She turned away without another word and walked toward the riverbank. Cord headed into the Waterside Bar.

Neither looked back.

Ashlynne walked along the river, following the path to the road leading to Waterside Lane. A picturesque name for an ugly street, filled with dilapidated old buildings housing the cheapest apartments in Lower Lyme Hill, Waysboro's most disreputable neighborhood.

She trudged up three flights of stairs to her family's apartment. The door was opened before she had a chance to pull out her key. Her pretty twelve-year-old sister Kendra was clutching a red-faced, screaming baby.

"She started crying right after you left, Ashlynne," Kendra said worriedly. "I think that tooth coming in back is really bothering her. Or else she missed you."

"Poor little Maxie." Ashlynne took the baby from her younger sister. "Where's Rayleen?"

"Watching TV." Kendra's wide dark blue eyes spoke volumes as they met Ashlynne's.

"Thanks for taking care of the baby, Kendra. You go on to bed now." Ashlynne carried Maxie into the tiny living room where Rayleen lay curled up on the worn old sofa. Rayleen didn't glance at her firstborn.

"I saw Cord Way tonight," Ashlynne said, sitting down beside her sister. The baby was whimpering now, her small body quivering. Ashlynne rocked her gently in her arms.

Rayleen didn't take her eyes from the TV screen. "Let me guess what happened. He told you it's not his problem and then he made some threats. Exactly what happened when I tried to tell Max about Maxie." She sighed. "I told you not to tell him, Ash."

"I didn't tell him anything, Rayleen. Cord said he was leaving town. It seemed hopeless to say anything after that."

Rayleen shrugged. "It's better this way, Ashlynne. It really is."

"Better for him, certainly. But it's going to be a whole lot harder for us, Rayleen. We're barely scraping by as it is and now we—"

Rayleen reached over and patted Ashlynne's arm. "We're still better off with the Ways not knowing, Ashlynne. Can you imagine what they would do to us if they found out? They could arrange to have Kendra and Maxie taken away—and this little unborn baby too." She patted her still-flat stomach protectively. "The Ways own this town, Ash."

Ashlynne's heart lurched. Her sister was right, of course. Whatever Rayleen's weaknesses, she did possess one vital strength—the ability to see things as they really were, untainted by such concepts as justice and hope, which Ashlynne frequently, foolishly succumbed to. It was her sense of unfounded optimism that had sent her to find Cord Way tonight, expecting him to do the decent thing once he'd heard the news.

Sitting beside her sister, the dozing baby in her arms, Ashlynne realized just how hopelessly naïve she had been, like a child blithely dropping a letter to Santa Claus into the mailbox and expecting it to reach the North Pole. Of course the Ways were a threat!

"I think Mama was looking down from heaven on us, protecting us by getting Cord Way out of town before you could tell him anything," Rayleen said. "It's for the best, Ashlynne."

"Maybe. But I hate him, Rayleen." Her young voice quavered. She felt duped and disillusioned by her own idiotic belief in Cord Way. She would not ever be so foolish again. "I hope he has a miserable life wherever he goes. I hope he's unhappy and alone till the day he dies."

Rayleen tore open a bag of sandwich cookies and helped herself to a few. "He's not a bad guy, Ashlynne. Don't blame him. We all play wicked games."

Ashlynne's blue eyes blazed. "Then it's time we either quit playing or start winning."

CHAPTER ONE

Six years later

"MORNINGS around here are like prison riots," observed Kendra Monroe as she watched her two small nieces, six-and-a-half-year-old Maxie and five-year-old Daisy race around the kitchen. Ashlynne was right behind them, stuffing papers into bookbags and food into lunch boxes. "All the noise, chaos, and confusion," Kendra continued.

Maxie accidentally dropped a full glass of milk on the floor and the liquid splattered everywhere. Without breaking her stride, Ashlynne seized a sponge and began to wipe up the milk, but not before Daisy skidded through it. The little girl lost her balance and grabbed a chair for support, overturning it in the process.

"Not to mention destruction," added Kendra, affecting a world-weary sigh as she righted the chair. She was a senior in high school, due to graduate in a few weeks. She dreamed of a day in the not too distant future with serene mornings on a sunny patio having breakfast served to her by a uniformed maid.

"Not to mention destruction," Ashlynne agreed, slipping a toaster waffle into Maxie's hand. She could tell by the faraway look in Kendra's eyes that her younger sister was having her breakfast-on-the-patio fantasy again. Kendra's fantasies of unbridled wealth amused her—except when they alarmed her.

"Mommy, don't forget, it's Maxie's show-and-tell day today," Daisy said, around a mouthful of her own blueberry-flavored waffle.

Both Ashlynne and Kendra groaned aloud.

"Show and tell *again*?" complained Kendra. "She's shown and told about almost everything we own!"

"Show and tell is stupid," grumbled Maxie.

"But you have to bring something!" Daisy exclaimed worriedly. She took her sister's first-grade assignments as seriously as she took her own kindergarten duties. "Mommy, help!"

Ashlynne looked at Daisy, her gaze flicking over the child's straight dark hair cut in a chin-length bob with thick bangs across her forehead. The little girl's eyes were dark brown, almost black, and almost always thoughtful and serious. Daisy was a highly intelligent child, the youngest in her class, a kindergartner who'd taught herself to read and was already doing math sheets that first-grader Maxie couldn't yet comprehend.

"Mommy, find something for Maxie to bring." Daisy's tone was both a plea and an order.

"Daisy, you are so obsessive!" Kendra shook her head, her expression a mixture of exasperation and affection.

"Daisy is conscientious," Ashlynne amended kindly. She knew that Daisy was storing the new words away and would know the meanings of both before she went to bed tonight. "Here, Maxie, take this to school." She pulled an object from a drawer.

Maxie stared at it. "What is it?"

"It's a potato masher," Ashlynne told her. "And we have to leave right now or you'll miss the bus."

Maxie shoved the utensil into her bookbag.

"A potato masher?" Daisy frowned. "That's not very interesting, Mom."

"What could be more fascinating to the first grade than mashing potatoes?" Kendra teased, hustling Maxie out the door.

Ashlynne followed with Daisy. She glanced at her watch, congratulating herself. It was eight-fifteen, and they were on time. Another morning rush successfully completed. And with considerably less chaos than a prison riot.

The business district of Waysboro, Maryland, was built around three sides of the town square with a wooded, grassy park in the center. A concave shell bandstand stood at one end of the park and a statue of Captain Henry Stafford

Way, the town's designated Civil War hero, kept watch at the other end.

During the day senior citizens claimed the park benches to feed the squirrels and watch as people went about their business in the shops, doctors' offices, and bank surrounding the square. After dark, especially on weekends, teenagers congregated in the interior of the park. If they grew too raucous, a police officer walking the beat would disperse them.

Directly in the middle of Main Avenue, between Waysboro Drugstore and The Needlepoint Shoppe, was a newly refurbished office building whose ultramodern style stood in jarring contrast to the Victorian-era buildings along the square. It was the office of Ethan Thorpe, a land developer who'd arrived unheralded in Waysboro three years ago. He had quickly won the zoning board's permission to build a sizable development of moderately priced condominiums on the tract of land bordering the grassy open fields known as Way's Run.

No one knew how he'd pulled this off. The leading citizens were shocked and outraged by the influx of "new people" who professed not to mind the sixty-mile commute into D.C.

"They're streaming into Waysboro like a swarm of refugees," wailed one of the older Way cousins as the priced-to-sell units were quickly snapped up.

"The social fabric of the entire town will be destroyed," protested a distressed friend and neighbor of the Ways.

Having become downright notorious, Ethan Thorpe proceeded to add insult to injury by hiring a Monroe as his secretary/receptionist. That Monroe was Ashlynne, who'd been thrilled to give up her low-paying job as the night-shift desk clerk at the Waysboro Hotel, where she'd met Ethan Thorpe when he was a guest. She had been working for him since, all the while planning her family's future exodus from Waysboro.

Buying and remodeling the office on Main Avenue had been Thorpe's pet project last year, and the high-end Waysboro natives were infuriated by the eye-popping, modernistic design, which clashed violently with the rest of the town square. Ashlynne knew this had been Thorpe's precise intention.

Privately, Ashlynne wondered about her boss's agenda, though she never dared to ask him. Ethan Thorpe was a mystery, but a Teflon one. Rumors and accusations might swirl around him but nothing ever seemed to stick.

She was in the office, gulping a cup of strong black coffee and grateful for its bolstering caffeine jolt, when Thorpe strode briskly through the door. In addition to his sleek leather attaché case, he carried a small paper bag that she knew contained two chocolate donuts. He purchased the same breakfast every morning at Letty's Coffee Shop.

Ashlynne handed him a mug of coffee, black with one teaspoon of nondairy creamer, just as she had every day for the past three years. Ethan had told her how he liked his coffee on the morning he had hired her and he'd only had to tell her once. Ever since then, he'd had his coffee waiting for him when he arrived.

"How does lunch at the Waysboro Hotel sound to you?" Ethan asked nonchalantly, biting into a donut. "I thought we would head over there today around noon."

"We?" Ashlynne stared at him, bewildered.

"We—as in you and I. I assume you don't have any other plans?" There was a hint of sarcasm in Ethan's tone. He knew she brought her lunch in a brown bag and ate it at her desk every day.

"You're taking me to lunch at the Waysboro Hotel?" Ashlynne was incredulous.

"Is that so difficult to comprehend?" Ethan smiled, but as usual, his smile did not reach his cold gray eyes. When Ashlynne had first met him, she'd been unnerved by those icy penetrating eyes of his. She no longer was. Though she had seen the hard, intimidating side Thorpe showed his adversaries, he had never been anything but polite—even generous—to her. Whatever Ethan Thorpe's quarrel with the world—and Ashlynne was certain he had one—she knew it didn't involve her.

But that didn't mean she and her boss were confidants. Thorpe knew a few basic facts about her life and she knew certain details of his: he was unmarried and childless. But that was as far as it went. Their smooth working relationship had never crossed the line into friendship.

"Don't I owe you a lunch or something for Secretary's Day?" Ethan said, further confounding her. This was the first time since she'd been in his employ that he had ever mentioned Secretary's Day.

"That was months ago. Not that I've been keeping track," Ashlynne hastened to add.

"I have been remiss, haven't I?" Ethan laughed. "Well, then, lunch it is! I take it you don't mind walking to the hotel?"

The hotel was a mere five-minute walk away. Ashlynne shook her head, bemused. Ethan's peculiar joviality was unsettling; it was as if Dracula were attempting to masquerade as Santa Claus. At the very least, one couldn't help but wonder why.

Ethan went into his own interior office where he would communicate with her by intercom, if need be. The morning passed quickly and uneventfully, and Ashlynne was feeling vague hunger pangs when Ethan reappeared at her desk.

"Ready to go?"

She wondered if she was imagining that unholy gleam in his eye. Reluctantly, she walked with him to the hotel wishing she were back at her desk with her brown-bag lunch.

Since Ashlynne was familiar with the Waysboro Hotel, she automatically cast a glance toward the lobby corner where a board announced the events being held that day.

The name Wyatt Way at the top of the board sent a frisson of apprehension through her. The name Way always disconcerted her, and Wyatt was Cord's younger brother, sort of a double whammy. She quickly looked away, her eyes colliding with Ethan's. It seemed that he had read the board too.

"A fund-raising lunch for Wyatt Way." Ethan's gray eyes were as cold as a winter sky. "I wonder how much they're charging per plate? Can one possibly put a price on the honor of dining with an exalted Way?"

Ashlynne managed a nervous smile. She always avoided the Ways as a topic of conversation, but Ethan was more direct. He was not a fan of the Way family. In fact, he was the major backer of the candidate running against Wyatt Way for the congressional seat. That rival candidate, Dan Clarkston, was launching a surprisingly successful drive.

"Shall we spy upon the opposition?" Ethan suggested with an evil smile.

"No!" Ashlynne exclaimed.

Ethan merely laughed. "Oh, come on, Ashlynne, just one quick look. We can see how many loyal supporters are willing to cough up two hundred and fifty bucks a plate to support dull young Wyatt. And we'll catch a glimpse of the family too. I expect Wyatt's mother, the Empress Camilla herself, will be there."

Two hundred fifty dollars a plate. The words raced through Ashlynne's mind. This was no casual spur-of-the-moment impulse of Ethan's. He'd known the Wyatt Way luncheon was scheduled, he'd known the cost! And for some reason, Thorpe deemed her presence at the hotel necessary.

Hopefully not to poison the food? Ashlynne tried a little black humor to ease her increasing anxiety as Ethan took her arm and propelled her to the door of the grand ballroom.

No one stopped them from slipping inside.

At the head table, ancient Archer Way, the district's current congressman, dozed as his grandnephew Wyatt Tyndall Way, the thirty-year-old new candidate for the job, delivered a less-than-rousing speech.

"Hardly Standing Room Only, hmm?" Ethan murmured, looking pleased at the number of empty seats at too many empty tables. "And by the looks of things, young Way's speech has put the poor old congressman into a coma. Level three, I'd guess."

"The rest of the crowd look bored too," Ashlynne remarked, glancing around at the fidgeting patrons. She'd seen Dan Clarkston deliver a speech and compared the wildly enthusiastic response he drew to this glazed-eye crowd. The voters might choose dynamic Dan over the charisma-impaired Wyatt Way in the November election.

It was almost unimaginable. A Way not serving in Congress? A Way failing? She felt a guilty pleasure at the thought.

And then her smile froze on her face and her breath seemed to become trapped in her throat. For at the right end of the head table, his eyes dutifully on his brother, was Cord Way himself!

A small gasp escaped from her lips. *Cord Way was back?* Fear pulsed through her, building and growing until it eclipsed everything else. The return of Cord Way was a development so horrifying she hadn't allowed herself to even consider it for the past six years.

She stared at Cord from across the length of the ballroom. Her heart was thundering in her ears, her throat felt dry. Though he was seated, she could see his striped oxford-cloth shirt, suit coat, and conservative tie. His hair was short now, and he was even wearing a pair of glasses. His un-Way-like ponytail had been abandoned, gone the way of his tight jeans and T-shirts.

The image of the way he'd looked the night he had told her he was leaving Waysboro flashed vividly before her mind's eye, superimposing itself on this new up-to-the-minute version of Cord Way.

Ashlynne was horrified. It was like conjuring up the devil and having him appear in an altered form. A more powerful-looking form. "Let's get out of here," she whispered hoarsely to Ethan.

He didn't seem to hear. He stood rooted to the spot, staring at the other end of the head table. Ashlynne's eyes followed his. "That's Camilla Way, Wyatt's mother," she murmured. "And her daughter Holly."

"Holly," Ethan repeated.

"She's Stafford and Cord and Wyatt's sister. Old Dayland Way's only granddaughter." Ashlynne's eyes flicked compulsively back to Cord as she recited the basic facts known to all longtime Waysboro natives. She knew she was babbling but couldn't seem to stop. "Neither Holly nor Cord live in Waysboro anymore, which is pretty radical behavior for a Way. Sort of like the Queen of England deciding to live in Brazil."

Wyatt finished his speech and sat down. There was polite but lackluster applause from the crowd but it became considerably heartier when Camilla Way herself rose from her seat and made her way to the dais.

Ashlynne looked at Cord's mother, so classy and impeccably groomed, still radiating beauty at sixty-something. Camilla was Daisy's grandmother, her only living grandmother, the grandmother she would never know. Ashlynne felt a shard of pain tear at her heart. The Ways would be appalled by their small Monroe connection; Camilla Way would probably prefer to be related to an extraterrestrial.

It was suddenly all too much. "It's too hot in here," Ashlynne murmured, edging toward the door. "I'm getting a headache. I—I'm leaving." Oh, her head was throbbing, all right. The sight of Cord Way was more than enough to induce a migraine.

She didn't wait for Ethan. She fled from the ballroom, her face flushed, her stomach churning. She remembered that there was a water fountain along a winding corridor to the left and quickly dashed off to find it.

When she did, she took a long drink then splashed water on her face. The icy cold restored her common sense. She launched into one of her pep talks to bolster herself. So Cord was in town—so what? He couldn't be here for long. Hadn't she heard that he owned some big resort out West? Had he not stated unequivocally that he intended to remain there? As far as she knew, this was the first time he'd been back to Waysboro in the past six years, and it was unlikely that he would look up Rayleen for old time's sake. And he wasn't dressed for the Waterside bar. He would go away soon, without ever seeing or learning about Daisy. All she had to do was to keep out of his way, which should be easy. It wasn't as if the paths of a Monroe and a Way crossed naturally.

Feeling a little calmer, Ashlynne raised her head from the fountain and straightened. And found herself face-to-face with Cord Way.

Ashlynne gasped. Water still dripping from her face, she reacted with sheer primal instinct and rushed off.

"Wait!"

She heard Cord's voice and hurried into a freight elevator farther down the corridor. She punched the buttons randomly and the doors began to close. But not fast enough. Cord caught the doors between his hands, forcing them apart, then quickly stepped inside the car.

"Rayleen?" he murmured, looking down at the panicked woman. He'd always thought fondly of Rayleen Monroe, that good-time girl with a wild streak combining sex and fun. "Why did you run away?" For just a second, he wondered if this was one of her crazy games. But the young woman's grim expression did not appear at all playful.

She dabbed her face with the sleeve of her prim white and blue blouse. "I'm not Rayleen," she said tersely. She did not look at him.

Cord realized his mistake. He knew her now—this was Rayleen's younger sister. He'd often chatted with her while waiting for the perennially tardy Rayleen to appear for their trysts. He searched his brain for her name and was surprised that he actually came up with it.

"You're Ashlynne, of course. Forgive the mistaken identity, but you do look like your sister." He remembered Rayleen as a beautiful woman and it appeared that her younger sister had developed into one as well.

"The Monroes do have looks," he remembered his sister Holly stating succinctly six years ago when she'd discovered his secret affair with a Monroe. *"Unfortunately, they possess neither brains nor consciences, so for God's sake proceed with caution."*

No one but Holly had known about his relationship with a Monroe—except this young woman who stood here glowering at him. Rayleen's younger sister Ashlynne.

"Why did you follow me?" Ashlynne demanded, sounding far more forceful than she felt. She couldn't believe that Cord Way himself was standing before her, tall and tanned and muscular, his hair and eyes as dark as she remembered. He must have taken off his glasses when he left the auditorium. His elegant, well-cut light brown suit probably cost more than she earned in a month.

"Well, I—" Cord paused, considering his answer. "Pure male instinct," he said with a grin. "When a beautiful woman runs, any red-blooded man is hell-bent on following."

Ashlynne rolled her eyes disdainfully. "If that's supposed to be a compliment, I'm not complimented. And if you were trying to be amusing, I'm not amused."

"None of the above." Cord smiled at her. "It was a heartfelt statement of fact."

Ashlynne heaved a sigh and punched another button on the panel. "Maybe Rayleen liked to listen to your slick lines, but I think they're as phony and sleazy as a—a—" She paused, searching her brain for the quintessential symbol of phony sleaze. Unfortunately, she was too frazzled to come up with any example at all.

Desperately, she hit the buttons again. "Why is this stupid car taking so long? We should be on another floor by now."

As if in response, the elevator lurched to a sudden halt.

"We're midway between floors now," Cord remarked.

"What? Oh, no!" Ashlynne began to frantically push all the buttons, including the red emergency one. It set off an earsplitting alarm but there was still no motion.

"It seems like something of a cliché, but we're trapped," Cord remarked dryly.

She was trapped in an elevator with Cord Way? Panic surged through her. Ashlynne began to pound the doors of the elevator. "Help! We're stuck! Get us out of here!"

The doors remained sealed. Cord calmly stopped the clanging emergency alarm by resetting the red button and then picked up the phone in the control panel.

"This is Cord Way speaking. Yes, I see," he said into the phone. "Yes, I understand. Well, please hurry."

Ashlynne tried to interpret his frown. "What happened? How soon before we can get out of here?"

"There was some kind of electrical mishap," Cord said slowly. His frown deepened. "The power to the ballroom has been cut off and this elevator happens to be on that same circuit. They're working on it now."

"The ballroom? That's where the fund-raiser is being held." Ashlynne thought of Ethan Thorpe and tried to fight the disloyal but insistent hunch that he was somehow involved. Oh, not that he'd personally tripped up the wiring but that he had encouraged someone else to do it. Perhaps monetarily encouraged. And that he'd brought her along as a cover, so that his presence here looked entirely innocent.

"There is no natural light in that place," Cord said grimly. "It'll be as dark as a tomb and we won't be able to show the film on Wyatt and his campaign either." He groaned. "Poor Wyatt, this was supposed to be a big day for him."

Ashlynne made no reply. After all, it was entirely possible that the electrical mishap had occurred due to faulty wiring, and that Ethan Thorpe really did want to bring her to lunch here to make up for missing Secretary's Day.

"I just want to get out of here!" she exclaimed. She was backed into a corner, as far from Cord as she could get. Which wasn't very far, given the small dimensions of the elevator. She delved into her purse and pulled out her key ring, which had a miniature flashlight attached. She switched it on, providing a reassuring spot of light.

"You're not going to go claustrophobic on me and pitch a hysterical fit, are you?" Cord asked lightly, his eyes sweeping over her.

The physical differences between her and Rayleen were more apparent under closer scrutiny. Ashlynne was tall and slender, almost angular, while Rayleen had been several inches shorter, her figure round and curvy and a bit overweight, which gave her a luscious aura of sexual ripeness.

Ashlynne wore no makeup, none at all, whereas he'd never seen Rayleen without plenty of it. And to say that their tastes in clothing differed drastically was an understatement indeed.

Ashlynne was wearing a pleated blue skirt and a buttoned-to-the-neck blue and white blouse with elbow-length sleeves and round collar. She looked demure to the point of prim. He remembered Rayleen favoring tight, skimpy neon-bright outfits that invariably clung to her ample curves.

Their choices in footwear were similarly diverse. What man could forget Rayleen's sexy strappy sandals with those pointed spike heels? Ashlynne's shoes were forgettably plain, dark blue pumps with a thick half-inch heel. A nun could respectably wear such a style, and probably did.

Ashlynne was excruciatingly aware of his scrutiny. She felt a peculiar tightness in her chest that spread to her belly, alerting every nerve ending. Fear, she decided. Loathing.

"I've never pitched a hysterical fit in my life," she said coldly. "But if I ever wanted to start, this would be the time for it."

"I'd appreciate your restraint." Cord slumped against the elevator wall. There was nothing else to do so he stared at Ashlynne, his gaze taking in her thick mane of blond hair that flowed around her shoulders, the stubborn set of her jaw. She was ignoring him so completely that he might as well have been invisible. Her oh-so-obvious dislike fueled the ornery streak in him.

"It's been a long time since I've been in town," he said in a blithe tone intended to raise her ire.

It did. "Not long enough," Ashlynne shot back.

Cord laughed. "I knew you were going to say that. In fact, I had a bet with myself that you would. Guess I win."

"Guess you're the same smug, self-centered jerk you've always been," Ashlynne muttered under her breath.

But she didn't mutter it softly enough. Cord heard, and the verbal attack surprised him. But he thought he understood. He'd spent enough time with women to recognize the old "all-men-are-pigs" maxim espoused by the bitter rejectee in a love affair gone wrong. Ashlynne Monroe had recently been either dumped or duped by some guy; he'd bet the lodge on it.

"Is it me you dislike so much or is it all men?" He prepared himself for her diatribe about the rat who'd done her wrong. Oh well, at least it would pass the time; this elevator showed no signs of going anywhere.

"It's you," she replied bluntly.

He was visibly taken aback. "Huh?"

"You asked if I disliked you," Ashlynne explained with exaggerated patience. "My answer is yes, I do. I detest you."

It occurred to Cord that this was the first time in his life he'd ever been told, face-to-face, that he was detested. He wasn't sure what to do with the information. "Why do you hate me?"

"A better question is, why wouldn't I?"

"I don't know. Before I left town, we were friends, weren't we?"

"No."

"Yes we were. It's all coming back to me now. I distinctly remember you and I having some friendly chats while I waited for Rayleen to show up."

"They weren't friendly. You blabbered on and on about yourself, assuming I was interested. Well, I wasn't."

Cord frowned, flushing slightly. "That's not the way I remember it."

"Well, that's the way it was."

Cord stared at her. She was cold, she was bitchy, and he knew she wasn't kidding when she said she disliked him. This was not a game of playing hard to get. And yet . . .

In spite of her blatant disregard—*because* of it?—his interest was piqued. His gaze traveled over her face, taking in the angles of her face, the high cheekbones, the deep blue eyes, and finally, the generous pink curve of her mouth. She was very attractive, she looked intelligent and alert, her clothes were tasteful. She had class.

That gave him pause. Rayleen's sister? *Class?*

A swift pang of guilt assailed him. How easy it was to revert to old Waysboro prejudices.

She glanced up at him, and their eyes met. Ashlynne held his gaze defiantly, determined not to be the one to look away first. She would display no signs of weakness to this man.

I hate you. She telegraphed her thoughts through the hot blue intensity of her stare. Her small breasts rose and fell beneath the thick starched cotton of her blouse.

Cord translated the silent message. It wasn't one he was accustomed to seeing in women's eyes. He'd been sought after by the opposite sex since his kindergarten days, thanks to the combination of his looks and the Way fortune. There had never been a woman he wanted that he couldn't have.

He was the one to finally break the eye contact between them, another first for him. When it came to sexy little gazing games, he'd always reigned supreme. But no one had ever gazed at him with such unbridled ferocity.

It was definitely unsettling. It was almost unnerving. Her hostility wasn't feigned, it was real and intense, and he knew it. He'd harbored enough anger himself in the past not to recognize genuine rage in another.

What would it take to turn that feminine fury into something else? he wondered. Six years ago, he would've made an instant pass at her, but the mature Cord Way suddenly perceived the situation with newfound insight. And was appalled by his own ridiculous predictability.

It was that age-old trap . . . the appeal of the resistant female, the ultimate challenge to the male's primitive hunting instincts. An age-old trap he was on the verge of mindlessly plunging right into . . .

Cord cleared his throat and straightened. He was no longer the rebel Way renegade, he reminded himself. He was a respectable thirty-four-year-old businessman, back in town to help his family. He would prove it by behaving like one. Which meant ignoring any feminine challenges, however enticing.

"Have you been following the election?" he asked with the bland politeness he might use to address the stranger behind him in a supermarket line.

Oddly, his impersonal tone and question irritated Ashlynne as much as his earlier attempt to rekindle their long-ago friendship.

"I've followed it enough to know that your brother Wyatt has a fight on his hands for that congressional seat." She decided that mentioning Ethan Thorpe and his support of Dan Clarkston would not be prudent. "I imagine that comes as a shock to all you Ways."

"Actually, it does," Cord said wryly. "A Way has represented the district ever since it was drawn over a hundred years ago. When Uncle Archer announced his retirement, we assumed Wyatt's election in November would be a mere formality."

"Dan Clarkston is very popular over in Exton and here in Waysboro too." She named the two major towns that comprised the congressional district.

"So I've been told." Cord heaved a sigh. "That's why I'm back in town, at the family's request. Holly too. To regroup, to brainstorm, to fight. We both arrived last night. Wyatt *can't* lose the family seat."

"The family seat," Ashlynne echoed, scoffing. "As if a Way has a God-given right to be in Congress! He's not the Prince of Wales, you know, and this district isn't the throne of England."

"Thanks for pointing that out to me," Cord said caustically. "Are you a Clarkston supporter or just doing a passable imitation of one?"

"I haven't decided," she lied. "I have till November to make up my mind."

"Well, think about this while you're deciding. The Ways have done a fine job of representing the district for the past hundred years. There has never been a whisper of scandal or corruption and Wyatt will continue that tradition. I know the theme of the opposition is 'It's Time for a Change,' but why change simply for the sake of change?"

Cord shook his head and laughed slightly at his own fervor. "Good Lord, I sound exactly like my mother and grandfather. I'm actually quoting them verbatim."

"That must be a strange experience for you," Ashlynne said coolly. "You've mostly been at odds with your family, haven't you? I remember that you were always called the 'closest thing to a black sheep the Ways have ever had.' "

"Deservedly so." Cord grimaced. That description of him had been painfully apt. "Insufferable" and "immature" also sprang to mind. It wasn't until he'd left Waysboro and its security and privileges, along with its traps and strictures, that he'd managed to become someone he wouldn't mind knowing. "But I'm in complete agreement with my family when it comes to Wyatt winning the election."

"Dan Clarkston's media consultant has managed to turn Clarkston into Good Old Danny, Man of the People, versus Wyatt Way, Candidate of the Elite."

"You really have been following this campaign, haven't you?" Cord's eyes narrowed.

Ashlynne felt her face flush. "Some." She shrugged, feigning nonchalance.

"Well, let me set you straight." Cord moved toward her as he spoke, his own face flushed with emotion. "Wyatt is anything but an elitist and I bitterly resent Clarkston's campaign for portraying him as one. We have to get Wyatt out and meet the voters, to let them know who he truly is. Unfortunately, he isn't a very good public speaker; he sounds like the quiet, mild-mannered tax attorney that he is. Wyatt doesn't stir up the crowds, he anesthetizes them," he added glumly.

Ashlynne stared at him in surprise. "I didn't think you'd admit that."

"I'm here to help turn things around. You can't do that till you've found and faced the prevailing weaknesses. Only then can you attempt to fix them. The same principles apply when it comes to running a business."

His dark eyes gleamed with enthusiasm and intelligence. Ashlynne found herself drawn into conversation with him, despite her attempts to remain aloof.

"I heard you own a hotel out West," Ashlynne said hesitantly. It was awkward to admit to someone that you knew things about them, things they hadn't told you.

Cord didn't take offense. Being a Way, he was accustomed to his doings being newsworthy to the citizens of Waysboro. "I bought the Glacier Lodge in Montana six years ago. I headed out West when I left Waysboro and ended up in Glacier. It's a small town near Glacier National Park, and this lodge and campground complex was in bankruptcy and on the market. So I bought it on a lark."

"And you figured out why it failed the first time around," guessed Ashlynne.

Cord nodded his head. "The main reason the lodge failed was because of poor planning. There was no cost containment at all. The management didn't order supplies in bulk but would wait until they were all out and then have to buy immediately, paying top dollar."

"That's like going to the store every day instead of making a list and watching specials and shopping weekly," Ashlynne murmured.

"Exactly." Cord looked pleased. "And, of course, sometimes what was needed wasn't readily available and that makes for unhappy guests. If you disappoint your clientele too often, word gets out. Word of mouth can make or break you in the travel industry."

"So you've become a bulk-buying warehouse shopper." Ashlynne had to smile at the image of a Way in that role.

But Cord nodded his head, quite serious. "I've also made expansions and improvements in both the lodge and the campgrounds. Business couldn't be better, though I refuse to become complacent."

"Weren't you worried about leaving and coming here?"

"Yeah, I had second thoughts—and third and fourth," he admitted. "But Wyatt needs me. Fortunately, I have a first-rate assistant manager in charge and a competent staff to run the place, and I'll be checking in by phone every day." He smiled wryly. "My brother Stafford is astonished. He can only remember what a lousy job I did in the position they created for me at Way Communications headquarters."

"I remember how much you hated that job," murmured Ashlynne, recalling one of their long-ago talks when Cord had confided just how much he loathed working for his grandfather, chairman of the board, and his older brother Stafford, CEO of Way Communications. "You said you'd rather work at the Waterside Bar than for your family's company."

"The Waterside Bar!" Cord gave a hoot of laughter. "That notorious mainstay of the Monroe clan, that landmark of Lower Lyme Hill! How is the old place, anyway?"

Ashlynne froze. No subject could have alienated her more. "It's still there," she said stiffly.

Cord was grinning reminiscently. "Do the old rules still apply? That whoever manages to start an all-out brawl is rewarded with a free drink as soon as they're released from jail or the emergency room?"

Ashlynne's lips tightened. "Everything is still the same in Waysboro. The Monroes are still considered a hopeless mixture of criminality, stupidity, and immorality. A blight on the town. You Ways, of course, are the crown jewels, as always."

The Ways had made their fortune nearly two centuries ago in tobacco and land holdings, invested the profits and diversified, now heading a communications empire spanning the country, including cable and broadcasting stations, news-papers, and preprinted advertising. Corporate headquarters for Way Communications was located in Washington, D.C., sixty miles away, and a heliport installed at OakWay, the Way family estate, provided a swift traffic-free commute for its executives.

The Way family was roundly lauded for preferring their hometown to the lures of big-city life. Conversely, the Monroes received no praise for staying; there were continual laments that they wouldn't leave.

It would never change, Ashlynne knew. For a Monroe, leaving Waysboro was the only way to escape the family's tainted-beyond-repair reputation. Occasionally, one did and succeeded. Her older brother Shane had joined the Navy and was living a respectable, productive life far from here. Ashlynne looked on Shane's escape as her inspiration.

"If you hate Waysboro so much, why don't you leave?" Cord asked reasonably.

Ashlynne thought of Kendra, of Daisy and Maxie and the expense of moving a family to a new town with no job or place to stay. It took money to relocate and she was saving as much as she could toward that end, but a family of four still had to live on something. She glared balefully at Cord Way. What would he know about any of that? When he felt like leaving town, he'd headed west and bought himself a lodge and a campground!

"Leave town? Gee, why didn't I think of that?" She affected a moronically stupid expression but her blue eyes flashed with fury. "You Ways sure are smart. I guess that's why you're so rich and why I'm so poor. I'm too stupid to comprehend the obvious."

Though her words were sharp, Cord saw the underlying hurt. She was pretty and smart and it must be a constant thorn in her side to be typecast as a typical Monroe by the town. He placed a consoling hand on her arm, just above her wrist. "Ashlynne, I didn't mean to imply—"

Ashlynne jerked away as if she'd been scalded. "Don't touch me!"

The touch of his hand electrified her. She could still feel its imprint, the heat on her bare skin. Worse, a current seemed to sizzle from that innocuous spot on her arm to every secret, wicked place in her body.

She had to get away from him! "I think maybe I'm claustrophobic after all. And if we don't get out of here right now, I really am going to pitch the first hysterical fit of my life!" Ashlynne warned.

Her nerves were overloaded. She did not consider herself a sexual being; she'd put a clamp on such thoughts and feelings long ago. She was Maxie and Daisy's mother, she was Kendra's sister; those roles were her whole identity. Her unexpected response alarmed her. And having those feelings for *Cord Way* horrified her. Feeling threatened, she glared at Cord, the cause of it all.

He reached for the phone again. "They're still working on the problem." Cord repeated the operator's message to Ashlynne. "And can't give an exact time when the power will be back. Maybe a few minutes, maybe—"

"If you're going to say a few hours, forget it! I am not staying in here that long!"

"Well, we do have another option." Cord studied the ceiling of the elevator. "Our freight elevator at the Glacier Lodge is almost identical to this one. There is a panel in the ceiling that can be removed fairly easily by unscrewing four bolts."

"And then we can climb out?"

"Onto the roof of the car. You'll be in the open elevator shaft and can assess whether or not it's possible to climb to the floor above. Of course, the doors on that floor will have to be opened but if I call—"

"We're going to do it," Ashlynne told him. She looked up at the ceiling and saw the panel. "Uh, how can we reach it?"

"You could sit on my shoulders and unscrew the bolts," Cord suggested. He could not suppress a smile at the look of horror that crossed her face. "No?" He shrugged. "Then I guess we can't do it. Neither of us is nine feet tall so we can't reach the ceiling on our own. And I sincerely doubt that you could hold me on *your* shoulders. We'll just make ourselves comfortable in here and wait it out."

Ashlynne knew she could not be comfortable with Cord Way in such close quarters. There was too much going on inside her, too much history. She had to do something, to divert all this energy into action.

"Okay, I'll do it." She gulped. "I'll sit on your shoulders and try to remove the panel."

"The lady's wish is my command." Cord stooped down. "Ready to climb on?"

CHAPTER TWO

VERY reluctantly, Ashlynne sat on his shoulders, draping her legs around him. When Cord stood up, she had easy access to the ceiling panel.

"See the bolts?" he asked. His body was already reacting to the soft feel of her bottom pressed against his shoulders. He'd clasped his hands around her thighs to steady her and he felt the enticing mixture of feminine softness and strength. Automatically, he spread his fingers to grasp tighter.

"Watch it!" Ashlynne snapped, her face burning. It was difficult to concentrate on unscrewing the stubborn little bolt when she was so excruciatingly aware of his nearness. Her thighs straddled his neck, she was pressed intimately against him. The feel of his hands moving over her legs jolted through her like a bolt of lightning.

"I don't want you to fall off." Cord's hands were under her skirt slightly above her knees, gripping her thighs. His eyes darted furtively along the length of her legs, dangling over his chest. His body grew taut and he stifled a groan. Why did she have to have such long, shapely legs? Slender ankles, firm calves, and rounded thighs, legs that inspired fantasies, like the one he was beginning to have right now. He imagined those luscious long legs of hers wrapped around his neck in entirely different circumstances . . . He imagined—

"I'll need my nail file to unscrew these." Ashlynne's voice jolted him. "Could you get it out of my purse?"

Cord fumbled in the bag. "This isn't a purse, it's a survival kit." He pulled out a candy bar, then a package of gum. "Aha, provisions. What else do you have in here? First aid supplies?" He held up a band-aid. "Maybe I'll find a flare if I dig deep enough."

"Just give me the nail file."

He obliged, still chuckling at his joke, and at her meet-every-emergency purse.

"I got one!" Ashlynne called out in triumph. She handed him down a bolt.

She was wriggling a little, shifting herself to better reach the second bolt. The muscular feel of him between her legs sent sparks of heat through her. She felt flushed and slightly dizzy. Automatically, she tightened her legs around him, to keep her balance.

They both drew in sharp, deep breaths.

"I—I'm having trouble with this bolt. It's stuck," she said breathlessly.

"Try another one." Cord's voice was husky and thick. He flexed his fingers against the warm softness of her thighs and closed his eyes. Sweet torture seemed a particularly apt description of the feelings roiling through him. He wasn't sure how much longer he could take it, but he didn't want it to end. Given the option of standing in the middle of the elevator, with Ashlynne Monroe wrapped provocatively around him, and the restoration of his freedom, Cord knew he'd choose to remain trapped.

But he wasn't given that option. The elevator gave a sudden lurch, then with a whoosh and a grinding sound, it slowly began to move.

"The power is back!" exclaimed Ashlynne.

Before either had a chance to move, the elevator doors snapped open. They were back on the first floor, where they'd started. But the corridor wasn't deserted as it had been then. A small crowd stood in front of the open doors, staring wide-eyed at Cord with Ashlynne perched upon his shoulders. Among them was Camilla Way, her son Wyatt, and her daughter Holly.

Ashlynne flushed scarlet from head to toe. "Get me down!" she hissed to Cord. She dug the heels of her shoes into his chest to emphasize her request.

Cord obediently dropped to his knees and Ashlynne scrambled off him, then raced from the elevator car, pushing her way through the throng without a word or backward glance.

"I won't even ask what that was all about," Wyatt Way said dryly, gazing down the corridor where Ashlynne had already disappeared, and then back to his somewhat disheveled brother.

"We were concerned about you, Cord," said their mother. She sounded vaguely censorious. "The security officers said you were trapped in here. I couldn't understand why you'd left the ballroom in the first place."

"I needed some air." Cord shrugged. It was partly true. He didn't add that he had been feeling so bored and restless he'd deemed a momentary reprieve from the tedious speeches as necessary as air. And in the corridor he'd run into Ashlynne Monroe—who had run away from him into the ill-fated elevator.

"I could've used a breather too," Holly piped up, grinning. "There really was a lot of hot air in that ballroom. Maybe from the concentration of all those old windbags?"

"You needed fresh air, so you got into the service elevator?" Camilla cut in, her dark brows arched. She pinned her son with a stern maternal stare. "Cord, I do not care to speculate on what sort of—of gymnastic stunt you and that young lady were attempting or what your actual destination was before the power went out. But let me remind you that you are not in your little western frontier town, but here in Waysboro. People in town are watching you, Cord."

Cord suppressed a sigh. It was as if he were a callow fourteen again instead of a seasoned thirty-four. The same old lecture, the same old family credo. "Remember: the Way-watchers are watching you." His mother ought to needlepoint it on one of those canvases she was forever working on.

"Now that the fund-raiser is officially over, why don't we go home and get something to eat?" Wyatt suggested. Wyatt was the family diplomat, who always tried to please. Both scholarly and quiet, his good nature was consistently taken advantage of by everyone in the family.

"I know I couldn't eat that rubber chicken they served for lunch here," Wyatt added grimly.

"At two hundred fifty dollars a plate, they could've

ordered in individual buckets of KFC," murmured Holly. "At least it would've tasted good."

Camilla shuddered. "I hope this is the last fund-raising luncheon of your campaign, Wyatt. The entire concept offends me—appearing in public to consume a mediocre meal for the sole purpose of asking people for paltry sums of money. It's so unnecessary. I don't know why the family can't finance the campaign as we have always done for Archer."

"Clarkston's campaign has accused the Ways of buying the congressional seat, Mother," Cord pointed out. "Wyatt's campaign advisers want him to have solid grass-roots support and that means soliciting funds from voters. Which means inviting them to the hotel for a rubber-chicken lunch," he added dryly.

"Whatever the reason, it is quite demeaning," Camilla said, frowning. As usual, she missed the note of humor in his statement. Camilla Way was not given to humorous observation, and Cord's penchant for it had always irritated her.

Her tone and imperial glare did not encourage debate. Giving Wyatt her arm, she permitted her youngest son to escort her from the hotel. Cord and Holly followed behind.

"Your little friend in the elevator certainly took off in a run," Holly murmured to her brother. "What were you two doing in there anyway?"

"Trying to get out. She did not appreciate being trapped in there with me." Cord realized at once that he'd said too much. He had no desire to explain either the interlude or Ashlynne Monroe to his sister.

Holly studied him curiously. "Was she an old flame? Or were you trying to make her a brand-new one?"

"None of the above. She's the younger sister of—uh—an old acquaintance." Cord knocked his palm to his forehead. "Oh no! I can't believe I forgot to ask her about her sister!" Not that Ashlynne had volunteered any information about Rayleen. Still, he conceded, not inquiring had been remiss of him.

"What an oversight!" Holly teased. "Sounds like Little

Sister knew just what buttons to press. And I'm *not* talking about the elevator."

Cord thought back to those intense moments when his body was strumming with sexual tension. No, he warned himself, he would not be at the mercy of his hormones, not at this stage of his life, and not with another Monroe sister. "Being stuck in the elevator had me frazzled," he countered.

Holly snickered. "If you say so, big brother."

Ashlynne made the five-minute walk from the hotel to Ethan's office in less than three. The office was empty and she gratefully sank into her desk chair and took her bag lunch from her desk drawer. She waited for her pulse rate to return to normal before she began to eat. And though she tried to concentrate solely on her lettuce and cheese sandwich, images of Cord Way kept flashing before her mind's eye.

She couldn't seem to sit still and ended up pacing the office as she ate, her body still wired and edgy. For years she had hated what he symbolized to her family—the danger and the careless unconcern. Now, his voice seemed to echo in her ears, his smile was imprinted in her brain, and the feel of his strong fingers on her thighs, of, the hard strength of his neck between them seemed to be branded on her skin.

Ethan returned an hour later. "I looked for you around the lobby but finally gave up and went into the dining room and had lunch."

"I—got trapped in an elevator during the power outage."

"Ah yes, the power outage." Ethan laughed. "It only affected a portion of the hotel, you know. The Way supporters streamed out of that ballroom like rats deserting a sinking ship. They seemed delighted to have an excuse to leave."

"I think this election has the Ways running scared," Ashlynne volunteered, remembering Cord's admission that the whole family was regrouping. "That's a first."

"And they're too late. The condo development was first

but they didn't catch on. The election is next and then the strip mall project." Ethan's lips curved into one of those nonsmiles of his. "The House of Way is long overdue for a fall and I am very well ensconced to provide it."

Ashlynne tried to keep her curiosity in check. This was the first time Ethan Thorpe had ever admitted that his actions here in Waysboro were deliberately aimed against the Way family. Now that he'd confirmed there was a motive, she wondered what was fueling his vendetta.

But she was too discreet to ask. Anyway, she didn't care to indulge in an in-depth discussion of the Ways with her boss, especially not with Cord back in town. Cord's dark brown, almost black, eyes that matched the shade of his hair drifted back to mind. And then she thought of little Daisy and those enormous, inquisitive dark eyes of hers. A secret would remain a secret if only one person knew it, she reassured herself. She was that one person.

Silence stretched between them, until Ethan himself broke it. "Look at the time!" He made the statement before he actually glanced at his watch, but Ashlynne wasn't about to mention the discrepancy.

"I have some calls to make and I know you've got things to do." He strolled through the reception area, past Ashlynne's desk, into his own spacious office, closing the door behind him.

Ashlynne wondered if he was going to take out little voodoo dolls and stick pins in them. If he did, would the Ways shriek with pain? The expression on Thorpe's face boded ill for whoever had inspired it. She felt a nervous relief that it wasn't her.

"So that's Dan Clarkston," Cord murmured to Holly.

They stood together watching the young congressional candidate move through the enthusiastic throngs that surrounded him, reaching to shake his hand and calling out friendly greetings and words of encouragement.

Cord and Holly had infiltrated the Dan Clarkston for Congress Picnic, being held in the bucolic picnic grounds of Way Park. After giving a short but dynamic speech, Clarkston mingled with his supporters, all of whom seemed positively enthralled with their candidate. Cord thought of the tepid response to his brother Wyatt yesterday at the Waysboro Hotel. The marked differences disturbed him.

"Young Danny Boy is accompanied as usual by his vivacious wife, Cindy," Holly said acidly. "That's how she is always described, and she certainly is, isn't she? Vivacious and then some. How does she do it? That great big smile and that sparkle in her eyes actually look genuine."

Cord stared at perky, brown-eyed Cindy Clarkston, who seemed to be enjoying the crush of people as much as her tall, dark, and handsome husband. "Maybe it *is* genuine, Holly. They look like they're having the time of their lives. Can anyone fake that kind of enthusiasm?"

"Wyatt certainly can't," Holly said grimly. "He looks pained when he's in a crowd; he's uncomfortable and stiff and it shows. Poor Wyatt. He's always been the quietest one in the family, the one who has the most trouble making small talk. I can remember him writing down topics of conversation to use on his dates."

"And now he's supposed to glad-hand every stranger in the county and treat them like longtime buddies." Cord shook his head. "I still don't understand why Grandfather and Uncle Archer and Stafford chose Wyatt to run for Congress. Why not one of the cousins? It seems any one of them would be a more likely choice."

"Because not one of the cousins would consider it." Holly heaved a sigh. "But you know Wyatt, he's so conciliatory and kind. The family drafted him and he willingly agreed to serve as the human sacrifice."

"Wyatt did say that he was bored with his job at company headquarters and wouldn't mind a change," Cord said. He hoped it was true and not simply a case of congenial, tactful Wyatt trying to put a positive spin on a hopeless entrapment.

The notion that his brother had been pressured into a position that didn't suit him troubled Cord greatly. It was what he had spent most of his youth fighting against—being forced by virtue of his name into a slot, a role, a life that didn't fit him. Had he escaped only to see his favorite brother caught in that very trap?

At that moment, Dan Clarkston and his vivacious wife Cindy veered to the left, heading directly toward Cord and Holly. The crowd followed the couple, pressing closer, calling their names. The Clarkstons eagerly responded, pausing to shake hands, kiss babies, and throw smiles and compliments to their well-wishers.

Cord watched them with a critical eye. There was no doubt about it; Dan and Cindy Clarkston were very good at this game. If they weren't actually enjoying the interaction, they were giving a flawless performance of doing so.

Within moments, the candidate and his wife confronted Holly and Cord. Mistaking the Ways for supporters, Dan flashed them a brilliant smile and thanked them for being there. Cindy urged them to "enjoy the picnic," adding that "the hot dogs look delish! I'm so sorry Danny and I can't stay but we have to get home to our little Scotty and baby Tiffany."

Before either Cord or Holly could reply, the couple were hustled toward a waiting car by members of their entourage.

"That devoted-parents' bit of theirs plays well," Holly grumbled. "Maybe we can rent Wyatt some adorable kids from the same casting agency where the Clarkstons got theirs."

"According to the Clarkston campaign literature I've seen, little Scotty is very much their own, as is sweet baby Tiffany," Cord said dryly. "Dan and Cindy are happily married and devoted to each other and to the children. She's a full-time homemaker and he's a worthy public defender in Exton, real people-of-the-people. And they do have charisma. No questions."

"Well, I don't think so," Holly countered crossly. "Their smiles were so blinding, they practically burnt out my retinas. I can't believe people are actually taking these fakes seriously. Oh Cord, I don't know if Wyatt will be happy as a congressman or not, but since he's agreed to run, I don't want him to lose!"

"Neither do I. And he won't, Holly. Wyatt will win, even if things look a little shaky right now."

"You're still laboring under the delusion that the Ways

will inevitably prevail. But this situation is different, Cord. Not only is Dan Clarkston a savvy campaigner, his main backer—the mastermind behind the scene, if you will—is a—a very influential man."

Cord laughed at that. "Oh, come on, Holly. Who is more influential than a Way in the Waysboro area?"

"You can't dismiss this man lightly, Cord. He's already established himself as a force to be reckoned with." Holly stared at the ground. "His name is Ethan Thorpe and he is the one responsible for that condo development near Way's Run, not to mention that eyesore of an office in the square. God only knows what else he has up his sleeve, or maybe I should amend that to only the *devil* knows, because I don't think God and Ethan Thorpe have even a nodding acquaintance."

There was a shout from the crowd and both Holly and Cord turned to look at the huge bunch of balloons being released into the air. Each bore the "Dan Clarkston: Time for a Change" message in bold black letters, visible even from a distance. The colorful spectacle inspired excited squeals from the children in the crowd.

"Good gimmick," Cord acknowledged grudgingly. "Gives the Clarkstons a memorable send-off."

"Those balloons are detrimental to the birds and animals that may ingest them," Holly said. "Releasing hundreds of them into the atmosphere is a slap in the face at environmentalists. But then, Ethan Thorpe and his stooge Clarkston don't even pretend to have an interest in preserving the planet. They oppose zoning restrictions, they'd like to cover every square inch of this county with buildings and roads. I wouldn't be surprised if there was a nuclear power station and a toxic-waste dump site in their future plans—to be located smack in the middle of the town square!"

Cord hid a smile. Holly had always been given to hyperbole. Still, he shared her anxiety about the threat to Wyatt's campaign—and Clarkston's potential plans to overdevelop the area. Family loyalty wasn't the only reason he'd returned to help his brother win. Since moving to Montana, he had become a firm believer in protecting the environment and preserving its resources.

"Ethan Thorpe is a law unto himself." Holly murmured almost to herself, her voice holding a hollow ring and her dark brown eyes haunted.

Cord stared at her, his curiosity roused.

On the drive back to OakWay where they both were staying, ensconced in their old childhood rooms, Cord tried to grill Holly for more information about Thorpe and Clarkston, but she abruptly changed the subject.

"Stafford and Prentice invited us to their house for dinner tonight. Actually, it's more of a command performance than an invitation, so don't even think of trying to get out of it, Cord."

Cord was already trying. He well remembered the dubious pleasures of dining with his elder brother, the pontificating, pompous Stafford and Staff's very proper wife, Prentice, a younger clone of Camilla. They had two teenaged sons, Dayland the Third, "Trip," and Stafford Junior, "Skip."

Though he hadn't seen his nephews since his return, Cord remembered them as rather likable kids, despite their preppy-to-the-point-of-parody nicknames. He wondered if being a Way in Waysboro had worked for or against the boys these past six years. It had definitely worked against him, as far as character development went, Cord acknowledged. Leaving town had been the best thing he'd ever done.

"I assume Mother and Grandfather will be there tonight too," Cord guessed glumly. "And Uncle Archer and Uncle Montgomery and Aunt Bitsy."

"Of course. And let's not forget Aunts Ella and Rhea. It's going to be a very long evening," lamented Holly. "With all of them demanding to know why you, Wyatt, and I aren't married yet. I wouldn't be surprised if they all have lists of names of suitable mates for each one of us."

"Do you think we could tell them we're all gay? That might dampen their enthusiasm for matchmaking."

"Except Mother would have a heart attack and Grandfather would take out his old Civil War dueling pistol and shoot us on the spot."

Cord grimaced. "It's enough to drive one to drink. In

fact, I used to think that getting drunk was the only way to survive life in the Way family prison. Now that I'm back, I fully remember why I felt that way."

"Well, don't even consider paying a visit to your old stomping grounds, the Waterside Bar," Holly warned.

"I understand the old place is still standing." He almost grinned, but Ashlynne's clear voice, taut and bitter as she described life as a Monroe in Waysboro, suddenly sounded in his head. He did not smile.

"And it's still run by the Monroes. They're as much a fixture in this town as the Ways, I suppose." Holly shrugged. "But may I recommend *not* resuming your fling with the Monroe girl you were romancing during your final wild phase, before you left town for good?"

Cord groaned. "Careful, Holly, you're sounding dangerously like Mother. But don't worry, that chapter of my life is closed."

"I've sworn the same thing about certain chapters of my life," Holly said cryptically. "And somehow they keep getting reopened."

"Well, I'm standing firm on this one. I'm not still crazy after all these years."

And he proved it by putting all thoughts of the Waterside Bar and his past indiscretions and temptations from his mind. He spent the evening being civil—and even charming!—to his relatives, and capped off the night by joining Wyatt for a strategy meeting with his top campaign staff. The name Ethan Thorpe kept surfacing.

"Dan Clarkston is Thorpe's puppet," the campaign manager said disparagingly. "If he wins, it'll be Ethan Thorpe calling the shots, make no mistake about that."

"But why didn't Thorpe run for office himself?" asked Cord. "Why bother with a middleman like Clarkston?"

"Thorpe doesn't want the restrictions that confine elected officials," Wyatt said solemnly. "His machinations and secret agendas wouldn't stand the glare of media exposure. Better to back someone malleable like Dan Clarkston and wield the power from behind the scenes."

"Wield the power behind the scenes?" Cord repeated. "It all sounds so melodramatic, practically medieval. Aren't you overestimating this guy? I mean, he's just a land developer who's new to the area, he's not the bogeyman. Or the devil," he added, remembering Holly's terse depiction.

"If he were the devil, that would explain the black magic he used on the zoning commission to get that condo development built," suggested one staffer. He was only half joking.

Thus it was a mixture of concern and curiosity that sent Cord to the town square late the next afternoon, to Ethan Thorpe's outrageously modern office, so at odds with the quaint country charm of Waysboro. If Ethan Thorpe was the force to be reckoned with, then Cord was going directly to the force to reckon.

Thorpe's office boasted a large reception area with low black leather couches and chrome and Lucite tables. The rug was a thick blood-red shag and the painting on the wall looked like a psychotic's interpretation of a Rorschach test. Cord's gaze flicked critically over the surroundings. There was modernistic decor and there was just plain ugly, and he placed Thorpe's office decor firmly in the latter category.

Farther in the back of the reception room was a small alcove with a desk, a hideous black and gold lacquered piece right in keeping with the rest of the place. A woman, presumably Thorpe's secretary/receptionist, was busy at a word processor, so completely absorbed in her task that she didn't hear Cord enter the office.

At least not at first. As he headed toward her desk, she looked up suddenly and gave a violent start.

"What do you want?" Her voice was sharp and held an unmistakable ring of panic.

"Is that the standard greeting visitors to Ethan Thorpe's office are given?" Cord asked a startled, wide-eyed Ashlynne Monroe. "No wonder people intimate there's something sinister about your boss."

Ashlynne stood up, clutching the edges of her desk, as if it were a shield to protect her.

"You work here?" Cord was incredulous. "For Ethan Thorpe?"

What an unexpected development! Seeing Ashlynne again—and here, of all places. Had any Monroe worked anywhere but the Waterside Bar?

Ashlynne fixed him with a piercing glare, as if she'd just read his mind. "No, I don't work here, I just broke into the office. I have the real secretary tied up in the back and as soon as I've finished looting the place, she can have her desk back again."

"Point taken." Cord's eyes swept over her. Her blue-gray knit dress was as modest and demure as the uninteresting outfit she'd had on yesterday. Yet somehow, the dull dress flattered the neat curves of her body, making her look delicate and feminine—and elegantly sexy. He swallowed. "I'm here to see your boss."

Carefully averting her eyes from him, Ashlynne punched the intercom button. "Mr. Thorpe, Cord Way is here to see you."

"I'm busy." Ethan Thorpe's voice sounded smoothly over the intercom. "If Mr. Way wants to see me, he'll have a very, very, *very* long wait."

"Well, you heard him," Ashlynne said dismissively. She sat back down in her chair, turning her full attention to the screen of her word processor.

"How long a wait?" Cord asked.

Ashlynne didn't look up. "I have no idea. But I've never heard him use three 'verys' before."

"Why do I have the feeling that Thorpe could be in there playing with a Gameboy? Or reading the tabloids? Or working on a paint-by-number kit? Anything to keep from meeting with me."

"If Ethan doesn't want to see you, he doesn't have to."

"Ethan?" Cord pounced on that. "So that's how it is? Are you involved in one of those torrid office romances with him, Ashlynne?" He was startled by just how much he loathed that notion.

Ashlynne took instant offense. "Oh, you would think that! In your mind, Monroes are for sexual use only— to be discarded immediately afterward. You can't imagine anyone hiring one of us because we might actually be able to do a good job or to—"

"Hey, lighten up. I was just kidding."

"No you weren't," Ashlynne said crossly. "But to set the

record straight, I am not now nor ever have been involved in a *torrid office romance* with Ethan Thorpe."

Cord sighed. He had never met a woman as edgy and chilly as she . . . and he couldn't understand why he was infinitely relieved that she was not involved with Ethan Thorpe.

Ashlynne didn't bother to disguise her impatience. "You can leave now."

Cord considered it. After all, he'd come to meet Ethan Thorpe, to evaluate and observe firsthand this shrewd manipulator who'd cultivated a mystique of power so convincing that even Wyatt and Holly were in awe of him. But Thorpe refused to see him and Ashlynne Monroe couldn't have been unfriendlier if he'd been a cannibalistic serial killer.

"Are you going to leave or shall I ask Mr. Thorpe to escort you out?" Ashlynne demanded, hoping he wouldn't choose the latter. Cord Way was perhaps two inches taller and far more muscular than Ethan Thorpe. "He knows karate," she added, trying to even the odds a bit.

"I'm terrified," Cord drawled. "But before you sic your boss on me, I'd like to ask about your sister Rayleen. How is she? What has she been doing these past six years?"

The question was so unexpected it struck Ashlynne like a physical blow. She blinked back the sudden tears that filled her eyes. "Rayleen hasn't been doing anything at all. She died a little over five years ago."

"She—what?" Cord stared at her, truly staggered by the news. An image of Rayleen, warm and laughing and vividly alive, flashed before his mind's eye. "She's dead?" he repeated in disbelief. "I don't know what to say. I'm shocked, Ashlynne. And truly sorry."

Ashlynne made an exclamation of disgust. "Oh, please! Spare me the phony sympathy. You didn't give a damn about Rayleen."

"That's not true," Cord protested. "I liked her very much. I—I have very fond memories of her."

" 'Fond' is an interesting choice of words." Ashlynne glared at him. Considering the type of relationship her sister had had with Cord Way, she could just imagine what kind of memories he harbored of her. "Anyway, you proved how *fond* you were of Rayleen when you walked out of her life six years ago and never bothered to get in touch with her again."

"Rayleen had no problems with me leaving town. We talked it over before I left and she wished me well. Why are you so . . . Wait a minute! I remember a certain conversation Rayleen and I once had about you way back when."

Cord stared at her, his eyes narrowing perceptively, as he recalled a portion of that conversation. "Rayleen told me that you thought she and I were in love." He also remembered laughing along with Rayleen at the younger girl's naïveté.

"We weren't in love, Ashlynne, not ever," he assured her. "Neither Rayleen nor I even pretended that we were. We were always honest with each other." But he was aware that trying to explain that good-times-with-no-strings affair to the tight-lipped, grimly disapproving Ashlynne seemed like a lost cause at this point.

"You used each other." Ashlynne's voice was cold and condemning. "Oh, I know how it was between you two."

Rayleen had always been outspoken when it came to men and sex, finding Ashlynne's views on the subject childishly romantic and hopelesly unrealistic. "*You don't have to be in love with a guy to make love with him, Ashlynne.*" She could hear her sister's voice, rich with laughter, echoing in her ears. Except, being Rayleen, she hadn't said "make love." She'd used another word, a tough street word that made Ashlynne flinch. And Rayleen laugh harder.

"Do you know, Ashlynne? Do you really? I understand why you would be angry with me if you thought I'd left Rayleen with a broken heart. But that's not the way it was." Cord wondered vaguely why he was trying so hard to convince her. Probably because her sister was dead and he wanted to ease the pain he saw reflected in her deep blue eyes. "Rayleen and I enjoyed each other's company, we were good buddies—"

"That's not quite the way I would describe your relationship, such as it was. Not that any of it matters now, anyway. That was a long time ago."

"And Rayleen is dead," Cord added quietly. "What happened, Ashlynne?"

Ashlynne did not reply.

"Was she sick?" Cord prompted.

Ashlynne shook her head. "She drowned." The memory of that awful night, the police banging at the door, the long hours of waiting for the grim results rushed to mind and she had to close her eyes to keep her composure. For a moment, she saw herself back in their decrepit old apartment, clutching the babies as she tried to absorb the shocking news. Daisy had been just a few months old then, Maxie not quite two.

She took a deep breath and forced herself to continue. "Rayleen went boating with some friends on the river. They'd been drinking all day and there was an accident later that night. Somehow the boat capsized. Rayleen wasn't wearing a life jacket, none of them were, and she wasn't a strong swimmer. Two guys managed to make it to the shore and call for help. The divers pulled Rayleen and three others out of the water the next day," she added bleakly.

Cord exhaled heavily. "God, Ashlynne, I am so sorry. She was so young and beautiful and full of life."

"She was reckless." Ashlynne's voice was taut. She twisted the band of her watch, an inexpensive but reliable drugstore brand. "Rayleen was wild, always seeking thrills, wanting to take risks."

Those thrills and risks had ended in pregnancy, producing two baby girls that Rayleen professed to adore but never bothered to take care of. That job had gone to Ashlynne, who'd accepted it, loving and caring for her two small nieces as if they were her own children. For they had become her own. She was the only mother they'd ever known.

"Ordinary everyday life bored Rayleen," Ashlynne added softly.

"I know. I was the same way myself for too long a time."

"Rayleen once said you were kindred spirits," Ashlynne murmured, remembering her sister's artless confidences.

And the memory sparked much more than that particular quote.

Her hypervigilant sense of danger kicked in. Kindred spirits, indeed! There had been nothing spiritual about Rayleen's affair with Cord Way. It had been strictly physical and not without consequences. Daisy was the result of their wild, hot nights.

Ashlynne's breath caught in her throat. Was she out of her mind? *What was she doing, standing around reminiscing about Rayleen with Cord Way, of all people?* He didn't know he had a daughter, he was completely unaware of Daisy's existence. But he wasn't stupid, and it wouldn't be too difficult for him to put the pieces together—if he were ever to get them.

Ashlynne thought back to that night she'd tried to tell Cord about Rayleen's pregnancy, the night he had announced he was leaving town and wouldn't be back. A cold, sick fear swept through her. Rayleen had cautioned her about the Ways' power. Her warning was as true today as it had been that night. For if Cord Way were to learn he had a daughter and decided to claim his parental rights, he would probably prevail, even at this late date.

She'd followed enough highly publicized custody cases in the media to know that the courts did not always consider the best interests of the child. The issue seemed to be the adults' legal rights to the child. Under that criterion, wouldn't the natural father be granted custody rather than a maternal aunt? And even more to the point, what court would favor a lowly Monroe over a rich and influential Way?

Cord could take Daisy away from her!

The possibility terrified Ashlynne, infuriated her too. She loved Daisy too much to ever give her up to this spoiled playboy who'd contributed nothing but his chromosomes to the child.

While she grew frantic over Daisy's fate, Cord was still mulling over the shocking news of Rayleen's demise. He gazed at Ashlynne, his dark eyes filled with sympathy and compassion.

"I'm sorry Rayleen wasn't granted the time to outgrow

her recklessness, Ashlynne." As he himself had been. "She would've, I'm sure."

Ashlynne's panic turned to rage. The last thing she wanted or needed was to have a Way feeling sorry for her, especially Cord Way! She had to get rid of him. Immediately, and hopefully forever.

"You have to leave right now, Mr. Way." Her voice was harsh, startlingly different from the soft, almost gently reminiscent tone she'd used only moments before. "You've taken up enough of my time. I have work to do."

Cord blinked. Her mood swings were as drastic as a Jekyll-and-Hyde personality shift. "What's with the 'Mr. Way'? Does this mean I'm supposed to call you Miss Monroe?"

"You'd find that impossible, wouldn't you? Showing me even the slightest respect?"

Exasperated, Cord threw up his hands, but before he could speak, the door to the office was flung open and two little girls, wearing bright blue tights and yellow leotards under their unbuttoned jackets, raced inside.

"Mommy! Hi, Mommy!" The children, one blond and one brunette, raced to Ashlynne's desk, both talking at once.

Cord stared from the children to Ashlynne. It was her they were calling Mommy, there was no mistake about that. He was floored. *She had two kids!* His eyes flicked immediately to her left hand, where no band of gold encircled her finger. Of course, the fact that she wasn't wearing a wedding ring didn't necessarily mean that she wasn't married, he reminded himself. She could have an allergy to metal, her husband could be too poor to afford a ring . . .

"I did a perfect cartwheel in gymnastics today, Mommy!" boasted the little blonde. "Want to see?" She dropped her overstuffed bookbag onto the rug and proceeded to do what was indeed a perfect cartwheel.

Ashlynne and the little dark-haired girl clapped their hands with enthusiastic appreciation. The small blond gymnast smiled and then turned to Cord and noticed that he wasn't clapping.

"Want me to do another one?" she offered.

"No, Maxie," Ashlynne interjected quickly. "The man was just leaving."

"The man definitely has time to see Maxie do another one of those perfect cartwheels," Cord said. He felt inordinately pleased at the annoyed flush that stained Ashlynne's cheeks.

Maxie needed no further urging to perform again. This time Cord joined in the clapping. "Bravo," he cheered.

"We go to gymnastics every Thursday," Maxie told him. "I'm the best one in the class." She turned to her sister for confirmation. "I am the best, aren't I, Daisy?"

Daisy nodded her head. "Yes, Maxie," she said kindly. "You're the best one. You're going to be a cheerleader."

Maxie looked euphoric at the prospect.

Cord lowered himself on his haunches, bringing him to the children's eye level. "So you're Maxie and Daisy, hmm?" he asked in a hearty tone.

"Maxie Kay Monroe and Daisy Marie Monroe," Maxie affirmed. "Who are you?"

"He's a stranger and you shouldn't talk to strangers," Daisy said sternly. She took a protective step in front of her sister and stared at Cord with her big, dark serious eyes.

Cord rose to his feet, uncomfortably ill at ease. The kid made him feel like a leering pedophile. He noticed Ashlynne give the child an approving smile. Oh, that little one was her mother's daughter, all right. Suspicious and outspoken with a knack for making him feel inane and unwanted.

"I can do cartwheels *and* work at Mommy's desk too," Maxie boasted expansively. Before Ashlynne could stop her, the little girl scrambled on top of the desk and pressed the intercom button. "You have a visitor, Mr. Thorpe," she said, attempting to imitate Ashlynne's professional tone and inflection.

Ashlynne and Daisy exchanged appalled glances.

"Maxie, get down!" wailed Daisy as Ashlynne plucked Maxie from the desk.

"Do I have a new secretary?" Ethan Thorpe's voice sounded over the intercom.

Ashlynne was relieved that he sounded amused rather

than annoyed. Though he permitted the children to be dropped at the office when their after-school day-care program ended to wait the fifteen minutes until her quitting time at five, she had always been careful to keep the girls from disturbing him.

Today, Cord Way's unsettling presence had made her less vigilant—and she'd had no idea that Maxie knew how to use the intercom!

"I'm sorry for the disturbance, Ethan," she apologized nervously. "Maxie would like to apologize too." She motioned the child over to speak into the intercom.

"I'm sorry, Mr. Thorpe," Maxie chirped, quite unrepentently, "but you do, too, have a visitor man here."

"Would you ask if the visitor's name is Cord Way?" Ethan asked.

"Is your name Cord Way?" Maxie asked importantly.

Cord nodded and Maxie nodded in turn.

"Mr. Thorpe can't see you, Maxie," Daisy pointed out, drawn into the exchange despite her initial horror. "You have to say yes."

"Yes," Maxie's voice boomed.

"Then please tell Mr. Way that Mr. Thorpe does not have time to see him today, and if he wants an appointment with me, he will have to make one in advance."

The message was too long for Maxie. "Bye," she called, running away from the desk. "C'mon, Daisy, let's practice our splits." She flopped onto the floor in a split, as limber as a bendable Gumby figure.

Daisy, sensing the tension, stayed by Ashlynne's side, clinging to her hand. Her presence bolstered Ashlynne's resolve. "I don't think Mr. Thorpe can make himself any clearer, Mr. Way," she said coolly, averting her eyes from Cord's. They were so like Daisy's, in color and shape, that it made her ache to look at them, to look at him.

"Very well, Miss Monroe." He mocked her icy professional tone. "I will leave this office at once and call tomorrow to make the necessary arrangements to be granted an audience with Mr. Thorpe."

He viewed Thorpe's snub today as the insult it had undoubtedly been meant to be and was more determined than ever to meet this hostile challenger to the Ways. Cord turned from the unsmiling faces of Ashlynne and Daisy and strode to the door.

"Bye, mister!" Maxie sang out from her position in a vertical split on the floor. She waved her small hand.

Cord couldn't resist waving back with a smile of his own. Little Maxie was a charmer. And he was struck by her close resemblance to Rayleen. He wondered if it was a comfort or if it hurt to see a dead relative in the person of a living child. Considering the life Rayleen had led and her unfortunate end, Maxie's lively blond prettiness was probably a source of anxiety to her uptight, cold-as-ice mother.

Maxie Kay Monroe and Daisy Marie Monroe. Quite unbidden, the children's names came to mind as he walked through the town square to retrieve his car, on loan from the company during his stay in Waysboro. The children shared their mother's surname, which was not her married name— undoubtedly because Ashlynne wasn't married now and hadn't been when she'd given birth to the two little girls.

Well, he wasn't a prude, and the scarlet letter days for unwed mothers were long gone. In some celebrity circles, it had become downright fashionable for single mothers to bear and raise babies without benefit of marriage.

Cord gave his head an impatient shake as if to physically derail his train of thought. He didn't care who had kids in or out of wedlock, be it in Hollywood or Waysboro, Maryland. None of it had anything to do with him.

But the memory of a long-ago conversation he'd once had with Ashlynne—in a parking lot of a convenience store while he waited for Rayleen to join him—commanded his attention . . .

"I don't make much money working at the Waysboro Hotel but I'm not leaving to work at the Waterside Bar, no matter how much they say I can earn in tips there," Ashlynne had said earnestly. Cord visualized her as she'd looked then, gazing up at him, her big blue eyes shining with sincerity. And anxiety. "I wish Rayleen would get away from that place. I'm worried about her, Cord."

"Hey, Rayleen's a lot of fun," he'd said blithely. "Everybody likes her."

"Rayleen has always been, uh, popular," Ashlynne had murmured.

Cord remembered what his response to her had been: "Well, you'd be popular, too, if you'd loosen up a bit." They had both known exactly what he meant.

He cringed at the memory. Ashlynne had been worried about her sister and he'd buzzed her off by suggesting that she adopt Rayleen's live-and-love-for-the-moment style.

He remembered that Ashlynne had turned away from him in weary resignation, agreeing, "It's true, nobody likes a Monroe girl who doesn't . . . party." Another candy-coated euphemism, just like his own "loosening up."

Cord frowned. He hadn't expressed a shred of empathy for her concern about Rayleen, a very viable concern considering Rayleen's untimely end. Who could blame Ashlynne for not viewing their past "friendship" in a warmly reminiscent light? However, the existence of Maxie and Daisy proved that Ashlynne Monroe had done her own fair share of "partying" after all.

Well, that was no business of his. He was back in town to get his brother elected and had already spent enough time thinking about Ashlynne Monroe, who was merely a peripheral figure from a regrettable but forgettable phase in his life.

CHAPTER THREE

BECAUSE it was less than a block from the campaign head-quarters of congressional candidate Wyatt Tyndall Way, Letty's Coffee Shop drew the hungry and caffeine-addicted staff members from the moment the office opened at nine until it closed at six. The staffers gave Letty so much business that she began to offer them some small perks generally not granted to coffee shop patrons. She instructed her employees to give the Way campaign workers straws for their soft drinks without them having to ask and to include extra napkins with the dripping ham barbecue sandwiches.

Letty also took it upon herself to send over a fresh pot of coffee to the headquarters at four o'clock every afternoon. The coffee wasn't free, of course. Letty didn't believe in giveaways, but she didn't charge for delivery. On Monday through Friday afternoons, the coffee was delivered by Kendra Monroe, who worked at the shop weekends and every day after school until closing time at seven.

Kendra liked the staffers, who were friendly and always gave her a tip, which they dutifully billed to the Way campaign.

It was on a Thursday afternoon coffee run that Wyatt Tyndall Way, the candidate himself, arrived at the head-quarters. There was an air of excitement mixed with a deference that Kendra found amusing. She'd never seen such sucking-up in her life, not even when the Waysboro High School chorus director announced the spring musical and every would-be star in the school began lobbying for parts.

So this was politics. Kendra stood apart from the gushing campaign workers and watched. She could understand the paid staffers a little better than the volunteers—at least they were earning money for the time they put in here. The volunteers did it all for free, performing tedious tasks that were supposed to get their candidate elected to Congress.

And then what? Kendra hadn't yet figured out what the dedicated workers would get out of all this. The purpose and the thrill of politics eluded her.

Kendra's eyes slid over Wyatt Way, lazily assessing him. He was not an irresistible hunk with a face and body to die for. If he'd been that, she would've clearly understood why the women in this office were slavering over him. But he wasn't.

He was not particularly tall, a few inches shy of six feet, and his conservatively cut hair was an undistinguished shade of light brown. He did have a nice smile, wide with astonishingly white teeth. A prerequisite for a politician and for a Way. When was the last time anyone had seen a Way with bad teeth? For that matter, when was the first time? Kendra smiled to herself, imagining a Way—any Way— flashing a grin filled with gaps and black decay. That would be a sure sign of the apocalypse, definitely more foreboding than those four horsemen they warned about in church.

Kendra continued her perusal of candidate Way. His gray suit—she knew it must be expensive—complemented an average frame. He looked proper, conventional, and dig- nified, interchangeable with every other boring politician she'd seen on TV.

Kendra stifled a yawn. She hoped Barry was the staffer to tip her today. He always gave her more than the others.

And then her eyes connected with Wyatt Way's.

Wyatt gulped for breath. The air seemed to have been temporarily trapped in his lungs. It was the strangest, most disconcerting sensation he'd ever experienced. One moment he was being hustled into the headquarters, surrounded by beaming staffers, all talking at once, reaching for his hand to shake, shouting into his ear to be heard. Then suddenly, unexpectedly, he was staring into the dark blue eyes of the most beautiful young woman he'd ever seen.

Girl, Wyatt quickly corrected himself. She wasn't a woman, she was a teenaged girl, dressed in the stu- dent uniform of jeans and T-shirt, except it looked so much better on her than on most. Her small breasts were full and softly rounded beneath the fitted cotton shirt, the jeans displayed her tiny waist and long legs to perfection.

Wyatt gulped. No, she didn't look like your average, everyday teen. There was nothing average about this girl. Her coloring was striking, her smooth skin a delicate ivory shade that had not ever been subjected to a sunbaking tan. She had an impressive mane of long, thick jet-black hair and dark, dark eyebrows that provided a dramatic contrast with her complexion. Her features were nothing less than exquisite: high cheekbones, large, wide-set deep blue eyes, her nose small and straight, her mouth red, sensually shaped, and sultry.

Their eye contact went on a moment too long but Wyatt couldn't seem to tear his gaze away from her. She was such a pleasure to look at, like a delicate porcelain figurine. A work of art come to life. The girl smiled slowly, and he knew she was aware of his scrutiny. He quickly dragged his eyes away from her, while groping in the pocket of his suit coat for a handkerchief. It was so warm and he was beginning to perspire. He wiped his brow and glanced furtively, guiltily, back at the girl standing quietly against the wall.

She was still watching him and she caught his eye again. Her smile widened, revealing small, straight white teeth. Wyatt felt as if he'd been drop-kicked across the room. A dizzying surge of heat flashed through his body, making him gulp for breath. He'd heard women described as "knockouts" before, he'd even used the term himself upon occasion, but this was the first time he'd ever experienced the phenomenon. That smile of hers had the effect of a sharp blow to the head.

Kendra was enjoying herself, her head tilted slightly as she smiled her special secret-weapon smile, complete with a dimple and sparkling eyes, the one she'd perfected in front of her mirror. She knew it packed a potent wallop on whomever she unleashed it on, and Wyatt Way proved no exception. She watched as he stood stock-still, flushed, his mouth fixed and his eyes glazed. Kendra felt a thrill of power. One of the illustrious Ways had seen her, and he couldn't take his eyes off her!

The beginnings of a plan began to germinate in her mind. Wyatt Way had definitely noticed her; now she must heighten his interest, intensify it. She had a part to play and she knew she would be superb. Her acting talents were top-notch, though Waysboro High's Drama Club had never validated her skills. Its membership was exclusive and she had not been invited to join.

The moment Wyatt finally managed to wrench his eyes away from her, Kendra walked slowly but purposefully toward the door, moving with the serene and self-possessed air she'd practiced and practiced until it appeared as natural as the slight, sexy sway of her hips. She'd practiced that as well.

"Oh, Kendra, don't leave without your tip," called Barry Lang, one of the younger, twenty-something volunteers.

"Thank you, Barry." Kendra beamed as he handed her a five-dollar bill. Five dollars! She was elated. "If you need anything else from Letty's, just give a call and I'll run it over." She paused at the door to give a quick wave.

"Isn't she fabulous?" Kendra heard Barry sigh as she sauntered through the door.

"Who is she?" asked Wyatt, straining to keep his voice at a natural pitch.

"That's Kendra, the high school girl who works afternoons in the coffee shop," replied one of the women. "She's a sweetheart. When she brings us coffee, she slips in extra packets of sugar and cream. That tight-fisted old bat Letty would probably behead her if she knew."

Kendra drifted across the street, back into the coffee shop. There were only two customers sitting in a booth, the same two she had waited on before leaving with the coffee. It was always slow this time of day, one of the reasons why Letty had instituted the free delivery service to the headquarters.

"What's happening over there?" Letty asked the same question she always asked upon Kendra's return. "You know, I've been thinking of switching to uniforms around here," she added. She said that at least once a day, too.

Kendra paid no attention to her last comment; she knew Letty was too individualistic to enforce a uniform rule. But she did have an interesting answer for her boss's question about Way campaign headquarters.

"Wyatt Way, the guy who's running for Congress, came in. You should've seen those campaign workers falling all over him. You'd think he was JFK or something."

"The Ways are the Kennedys of this town," Letty pronounced. "They're our royal family, too, all wrapped up into one."

"It must be great to have all that money," Kendra mused. "To live in a big house and wear beautiful clothes and never have to look at the prices on anything. I can't think of anything more wonderful."

Letty snorted. "I guess this is when I'm supposed to give you some kind of a lecture about money not being important and how money can't buy happiness."

"That's as untrue as that stupid myth about how it's better to be beautiful on the inside instead of on .the outside," Kendra scoffed. "Like it's cool to be ugly or something! Puh-leeze! Be honest, Letty, wouldn't you rather be rich and beautiful and wicked instead of poor and homely and virtuous?"

"What a question!" Letty shook her head.

"Yeah. As if anybody gets the chance to choose," Kendra said darkly. She began to set clean place settings at each seat at the counter, preparing for the regulars who came in for dinner starting around five o'clock.

While she worked, she started formulating a plan. It would take nerve and resolve but she had plenty of that. At last she was going to turn her dreams of escaping from Waysboro into reality!

Everything would be financed by the enormous sum of money Wyatt Way would pay her in exchange for keeping her mouth shut about their torrid affair. Kendra contemplated exactly how much money she should demand: certainly enough to cover travel expenses for her, Ashlynne, Maxie, and Daisy—even if they chose to go by jet. Certainly enough to get them a nice apartment in a big exciting city. Like New York! And of course, they would all need new wardrobes for their new lives. She didn't want to be greedy, but her payoff would have to be substantial to meet all their expenses.

But first things first. Kendra dutifully refilled the salt and pepper shakers while she contemplated how to begin a torrid affair.

Sunday dinner at OakWay was served at two in the afternoon, a ritual as unshakable as roasting a turkey on Thanksgiving Day. Cord joined the clan for the event, which marked the end of his first week in Waysboro. It was exactly as he'd remembered, right down to the standing rib roast, mashed potatoes, and thick gravy. The meal was Grandfather Way's favorite, and the old man sat at the head of the table, wolfing it down with relish.

At ninety, Dayland Way Senior confounded medical science by remaining in perfect health, despite consuming enough cholesterol to clog the arteries of a small city. He ate red meat at least once a day, loved anything fried, and breakfasted on bacon and eggs each morning. He also had a seventy-five-year pack-a-day smoking habit. The old man had long outlived his only son and Cord figured he would probably outlast his grandchildren as well.

Cord watched his brother Stafford eye their grandfather's plate with disapproval, but no one dared to challenge Dayland. So Stafford directed his lecture on the evils of cholesterol, including figures and stats, to the rest of the family, loading his own plate with salad and vegetables to serve as an example. While he spoke, sons Trip and Skip poured ever more gravy on their slabs of meat and slathered their biscuits and potatoes with gobs of butter. Cord recognized a dietary rebellion when he saw one. He silently cheered his nephews on. There was just something about Stafford that made you want to do the opposite of whatever he happened to advocate.

"Killer cholesterol levels are beside the point," Holly snapped.

Stafford shot her a killing look; Prentice gasped at such heresy. Holly ignored them and launched a diatribe of her own. "What we should all be concerned about is the fate of our fellow living creatures! For far too long, humans have arrogantly slaughtered animals for sport, for fur and for food. It's long past time that we recognize how cruel and repulsive our behavior has been and take steps to remedy it before it's too late."

Everyone kept on eating. Holly gripped her fork like a spear, her face taut with frustration. "I eat nothing with a face and I find it unconscionable that my own family is sitting around me *wolfing* down a poor defenseless cow that possessed one."

"Potatoes have eyes, Aunt Holly," Skip said tauntingly as Holly took a bite of an oven-roasted spud. "And eyes are features on a face. Better put down that fork."

Cord chuckled. He couldn't help himself. That earned him a stern rebuke from Prentice for encouraging her son's insolence.

"Will you people kindly shut up so I can eat in peace!" thundered old Dayland. Silence descended. Dinner at OakWay had never been one of those family affairs where everybody, from the youngest child on up, was encouraged to contribute to the conversation. Dayland Way preferred and often demanded "blessed silence" while surrounded by his progeny.

"When did Holly go crazy?" Cord asked Wyatt as they exited the dining room together at the end of the interminable meal. "All that crap about not eating anything with a face! I remember how much she used to love honey-baked ham and veal medallions. Those are pigs and calves, and they most definitely have faces. What happened?"

Wyatt answered him quite seriously. "Something happened to Holly a few years ago, Cord. I don't know what. She's never confided in me. But remember when she left that job of hers in Columbus to move to Atlanta? You'd been in Montana for a couple of years at that point."

Cord nodded. "I remember. I was told she was tired of Columbus, tired of the Midwest and her job with the newspaper. She wanted a change, so she switched jobs and cities. Good-bye, Columbus and print journalism; hello, Atlanta and broadcast news. Made sense to me."

"I think there was more to it than that," said Wyatt. "I haven't seen too much of her since then, but she's definitely been different. Sadder, more cynical and guarded. Prentice thinks it was a love affair that went sour, but Holly's never said."

"Well, a man does have a face," Cord acknowledged. "And if Holly had a sour love affair with a guy and his face, then why not boycott eating all creatures that have faces? Makes perfect sense. Not!" he added, lapsing into Trip and Skip's vernacular.

Wyatt tried and failed to stifle a grin. "Sometimes you say the things the rest of us only dare to think."

"That's because I'm as nuts as Holly. And after another week here in Waysboro, I'll be genuinely certifiable."

Actually, he already seemed to have reached the certifiable point, Cord decided as he stood in the foyer of the white frame building that housed four separate apartments. It was several hours after the Way family Sunday banquet, and he was holding a potted plant as he read the names on the mailboxes.

There it was: Monroe 3C. He'd been surprised that Ashlynne did not live in Lower Lyme Hill with the rest of the Monroes; he'd never heard of any of them leaving their enclave. But this apartment building was located in a solid middle-class neighborhood where there were strict zoning restrictions against places like the Waterside Bar.

He walked up the stairs and pressed the doorbell without giving himself time to reconsider. He really was crazy, he must be. Why else would he be at Ashlynne Monroe's door when he knew she loathed him? A diagnosis of insanity would also explain why he couldn't make himself stop thinking about her, of reviewing every minute detail of their less-than-friendly encounters. Of trying to come up with a good reason to have another.

There was no good reason, so he'd manufactured a lame one. Oh yes, this past week in Waysboro had addled his brain, all right.

The door to the apartment was opened by a pretty teen-aged girl who stared at him and the plant in his hands as if he'd just been dropped to earth from a spaceship.

"I'm here to see Ashlynne Monroe." He spoke first as the girl seemed too astonished to utter a sound.

"You are?" She continued to gape at him. "And you brought her those flowers?"

"Well, actually, I want to ask her to—uh—show me the location of—of where her sister Rayleen is buried. These flowers are for—"

"You want to ask Ashlynne to go to the cemetery with you to plant those flowers on Rayleen's grave?" the girl asked incredulously. "Who are you?"

"Oh, just a lunatic passing through the neighborhood." He guessed he appeared as stupid as he felt. "Who are you?"

"I'm Kendra Monroe, Ashlynne's sister. And I know she doesn't know you. She makes it a point to steer clear of weirdos."

"Very commendable of her. But unfortunately for Ashlynne, she does know me. You see, I was a friend of Rayleen's before I left town six years ago. I recently returned and learned of her death." He nodded toward the plant. "I'm Cord Way, and I was very sorry to hear the sad news."

"Cord Way?" Kendra repeated. "You're not—one of *the* Ways?"

"Guilty as charged, I'm afraid".

"And you knew Rayleen six years ago?" Kendra was staring oddly at him. "How friendly were you with her? Did you, like, date her?"

"Well, yes." He supposed what they'd done might be construed as a form of dating.

"Holy God!" Kendra swayed slightly and stared at him, her blue eyes wide and shocked. "Now I know—" She gasped and clapped her hand over her mouth.

"Now you know what?" Cord asked curiously.

"—Uh, uh, two Ways," Kendra improvised quickly. "Now I know two Ways. I met Wyatt Way, the one who's running for Congress, a few days ago, and now here you are, another Way." She ran her hand through her long, dark hair, tousling it. "Wow, listen to me rambling on and on. I must sound like a real jerk. But it's so exciting to meet a Way, sort of like meeting—um—Axl Rose or—or—Bono."

Kendra wondered if she were laying it on a bit too thick. She wanted to sound like the sort of airhead who would completely blow her cool upon meeting a Way, but perhaps she'd overdone it? She strove to regain credibility. "Oh, I can't believe I said that! You probably think I'm an idiot."

"If you are, then so am I." Cord grinned. "So you've met Wyatt? He's my brother."

"Oh, wow!" exclaimed Kendra. The blood was roaring in her ears and she thought her heart was going to burst with excitement. This man was Daisy's father, she was sure of it. There was a resemblance that was unmistakable, plus the timing, the fact that he'd dated Rayleen—it all fit. She was under no illusions about her late sister. Rayleen slept with every guy she dated—and that meant she'd slept with a Way!

And it also explained the secrecy surrounding the identity of Daisy's father. Kendra had always known who Maxie's father was; she and Ashlynne even mentioned him from time to time. But never a word about Daisy's father. Kendra had assumed that Rayleen herself was unsure who had impregnated her the second time. But if it was a Way . . .

Kendra stared at Cord, her eyes drinking in every detail. Why, it had been a Way, she was sure of that now! Cord and Daisy had the same coloring, those same dark eyes that oddly matched the shade of their hair. *Daisy was a Way!*

Cord watched the girl appraise him. Her reaction to him was amusing. And her enthusiasm over meeting him was in stunning contrast to her sister Ashlynne's utter disdain.

"So is Ashlynne here?" he asked lightly, figuring that she wasn't. Otherwise, she would've already appeared and thrown him out of the building.

"She went to the store. I'm here baby-sitting my two little nieces." Kendra eyed him slyly. "Want to come in and meet them?"

"Sure. Although I think I already have. Maxie and Daisy, right? Ashlynne's little girls."

"That's right." Kendra didn't correct his misassumption that the children were Ashlynne's. The sisters had decided years ago to maintain the fiction of Ashlynne's motherhood, not mentioning the truth about Rayleen to anyone who didn't already know.

"Come on in and remeet them." Kendra took his arm and fairly dragged him inside. "You can put the plant on that table. It's pretty. I'm sure Rayleen will love it on her grave. And if she has too many flowers, we'll put it on one of the others. Maybe on our mother's grave. I bet she'd like having something from you, considering who you are."

Cord winced at that. Their mother was dead, too? All this talk of cemeteries and dead Monroes seemed to underscore how very downtrodden they actually were. Suddenly, he felt trapped, yet he couldn't seem to come up with an acceptable reason to leave the premises immediately. Kendra had a viselike grip on his arm and was calling the children. He was well and truly stuck now.

When Ashlynne arrived nearly a half hour later, he was sitting on the sofa reading a storybook to Maxie, who sat snuggled on his lap. Daisy sat cross-legged on the floor several feet away. She was listening to the story but wouldn't come any closer. He didn't know much about kids, but Daisy was such a wary, reserved child that she struck him as a bit spooky, especially in comparison to open, lovable Maxie.

Kendra sat on a chair opposite the sofa, staring at him, her eyes intense as lasers, never leaving him. Cord decided she was a little spooky too.

Ashlynne walked through the door and gaped at the cozy scene. The bag of groceries she carried slipped out of her hands and fell to the floor. Everybody jumped at the sound.

"What's going on?" she asked. It was hard to breathe. Cord Way was in her living room! With the children, with Daisy!

"Mommy, Uncle Cord came to see us and he's reading *Candy for Penny*," Maxie cried happily.

"*Uncle* Cord?" Ashlynne repeated. Her eyes met Cord's. He shrugged nonchalantly and resumed reading.

Daisy jumped to her feet and hurried to Ashlynne's side. "Mommy, he's not a stranger," she said reassuringly. "He knows Kendra and that Rayleen, the one who's in heaven."

"Yeah, he knew Rayleen real well," added Kendra. She stared pointedly from Daisy to Cord.

Ashlynne's heart sank. She knew by the look on her younger sister's face that Kendra had figured out Cord Way's role in their family. It was probably why she'd invited him in.

"He brought Rayleen a plant." Kendra pointed to it. "Isn't that amazing? Guys are still bringing Rayleen presents, even though she's been dead and buried for years. Talk about having long-lasting appeal!"

"Kendra!" Ashlynne's voice quavered on a warning note.

Kendra flashed an acquiescent smile. "Hey, I have an idea. Why don't you two take the plant over to the cemetery? I'll give the kids their bath and get them ready for bed."

"I'm not going to the cemetery. It'll be dark soon. Anyway, Mr. Way has to leave immediately," Ashlynne added firmly.

"Come on, kids, let's get that bath." Kendra grabbed each child by the hand. "Uncle Cord and Mommy want to talk about Rayleen and heaven and flowers, you know, stuff like that." She hustled them from the room, talking as they went, successfully stifling any possible protests.

Ashlynne and Cord faced each other. "What is this all about?" she demanded, trembling with fright and anger. What kind of game was he playing?

"Like Kendra said, I wanted to pay my respects to Rayleen." He felt as foolish as a gauche adolescent. "If you'll—er—come to the cemetery with me, we can have this planted and be back before it gets dark." Now there was an enticing offer, he silently mocked himself. What woman could possibly resist?

"I'll put it on Rayleen's grave the next time I visit. You don't have to be there."

"So much for that." Cord sighed. "Okay, I admit it was a lame excuse but it was the only one I could come up with on short notice."

"An excuse for what?"

"To see you." He shrugged. "I wanted to see you, Ashlynne. I mean, Miss Monroe," he amended drolly. "For a minute there, I forgot that I didn't have your permission to address you by your first name."

"Did you weasel your way into my home to make fun of me?" Ashlynne was incensed.

"Not at all, Miss Monroe. I was showing you the respect you demanded in Thorpe's office, remember? You said that you wanted to be—"

"I remember what I said," she snapped. Except hearing him call her "Miss Monroe" sounded pretentious and phony. Maybe it was the way he said it? "Forget it. Just call me Ashlynne, tell me what you're doing here, and get out."

He smiled ruefully. "You're not going to make it easy for me, are you?"

Icy fingers of apprehension froze her to the spot. "I don't know what you're talking about." Why was he here? Had he already learned about Daisy? "I—I'll never make anything easy for you, Cord Way," she promised.

"I figured as much." He smiled a smile that managed to be both boyish and seductive. "Well, nothing good comes easy, I guess, so here goes. I want to ask you out, Ashlynne."

There, he'd said it. He was proud of himself. He'd abandoned the game-playing strategies of his past and opted for the truth. He wanted to go out with her, to get to know her better. It was a relief to face the facts and state them plainly, to put aside schemes and stratagem—

"Go out with you?" Ashlynne exclaimed. She didn't look pleased by his straightforward lack of maneuvering, not at all. Instead, she appeared—aghast?

"I—I'd rather have a kidney removed than go out with you. I can't believe you have the gall to even ask. Just get out and stay away from us. We don't want you anywhere near us."

Anger flashed through him, a combination of frustration and exasperation. "Your sister and your daughters don't seem to mind having me around."

"They're minors, what do they know?" Ashlynne retorted furiously.

How dare he barge into her own home and try to insinuate himself with the kids? Did he suspect something? Had Kendra given away their secret the moment she'd worked out Daisy's parentage or had he figured it out on his own? *What if he knew?*

Panicky with fear, Ashlynne struck out blindly, giving him a hard shove toward the door. "Get out of here! And don't you ever come back."

She pushed him again harder. Swaying slightly, he stepped backward to steady himself, both feet coming down flat on the bag of groceries that she'd dropped on the floor. There was a sickening squish and a crunch as he landed.

He quickly stepped aside and looked down. The bag was squashed flat.

"Oh, look what you did!" Ashlynne dropped to her knees and opened the bag. She removed a crushed loaf of bread and a bag of grapes that looked as if they'd been stomped to make wine. The bunch of bananas hadn't fared any better—they were flattened and bursting out of their skins. Since the box of graham crackers was smashed, one had to assume that its contents had been pulverized. And then there were the dozen eggs . . .

Cord groaned. Naturally, there weren't any canned goods, no paper products—everything in the bag was something eminently squashable. And it appeared that his flat-footed landing had destroyed every single item.

"You clod!" Ashlynne exclaimed. "Everything is ruined. Everything I bought!" She shoved the damaged goods back in the bag and stood up, gripping it.

Cord was certain that she intended to hurl the whole sorry mess at him. And while being hit with a loaf of smashed bread wouldn't hurt him, he did not relish the impact of the crushed grapes, bananas, and eggs.

"You're as much to blame as I am." He held out his arm, to ward her off. "If you hadn't pushed me, I wouldn't have—"

"Oh, that's your theme song, isn't it? 'It's not my fault.' " Her voice rose to a mocking trill. "Cord Way is automatically absolved of responsibility. It's never your fault, is it, Cord? No, it's not your problem. Nothing ever is."

She drew back her arm, the bag dangling threateningly from her hand.

Swiftly, in self-defense, Cord's hand snaked out to fasten around her wrist. "You're crazy, do you know that? Going ballistic over a bag of groceries that *you* pushed me into!" He tugged at her arm until the bag slipped from her fingers. "I've never met anyone as volatile as you are. You're as explosive as a live grenade."

"Let me go!" Ashlynne tried to wrench her arm from his grip. When he didn't release her, she swung wildly at him with her other hand.

Cord grabbed that one too. "Will you calm down?" It came out more a desperate plea than an order. She continued to struggle as he continued to hold on to her. "Ashlynne, stop this. I—*ouch*!"

She'd kicked him in the shins. When she drew back to do it again, Cord automatically yanked her against him, pinning her arms behind her back and anchoring his legs between hers, effectively halting her attack.

"Let me go!" She gasped, her face flushed and furious. She glared up at him, her eyes blazing.

"You really are nuts if you think I'll turn you loose without some kind of assurance of amnesty," Cord said wryly. "You'd like to flatten me as thoroughly as that box of crackers."

"That *you* stepped on and ruined, you—you oaf!"

"Doesn't sound like you're quite ready to negotiate." He laughed huskily.

The feel of her soft, warm body against his was already wreaking havoc with his senses. He stared down into her luminous blue eyes, then lowered his gaze to her lips, which were parted and trembling. She had the most sensual mouth he'd ever seen, he thought dazedly. Soft and full and pink.

He felt the thrust of her breasts against his chest, the tight beads of her nipples a provocative lure. Her long slim legs were entwined with his. A dark, rich rush of desire surged through him.

Ashlynne drew a shaky breath. She tried to move but couldn't; his superior strength subdued her own. More alarmingly, the urge to fight had been replaced by a pulsing tension that completely immobilized her. There didn't seem to be an inch of her that wasn't plastered against the hard, muscular frame of his body. She felt the beat of his heart against hers, felt every breath he took . . . and she was aware of the exact moment when his body tightened and hardened into blatant male arousal.

A bolt of sensual electricity sent shocking streaks of sensation from her belly to the insides of her thighs, which were straddling his. His hands cupped her bottom, crushing the cotton fabric of her skirt with his fingers as he pressed her even more intimately to the contours of his body. She felt the taut shape of him straining against the denim of his jeans, straining against her.

She gasped and her eyes flew to his. Their gazes locked and held for a long moment. Ashlynne's mind seemed to splinter, and her eyes fluttered shut. His dark gaze was too searing, too intimate. She couldn't think, couldn't move. She couldn't do anything but lean into the strong masculine planes of his body as a strange and enervating syrupy warmth coursed through her.

She heard him murmur something unintelligible and then his mouth was on hers, hot and hard and hungry. The taste of his mouth was delicious and went straight to her head like a shot of the potent whiskey she had always been careful to resist. But she couldn't resist him. Held so close against him, the thought of resistance never entered her muddled mind. Her lips parted instinctively for his tongue, which surged, bold and insistent, into the warm, moist hollow of her mouth.

Ashlynne clung to him, rocked by the shattering sexuality of his kiss. She'd never known anything like the explosion of desire that rocketed through her, making her feel daring and sensual and free. She met his tongue with her own, rubbing and teasing. She threaded her hands—somewhere along the line he'd freed them but she had no idea when— through his dark, thick hair and melted against him.

Her breasts swelled and her loins felt full and achy. A wild little cry escaped from her throat. The exquisite pleasure of his hands and lips was making her burn with helpless urgency. She'd never been kissed this way before, so deep and intimate, so primitively possessive.

She was aflame with passionate excitement she had never before experienced. Clinging to him, she kissed him back with an ardor that equaled his own. Nothing mattered right now except that he go on holding her, kissing her . . .

Cord was more than willing to do just that. Her open, uninhibited response unleashed a passion within him that electrified him, astonished him too. He couldn't remember the last time he'd been aroused so hard and so fast by a kiss, but it was probably back in his early high school days when kissing was a new and exciting sensual pleasure.

And now, in Ashlynne's arms, he felt wonderfully renewed, as if he'd been given the chance to start all over again. Passion coursed through his veins like a drug. He was elated. And very, very turned on.

"Let's get out of here," he whispered urgently, his lips against her ear. He reluctantly lifted his mouth from hers, unable to postpone the need for oxygen. They were both panting and breathless and gulping for air. "I want to be alone with you, Ashlynne."

His words penetrated the sensual cloud enshrouding her with the force of a verbal atomic bomb. The passion drained from her as if some invisible plug had been pulled. There was only one reason why he wanted to hustle her out of the apartment, only one reason why he was so eager for them to be alone. Ashlynne's face burned. Worse, her own shocking, unexpected response to him had given him every reason to believe that she was ready and willing to accommodate him.

She pulled back from him, horrified. Cord Way had taken her into his arms and she'd responded as if she'd spent her whole life yearning to be there. She'd melted like a crayon in the sun under his sensual heat. It was an appalling realization.

"So now you expect to take me to bed?" She pushed against his chest with her hands. He hadn't been expecting any resistance. Before he could make a move to keep her close, Ashlynne had effectively freed herself from his embrace.

"Well, from your point of view, why not?" Her voice shook. "You were having an affair with Rayleen when you left town, so it probably seems quite natural for you to take up with her sister, since she's not around to—to service you. After all, one Monroe tramp is as good as another. It's common knowledge that we're all interchangeable, like grains of wheat."

She turned away from him and strode across the room to stare out the window, determined that he wouldn't see the hot tears shimmering in her eyes.

Cord stood still, his body tense and wired, his unsatiated passion rapidly transforming itself into frustrated anger. "That's not true," he growled.

"Yes it is. That's why you came here tonight, that's why you grabbed me—"

"I didn't grab you!"

She whirled around to face him. "Yes you did. And now you're going to rant and rave and accuse me of leading you on, of being a trashy tease who—"

"Still working out the details of that trip to the cemetery?" Kendra's voice, clear and playful, joined the fray. She stood on the threshold of the room, eyeing the two of them with undisguised amusement. "Sorry to interrupt. I was on my way to the kitchen to get the plastic measuring spoons. The kids want to play with them in the tub."

"I'll get them. And I—I'll take over with their bath now, Kendra." Ashlynne raced into the small kitchen, snatched the spoons from the drawer, and headed into the bathroom where Daisy and Maxie were splashing in the bathtub surrounded by mermaid dolls and animal-shaped sponges.

Cord watched her leave the room and heaved a sigh of resignation. Her hasty exit had ended any chance they might've had to—To what? Settle the argument or continue the love scene? Or both? He wasn't sure. He hadn't felt this confused since . . . Had he *ever* felt this confused?

Kendra came closer, scrutinizing him with the avid curiosity of a scientist observing a newly discovered species.

"It didn't look like things were going too well," she said bluntly.

"That's one way of putting it. Here's another—your sister would rather be an organ donor than go out with me."

"You asked Ashlynne out?" Kendra's voice rose with excitement.

Had he? Cord frowned thoughtfully. Well, not exactly. He'd said he wanted to ask her out, but he had never gotten around to actually extending an invitation. No, he had argued with her, stomped on her groceries, and then seized her in a hot clinch. The last of his self-righteous anger abruptly dissolved. Considering his past history with Rayleen, no wonder Ashlynne had reacted as she had. He'd acted with all the finesse of a bull in heat. He stifled a groan.

"You asked her out and she turned you down?" An incredulous Kendra was mulling that one over. "I don't get it." She moved closer and stared even harder at him. "You're cute, you're successful, and you have more money than God. What else is there?" She appeared genuinely baffled.

Cord brightened. "Thanks, Kendra. You've put it all in perspective for me." Looks and money might be enough for Kendra, but not Ashlynne. Cord found that intriguing, refreshing.

A swirl of sensory memories clouded his brain. Her warmth and softness, the taste of her, the sweet urgency of her lips and her body . . .

In spite of her professed antipathy to his money and his looks, Ashlynne wanted him. As much as he'd wanted her.

"I guess you won't be asking her out again," Kendra speculated glumly.

"You guess wrong, honey." He headed buoyantly for the door. And managed to sidestep the hapless bag of groceries. "Here, Kendra, take this." Cord reached into his pocket and pulled out some bills. "For the groceries," he added, not bothering to explain.

"Thanks." Kendra accepted the money without question. It wasn't until he'd left the apartment that she allowed herself to look at the bills in her hand.

"A fifty and a twenty?" She gasped and studied the bills closely, as if expecting them to change denominations before her very eyes. "Ashlynne, he gave us seventy dollars," she cried joyfully, running into the bathroom. "He just reached into his pocket and pulled out a fifty and a twenty without even bothering to look!"

"If that snake thinks he can—can buy his way . . ." Ashlynne muttered. Her voice trailed off. She didn't dare lose control of her temper with the little ones present, although she was sorely tempted to snatch the money from Kendra's hand and set fire to it.

Not that she would've been able to pry the money from Kendra's inexorable grip. "I bet he had hundred-dollar bills in there too," the girl murmured, gazing at the faces of the presidents engraved on the bills. "Too bad he didn't pull out one of those. Maybe next time he will."

"There will be no next time, Kendra," Ashlynne said through gritted teeth.

"He said there would be."

Ashlynne's heart jumped painfully in her chest. "No. There won't be, Kendra."

"Have you always known he was Daisy's father?" Kendra asked, lowering her voice to a confidential whisper.

Ashlynne nodded. "From the very beginning. Rayleen didn't want him to know about the baby and she was right. We're no match against the Ways, Kendra. If they ever found out about Daisy . . ." Her voice trailed off ominously.

"And so that's why you won't see Cord Way again, even if he asks you out?"

"I can't, Kendra," Ashlynne said impatiently. "Surely you understand how dangerous that would be."

"Dangerous good or dangerous bad?" Kendra looked thoughtful. "There is a difference, Ashlynne."

Ashlynne cast a quick glance at the little girls playing in the tub, then looked squarely at her younger sister. "No there isn't," she said fiercely. "That's the kind of stupid thing Rayleen would've said. The same kind of faulty thinking. And look where it got her, Kendra. Look how it ended for her."

"I'll never be like Rayleen," Kendra assured her. "But sometimes you gotta take a risk, Ashlynne. Don't the means justify the end or something like that?"

Ashlynne rolled her eyes heavenward. "In my mind, the end does not justify the means, although I'm not exactly sure what means and what end you're referring to."

Kendra merely smiled enigmatically and turned her attention to the children in the tub.

CHAPTER FOUR

"I CAN'T believe I let you talk me into this, Kendra." Josh Overly huddled behind the wheel of his blue Ford Tempest and glared balefully at Kendra, who sat in the seat next to him. "I must be out of my mind."

Kendra reached into a box of dog biscuits and pulled out a bone-shaped treat. "Here, Judge." She offered it to the black Lab that stood on the backseat, his head hanging over the front as he drooled happily. The dog accepted the milkbone biscuit graciously, though he wasn't quite as eager for it as he'd been for the previous eight treats she had given him.

Kendra patted his big head and the dog gazed lovingly at her with his soulful brown eyes. "You're a sweetheart, Judge. Yes, you are." She turned to Josh. "He likes me. He likes being with us. Look how happy he is."

Josh shrugged. "He's a Lab and Labs are people-friendly. We're lucky that Wyatt Way didn't have a Doberman or a Rottweiler or we'd be in the emergency room right now, getting ourselves stitched back together." He shook his head, groaning. "Dognapping! I can't believe we did it! Sneaking into Wyatt Way's backyard and taking his dog and holding him hostage! I think we could be arrested for this, Kendra!"

"We haven't kidnapped him and we're not holding him hostage," Kendra said patiently. "We simply borrowed him for a little while. We'll be taking him back." She glanced at her watch. "Right about now. He's been gone for over an hour." She patted the dog's head. "Want to go home, boy? Want to see your daddy or your master or whatever Wyatt Way calls himself?"

"I call him a poor sucker," Josh said trenchantly. "He

doesn't know what he's in for, getting tangled up with you."

Kendra leaned over and patted Josh's knee, in the same lightly affectionate way she'd patted the dog's head. "You're a good friend, Josh. The best."

They'd met two years ago when Josh had moved to Waysboro. The high school, thrilled to finally have an Asian student, automatically assigned him to advanced math classes and recruited him for the orchestra. But Josh possessed no particular mathematical talent and had never touched a violin in his life. The school's upper echelon quickly lost interest in him and the lower echelon, Kendra and other outcasts, were quick to befriend him.

"I should be trying to talk you out of this stupid scheme of yours instead of helping you along with it," Josh grumbled. He gunned the engine of the car and pulled out of the secluded parking spot in woodsy Way Park.

Ten minutes later, they arrived at Wyatt Way's Georgian-style brick house on Applegate Lane. Wyatt was walking along the sidewalk, whistling for his dog and calling its name.

"The poor guy. Look at him. He's all worried about his dog," Josh said, shooting a reproachful glance at Kendra.

"He's wearing a suit to look for his dog?" Kendra's voice was tinged with disbelief. "It's nearly ten o'clock at night. What's he doing in a suit at this hour?"

"The guy's a politician, Kendra. They live in suits. Maybe he just got in from a meeting only to discover his dog was missing, and he rushed right out to find him without even taking the time to change his clothes."

"Then he'll be so happy to see Judge, just like we planned!" Kendra's blue eyes sparkled with excitement.

"Just like *you* planned," Josh reminded her. "You're the mastermind, you can have full credit. I'm just the idiot accessory to the crime."

Kendra was undaunted. "Come on, Judgie boy. Let's go home!" She opened the car door and the dog bounded out, running up to his master to bark joyfully.

Judge stood on his hind paws, bracing himself against Wyatt and slobbering ecstatically all over his white shirt, suit, and tie. Wyatt didn't mind. "Judge!" He patted the dog's big head, beaming his relief. "Where were you? And how did you get out of the yard?"

"It looks like we brought him to the right place," Kendra observed, smiling at the man and his dog.

Wyatt looked up to meet her warm blue eyes. He recognized her instantly—the beautiful girl from Letty's Coffee Shop. He had looked for her his next time at campaign headquarters and been disappointed to be told he'd missed her. Immediately after, he'd fought his sudden craving for some of Letty's thick, greasily delicious vegetable soup, which would've required a trip to the coffee shop—and another look at this breathtakingly beautiful young woman, now standing in front of him, smiling a smile that sent his pulses racing faster than thirty minutes on the Stairmaster.

An unnerving surge of heat suffused him. "You brought him home?"

Kendra nodded her head and continued to smile that smile. "Josh and I saw him running along Way Boulevard. We thought he looked lost, so we called him into the car. We read his name and address on his collar and here we are."

"We stopped to get him some doggy treats," Josh added.

Wyatt dragged his eyes away from the girl to her companion, a stocky teenaged Asian boy about her height, who was clutching a box of dog biscuits. The boy extended his hand to shake. "I'm Josh and this is Kendra. You're running for Congress against Dan Clarkston, aren't you?"

"Yes, I am." Wyatt shook the boy's hand, a bit unnerved by his easy reference to the candidate running against him. Was Clarkston becoming such a household name in Waysboro that even high school kids knew it?

Wyatt stroked Judge's smooth coat, fighting the unease that gripped him. Lately, any mention of his congressional campaign brought on a sense of impending doom.

Kendra was watching him closely. She'd always been perceptive in gauging others' moods and his was definitely bleak. She wondered why. If she were as rich as Wyatt Way, she would be happy all the time. Well, she didn't have time to puzzle out his dark mood, she had a plan to implement.

"I deliver coffee to your staff on weekdays from Letty's Coffee Shop, Mr. Way," she piped up, determined to reclaim his attention. "I like your staff very much. They work so hard for you. I hope you win."

Her voice was soft and cool. Wyatt's attention was immediately reclaimed.

"That's very kind of you—Kendra." When she looked at him in that certain way, with those shining blue eyes of hers, it was impossible for him to feel unease or doom or anything but pure pleasure.

Kendra nodded imperceptibly at Josh. They were back on track. Now if only Josh remembered what he was supposed to say . . . He'd been joking around so much during their practice session, she wasn't sure what he would come out with.

"Hey, Kendra, if his staff works so hard, then how come they're not out there trying to reach new voters? Know what I think? That staff of his just sits around, drinking too much coffee and taking Mr. Way's victory for granted." Josh's tone was challenging, almost taunting.

Kendra suppressed a smile. He'd nailed it!

Wyatt bristled, but before he could defend his staff, Kendra spoke up. "Josh, that's not true! Don't pay any attention to him, Mr. Way." She turned earnest blue eyes on Wyatt. "He's been critical of your staff ever since Dan Clarkston came into the senior high to recruit volunteers for his campaign. I told Josh that your staff probably has a similar plan—an even better one—for encouraging eighteen-year-olds to register to vote. You see, most of the senior class is eighteen and—"

"Clarkston came to the high school?" Wyatt cut in. He knew for a fact that his staff hadn't given a thought to the high school and its young voters who'd come of age and would be voting for the first time in the November election. He hadn't either.

Kendra nodded. "It was an informal thing. He talked to the students about voting. Made a few jokes."

"Some were about the Way dynasty," Josh added. "Mr.

Clarkston was real friendly. He passed out candy bars too. Clark bars. Good name recognition, huh?"

"I don't like Dan Clarkston," Kendra said. "He smiles too much. I would rather vote for you, Mr. Way." She sidled closer to Wyatt.

Wyatt breathed in the alluring, exotic scent emanating from her body. His blood seemed to thicken. So did another, crucial part of his anatomy. It was hard to keep his mind on the campaign with her standing so close.

"Thank you," he said huskily. "But Josh's criticism is valid. My staff and I have been remiss. We don't have a plan to reach the youngest, newest voters or—"

"You should get one," Josh interjected bluntly.

Kendra cleared her throat, glanced at Josh, and raised her eyebrows, their prearranged signal. Wyatt, lost in a Kendra-soaked haze, missed the subtle exchange.

"You could hire me and Kendra to run a student campaign for you, Mr. Way," Josh continued. "We have some great ideas."

"We will *not* be hired, Josh," Kendra told him sternly, then turned to face Wyatt. "We'll *volunteer*." Her gorgeous blue eyes shone with intelligence and determination. "If you want us, Mr. Way."

"Oh yes," Wyatt said quickly. "I want you." His face was flushed.

Kendra could hardly restrain herself from jumping up and down with glee. Her plan was working! Wyatt Way had taken the bait.

Josh grinned. "I'm sure this will be an interesting experience for all of us, Mr. Way."

Wyatt cleared his throat. "Uh, call me Wyatt. When I hear 'Mr. Way', I expect to turn around and see my grandfather, or perhaps my rather formidable older brother Stafford."

"Stafford and Wyatt." Josh chuckled. "Sounds like a law firm. Your family doesn't go in for normal guy names like Bill or Nick or Steve, huh?"

"What about your father?" Kendra asked, fixing Wyatt with a piercing, inquisitive gaze. "Why don't you think of him when you hear 'Mr. Way'?"

Wyatt shifted uncomfortably. She had unknowingly honed in on a most vulnerable point. "I didn't deliberately exclude my father. He . . . was killed in a plane crash when I was a boy and therefore doesn't automatically come to mind."

"I know what you mean." Kendra nodded her head. "My father died when I was eleven. I was furious with him for leaving us, so I made myself stop thinking about him. It kind of gets to be a habit. Now it's hard to remember him, even when I want to."

Wyatt was flooded with unwelcome memories of those dark days following his own father's death: the funeral, the terrible grief—and the irrational yet powerful rage he had felt at being abandoned. He gazed at Kendra, surprised at her insight, a bit unnerved by her honesty. He had never admitted to anyone that his father's death had infuriated as well as saddened him.

"Hey, Wyatt." Josh's voice broke the sudden silence. "Since we're going to be working together, I guess I should start talking strategy. And the sooner the better."

"I agree completely." Wyatt was eager to change the subject. "Would you two like to come inside?" He gestured toward his house.

"I'd like to, but I can't. Not tonight," Kendra said, her voice tinged with regret. "I have to get home or my sister will freak. She's watched too many episodes of *Unsolved Mysteries*. If I'm twenty minutes late, she assumes I've become one."

Wyatt smiled. "Well, what about tomorrow?"

"I work at the coffee shop till it closes at seven. Could you come then?" Kendra asked sweetly. "After I close the place to customers we can talk there."

"Cool!" Josh enthused. "Can you make it, Wyatt?"

Wyatt nodded. "I'll look forward to it." He was gazing at Kendra. "And I want to thank you again for bringing Judge home." He frowned slightly. "I put him in the yard and locked the gate before I left for my meeting with the chamber of commerce. I don't understand how he could've gotten out."

"Maybe some bratty neighborhood kids did it," Kendra suggested.

"Yeah, it's amazing what some brats will do," Josh said dryly.

Wyatt frowned. "I hate to think that's the case but, from now on, I will definitely have to be more careful." He stroked the dog's silky black coat. "I'd hate for anything to happen to Judge. We've been together seven years now."

"Ah, that's sweet." Kendra gazed at the man and his dog fondly. "Don't worry, Wyatt. I'm sure Judge isn't in any future danger."

"Judge might not be in any danger but Wyatt Way definitely is," Josh muttered as he steered his car away from the curb and into the street.

Beside him, Kendra smiled beatifically. "You were great, Josh. You said your lines exactly right. I think you should consider being an actor, I really mean it."

"I did sound like a smart-ass dude with an attitude. And you just ruled as Little Miss Vote-Getter. 'We will *not* be hired, we *volunteer*.' " His imitation of Kendra was right on the mark.

They both laughed.

"Everything seemed to work," Josh admitted. "He didn't even suspect us of taking the dog. I was worried about that. It was kind of weird when you two were talking about your dead dads, though. We hadn't rehearsed anything like that."

"I didn't know his father was dead. I feel sorry for him there. It's crummy to lose a parent when you're a kid. I sure know what that's like—my dad one year, my mom the next." Her expression grew bleak but she determinedly plastered a smile on her face. "Well, like my brother Shane says, 'you play the hand you're dealt.' "

"And you're really good at it. I bet that someday you'll be dealing your own deck, Kendra," Josh said admiringly. "One thing I don't understand, though, is how come you said no when Wyatt Way invited us inside his house tonight? I thought you'd jump at the chance."

Kendra shrugged. "It's getting late and Ashlynne really does worry about me."

"Yeah, but you could've called her."

"I don't want to seem too eager." Kendra smiled slyly. "Haven't you ever heard of playing it cool, Joshua?"

"Well, *he* sure was eager. I saw the way he was looking at you, Kendra. I think you've already got your hooks in him. But we do have a problem. What if he finds out that Clarkston never came to the high school? And what are we going to say when he asks our ideas for planning a student voter drive? We don't have any ideas."

"I'll have some," Kendra assured him. "Tomorrow at lunch, we'll rehearse for our scene at the coffee shop with him. Don't worry, you won't have as much to say as you did tonight."

"I'm getting written out early, huh? You plan on doing your best work alone?"

She nodded. And then: "Was he really looking at me, Josh? I mean really looking, like man to woman?"

"He was looking at you like horny man to woman," Josh said baldly. "He was practically drooling over you, like Judge with those dog biscuits." He paused. "Kendra, are you sure you know what you're doing? Wyatt Way isn't some high school guy, you know. He's thirty years old and he's rich and probably used to getting whatever he wants. That could mean big trouble for you."

"Trouble is exactly what I'm looking for," Kendra said. Her expression was nothing less than calculating, her beautiful blue eyes glittered like polished jewels. "And when it comes to payoffs, the bigger the trouble, the better for me."

"And the worse for Wyatt Way," finished Josh. "If he wasn't a Way and a politician, I might almost feel sorry for him. But since he's both, I don't."

"Me neither," seconded Kendra. She closed her eyes and began to plot. Scene: Letty's Coffee Shop. Time: seven P.M. tomorrow night. Characters: Kendra, Wyatt, and Josh, for about ten minutes. The phone rings and Josh is summoned home, leaving Kendra and Wyatt alone . . .

Cord stood in front of the window of his bedroom, staring out at the perfectly landscaped lawn. To the left were the famed OakWay gardens, his mother's pride and joy. Every year, garden clubs from the tri-state area were permitted to tour the grounds and admire his mother's horticultural talents, then were served tea on the spacious patio. For a fee, of course, which was always donated to Camilla's current pet charity.

Cord closed his eyes and visualized another view from another window, his office at the Glacier Lodge in Montana, where spectacular jagged mountain peaks rose to the sky in the horizon. He mentally transported himself back there as he phoned his assistant manager for the daily update on the lodge and campgrounds.

"How's it going, Mary Beth?" he asked. A pang of longing assailed him. He wanted to be back home, for Montana had long ago become home to him in a way that OakWay, the venerable old family homestead, would never be.

"We're surviving, but we wish you were here," Mary Beth Macauley replied, diplomatic as usual.

Cord grinned, picturing the competent and affable woman, a divorced mother of two college-age sons, who had worked in hotel management all her adult life. He had been fortunate, indeed, that she wanted to live and work in Glacier, for her presence at the lodge was invaluable.

"It wouldn't do to let the boss think that his absence isn't even noticed," he said dryly. "What's the occupancy rate today?"

"Same as yesterday, twenty vacancies, two hundred occupancies. We have the Hyland corporate retreat checking in this weekend. Ten rooms have been set aside for it."

"And the preparations are under way for the campground's opening next weekend? Since this is the first year we'll be opening before the Memorial Day weekend, we need to—"

"Keep accurate records so we'll know if it's worth our while," Mary Beth cut in.

"I guess you've heard that lecture a few times before, huh?" There was a smile in Cord's voice.

"Just a few—hundred." Mary Beth laughed. "By the way, I heard a rumor that a KOA inspector is in the state. He was allegedly sighted in Yosemite and might be headed our way."

Cord felt a frisson of anxiety. "Kampgrounds of America has always given us their superior rating, we can't lose that." He wished once again that he were there, he *should* be there!

"Don't worry, the campgrounds will pass with flying colors even if Herr Inspector arrives on opening day," Mary Beth assured him. She paused. "Have I mentioned that there might be just a little problem with the chef?"

"A problem with Jack?" Cord's voice deepened ominously. "No, you haven't mentioned a word of that, Mary Beth."

"I didn't want to bother you, I thought I could handle him." Another pause. "Jack is thinking of quitting, Cord."

"He's *what*?" Cord nearly dropped the cordless phone. This was not the sort of thing he wanted to hear while he was hundreds of miles away. The Glacier Lodge's cuisine had garnered raves, stars, and diamonds from travel-industry mavens, last year securing their first coveted four-star and four-diamond rating. Cord scowled. Losing Jack Townsend, their brilliant and innovative young chef, was not an option he was going to consider. "What's going on, Mary Beth?"

She sighed. "Remember that travel agent who was here last month, Tari Keene of Tari's Triumphant Tours?"

"The flaky one who wore turbans and read tarot cards?" Cord shuddered in remembrance. "I remember."

"Well, apparently she read Jack's cards or something, and now he's convinced that his true destiny lies in France where he's meant to study French country cooking. He feels restricted and restrained here in Montana and—"

"He is restricted to Montana because he signed a contract with me that runs for another two years. If he dares to quit on me, I'll sue him until he's so broke he won't even be able to afford a spatula, let alone airfare to France!"

"I won't quote you on that," Mary Beth said calmly. "Making threats is only going to make Jack feel more constrained. I mean Jacques. That is what he prefers to be called now."

Cord gripped the phone so tightly his knuckles turned white. "I think I'd better fly back there tonight."

"He is determined to go to France and you won't change his mind by threatening to sue him," countered Mary Beth. "My advice would be to stay there and help with your brother's campaign and let me try to convince Jack that his destiny really lies here in Montana."

"How do you intend to do that? By reading his palm? Or do you plan to begin studying tea leaves, Madame Swami?"

Mary Beth laughed. "I'm sorry I mentioned it, but—well, I thought you should be aware of the potential situation. Seriously, though, Cord, I don't think it's critical. Yet. Stay and help your brother."

"Wyatt's campaign is in worse shape than I thought," Cord admitted. "Much as I want to come back, I feel I owe it to Wyatt to stay around for a while. But I can't if—"

"Let me work on *frère* Jacques for a while," Mary Beth suggested. "I'll keep you posted."

After a few more assurances that the lodge kitchen wasn't in imminent danger of losing its chef, Cord decided to stay in Waysboro as he'd promised. It was frustrating, but he had a feeling that having to listen to Jack spout nonsense about destiny and tarot cards while calling himself Jacques might be more detrimental to the lodge than remaining here and letting the implacable Mary Beth deal with the impressionable young man.

"Are you all right?" Ethan Thorpe took Ashlynne's arm as they left the hospital auditorium, which had been set up as a clinic to accommodate the donors for the emergency blood drive. "You don't seem very steady on your feet."

"I'm fine, just a little light-headed," Ashlynne hoped to convince him as well as herself. She'd been feeling weak and dizzy since she'd donated a pint of blood fifteen minutes ago, and the few sips of juice she'd managed to swallow hadn't helped quell the feeling.

"Step back out of the way." Ethan pulled her toward the wall. "The photographers are taking pictures of Dan and Cindy."

Ashlynne glanced at the Clarkstons and marveled at their robust energy. The candidate and his wife had also donated blood, but they looked hearty and hale, ready to bound into a rally and shake a hundred hands. Dan Clarkston was even joking with the reporters and photographers from *The Waysboro Weekly* and *The Exton Evening Post*. Ashlynne had personally called the papers this morning to tip them off about the Clarkstons' appearance at the blood drive.

"Cindy and I give blood several times a year, and always when we hear there is an emergency," Dan told the press. "When we heard about the blood bank's critical shortage on the radio this morning, we knew we had to get over here and, well, open a vein."

The reporters chuckled, scribbling down the quote. The photographers snapped pictures of the photogenic candidate and his vivacious wife.

Ashlynne leaned against the cool tiled wall, watching and listening. Ethan Thorpe had been the one to hear about the emergency blood drive and had phoned the Clarkstons from the office, suggesting that the two of them get to the hospital immediately. Thorpe's suggestions had a way of sounding like orders but the Clarkstons always complied.

It had been Ethan's idea, but that was politics, wasn't it? Ashlynne was both amazed and disconcerted at how easily image and reality seemed to blur, creating something not quite fake and not quite real.

However, now was hardly the time to ponder great truths. She was feeling queasier by the minute and a misty haze shrouded her vision.

"Maybe you shouldn't have done this." Ethan frowned at her. "You are so slender. Maybe you're too thin to give blood."

"I wanted to," Ashlynne murmured. "There's a critical shortage and I met their weight requirements." Except it felt as if they'd drained all her blood instead of the regulation pint.

"Well, you look terrible. You're not going to faint, are you?" Ethan asked apprehensively.

"Of course not. I wouldn't upstage Dan and Cindy like that." She attempted to smile.

"Since we're here at the hospital, Cindy and I would like to visit the children's wing," Dan was saying with his usual upbeat enthusiasm. "You know, we are so grateful every minute of every day that our little Scotty and baby Tiffany are healthy. We'd like to offer our support to the parents of the sick little ones upstairs." He cast a quick glance back at Ethan, who gave a subtle nod of his head.

Ashlynne and Ethan watched the Clarkstons depart with an ever-growing group trailing in their wake.

"I hadn't thought of them visiting Pediatrics," Ethan murmured, smiling his approval. "Dan is really good at this. And Cindy has—"

All at once, he stopped talking. And stopped walking. They came to an abrupt, silent halt in the middle of the corridor. Ashlynne, who'd been stumbling along beside him, her eyes fixed to the floor, jerked her head up to look. And instantly regretted it.

As if the lurch of nausea and head-spinning dizziness weren't enough, she was faced with the disquieting sight of Cord Way and his sister Holly walking directly toward them. She heard Ethan draw in a sharp, audible breath. And then they were face to face with Cord and Holly.

Ashlynne decided she was glad she was having trouble focusing. That way, she didn't have to look at Cord, who was staring at her, his black eyes intense. The last time she'd looked into his eyes, she had been in his arms. Had he given her a thought since? She had spent entirely too much time thinking about him, about their passionate kiss, reliving it, actually.

She tried to block out everything, those memories, those feelings. She couldn't cope with them, not now, when it took every bit of her energy and willpower to remain standing.

"Hello, Holly." Ethan was the first to speak.

His voice sounded strange to Ashlynne, deeper and thicker than usual, but then, right now every sound seemed to be reverberating inside her skull. She didn't attempt to speak.

Ethan paused, then added. "It's good to see you."

"Well, one big lie deserves another, so I suppose I should say it's good to see you too," Holly replied coldly. "But I won't. It isn't."

Any prospect of conversation, even stilted, seemed

doomed after that. A tense, awkward silence fell over
the two pairs. Again it was Ethan who attempted to break
it. "We heard about the blood shortage over the radio this
morning, so here we are."

"Did you come to donate blood?" Holly asked caustically. "Or to drink it?"

If Ashlynne hadn't been feeling so wretched, she might
have laughed. There *was* something vampirish about Ethan
Thorpe at times—his brooding intensity and chilling false
smile came to mind—though she never would've had the
nerve to say so.

"I—uh—think introductions are in order," Cord said, his
gaze darting from his sister to Ashlynne and the man at
her side. He'd noticed instantly that the man was holding
Ashlynne's arm and the possessive surge that swept through
him alarmed him. Though he'd never met the man, he
felt an animosity toward him that equaled the one Holly
was displaying. He looked at his sister, saw her dark eyes
smoldering as she stared at the man.

"I'm Cord Way," Cord said, though he didn't offer his
hand to shake.

"Ethan Thorpe." He didn't offer his hand either.

The name caught Cord off guard and he studied the other
man even more closely. He was tall and wiry, impeccably
dressed in his custom-tailored navy suit. His thick blond
hair was streaked with silver, his face deeply tanned.

So he'd finally met Ethan Thorpe. Cord studied the other
man's cold, assessing gray eyes and decided he didn't like
the guy, not at all. He had all the warmth and geniality
of a jackal—and he was still holding on to Ashlynne's
arm.

"I assume you're here for the blood drive too. Where is
your brother, the candidate?" asked Ethan. "Unfortunately,
you missed the press. They're with Dan." He smiled with
satisfaction at that.

"Unlike you and your flunky Clarkston, we're not here
to put on a media show," Holly said sharply. The hostility
radiating from her was palpable. "And I pity the recipi-
ents unlucky enough to be transfused with your donation
because whatever flows through your veins certainly isn't

blood. Poison is closer to the mark. I'm sure the same holds true for Clarkston."

"Whatever runs through his veins, Dan Clarkston is going to be our next congressman, after your venerable great-uncle retires in November," Thorpe said, still smiling smugly. "Your brother Wyatt is going to get trounced."

Both were so absorbed in their war that they seemed oblivious to the presence of Cord and Ashlynne. Who were acutely aware of each other.

Cord's eyes met Ashlynne's. "We brought our grand-father in today for his annual physical," he explained, willing her to reply. To say anything to him.

She didn't, and frustration surged through him. She hadn't said a single word to him, and he was vexed by how much her silence bothered him.

But Ashlynne remained mute, and it was Ethan Thorpe who picked up the conversational slack. "I hope the exam is strictly routine and that the old gentleman isn't experiencing any problems with his health," he said smoothly.

"Don't try to pretend that you care about our grand-father," Holly snapped. No faux friendliness for her. If looks could kill, Ethan Thorpe would already be on life support.

"You two seem to know each other," Cord observed, his gaze darting from Holly to Thorpe. "Unless you're experiencing an acute case of hate at first sight?"

Nobody laughed. "But I don't know if you know Ashlynne, Holly." Cord noticed that his sister had her eyes fastened on Ethan Thorpe's hand, which was fastened on Ashlynne's arm. "Holly Way, Ashlynne Monroe."

Ashlynne looked at Holly, whose beautiful auburn hair hung to her shoulders thick and straight, the ends turning under in perfect symmetry, not a single strand out of place. She recalled other times she'd glimpsed Holly Way over the years, the first when they were both teens—Ashlynne a skinny, self-conscious thirteen and Holly a gorgeous, self-assured goddess of eighteen. Holly possessed, then and now, a terrifying self-confidence.

Ashlynne smoothed her damp palms over the long skirt of her floral-patterned cotton dress, feeling like an awkward schoolgirl. Holly wore tailored beige slacks and an orange silk blouse, a color that heightened her lovely peaches-and-cream complexion. As perspiration bathed her face, Ashlynne guessed her own skin tone must be a ghastly green by now.

Suddenly, a sickening pattern of too-bright lights flashed before her, blinding her, as a dreadful wave of nausea crashed over her. The hospital corridor was spinning around her and Ashlynne swayed, trying to keep her balance. But her knees buckled, unable to support her.

"Ashlynne!" She heard her name being called and it echoed in her head as she lost consciousness and keeled forward.

Cord had been watching her and took instant action. He caught her before she fell, sweeping her up in his arms to hold her high against his chest. "I'm taking her back in there," he said, striding toward the auditorium where a nurse quickly directed him to lay her down on one of the cots that lined the walls.

Ethan and Holly followed. Neither glanced at each other; both were careful to keep their eyes fixed on Cord and Ashlynne.

"She fainted," Ethan told the nurse with concern. "She hasn't been well since she gave blood a short while ago."

"You brought your girlfriend to a blood drive so you could donate together?" Holly murmured sarcastically. "You always did know how to show a girl a good time, Ethan."

"She is my secretary, Holly," Ethan said through gritted teeth.

Ashlynne's eyelids fluttered as the nurse took her blood pressure. Opening her eyes, she glanced at the group assembled around the cot. There was Cord on her left side with Holly beside him, Ethan on her right, and a strong strapping nurse hovering above her, waving a carton of pineapple juice with a straw sticking out of it.

It was all too much to cope with in her weakened state. "May I have some coffee?" she asked, closing her eyes again. "I could really use the caffeine." Preferably mainlined directly into her veins.

"After you get your blood sugar up, honey," the nurse

said briskly. She turned to Cord, thrusting the juice into his hand. "She has to drink it all and eat a donut—and I don't want her to leave until I check her pressure again."

Cord sat on the edge of the bed and held the straw to Ashlynne's lips. "You heard her, *honey*. You have to drink it all up."

"I can't," Ashlynne moaned. "It's disgusting. It's as thick as glue. That's why I didn't drink it the last time."

"And look where it got you—right back in here with Super Nurse and her high-tech blood-pressure gauge." Cord slipped his arm around her and lifted her slightly, so that her head was resting against his shoulder. He put the straw between her lips. "Just sip it slowly." His voice was soft and soothing. "Just take a little at a time. You can do it."

Ashlynne sipped the juice. It was warm and syrupy-sweet. "It's still awful. And I don't like pineapple juice." She shuddered and pushed it away.

"It wasn't that bad, Ashlynne," Ethan reproved. "After all, I drank it myself."

"A creature like you would think battery acid was tasty," Holly interjected. "She obviously wants something fit for human consumption."

Holly and Ethan continued to glower at each other across the cot.

Cord felt caught in the crossfire. Well, he had two options—attempt to make peace between them, or get rid of them. The latter held immense, immediate appeal. "I have an idea," he said heartily. "Why don't you two go to the cafeteria and get Ashlynne some cold orange juice? You like OJ, don't you?" He didn't wait for Ashlynne's answer. "And get some coffee too. For her and for me."

"You must be joking." Holly eyed her brother with disbelief. "Why not just ask me to take a swim in shark-infested waters?"

"I see your gift for dramatic exaggeration is still intact, Holly," Ethan drawled. "All he asked you to do is to go to the cafeteria to buy juice and coffee."

"I'll go—but not accompanied by *you*," Holly retorted. "Not that you dare leave, anyway. You have to stay here and stake your claim, don't you?" She stared pointedly at Ashlynne then stalked off.

Ethan followed Holly down the hallway, taking giant strides to catch up to her. "Stake my claim?" He repeated. They walked along the corridor, side by side. "What is that supposed to mean, Holly?"

"It means that my brother once had a fling with your little girlfriend who's laid out on the cot back there," Holly said tightly. "I put it together the moment he said her name. Monroe. Well, it looks like Cord is not averse to picking up where he left off, and being a Monroe, *she* certainly won't be."

"You don't listen very well, do you, Holly? Ashlynne is my secretary."

"Is that what they're calling it these days? Well then, it appears that Cord is interested in procuring her secretarial services for himself."

"Exactly when did your brother have this affair with Ashlynne Monroe?" Ethan asked, his eyes narrowing shrewdly.

"Before he left for Montana—about six years ago, I guess."

"Ah."

"Why are you smiling that—that shark's smile, Ethan Thorpe?" Holly paused, catching his arm. But the moment she touched him, she quickly drew her hand back, as if the sleeve of his suit coat were fiery hot. She continued walking, at a quicker pace. Which he easily matched.

"You are obsessed with sharks today, aren't you, Holly?"

"It's a species that naturally comes to mind when you're around. Although rats are a suitable alternative." The angrier she grew, the more his smile widened, perpetuating her cycle of rage. "So you find it funny that my brother and your cheap little—"

"—secretary," Ethan said firmly. "Who is not at all cheap. I pay her an above-average wage for this town. She is a single mother with two small children, and I admire her for the sacrifices she's made to raise them. Of course, sacrifice and motherhood are two alien concepts to you, isn't that right, Holly?"

"Shut up, Ethan! And wipe that phony grin off your face."

"My grin isn't phony, Holly. I'm genuinely pleased. You've provided me with some very interesting information."

"You mean about Cord's tawdry affair with that Monroe girl? Well, if you're hoping to work up some kind of a blackmail scheme, you can forget it, Ethan." Holly laughed off the threat. "True, the Monroes are sleazy, but it isn't a crime to screw around with one."

"Whereas the Ways are blue-blooded through and through. How grand it must be to stand on your pedestal, judging the rest of humanity, knowing that you and your esteemed family are noble, brilliant, and pure right down to your illustrious DNA."

Holly stopped in her tracks, her face flushed, her dark brown eyes snapping with fury. "You're still the same arrogant, insufferable bastard you've always been, Ethan."

"And you're still the same cold-blooded bitch."

Holly stared at him and opened her mouth as if to speak. But instead, she whirled swiftly in the opposite direction and rushed down the hall, away from him.

"The cafeteria is this way, Holly," Ethan called after her, his voice taunting. Holly picked up her pace, until she was almost running. Ethan watched her until she'd disappeared from view.

CHAPTER FIVE

"At least drink some water," Cord insisted, offering Ashlynne a glass of ice water. He was still sitting on the edge of the cot, still holding her as she lay passively against him. He guessed she was too weak to offer any resistance. He was glad, he acknowledged a little guiltily. He liked comforting her like this. She felt small and soft and sweet in his arms.

He stroked her blond hair gently. It was long and silky, a spectacular mane of thick natural curl that flowed over her shoulders.

Ashlynne obligingly sipped the water. It soothed her parched throat, and though the nurse would probably claim that it didn't have the restorative powers of that wretched juice, she began to feel better anyway.

"I'm glad you sent Heckle and Jeckle on an errand," she murmured. "They needed a diversion."

Cord chuckled.

"Why don't they like each other?" Ashlynne asked, more languid than curious.

"I know that Holly is upset because Thorpe is backing the candidate who's running against our brother Wyatt."

"No, their kind of anger is personal," Ashlynne said thoughtfully. "Ethan has made a lot of people in this town mad and vice versa, but he seems more indifferent to them than hostile. But with Holly . . ." She paused to take another long, cold gulp of water. "He certainly wasn't indifferent to her."

"Far from it."

Ashlynne gingerly nodded her head. The tentative movement didn't shatter her equilibrium as it had before. The terrible dizziness was fading too. She drank some more water; she was feeling much better.

She closed her eyes and allowed herself to relax against the hard strength of Cord's chest, savoring the comfort and the warmth. It felt so good, being held like this. She couldn't remember the last time she'd been held. Of course, she was always holding Maxie and Daisy, but this was different. This time she wasn't the one doing the holding, the protecting, the comforting. For the first time in years, she wasn't the strong one, the one in charge. She had someone to lean on.

"Do you realize that we actually managed to have a civil conversation?" Cord murmured huskily. "We've been together for at least fifteen minutes and you haven't told me to get lost once."

Ashlynne felt his arm tighten around her. His fingers were caressing her hair, his lips brushed her temple. And what had been a comfortable, comforting nonsexual interlude suddenly throbbed with a tension and awareness that was intensely sexual.

The abrupt transition served to emphasize what she already knew—that there was a price attached to depending on anyone but herself. Leaning on someone else was a luxury and when that person was Cord Way . . . It was definitely time to end this little fantasy idyll and rejoin real life.

"Well, don't let it go to your head." Her tone was light but cool. "My blood volume is lower than usual, remember? And my blood chemistry is still out of whack." Carefully, deliberately, she sat up straight in the cot, moving out of his embrace.

"Does that mean that after a glass of juice and a donut restores you to your usual stalwart self, you'll go back to hating my guts?" Cord resisted the impulse to pull her close again. His arms, empty now, seemed to ache for the feel of her.

His arms ached for the feel of her? Cord was horrified. Since when had his thoughts started to sound like the lyrics of some weepily sentimental country song? Adrenaline pumping, he pondered the powerful effect Ashlynne Monroe had on him. He needed a cure for it, and fast.

"What makes you think I ever stopped hating you?" Ashlynne asked. Her tone, challenging and defiant, blasted through his panicky reverie.

"Back to your normal charming self, I see." Cord stood up abruptly. Her hostility actually came as a relief. If she'd cuddled up to him while he was in that horrifyingly weak emotional state, Lord only knows what he might've promised. "I think it's safe to leave you alone until your friend Thorpe returns."

"Feel free to leave at any time." Ashlynne dismissed him airily.

"I will."

But before he could leave, Ethan Thorpe was back, carrying two cans of ginger ale. "Here." Thorpe thrust one can at Cord, then handed the other to Ashlynne.

"She's supposed to have juice, not soda," Cord pointed out. "And I won't even mention the coffee you were going to bring us."

"You just did," Ashlynne retorted. She popped the tab on the can and began to drink. "This is fine, Ethan. Thank you."

"No it isn't. You shouldn't be drinking this now. Damn! I forgot what I went for." Thorpe appeared both stunned and agitated by his own uncommon lapse. "When I saw the soda, I grabbed it . . ." His voice trailed off. "I'll go back and—"

"No, *I'll* go this time," Cord cut in. He shot Ethan an inquiring glance. "Where's Holly?"

"How should I know?" Ethan snapped. "I'm not obliged to keep tabs on her whereabouts."

Cord arched his brows but said nothing. He left the auditorium, casting a quick departing glance at Ashlynne lying on the small cot, with a preoccupied Ethan Thorpe standing at her side.

Ashlynne stared up at Ethan, surprised that the appearance of Holly Way seemed to have derailed her boss's thought processes in a way she had never seen before.

"The House of Way is long overdue for a fall." She remembered Ethan's threat and his anti-Way deeds: the condo development near Way's Run, backing Clarkston

against Wyatt Way for Congress, and the newest, secret project yet to be unveiled—Thorpe Development's giant strip mall of discount stores and outlets, including a motel and fast-food restaurants to house and feed the busloads of bargain hunters the mall expected to attract.

The location of the shopper's paradise was to be near the Seneca Creek River, which would require environmental approval from the Corps of Engineers. Pressure from the district's congressman could secure it, thus Dan Clarkston's victory meant a developer's bonanza for Ethan Thorpe. Yet it was defeating Wyatt Way in the election that seemed to fire Ethan's enthusiasm.

Was Holly the reason behind it all?

Being a discreet and loyal secretary, Ashlynne didn't ask any questions or offer speculations. She didn't really want to know, she decided. She had her own secret concerning the Ways, she didn't need to become involved in someone else's.

Cord made a quick return and stayed just long enough to hand Ashlynne a carton of cold orange juice and a Styrofoam cup filled with coffee. He made his getaway before she could murmur a word of thanks.

Ethan noted his hasty departure. "Lovers' spat?" He was back in control, as cool and collected as ever.

Ashlynne managed not to choke on her juice. "Cord Way is not my lover."

"But he used to be. He's Daisy's father, isn't he, Ashlynne?"

Ashlynne stared up at him with wide, scared eyes. "What—How . . . did you ever come up with that?"

Ethan shrugged. "It wasn't hard. Now that I've seen both Cord Way and Daisy, the resemblance between them is unmistakable. Daisy has his coloring but she looks uncannily similar to pictures I've seen of Holly as a child and—"

"You've seen pictures of Holly as a child?" Ashlynne asked. Despite her don't-ask-don't-tell policy, she simply couldn't let that one pass. "So you know her—um—pretty well?"

"Let's just say that I knew her very well at one time. But we're not talking about Holly, are we? The subject at hand is your little Daisy. She's a Way, Ashlynne. Don't bother to deny it."

Ashlynne did anyway.

"Holly mentioned Cord's fling with one of the Monroes six years ago, Ashlynne," countered Ethan. "That would be you, of course. And the timing coincides with Daisy's age."

She'd seen her boss in this mood before. Ethan Thorpe was nothing if not tenacious; he was not going to give up or back down. She could deny Daisy's paternity until she turned blue, she could lie that Cord's affair had been with some other Monroe, but Ethan would keep digging until he got all the facts. And if he were to learn about Cord's affair with Rayleen, he would know the full truth about Daisy's parentage.

She couldn't allow that to happen. The old tactic of throwing a dog a bone to distract him from the main course seemed entirely apropos. She would admit some, but not all. Never all.

"Cord doesn't know about Daisy. I don't want him to know, Ethan. You have to promise me that you'll keep this our secret."

"That's an easy enough promise to make," Ethan said, shrugging. "Cord Way doesn't interest me. Now if Wyatt Way were the daddy, it would be a whole different ballgame." His eyes gleamed. "Ah, the thrill of disclosing the shocking news of the upright, moneyed, conservative candidate's illegitimate child! It's an opponent's dream. Daisy is not much older than little Scotty Clarkston, is she? Can you imagine the mileage Dan and Cindy could get—"

"I've never even met Wyatt Way, let alone had a fling with him, let alone had a child by him," Ashlynne felt compelled to remind him.

"I know." Ethan sighed. "I've done a thorough background check on Wyatt Way. His past is as dull as his speeches. He's never done a damn thing wrong, not even gotten a parking ticket. His few relationships have all been correct and depressingly dull with women of impeccable bloodlines and credentials. The breakups, such as they were,

were friendly and passionless with each wishing the other well."

"Unlike your breakup with Holly," Ashlynne surmised.

Thorpe gave her a look that could freeze fire. Ashlynne realized at once that she'd overstepped her bounds and quickly sought to make amends. "But that's none of my business and it's all ancient history, just like my, uh, relationship with Cord."

Ethan allowed himself to be appeased. He sat down on the edge of the cot. "Each member of the Way family is individually wealthy in his own right, and you have to struggle for every dollar. Doesn't that ever strike you as unfair, Ashlynne? Daisy is entitled to her share of that fortune. Haven't you ever considered going after it?"

"No." Ashlynne shook her head. "I've always been afraid that if the Ways found out about Daisy, they'd take her from me. Not because they wanted her but from sheer spite. I could never win a custody fight against them."

"Hmm, I see your point. You do have the other illegitimate child by another man. Their lawyers would crucify you for that."

Ashlynne's face burned. She was the Scarlet Woman times two, and she'd never even had a lover! But she was not about to confide *that* to Ethan Thorpe. She didn't trust him enough; both habit and instinct compelled her to stick to her and Kendra's pact to keep the truth of Rayleen's motherhood from anybody who didn't already know. It was so much safer that way.

"Please don't tell Cord about Daisy, Ethan. Or—or Holly either," she felt compelled to add. "I don't want any of the Ways to know."

"I said I wouldn't tell," Ethan said impatiently. "Ashlynne, the strongest bonds are created when people share a common loss or a common enemy. Well, we share a common enemy—the Ways."

She nodded her head warily.

"So there is a bond between us. And I know I can count on your cooperation and loyalty, just as you can count on my promise to keep your secret."

Ashlynne knew he was making a point, subtly warning

her. "Of course." She smiled reassuringly at Ethan.

He didn't know that his threat was an empty one, but she did. Even if Ethan were to tell Cord that Daisy was his child, Cord would never believe it was true. Because Cord thought Daisy was *her* child, and he knew very well that he hadn't had an affair with Ashlynne Monroe.

Ethan didn't know that, of course. In this bizarre game, only she had all the necessary pieces to be a player; Ethan had a few, Cord had none. Ashlynne intended to keep it that way. She might not win, but she wasn't going to lose. Not ever again.

"So what do you think?" Kendra asked eagerly. She and Wyatt were sitting in a back corner booth in the coffee shop, and she leaned forward a little, treating him to a brilliant smile.

Wyatt felt its effect all through his body, and he shifted uneasily in his seat. It was unnerving, it was insane. He was acting like a dumbstruck schoolboy granted an audience with the Prom Queen. For the past half hour, he'd been gazing at her while listening to her plans for the Way campaign to appeal to teen voters. She'd suggested sponsoring a vote-getting concert, bringing bands he'd never heard of to Waysboro and Exton. She was also not averse to simply handing out ten-dollar bills to every prospective student voter. The concept of buying votes did not offend her, not even when Wyatt pointed out that it was illegal.

And instead of telling her that her ideas were totally unacceptable and leaving, he had stayed in his seat, watching her, listening to her, his every sense reacting to her beauty and her vibrance.

"You've obviously given this a lot of thought." Wyatt cleared his throat. He wished he could clear his head as easily. "And I appreciate your efforts . . ." He stopped in mid-sentence. Underneath the table, one of her slim, nylon-clad legs slipped subtly between his. His mouth grew dry.

"Those were Josh's ideas," Kendra said, rubbing her leg lightly along his, her expression innocent. "I told him they wouldn't work, but he insisted I pitch them to you."

Wyatt tried to alter his position but the booth was small

and the legroom limited. It seemed no matter how he sat, their limbs were touching. "It's too bad your friend Josh couldn't stay tonight and pitch them himself," he said a bit desperately.

Too bad, indeed. Five minutes into their meeting, an urgent phone call had sent Josh fairly zooming out the door.

"Do you want to hear my ideas for a student voter campaign?" Kendra asked sweetly. "They're not as grandiose as Josh's but I think they're more usable."

She watched his face as her now shoeless foot slipped beneath the cuff of his trousers. Her toes teased the muscle of his calf. He was not as skilled at managing his facial expressions as she was. Unlike her own, his face was as readable as an open book. Her nearness was affecting him, arousing him. And alarming him too.

Kendra was disconcerted. Scaring him off was not part of the plan.

Wyatt abruptly rose to his feet. "I really can't stay." His breathing was shallow and quick, his whole body taut.

"But—" Kendra jumped up, following him as he practically raced to the door.

The sudden appearance of four young men who began to pound on the other side of the door startled them both. Wyatt stared at the foursome through the glass. They were young, in their late teens, unkempt and disheveled—and very, very drunk.

Wyatt turned to face Kendra, who was standing behind him, looking dismayed. "They look like they could be trouble," he cautioned. "I think we'd better call the police."

Wyatt's eyes swept over her protectively. She was wearing a short blue skirt, a black cotton shirt, and long black crocheted vest; her thick dark hair tumbled alluringly over her shoulders. She looked beautiful and defenseless, certainly no match for those creeps at the door.

"Let us in!" one of the boys shouted and threw himself against the glass-paneled door.

"You're right," Kendra said with a sigh. "They are trouble." She unlocked the door, frowning grimly. "But they're my cousins and they're probably *in* trouble too. Welcome to the Wonderful World of the Monroes."

She saw Wyatt's appalled expression and silently kissed her plans of seduction and blackmail and riches good-bye. She hadn't planned on his learning that she was a Monroe until much, much later in the game, when she had the evidence she needed to use against him. Now that he knew her identity, she knew he wouldn't come near her again. Wyatt Way might be captivated by her beauty but that would not be enough for a respectable, uptight, do-right guy like him.

And here were her four cousins to remind him of how very low on the evolutionary chain the Monroes actually were. Kendra sighed again as the four boys staggered into the coffee shop.

"Ben needs some coffee real bad," said her cousin Lonnie Joe, shoving short, skinny Ben into a chair.

Kendra stared critically at him. "He looks like he needs more than coffee." She touched the boy's cold, clammy skin. His color was terrible, his breathing labored. "He looks half dead. How much did he drink? And how fast?"

"He chugged almost a quart of vodka behind the bandshell," giggled cousin Mitch. "And he was laughin' an' then he jus' passed out cold. We had to carry him here."

"Well, he should be in the hospital," Kendra said grimly. "He's not just drunk, I think he's got acute alcohol poisoning. Again. Which one of you is driving?"

"Me!" Cousin Philly raised his hand, eager as a schoolchild with the correct answer to the teacher's question.

"Show me the car keys." Kendra challenged.

Philly dug them out of his pocket and triumphantly jangled them, and she snatched them away.

"I'm driving Ben to the hospital and you three are riding the bus home."

"We don't like the bus," whined Philly.

"Well, you're all too drunk to drive," Kendra replied firmly.

"But I wanna!" Lonnie Joe lunged for the keys. "Gimme 'em."

"No." Kendra adroitly sidestepped him. "Look, there's the bus now. Come on." She grabbed Philly and Mitch by their arms and propelled them out the door. The hapless Lonnie Joe shuffled after them, looking confused.

Wyatt watched through the window as Kendra half pushed, half dragged each boy onto the bus, inserted the necessary tokens, and spoke with the bus driver. He glanced at young Ben, who was sprawled pale and unconscious in the chair. Common sense told him to leave. His presence was not required here. Kendra was cool and calm and self-possessed, obviously accustomed to handling such situations.

He suspected that she could handle anything! Thinking clearly for the first time that evening, he assessed his own current situation.

One look at her, and his good judgment had abruptly deserted him. She had been playing a game of temptation with him and he had been so entranced that he'd very nearly succumbed. It was a humiliating admission for him to make. A man of his age and position, to be beguiled, even temporarily, by a conniving Lower Lyme Hill Lolita!

Having loaded the trio onto the bus, Kendra returned to the coffee shop. She seemed surprised to find Wyatt still there. "I'm going to take Ben to the hospital now." She looked and sounded dispirited but resigned. "Their car is parked behind the bandshell so I'll drive it over here to pick up Ben. You'd better go now."

Wyatt was about to do exactly that. Except when he cast a final glance at her, he saw something unexpected. He assumed her lack of morals and class would now become apparent to him. Instead, he saw a beautiful girl who looked very young and very weary, someone who had not asked for help and clearly didn't expect any.

"I don't think you should waste time walking to the square to get the car," Wyatt the attorney and knowledge-able adult said. "I agree that the boy needs medical attention as quickly as possible. Call an ambulance from here."

"We're not allowed to use the ambulance service." Kendra headed toward the door, car keys in hand.

"What do you mean, you're not allowed?"

"Some of my relatives—old Great-aunt Carolyn in particular—used to call for the ambulance too often. She'd call them for a ride into town because it was raining and she didn't want to get wet and catch cold, she called when her cat got stuck in a tree. Stuff like that. The city got mad and wrote her up for abuse of the service and refused to answer any more of her calls. Unfortunately, some others in the family also started calling the ambulance for nonemergencies. So the ban was extended to all Monroes. We don't dare call for an ambulance now. Not only won't they come, according to the police we could get arrested."

"But that's unfair." Wyatt followed her to the door. "It's also illegal."

Kendra shrugged. "Well, I don't think there's a single lawyer in Waysboro who would want to take the case."

Wyatt knew that was true. But being permanently boycotted by emergency services struck him as excessively punitive.

He considered how firmly and cleverly Kendra had managed her cousins, taking charge of them though she was younger and smaller. He felt a reluctant admiration for her loyalty as well. It couldn't be easy, having that crew for relatives. And he wasn't making things any easier for her.

He felt ashamed of himself. "There's my car." Wyatt pointed to the gray Lexus parked alongside the curb, in front of his campaign headquarters. "I'll drive you and the boy to the hospital."

He looked over at Ben, who had not moved and appeared to be barely breathing. For the first time, he felt a thrust of fear. The kid's condition was deteriorating rapidly. "We can't waste any more time, Kendra."

He carried Ben Monroe to his car, placed him in the backseat, and took off for the hospital, Kendra sitting beside her cousin. "His pulse is so fast and weak," she said gloomily. "I can't believe he did it again. Poor Aunt Debbie, she's had such a hard time. Her husband ran off, her boyfriend is in prison, and her twins are both pregnant and they're only sixteen. Ben is the one bright spot in her life and now she might lose him."

Wyatt said nothing. He was already regretting his involvement in this crisis. He wanted to go home, to his dog and his books and magazines, to his quiet, sedate, and blessedly peaceful existence where drunken teens didn't have near-fatal collapses and their mothers didn't have boyfriends in prison.

"Just dump us out here," Kendra instructed as he pulled in front of the hospital's emergency entrance. She opened the back door and stepped out, grasping Ben under the arms and dragging him bodily from the car. "Thanks for the ride, Wyatt."

As she pulled her cousin closer to the sliding doors, she gestured for assistance, and hospital personnel hurried out. Ben's limp form was hoisted onto a lift and rushed inside.

Wyatt drove halfway home before he turned his car around, his conscience smoting him. What if the boy, Ben, were to die? Kendra would have to deal with it all alone. He simply couldn't abandon them this way.

He found a forlorn Kendra standing beside the pay phone in the hospital waiting room. When she saw Wyatt, her blue eyes widened.

"How's Ben?" he asked.

"Not good. He has acute alcohol poisoning and is on kidney dialysis and a respirator, just like the last time. He may or may not die, just like the last time. I'm calling his mother now."

After relaying the news, Kendra hung up, leaned against the wall, and closed her eyes for a moment, before phoning her sister Ashlynne. Their conversation was brief and terse.

"Don't cry," Wyatt said softly, after she'd replaced the receiver in its cradle.

"I'm not crying." Kendra blinked back her tears. "But I hate it when Ashlynne gets mad at me and right now she's furious. She doesn't want us to have anything to do with the Monroe cousins, but I had to step in. Those guys were so dumb and so drunk that they thought a cup of coffee would fix Ben right up."

Wyatt slipped his arm around her slim shoulders. She felt small and delicate under his hands and he felt a powerful urge to pull her closer, to take her fully into his arms.

But Kendra walked away from him, her expression bleak. "Ashlynne feels differently about the Monroes than I do. She was twelve when we moved here but I was only four, so I grew up with the cousins, I got to know the aunts and uncles pretty well. Ashlynne and Shane and our mom didn't want anything to do with any of them. They remembered life in the army with Dad, when we weren't considered trash."

"Your father was in the army?" prompted Wyatt. That surprised him.

Kendra's lips tightened. "My dad seemed to be one of the rare Monroe success stories. He graduated from high school and joined the army right afterward. He met my mom when he was stationed in New Jersey and they were married and had us four kids. We lived all over the world! Daddy did real well in the army but when his twenty years were up and he retired, he made the biggest mistake of his life. He brought us here to Waysboro.

"Ashlynne says that everything changed for the worse when we moved here." Kendra shrugged. "But I was too little to remember anything else. All I saw was my dad drunk and hanging out at the Waterside Bar, and Rayleen slutting it up with any guy who wanted her, and believe me, there were plenty of those. Mom and Shane and Ashlynne kept apart from it all. They said we were different from the other Monroes, but I couldn't see how or why."

"You are different, Kendra," Wyatt said quietly. "When I look at you, I see a smart and loyal young woman with a strong sense of responsibility. Those are not qualities that one readily identifies with—er—the average Monroe."

"Does that make me an above-average Monroe?" Kendra smiled, her blue eyes suddenly lighting with humor. "I remember playing with the cousins you met tonight when we were all little kids. Their stupidity fascinated me. It sort of still does. Sometimes I get transfixed listening to them try to make plans or figure something out."

Wyatt grinned. "The mind reels."

Her smile faded and she stared at the waiting-room crowd, pacing, sitting, or talking quietly among themselves. "You ought to go home now. You don't want to be here when Aunt Debbie arrives. She'll cry and yell and start criticizing the hospital. You can guess how the staff will react to that."

Wyatt envisioned the appalling scene. "I'll . . . stay," he said dubiously.

Kendra bristled. It was as if he were reluctantly agreeing to having a cavity filled without novocaine. "Think you're man enough to handle it?" She gave him a cool, sultry glance, then strolled to the row of chairs and sat down, gracefully crossing her shapely legs.

Wyatt felt a thrill of alarm. There was not a trace of the sad little waif who had so effectively aroused his protective instincts earlier. She looked like the exciting temptress who lately had been haunting his dreams, awakening him nightly with a steamy, sweaty jolt.

Who was she? What was she? A heartrending Little Girl Lost who'd had the misfortune to be born intelligent and beautiful into the lowest clan in Waysboro? Or a scheming, seductive young woman, using her beauty and intelligence and amorality to lure him into something he would regret for the rest of his life?

Whatever Kendra Monroe was, she fascinated him. Never before had he found a woman irresistible; he didn't believe himself capable of such hunger. In recent years, he'd begun to think of himself as one of those resolute, inflexible types who preferred his solitude, aged thirty-going-on-seventy. A man with a low sex drive. Certainly not the sort of man who could take one look at a young woman and lose his head. Who could see the danger she presented but was unwilling to walk away from her.

But it was that man who returned to Kendra's side, taking the seat beside her. "I've decided to stick around and meet Aunt Debbie."

Kendra stared at him, incredulous. "Why? She'll drive you crazy. She drives everybody crazy."

Wyatt shrugged. "Maybe this is the Year of Living Dangerously."

"More like the Year of Living Stupidly," countered Kendra.

Or perhaps it was the Year of Living, instead of merely

existing. Wyatt took her hand. It was small and delicate and cold in his big, warm one.

Their eyes met and held for a long, quiet moment.

"You didn't have to wait up for me, Ashlynne," Kendra said breathlessly as she let herself into the apartment.

Ashlynne stood up, laying the book she'd been reading facedown on the sofa. "How is Ben?"

"Still among the living. They say it's touch and go for the next forty-eight hours, but I have a feeling he'll make it."

"Kendra, I'm sorry I snapped at you over the phone." Ashlynne stood beside her sister and lightly laid her hand on the younger girl's shoulder. "I know you had to help the boys, you had no choice. They certainly aren't capable of taking responsibility for themselves. I guess I was just mad that you had to be involved with them at all. We try so hard to live decent lives but then they show up to drag us back into their messes and their crises. Which are never-ending."

Ashlynne gave Kendra a quick, apologetic squeeze. "I sound as cold and judgmental as anyone in this town, don't I?" She laughed ruefully. "I probably sound like—like one of the Ways describing the Monroes."

"Interesting that you should mention the Ways," Kendra said casually, sliding a sidelong glance at Ashlynne. "Wyatt Way was at the hospital tonight. He was there when Aunt Debbie arrived and—and he stepped in when she started going mental. He calmed her down and then talked to the hospital staff. He said that when Ben is discharged, he's going to get him into a drug and alcohol program at the state hospital. The doctor said if a Way arranges for Ben's admission to the program, it's as good as done."

"Oh, brother!" Ashlynne rolled her eyes heavenward. "I'm glad I missed that performance."

"Performance?" echoed Kendra, confused.

"Of course! It's so obvious. Dan Clarkston was photographed at the hospital giving blood, so Wyatt Way felt *he* needed to do something to show that he's a humanitarian too. He was probably trolling the hospital, looking for just the right opportunity. By using Aunt Debbie and Ben,

Wyatt Way gets to pretend he's a friend of the downtrodden and he plays out the scene in front of an audience, potential voters, who'll tell their family and friends what a great guy he is."

A dark blush suffused Kendra's cheeks. Had she misinterpreted political showboating as kindness and personal interest in her? The thought galled her. She'd always considered herself too cool and too savvy to be taken in by anyone.

"Did you have to wait a long time at the hospital for a bus?" Ashlynne asked as she walked around the room, turning out the lights, one by one. "They're never on time at night."

Kendra stared out the window into the night. "I didn't have to wait." She didn't add that she hadn't taken the bus home, that Wyatt had insisted on driving her here. They'd talked the whole way, so easily and naturally. She hadn't had to plan a single sentence.

When they'd reached the apartment, Kendra felt proud that the building and the neighborhood they lived in was a good one, not that old dump in Lower Lyme Hill. Buoyant from Wyatt's attention and the unaccustomed respect shown her at the hospital after his intervention, she had leaned across the seat and kissed his cheek. She could still feel the warm pressure of his hands closing around her shoulders. For a few moments, he'd held her still, their faces very close. He wanted to kiss her; she'd been sure of that.

But he hadn't. He had released her without a word.

She thought he had been too shaken by their near-kiss to speak. But now, doubts sprang to life. Maybe he hadn't been dumbstruck by the chemistry between them but simply eager to be rid of her. Maybe the only reason Wyatt had stuck around tonight was to have a chance to befriend the lowly Monroes for political gain!

Kendra followed her sister down the narrow hall to the small bedroom they shared. Ashlynne was very smart, Kendra reminded herself. Ashlynne was the sole reason they were in the good building in the decent neighborhood and not slutting around the Waterside Bar with a raft of illegitimate children crammed into a roach-infested hellhole.

She'd listened to her big sister her entire life. So far Ashlynne had yet to be wrong about anything.

Kendra lay in bed, scowling. Wyatt Way had faked her out! It was embarrassing how completely she had been duped by him. "Ashlynne, you know that saying, 'revenge is sweet'? Well, is it?"

"I wouldn't know." Ashlynne laughed as she slipped under the covers of her own twin bed, just a foot away from Kendra's. "But I like the idea that 'living well is the best revenge.' That can be ours when we get out of this town and are happy and successful. And it *will* happen, Kendra. I promise."

Kendra closed her eyes. "I can't wait for that day, Ashlynne."

"Neither can I, Kendra. Neither can I."

CHAPTER SIX

THE late-afternoon thunderstorms had cleared the town square of shoppers, giving the streets a deserted, eerie feel. Torrents of rain continued to fall, and the dark sky and empty stores and sidewalks made it seem more like midnight than five-thirty. Ashlynne stood at the bus stop, clutching her umbrella and counting the seconds between lightning flashes and booms of thunder. She didn't even make it to one. The storm was directly overheard.

She glanced nervously at the sky, and then at the umbrellas she and Maxie and Daisy hovered under. There was no kiosk in which to seek shelter. In Waysboro, one was expected to own a car and drive from place to place. Few depended on the public transit system, which was less than reliable on good days, wholly unreliable in bad weather such as this.

"I'm getting all wet," Maxie complained as she stomped in a puddle. "And I don't like this noise but I can't cover up my ears 'cause I have to hold my stupid umbrella."

"Your umbrella isn't stupid, Maxie," Daisy attempted to assure her.

"Yes it is," countered Maxie. "I wanted pink and I got this dumb green one." She waved the small, bright green umbrella high above her head, chanting in a sing-song voice, "I hate green, I hate green. I wish dumb green would blow away."

The dumb green umbrella looked like a lightning rod to Ashlynne, practically inviting an errant bolt of electricity to strike them. "Maxie, stop doing that," she admonished anxiously. Where was the bus? It was already nearly a half hour late.

"Green is pretty," Daisy said doubtfully, looking up at

her own green umbrella. "But purple is better," she mumbled under her breath.

Ashlynne made a silent vow that the next time the girls needed umbrellas, she would pay the extra few dollars to purchase the colors of their choice, rather than shopping the sale bins. She found it depressing that she'd never bought a single item for either of the children that wasn't on sale.

"Daisy, let's practice our new dance steps," Maxie suggested, dismissing the ugly-umbrella issue. She attempted to tap-dance right there on the sidewalk, despite her umbrella and bookbag, the puddles of water, and her thick-soled bulky sneakers.

Daisy was game. The two of them launched into their routine, Daisy laughing, Maxie focused and concentrating.

Ashlynne watched them, smiling, despite the terrifying sound-and-light show provided by the thunder and lightning. Maxie was currently torn between a future career as a cheerleader or a dancer, so she took her gymnastic and dancing lessons quite seriously. Daisy was not under such pressure; she planned to be a doctor, though she hadn't yet decided if her patients should be dogs or cats or babies.

A deafening crack of thunder made Maxie stop dancing and shriek. "I want to go home, Mommy!" she wailed. Ashlynne put a comforting arm around her and hugged her close.

"I wish the bus would come, I wish the bus would come," Daisy whispered under her breath.

"It was wonderful getting together with the old crowd this afternoon, wasn't it, Cord?" Leigh Harrison inched closer to Cord as he steered the borrowed company car through the driving rainstorm. "Having you there today made it even more special."

"If you'll remember correctly, I wasn't exactly a member in good standing with that crowd," Cord remarked.

"But we were always intrigued by you, Cord," Leigh purred. "You were simply more than we good little girls could handle back in those days."

Cord thought back to "those days." The luncheon today, which had extended into a party lasting the entire afternoon, had been hosted at the country club by fellow Waysboro Academy alumni. The seemingly endless day spent among Waysboro's elite had dredged up unwelcome memories of his wild past. He hadn't liked his fellow classmates when they'd all been prep school teens together but his attendance at today's event was a necessary evil. Wyatt's campaign made cultivating the old crowd's goodwill necessary. Cord was not surprised that he liked them even less in their roles as the movers and shakers of Waysboro, but all had pledged support to Wyatt, as expected.

Leigh Harrison was the unexpected development of the afternoon. Divorced and on the lookout for a new man, she had attached herself to Cord the moment he'd arrived, making it clear that she was ready to party privately into the night.

To his own surprise, Cord was beginning to consider it. The evening loomed endlessly before him. He had already made his daily call to Mary Beth at the lodge to hear that things were running smoothly, that Jack Townsend was still cooking, though he hadn't given up his plans to seek his destiny in France. The campground had opened without a hitch but there were only seven families currently using the facilities; in peak season the number quintupled. The KOA inspector hadn't yet made an appearance.

With his business concerns taken care of, Cord had paid a brief visit to his grandfather and an even briefer one with his mother. He'd hoped to spend the evening hanging out with Wyatt and/or Holly, but both had plans. Even Stafford and Prentice and the boys had plans.

Cord frowned. It appeared that his choice was to spend another evening alone, or take up Leigh Harrison on her offer of whatever she was offering tonight. Cord glanced at her. She was an attractive woman, sending all the obvious signals. He didn't have to be a mind reader to know that she was offering him whatever he wanted from her.

At that moment, he spotted the three figures at the bus stop in the middle of the square, standing in the rain, getting soaked despite their umbrellas. Without pausing to think, he swung his car over to the curb in front of Ashlynne and the little girls.

"Cord, what are you doing? Why are you stopping?" Leigh demanded. There was a sharp, disapproving edge in her tone.

Cord ignored it and lowered the electronic window, leaning his head out. "Need a ride?" he called to the trio.

Ashlynne's heart jumped at the unexpected sight of him. She saw him squint as heavy drops of rain hit his face. He grinned as one drop splashed squarely on the tip of his nose. His smile sent a flood of heat surging through her. Ashlynne knew she should refuse. The chance of getting struck by lightning was not as risky as the three of them getting into that car with Cord Way.

But the children had no such qualms. "Uncle Cord!" squealed Maxie. "The bus won't come."

"We need a ride," Daisy affirmed, casting a questioning glance at Ashlynne. "Right, Mom?"

"Yes," Ashlynne said resignedly. What else could she say? Making two small children stand outside in an electrical storm when an alternative was offered was not only stupid, it bordered on neglect.

"Hop in," Cord said.

Ashlynne opened the back door and the two little girls tumbled in with their wet shoes and umbrellas and bookbags, spraying droplets of water throughout the car. Leigh didn't bother to conceal her disapproval, she broadcasted it with distinct, impatient "tsks" of indignation.

Ashlynne slipped into the backseat and pulled the door closed. Seconds later, they were on their way.

"You're looking much better than the last time I saw you, Ashlynne," Cord said heartily.

That was when she'd been chalk-white from blood loss, Ashlynne remembered with a grimace. How ungracious of him to remind her!

"Really?" Leigh Harrison cast a cold, condescending glance at Ashlynne. Her expression and tone clearly implied that Ashlynne must've looked subhuman to have looked any worse than she did now.

Ashlynne ran her hand through her hair in a futile effort to tame it. She guessed she looked like a half-drowned rat, and the intimidatingly elegant, expensive-looking woman in the front seat confirmed it. The woman did not want them intruding and didn't bother to conceal her hostility.

And then Cord made things even worse. "Leigh, meet Ashlynne, Maxie, and Daisy. Group, meet Leigh Harrison."

He didn't bother with their last names, Ashlynne noted grimly. He didn't want his high-class friend to know that she was vehicularly trapped with Monroes.

"Quite a storm, eh?" Cord remarked. Neither woman responded to his conversational sally and he dropped it.

Maxie had discovered the electronic windows and the button that regulated them, pushing it over and over again, sending the back right window, up and down, down and up. She giggled with delight, then stuck her umbrella out the window, trying to pull it back in before the window closed on it.

A moment later, she screamed in pain. And kept screaming. The window had closed tightly, trapping Maxie's small hand.

"Her fingers are caught in the window!" cried Ashlynne. She pressed the control button once, twice, three times, but nothing happened. The window remained locked shut.

"That lady did it!" Daisy howled. In an instant, she hurled herself over the seat and climbed across Leigh Harrison to press the master control button in the front, which overrode the controls in the back. The window went down and Ashlynne pulled Maxie's fingers free.

Three little fingers were dented and turning purple, and Ashlynne automatically kissed and rubbed each one. "My poor baby. I hope they're not broken." She cuddled the wailing Maxie on her lap.

"My fingers are broken off?" Maxie started to scream again.

"No, not broken off." Ashlynne hastily corrected herself and showed Maxie that her fingers were indeed intact. "It's all right, sweetheart. It's okay."

Things were not okay in the front seat. "Get away from me!" Leigh Harrison ordered Daisy, who was still sprawled across her. "You're all wet and your shoes are filthy. Don't touch me!"

Daisy quickly scrambled to the middle of the seat, her head brushing Cord's forearm. Undaunted, she returned Leigh Harrison's scowl with an even fiercer one of her own.

"You did it on purpose!" Daisy accused. "You pushed that button and made the window get stuck on Maxie's fingers."

"That's ridiculous!" snapped Leigh. "How dare you make such an accusation! Furthermore, your tone is inexcusable. I demand an apology from you immediately."

Cord was startled by the venom in her voice, the fury in her eyes. Daisy was just a little kid, hardly a worthy target for such wrath. Any interest he'd had in spending another moment in Leigh Harrison's company disappeared. He couldn't quite bring himself to admit that Leigh was history the moment he'd seen Ashlynne standing in the rain.

"Well?" Leigh snarled. "I'm waiting for an apology, young lady."

Daisy was not at all cowed by the woman. And certainly not in the mood to apologize. "I saw you do it," she insisted. "You hurt Maxie on purpose. I saw you and God saw you and all the angels did too."

Leigh's laugh was shrill and unpleasant. "Good heavens, a pint-sized Holy Roller! Honestly, Cord, I think—"

"I think you should apologize to Maxie, Leigh," Cord cut in.

"Me? Apologize?" spluttered Leigh. "You can't actually believe that I . . . Why, if that little brat got hurt, it's her own fault! She was playing with the windows, carrying on like a—a wild chimpanzee. And as for this rude, insolent little monster—"

"You did it on purpose," Daisy said flatly.

"Daisy, come sit with us," Ashlynne commanded and Daisy immediately somersaulted into the backseat.

The three huddled together in silence while Leigh Harrison kept up a steady tirade, issuing threats and complaints, until Cord braked to a stop in front of her big brick house on Applegate Lane.

"You haven't changed a bit, Cord Way. And your taste in companions hasn't improved either," Leigh hurled as her parting shot. She stalked out, slamming the car door so hard that the whole car shook.

Cord glanced at the trio in the back seat. "An old acquaintance." He shrugged. "She never liked me much."

"Well, I don't like her." Daisy gazed at him with her enormous dark eyes.

"I don't either," Cord agreed. "I'm surprised she risked venturing out into the rain. Aren't witches supposed to melt in water?"

"Like in *The Wizard of Oz*." Daisy recognized the reference. "A house fell on the other witch." She glanced hopefully out the window, but the brick house remained intact, with Leigh Harrison entering it, not under it.

"She's mean!" Maxie proclaimed, venturing off Ashlynne's lap.

"I'm sorry for what happened," Cord said quietly.

Maxie stood up and leaned over the seat, showing Cord her small fingers, still purple and still dented, though not as badly.

Cord grimaced. "That must've hurt a lot, Maxie."

"It did. But they're feeling better. You can kiss them," Maxie offered. She pressed her hand to his mouth.

Feeling self-conscious and out of his depth, Cord removed the little fingers, patting them awkwardly with his hand. "You're a very brave girl," he murmured.

Ashlynne watched the interaction, thoroughly bemused. She still hadn't gotten over the shock of Cord taking their side, that he'd believed Daisy's account of the incident. If she hadn't been there to see and hear for herself, she never would have believed it.

"Do you think she should have her hand X-rayed?" Cord asked Ashlynne, examining Maxie's little fingers. She was wiggling them easily, without any pain.

"No, I think she's okay." Ashlynne sank back against the seat and glanced out the window at the rain streaming in rivulets down the glass. "We'd like to go home now, please."

"What about dinner?" Cord asked impulsively. "Have you eaten yet?"

"No," Maxie and Daisy chorused together. "We're real hungry," Maxie added.

"I have an idea. Why don't I take you three ladies to dinner?" Cord cast a quick glance at Ashlynne, expecting, waiting for her refusal.

Part of him already regretted his spontaneous invitation and hoped she would refuse. An evening with edgy, skittish Ashlynne and the two lively little girls was hardly a relaxing way to pass the time. But another part of him—the old incorrigible Cord he thought he'd exorcised forever—dared her to refuse. Because he knew he would overrule her, and use the children to do so. It was all in the game.

Ashlynne was caught completely off guard. Cord Way was inviting them to dinner? She was too astonished to reply.

Maxie wasn't, however. "Could we go to Chuck E. Cheese? They have pizza and hot dogs and video games and skee ball and puppets and a room filled with balls and a slide and—" She had to pause to breathe.

"Sounds like a regular nirvana for kids," Cord said dryly.

"I went there for my friend Lissy's birthday party," Maxie told him. "It's the best fun I ever had."

"Maxie," Ashlynne warned, finally finding her voice. "We can't—"

"I've never heard of the place. Where is it?" Cord asked.

"In Exton on that big road by the mall," Maxie said breathlessly.

"Well, it sounds good to me." Cord grinned at the two girls. They were really very cute children, he decided, Maxie with her curly blond hair and light blue eyes and Daisy with that straight dark hair and equally dark brown eyes. Though they hardly looked like sisters. Their different fathers' genetic influences, perhaps? He quickly banished the thought. "I like to try new places. What about you,

Daisy? Any suggestions on where we should go?"

"I always wanted to go to Chuck E. Cheese, but I never thought I would," Daisy whispered almost reverently.

"That leaves your mother's vote." He turned to Ashlynne, his dark eyes alight with triumphant laughter. He'd won this round hands down and the victory was oddly exhilarating. "How about it, Mom?"

Ashlynne met his eyes. All things considered, she knew she should say no and insist that he take them home immediately. But a rare reckless impulse sparked within her. Why couldn't they do something spontaneous and out of the ordinary, just this once? They were so regimented, following their busy schedules, living on their always too-tight budget. Other Monroes might lack structure and routine in their lives, but not Ashlynne's branch of the family. But at this moment, all that structure and routine suddenly seemed suffocating. To break out, just this once . . .

Rayleen's face flashed before her mind's eye and Ashlynne felt a frisson of fear. She was in no danger of becoming a thrill-seeker, she quickly reassured herself. This was for the children. Didn't Daisy and Maxie deserve an unexpected special treat now and then?

"Well?" Cord challenged. "We're eagerly awaiting your decision."

"Please, Mommy!" the girls cried, their faces flushed with excitement.

"I'm not a killjoy out to ruin everybody's fun," Ashlynne said, smiling at them. "I'd like to see this place myself."

The children cheered. Cord was astonished. She hadn't said no. He'd been so sure that she would that he was unprepared for her assent.

"Are you sure you want to take us?" Ashlynne said. "It's not too late to back out."

Cord stared at her, nonplussed by her tone. Was she teasing him? Was it possible that rigid, wary Ashlynne was capable of having a playful moment? She looked at him, her smile for the children extending to him.

Cord drew a deep breath. "I want to take you," he murmured.

After calling Kendra at the coffee shop to inform her of their whereabouts, Ashlynne joined Cord and the kids for an evening of junk food, games, and prizes.

"They're euphoric," Cord marveled, watching Maxie and Daisy run from one room to another, trying one activity after another, returning to gulp a bite of pizza and a sip of soda, animated and laughing, their eyes bright. "I've never seen Daisy smile so much. Come to think of it, this is the first time I've ever seen her smile."

"She's a serious child and she's reserved around people she doesn't know. But she's happy," Ashlynne added quickly. "She loves all-day kindergarten and has lots of friends, and at home she's—"

"You don't have to get defensive. I wasn't criticizing, just making an observation." Cord took her hand. "Come on, let's try to grab some dinner while the kids are occupied in the playroom."

His hand was big and warm and completely encircled hers. Ashlynne's heart thumped heavily against her ribs and a syrupy warmth flowed deep inside her. He needed only to take her hand in his to evoke the wild, exciting rush she'd felt during their first and only kiss.

They sat side by side on a long bench behind their table. Ashlynne reached for a slice of pizza. Though there was no one else on the bench, Cord was sitting so very close to her that her shoulder brushed his, and his thigh was pressed along the length of hers.

She took a bite of pizza but her mouth was dry and it was difficult to chew. His body felt big and warm and strong next to hers, and she was swamped by another surge of potent memories, of the feel of his body against hers, when he'd held her in his arms.

Ashlynne gave up trying to eat and concentrated on sipping her Coke through the straw.

"Maxie is fearless," Cord observed. If he were aware of Ashlynne's flushed cheeks and the trembling in her limbs, he didn't let on. "I couldn't believe it when she cartwheeled down that slide. If they had bungee-jumping here, I bet she'd be the first in line."

He smiled at Ashlynne, a smile so potent it sent her already befuddled mind whirling in giddy confusion. It was impossible not to respond to him and to the effervescent excitement he generated within her.

"Maxie's dancing and gymnastic teachers in after-school day care both say she's exceptionally limber and well coordinated," Ashlynne told him proudly. "Of course, considering who her father is, that should come as no surpri—"

She broke off abruptly. That was the sort of remark she and Kendra made to each other, but never to outsiders! Whatever had possessed her to talk to Cord Way as if they were confidants? Her heart was still pounding but this time with anxiety. She couldn't trust herself around him. If she were ever to let Rayleen's other secret slip . . .

Cord noticed her instantaneous withdrawal, of course. His curiosity was piqued, along with another, unfamiliar but definitely darker emotion. Jealousy? Of the man who'd been Maxie's father? He rejected the notion. And was determined to prove just how casual he really felt about the matter.

"Who is Maxie's father?" he asked, pleased by the indifference in his tone.

Ashlynne swallowed hard. "I don't like to name names."

"So don't. Although you might clue me in on his profession. Let's see, who could Maxie have inherited her well-coordinated daring from? A sky diver? A mountain climber? I've got it," he guessed jovially. "A stuntman!"

Ashlynne willed her cheeks not to redden. She ordered her expression to remain blank. And was betrayed by her own reactions. Cord stared at her, astonished.

"Good Lord, did I actually call it right? Was he really a *stuntman*?"

"I don't want to talk about it!" Ashlynne fled into the playroom.

Cord followed her to see Maxie jumping off the top of the slide into the pool of soft colored balls. Daisy watched her, awestruck and horrified. He smiled wryly. One thing was certain, cautious little Daisy was not the stuntman's kid—though she was feisty in her own way. He thought of the way she'd stood up to Leigh Harrison, whose rage would've scared the breath out of a lot of little kids.

"Maxie, stop doing that!" Ashlynne ordered the bouncing little girl. "Go back to the table and eat some dinner or we'll leave right now."

Maxie and Daisy obediently charged back to the table to stuff a few more bites of pizza into their mouths. They agreed to have some ice cream for dessert.

When the four of them finally emerged from the cavern-ous building shortly before eight, Daisy and Maxie each clutched troll dolls, bendable pencils, candy, and pink and purple combs. Seating arrangements were not discussed, but Cord buckled the two little girls into the backseat, then took Ashlynne's arm and escorted her into the front seat, beside him.

"The kids had a wonderful time," Ashlynne said politely as they drove through the rain, which had lightened to a drizzle. "Thank you. It was very generous of you."

"Amazingly enough, I had fun too. I wouldn't have believed I could endure an evening spent with shrieking children, flashing lights, and lousy food, let alone enjoy it, but I did. We have a game room at the lodge—some video games, a Ping-Pong table, and table hockey, nothing on a scale like tonight—but I assiduously avoid it when kiddies are in force. But your kids . . ."

His voice trailed off. He liked her kids. But this was his first time playing the role of a treat-dispensing benefactor and he wasn't quite comfortable with it. "Anyway, I owed the kids some fun. After their encounter with the dragon lady, it was the least I could do."

"Your dragon-lady friend wasn't very happy with you when she slammed out of the car," Ashlynne reminded him. "You'll have to work hard to get back into her good graces."

"Honey, all I have to do to get back into Leigh's good graces is to pick up the phone and ask her to meet me. And that's not so much a reflection of my charm as it is her desperation."

"I—uh—I'm sure you're just being modest," Ashlynne murmured, distracted.

"I'm sure I'm not." Cord laughed. "I've never been known for my false modesty." He cast a quick glance at the two little girls playing contentedly in the backseat. Then he leaned closer to Ashlynne. "You met the stuntman when that movie company was in Waysboro filming, didn't you?" His voice was low and quiet. He'd been thinking of her former lover since she'd inadvertently revealed him. And though he knew it was none of his business, he couldn't seem to put it from his mind.

He didn't give her a chance to reply. "I remember when they were filming that movie. It's the only one ever to be shot anywhere near Waysboro so it was a big deal around here." He shrugged, smiling slightly. "And where else would you meet a stuntman?"

"A stunt coordinator," Ashlynne corrected. "He'd been a stuntman for years and then injured his back and couldn't work as one anymore. So he moved on to coordinating stunts for movies."

She remembered Rayleen's excitement about the movie, how thrilled she'd been to meet the stunt coordinator in the Waterside Bar, which had quickly become the watering hole for certain members of the production crew. She remembered everything Rayleen had told her about the man who was to become Maxie's father.

"His career must've been on the downslide if he was working on that movie," Cord said dryly. "It was about demons taking over the world, although the plot was so convoluted, I'm not entirely sure. What was it called? *The Plan from Hell?*"

"Plan 666 from the Devil's Den," Ashlynne corrected.

"It was such a bomb, it couldn't find a distributor and went straight to video. There were a lot of stunts in it, though. Ever see it?"

"Once, on my aunt's VCR. Rayleen was an extra in it. She was one of the possessed villagers in the crowd scene. Max arranged it."

"Max," Cord repeated. "The stunt coordinator." Ashlynne's lover, father of little Maxie, his namesake. "Did he get you a part in the picture too?"

"No." For a split second, Ashlynne was confused. Why would Max Mathison arrange for *her* to be in the movie? He didn't even know her. Getting to be an extra in the crowd scene had been Rayleen's "payoff for showing him such a good time out here in hicksville."

Ashlynne glanced at Maxie, who was methodically combing her troll doll's long pink hair. Maxie might be considered another payoff of that affair, but Max Mathison had left town after informing Rayleen that her pregnancy was not his problem and threatening her if she dared to try to make it his. Rayleen hadn't, and she'd never heard from him again. Max Mathison was unaware of his daughter's existence.

Rayleen had cried when he left. It was the only time Ashlynne had ever seen her sister shed tears over a man.

"Why weren't you in the movie?" demanded Cord. "Why was Rayleen an extra and not you?"

Ashlynne started, jolted from her reverie. "I—I didn't want to be in the movie," she said quickly.

"Does this guy Max ever see Maxie?" Cord pressed. "Does he support her?"

Ashlynne nervously twisted her fingers. Rayleen had always maintained that when lying, it was best to stick as closely to the truth as possible to avoid future trip-ups. That's what she would do now. "No, he was gone long before she was born. He said the p-pregnancy wasn't his problem and he didn't care what happened to the baby. He—he was married."

"With no intention of leaving his wife," Cord surmised.

"Not for an on-location fling." Ashlynne quoted the hurtful words Max had given Rayleen when he told her it was over. "So now you know." Her whole body flushed with vicarious shame. She stared straight ahead, her eyes fixed on the windshield.

"You were very young." Cord gripped the steering wheel tighter. "I was no angel either, when I was younger." He cleared his throat, a fact dawning. "So you already had Maxie when I started—er—seeing Rayleen."

He remembered the Ashlynne of those earlier days. She'd seemed so innocent and reserved, to the point of being inhibited, certainly not the type to have had a fling with a married stuntman and given birth to his baby. Of course, she seemed the same way now, which just went to show that appearances could be deceptive.

Ashlynne was remembering how she'd taken care of Maxie all those times Rayleen had left the baby to go out with Cord. "Yes, I had Maxie when you started seeing Rayleen," she said coolly.

"What about Daisy? Who is her father?" Cord felt testy and on edge. He knew his questions were intrusive but he didn't care, he couldn't stop himself from asking them. "Was he married too? I'm assuming he wasn't the stuntman back in town for a return engagement."

"No, he wasn't the stunt coordinator and he wasn't married. He was a big mistake, that one. He was a jerk. Some might even say a classic jerk."

Cord's lips tightened. "Does the classic jerk know he's a father? Did he walk out too?"

"No and yes," she snapped. An almost tangible tension built and stretched between them. "And I don't appreciate your FBI-agent routine. Stop grilling me."

"I was simply expressing interest."

"In a condemning, self-righteous way."

"I'm not condemning you for your affairs or for having the children but I do think you should inform those men that they are fathers and demand child support from them."

"Oh, do you?"

"If a man makes a woman pregnant, he shouldn't be allowed to walk away scot-free, Ashlynne. And the children have a right to their father's support."

"That's true. And in an ideal world, that's the way it would be. In an ideal world, you wouldn't be a sanctimonious judgmental snoop either. But here's a news flash for you, Cord. We don't live in an ideal world so we make the best of what we can in this one."

Cord bristled. A sanctimonious judgmental snoop? Him? He thought he'd been the soul of understanding! He switched on the radio, turning up the volume so loud it precluded any further conversation.

Ashlynne was relieved. The less she told Cord Way about Rayleen's past—which he thought was her own—the better for all of them.

"You should inform those men that they are fathers." His words, stern with censure, kept echoing in her ears. She was frightened, certain now that Cord would be enraged if he ever learned the truth about Daisy. There was no question in her mind that he would pull out all stops to gain custody, if not simply to punish Ashlynne for her alleged duplicity.

"We're home!" Maxie sang out as Cord braked to a stop in front of their apartment building. "Thank you, Uncle Cord," she added exuberantly. "I'm taking all my stuff to school tomorrow to show everybody. I'm so glad you came to be our uncle, Uncle Cord!"

"He's not really our uncle, he's a pretend uncle," Daisy corrected.

"Well, I'll just pretend he's our real uncle," Maxie said blithely. "Okay, Uncle Cord?"

Cord was touched. "That's fine with me, sweetie."

Ashlynne found the heartwarming camaraderie taxing. She quickly herded the children out of the car, helping them with all their gear. "Never mind getting out," she instructed Cord when he started to do so. "We can manage just fine on our own. We always have."

Her tone was as cold as ice, and Cord recognized her dismissal for exactly what it was. An order for him to get lost and stay lost. He watched her, her back ramrod straight, her head held high. Oh, she was an ice queen, all right. She'd frozen him out, when he'd merely been trying to be helpful.

Feeling irked and misunderstood, he waited until the three of them were safely inside the building—Ashlynne Monroe could not accuse him of simply dumping them out into the rain!—then pulled away from the curb with a squealing of tires, reminiscent of the dramatic departures of his earlier years.

"I won't bother you again, lady," he promised. He was only sorry she wasn't there to hear it.

Ashlynne and the chattering children climbed the stairs, almost colliding with a well-dressed man in a suit and Burberry raincoat on the second flight. He murmured a distracted apology, and continued down the steps at an even faster clip.

Ashlynne stared after him, astounded. That was Wyatt Way. And he was coming from the third floor. *From their apartment?*

Kendra was sitting on the sofa watching TV when they entered. Daisy and Maxie swarmed over her, giving a breathless detailed account of their most exciting evening.

"And you were with Uncle Cord, huh?" Kendra looked over her nieces' heads to grin at Ashlynne. "Cool!"

"It was just an accidental meeting," Ashlynne felt compelled to assure them all. "A one-time thing."

Kendra snickered. "If you say so."

"Kids, how about taking all your stuff to your room?" Ashlynne suggested. They complied, leaving the room with their arms full. Ashlynne turned to Kendra. "I saw Wyatt Way on the stairs. He . . . looked as if he were coming from here."

"Yeah, he was." Kendra tucked her jean-clad legs beneath her and smiled. "He wanted to assure me that he hadn't been using Aunt Debbie and Ben for publicity purposes. He promised the story would never reach the papers."

Perplexed, Ashlynne dropped onto the sofa beside her sister. "Why would he come here to tell you that?"

"Maybe because I wouldn't speak to him in the coffee shop when he dropped by this afternoon." Kendra shrugged. "And Josh told him I was mad because he'd used our family problems to make himself look good to the voters."

Ashlynne felt an ominous foreboding. "I didn't know you knew Wyatt Way well enough to get mad at him, Kendra. Or that he knew you well enough to mind."

"Oh, he minded that I was mad." Kendra looked pleased. She turned to Ashlynne, her dark blue eyes glowing. "He was desperate to convince me that he hadn't helped Aunt Debbie and Ben for political reasons."

"Then why did he help them, Kendra?"

"Never mind. You wouldn't believe it anyway." Kendra stood up and stretched, raising her arms high above her head. She looked beautiful and sexy and too alluring for her own good.

Ashlynne's stomach muscles clenched. She could imagine Wyatt Way viewing her younger sister that way, as an enticing, seductive woman rather than the innocent girl she actually was. She took a deep breath. "Kendra, I don't know what's going on, but for God's sake, stay away from Wyatt Way."

"You're overreacting, Ash. Everything is going to be all right," Kendra promised with the same exuberance that Maxie had displayed during a headfirst plunge down the slide. "Hey, you've had a long day. Just sit here and relax and I'll help the kids get ready for bed."

"Kendra, how can I relax when I have the awful feeling that you're heading straight for—"

"No awful feelings allowed!" Kendra decreed gaily, prancing out of the room.

How could she help but feel awful? Ashlynne worried. Tonight she'd had to contend with Cord Way's condemnation and Kendra's alarmingly Rayleen-like giddiness, not to mention Wyatt Way racing down the stairway like a bat out of hell. Because he'd heard her and the children coming?

Wyatt and Kendra had been alone here in the apartment. About to do what?

Ashlynne tried to reason with herself. Maybe she really was overreacting. Wyatt Way would have to be crazy to get involved with a teenager during his congressional campaign! She had never heard that he was self-destructive.

But the clues she'd gathered tonight were disturbing, adding up to a troublesome picture.

And even if her speculations were all wrong, she'd worked for Ethan Thorpe long enough to know that facts were irrelevent if a more interesting story could be gleaned through innuendo. Oh, the story Ethan could glean from these innuendos!

Ashlynne shivered.

CHAPTER SEVEN

IT was mid-morning, and Ashlynne was working on a spreadsheet when Ethan's private telephone line rang. Though he usually answered it himself, she knew he was on another line with a realtor from Exton whose calls were always considered high priority. In such cases, she was to answer his private line herself. His aging parents in Columbus and an aunt in Cincinnati sometimes called Ethan here, and there were occasional calls from various women, none of whose voices were familiar to Ashlynne.

But this time she instantly recognized the woman's voice.

"I want to speak to Ethan immediately. It's extremely important." It was the same waspish snarl that had lashed out at Daisy yesterday. Even before she gave her name, Ashlynne knew who it was.

"This is Leigh Harrison."

Ashlynne told her that Mr Thorpe was otherwise occupied and suggested that she leave a number for him to call her back.

"What do you mean, he'll call me back? You obviously did not convey the importance of this call to your boss." Leigh went from testy to irate. She was clearly the kill-the-messenger sort. "Tell him it involves the Way campaign."

Ashlynne went still. The woman certainly knew which buzzwords to use. "Just a moment, please." She wrote down the message and crept quietly into Ethan's office.

Ethan, deeply absorbed in his phone conversation, looked annoyed when he saw her and impatiently waved her away. Ignoring him, Ashlynne slipped the note onto his desk, in front of him. Scowling, he scanned it, then crumpled it up and threw it in the trash.

Ashlynne understood. Ethan did not deem Leigh Harrison's important call worthy of taking precedence over his current business. She politely conveyed the news to Leigh, in the most diplomatic terms, careful to keep the glee from her tone.

When Ethan emerged from his office a while later, she stifled her curiosity and didn't mention Leigh Harrison. But he did.

"I returned the persistent Ms. Harrison's call."

"She was persistent," agreed Ashlynne. "Not to mention furious. She cursed a blue streak when I told her you absolutely could not take her call."

"Your ears are still burning, hmm?" Ethan appeared to be in an exceptionally good mood. "Hardly the language you'd expect from a highborn Waysboro lady, is it?"

"She could hold her own at the Waterside Bar," Ashlynne murmured.

"Perhaps I'll suggest having lunch there." Ethan grinned wickedly. "That is, if they serve lunch."

"They don't even open till five in the afternoon. And you wouldn't want to eat the food they serve there, no matter what time it is."

"Not a gourmet's paradise?"

"Nobody goes to the Waterside Bar to eat." She eyed him curiously. "Are you having lunch with Leigh Harrison?" She wondered if the question was out of line. But Ethan seemed to want to discuss Leigh Harrison.

"Surprised?" Ethan chuckled. "Yes, I'm having lunch with Leigh Harrison. As angry as she was at me for not taking her call immediately, she's even angrier with the Ways. Compared to theirs, my offense was judged forgivable."

"She's angry with the Ways? With—With Wyatt?"

"Who could get angry at Wyatt Way? He's too bland, too vanilla. It would be as futile as raging against Casper the Friendly Ghost. No, it's Cord Way who's infuriated our Ms. Harridan."

Ashlynne shifted in her chair. Her breath seemed trapped in her throat. She knew why the woman was furious at Cord.

Ethan noticed her discomfiture. "I wanted to share the information because I thought you would be interested in hearing about Cord Way." His voice was smoothly solicitous. "I'm sorry if mentioning his name upsets you, Ashlynne."

Ashlynne forced herself to meet his gaze. "It's okay, it's just . . . strange hearing his name. Strange talking about him and—and strange running into him at places like the hospital. He's been gone for such a long time."

"And now he's back and you have to deal with his presence in town." Ethan nodded. "I understand. But with any luck, he won't be around too long. His brother's campaign is going to become so hopeless that he'll decide it's no use to stay and fight the inevitable. He'll throw in the towel and return to Wyoming."

"Montana," Ashlynne automatically corrected.

"Wherever." Ethan shrugged. "Meanwhile, the Clarkston bandwagon continues to roll on. Leigh Harrison has offered her help in defeating Wyatt Way. She wants to meet with me today to discuss a financial contribution to Dan's campaign as well as aiding us as a Way insider."

Ashlynne's jaw dropped. "I thought she wasn't mad at Wyatt. Oh . . . I see. She intends to get back at Cord by hurting his brother."

"Bingo. I think she knows she couldn't get to Cord any other way." Ethan laughed. "She wouldn't give specifics but I know enough about Leigh to figure that she made a play for your ex and he turned her down. Hell hath no fury like a woman scorned—or sentiments to that effect."

Ashlynne didn't move or even blink.

"That woman is a piranha," Ethan continued cheerfully. "The type to attach herself to a man and then strip him of all his assets. But apparently, she's forgotten how to sweeten the bait and is beginning to get desperate. Her potential prey keep eluding her. I was one myself, but I managed to extricate myself deftly and smoothly enough to avoid activating her vicious streak. Cord Way obviously did not choose to nurture her ego when he rejected her."

Ashlynne gulped, feeling a twinge of guilt. By siding with her two little girls, Cord had detonated Leigh Harrison's vicious streak. Now the woman spurned was seeking revenge by offering to work as a campaign spy against the Ways.

"Ashlynne, make reservations for two for lunch at the Exton Crab House at one o'clock," Ethan instructed. He sauntered back into his office, looking well pleased with himself.

Before Ashlynne could pick up the phone, the front door of the office was flung open.

"I want to see Ethan Thorpe!" Holly Way stood at the threshold, and her tone of voice, her stance, and the expression on her face all bespoke fury.

"I'll tell him that you're here," Ashlynne said quickly.

"Never mind. I'll tell him myself." Holly strode past her, just as Ashlynne said hurriedly into the intercom, "Holly Way is here to see you, Mr. Thorpe."

Ethan opened the door to his inner office just as Holly reached it. For a moment, her eyes clashed with Ethan's, then she pushed past him and stepped inside. "You are not going to get away with this, Ethan."

"I don't know what you're talking about, Holly," Ethan said coolly. He didn't close the door, and Ashlynne moved her chair a little to the left and leaned forward to peek inside.

"Then I'll just have to make myself understood, won't I?" With one arm, Holly swept the filled-to-the-brim in-basket from Ethan's desk, sending it crashing to the floor. Papers were still fluttering to the ground when she kicked over the trash can, scattering the contents onto the rug. His out-basket, also full, was the next to go.

"Stop it!" Ethan roared, going after her. Holly ran behind his desk and grabbed his chair, using it like a lion-tamer holding off a ferocious beast. There was a momentary standoff, then she threw the chair at him. She hit her target, almost knocking Ethan off his feet.

Ashlynne jumped up from her seat as if she'd been ejected by an automatic spring. She rushed into the office and ducked as a book came whizzing through the air. Holly was attacking the bookshelves that lined one wall, throwing volume after volume alternately onto the floor and at Ethan

Thorpe. Anytime he advanced toward her, he was smacked by a flying book.

"Should I call someone?" Ashlynne asked uncertainly, cowering behind the doorjamb. Ethan, who had just been struck by a particularly thick reference book, gasped and did not answer.

"Call the Federal Election Ethics Committee," Holly replied. "I want to report the dirty tricks this devious, rotten bastard is perpetrating against my brother's campaign."

Ashlynne watched in awe as Holly rapidly emptied the shelves of all the books and then started in on Ethan's desk. She emptied the drawers, upending the contents onto the floor, then hurled the drawer itself at Ethan. Her precise aim kept him safely at bay.

"I went to the Waysboro Hotel this morning at eight, where Wyatt was to address the Wetlands Coalition at a breakfast meeting." Holly was panting from the force of her exertion, but she didn't stop heaving and hurling. "The room wasn't set up, no food had been prepared or extra wait staff called in. The meeting wasn't even on the hotel's schedule! It seems someone had called several days ago to cancel the event."

Holly pointed her finger at Ethan, her deep brown eyes glittering with rage. "It was you!"

"So that's what this is all about?" Ethan sounded the soul of calm. "You're blaming me for the ineptitude of your brother's campaign staff? More likely, they accidentally canceled the breakfast themselves—or perhaps forgot to make the reservations in the first place."

Ashlynne knew by the smooth diffidence in his voice that he was lying. She'd observed her boss carefully over the years and was perceptively attuned to his most subtle nuances.

Apparently, so was Holly. "Don't bother to lie to me, you vile, arrogant weasel!"

Ethan merely smiled. "So there was your hapless brother Wyatt and his staff standing around the Waysboro Hotel looking inept and upset while the Wetlands Coalition watched and wondered, 'Is this the kind of guy we want to send to Congress?' " His smile broadened. "Gee, that is upsetting, Holly. Makes you want to go out and trash someone's office, doesn't it? But why mine? You don't have a shred of proof that I had a thing to do with your brother's hotel blunder."

Ashlynne winced. She did not think that provoking the volatile Holly was in anybody's best interests at this time.

"Just knowing you is all the proof I need! You're underhanded and scheming and totally unscrupulous." Holly picked up a red and black ceramic urn that had somehow been left standing and smashed it against the wall. It shattered and left a dent in the wall.

"We postponed the breakfast for an hour, giving the hotel some time to get things together," Holly said tightly. She was trembling. "My brother Cord started a discussion with the coalition members about environmental issues out West that held their interest while we waited. Everything seemed back on track when—in the middle of the meeting—Wyatt's campaign headquarters got a call from the Sheridan Hotel in Exton. They were wondering where Wyatt was. It seemed someone had booked a breakfast meeting there for Wyatt and the Exton Junior Chamber of Commerce. They had a room set up, prepared breakfast for fifty, and the Exton Junior Chamber was ready and waiting for Wyatt."

"And he didn't show up?" Ethan gave a whoop of laughter. "What a disaster! Your pitiful brother looks unorganized and incompetent in front of two different groups in two different towns, and both hotel staffs are convinced that Candidate Way and his organizers don't know what they're doing. Finally, adding insult to injury, the Way campaign is billed for the costs of two separate breakfasts for fifty! Good golly, Miss Holly, what could go wrong next?"

"You were behind this entire debacle, Ethan Thorpe," Holly accused him wrathfully. "You canceled the meeting at the Waysboro Hotel and set up the bogus one in Exton."

"It's too bad you have no evidence to back up your theory, isn't it, darling?" taunted Ethan.

Ashlynne watched wide-eyed as Holly picked up his desk chair and turned toward the wide picture window with its bucolic view of the park.

"Don't do it, Holly," Ethan warned. "You've gone far enough today."

"I haven't even begun, you son of a bitch!" She flung the chair directly into the window.

Ashlynne gasped. Holly was strong! The chair hit with such force that it shattered the glass. But before Holly could grab the chair again, Ethan charged her. And though she fought him fiercely, her physical strength was ultimately no match against his.

Ashlynne watched, fascinated and horror-struck, as Ethan finally overpowered Holly, grabbing her in a choke hold used by tough cops to subdue violent criminals. Holly continued to struggle for a few minutes, then began to gasp for breath.

"No!" cried Ashlynne, running over to them. "Ethan, stop. You're choking her!"

"No, I'm throttling her. There's a difference." But Ethan eased his grip.

"Let her go!" pleaded Ashlynne.

"You must be joking. I'm not turning her loose in here." He half dragged, and half carried a flailing Holly from his office, outside to the sidewalk.

Ashlynne trailed after them, shuddering as she saw him give Holly a hard push away from him. Holly stumbled, bumped into a curious passer-by, then grabbed a parking meter with both hands and held on to it, to steady herself.

"Stay away from here, darling," Ethan commanded. "Or I'll make you sorrier than you've ever been in your life."

"I'll make you even sorrier." Holly flung the words at him.

Ashlynne followed Ethan back inside, and through the window kept a nervous eye on Holly, who was staring murderously at the office building, its overdone modern design so at odds with the rest of the village square. After a few more tense moments, Holly finally walked away. Ashlynne breathed an audible sigh of relief.

Ethan stood in the doorway of his office, surveying the damage. Ashlynne came to stand behind him. The place was wrecked, with papers, books, and broken glass littering the floor, furniture overturned, pictures and certificates torn from the walls.

"It looks like a hurricane hit," marveled Ashlynne.

"Hurricane Holly. A Category Five."

"The Waterside Bar has never looked this bad, not even after a Saturday-night brawl." Ashlynne slipped by him and began to pick up the books from the floor and return them to their rightful place on the shelves. It was going to take hours to restore the office to order.

Ethan watched her. "Call Larimer's and order a replacement window. I'll be gone for the rest of the day. I can't get anything done in this disaster zone. Oh, and don't forget to make those reservations at the Exton Crab House today."

Ashlynne's eyes widened. "After all this, you're still taking Leigh Harrison to lunch?"

"Of course. I'm even more interested in what she has to say—and what she's willing to do to help defeat the Ways. You don't think I'd let Holly's little tantrum here deter me, do you?"

"It would deter me," Ashlynne said earnestly, gazing around at the destruction.

Ethan laughed. "That's where we differ, Ashlynne. You let Cord Way walk away from you without paying any price for the damage he caused. I will never, ever let Holly off so lightly."

His cold, steely tone gave Ashlynne the creeps. "Your relationship with Holly must have been—" She paused, trying to come up with a tactful word. She had to settle for "—quite something."

"You don't know the half of it," he mumbled.

Ashlynne was glad she didn't. Ethan's taut intensity and Holly's explosive temper, combined with their mutual taste for vengeance, qualified them as the couple from hell. But she continued to wonder about them while she straightened up Ethan's office.

She took a break for lunch, brown-bagging it, as usual. It had been Kendra's turn to prepare all four lunches and she'd fixed peanut butter and jelly sandwiches, as usual. Ashlynne poured herself a cup of strong black coffee and sipped it, enjoying the silence. It was nearly one-thirty, and she imagined Ethan and Leigh Harrison at the Exton Crab House, plotting skullduggery over a seafood feast. She'd heard the food at the popular restaurant was delicious but knew she would rather eat PB&J here at her desk than join that ruthless pair in dining on the finest cuisine.

"I want to see Ethan Thorpe!"

The last time she'd heard those words, an orgy of destruction had followed. Ashlynne looked up, alarmed.

Cord Way was standing in the doorway, his arms folded in front of his chest. He was as handsome as ever, and looked imposing and executorial in his dark blue suit. He also looked furious.

"Mr. Thorpe isn't here," Ashlynne said, trying to keep her voice from quavering. Every time she saw Cord, her heartbeat seemed to go into overdrive. She decided that she would've rather had Holly back for a return visit than Cord Way walking toward her, his mouth hard and defiant, his dark, dark eyes piercing her.

"I don't believe you. I'm going in." Cord kept walking until he reached the door to Ethan's private office. He opened it.

Chaos still reigned within. Besides the damage, Ashlynne wasn't even half finished putting the place back together. Sorting out the papers from Thorpe's separate in-and out-baskets was tedious and time-consuming, and she had yet to start on the contents of his drawers.

"Good God!" Cord gasped. "What happened? It looks like a replay of Sherman's march through Georgia in here."

Ashlynne stood up and joined him in the inner office. "Your sister paid a visit earlier."

Cord turned to face her. "Holly did this?" He gazed around, awestruck. "*All* of this? It looks like a hurric—"

"Yes, Hurricane Holly," Ashlynne interjected. "A Category Five. We already did that one."

"Was Thorpe here when she—uh—blew in?"

"Oh yes, he was here. I think he'll be black and blue from getting hit with all the books and pictures and furniture she threw at him."

Cord walked to the shattered window. "And this?"

"She threw a chair at it."

"Whew!" He dropped onto Ethan's desk chair, which wobbled precariously, almost tipping over. Cord stood back up and the chair fell over on its side. He stared at it. "The result of today's—uh—war?"

"It was wounded in action," Ashlynne said dryly. "After what the poor thing went through, it's a candidate for the Purple Heart."

Cord grinned. He knew he shouldn't. But he couldn't help himself. He looked over at Ashlynne and started to laugh.

And so did she. She'd been so tense since this morning's brouhaha and Cord's appearance had sent her adrenaline level surging. A wave of giddiness swept through her, making her laugh until tears were streaming from her eyes.

Their shared laughter broke the tension between them. By the time they'd gained control of themselves, a kind of comfortable intimacy enveloped them. Cord leaned against the windowsill and Ashlynne sat on a corner of Ethan's desk, the contents of one of the drawers littered around her. She began to idly sift through it.

Cord picked up Ethan Thorpe's framed university degree, summa cum laude, which lay facedown on the floor. A thick crack ran across the length of it. "What do you think Thorpe is going to do about this mess?"

"Have me clean it up. Get a new window and a new chair and a new decorative urn. Replace the glass in the frames."

"Do you think he'll have Holly zapped with some kind of vandalism charge?"

Ashlynne shook her head. "This sounds odd but he sort of accepted her right to do it. I mean, he was furious, but it seemed like some private battle in their own personal war. If anybody else had come in and done this, he would've already called the police. He'd've probably called the FBI too! But I just don't see him pressing charges against Holly. Besides, he's already working on his revenge, even as we speak."

"Oh?" Cord hung the degree on a hook on the wall, then reached for Ethan's framed MBA, which was leaning precariously against the side of the desk. The frame was dented but the glass remained intact. He hung it up too.

"I—know I shouldn't tell you this, but you did take Maxie and Daisy's part yesterday." Ashlynne continued to sort through the pile of papers. "You didn't have to, but you did and I—I feel as if I owe it to you. You have to swear not to tell anybody who told you, though."

"I won't be able to tell anybody anything because I have absolutely no idea what you're talking about, Ashlynne," Cord said, with humor in his voice.

"Ethan is having lunch with Leigh Harrison today," Ashlynne blurted out. "She called this morning and told him she wants to contribute to Dan Clarkston's campaign and to work as a spy in your brother Wyatt's campaign— because she's angry with you, Cord. Ethan thinks it's because you rejected her—uh—romantically but I know it's because of last night, when you sided with Maxie and Daisy against her."

She stood up. "I thought you should know. But you can't say I told you."

"Well, Thorpe isn't too far off. I would've rejected her— uh—romantically." He imitated Ashlynne's hesitant inflection. She blushed. "But before the kids laid a finger on the window controls, I'd already decided that Miss Leigh was not my type."

"Ethan called her a piranha. He said she's nobody's type. He rejected her too, but diplomatically."

Cord rolled his eyes. "Do you and Thorpe sit around here gossiping? He tells you how he gracefully dumped Leigh, you tell him—"

"No! He just happened to mention Leigh and I—"

"—decided I had a right to know what she was up to. Well, thanks for the tip. We'll keep an eye on her, but I don't think she could cause any more harm than the *diplomatic* Mr. Thorpe himself."

Ashlynne tensed. "Is that why you're here? To blame him for those mishaps at the hotels this morning?"

"They weren't mishaps, they were deliberate acts of political sabotage."

"Holly called them dirty tricks. She said she knew Ethan was to blame."

"Did he deny it?"

"Well, sort of. But in a taunting way."

"In such a way that even you believe he was behind it," Cord said grimly.

Loyalty kept Ashlynne silent, though she believed it was possible that Ethan could've been behind the incidents. On the other hand, it was also possible that Wyatt's campaign staff were disorganized idiots. She decided it would be wiser to keep that observation to herself as well.

"I wish Thorpe was here." Cord removed the two degrees he'd just hung on the wall and dropped them both to the floor. "I'd like to confront that—"

"I'm glad he's not here," Ashlynne said trenchantly. "I'm not up for another round of Way versus Thorpe. Besides, there's nothing left to trash in here. My desk would be the next battleground and I—"

She broke off abruptly. She'd been stacking papers, wondering what drawers they belonged in, when a packet of photographs slipped through her fingers. One picture fell out of the envelope onto the desk. The sight of it made her completely lose her train of thought.

She gawked at the photo, then impulsively held it up to Cord. "Look at this."

Cord took it from her. "Good Lord, it's Holly!"

"Sitting on Ethan's lap," added Ashlynne. Nothing could've stopped her from delving into the envelope to look at the other pictures. It seemed that she was not such a discreet secretary after all. "There's more. They're of Ethan and Holly together or ones just of her."

"The date is imprinted on the photograph." Cord was still studying the first picture. "It was taken five years ago."

"Here's one from seven years ago. Looks like they're at a beach." Ashlynne showed him a photo of a bikini-clad Holly, gazing up adoringly at a tanned, smiling Ethan Thorpe, whose one arm was hooked possessively around her waist.

Cord reached for the pictures. "Let me see the rest of them."

Ashlynne handed him the packet, holding several photos back. "Since you're her brother, I don't think you'd want to see these."

Cord groaned. "Oh God."

"Not pornographic," Ashlynne soothed. "Let's just call them—um—intimate. Ethan must've taken them of her in a . . . private moment."

Frowning, Cord leafed through the photos Ashlynne had handed him. "They range over a five-year period. Holly was in Columbus, working for the paper owned by Way Communications during those years."

"Ethan is from Columbus. He lived there until he moved here. His parents still live there."

"Were Holly and Thorpe together all that time? For five years?" Cord looked thunderstruck. "She never said a word about him. I never met the guy, I never even heard his name until I came back here to help with Wyatt's campaign."

Ashlynne gazed at a picture of Holly and Thorpe entwined in a loving embrace. "Look how tenderly he's holding her. It's hard to believe he's the same guy who had her in a choke hold a few hours ago."

"A choke hold?" Cord echoed, outraged.

Ashlynne nodded solemnly. "Watching them fight was kind of scary. Like watching a documentary on domestic violence. Except I was a live audience."

Cord looked from the pictures of the happy couple to the wreck around him. "I wonder how it happens. How do two people go from being in love to—choke holds and mass destruction?"

"I don't know how it happens but it happens often enough. Holly and Ethan sure aren't the only couple to end up on the rocks." Ashlynne gazed pensively out the shattered window to the leafy green trees lining the park. "I watched it happen to my own parents."

"Did they fight a lot?"

"After we moved to Waysboro and Dad started drinking, they did. They yelled and cursed and made threats but there was never anything physical. No hitting, no flying plates— or chairs. I'm grateful for that. How about yours?"

Cord shook his head. "Holly didn't learn this at home, if that's what you're suggesting. My parents were always very proper and polite to each other. Of course, my grandfather lived with us and he was the alpha male in the house.

Mother always deferred to him, always allied herself with him, often at Dad's expense. Dad was quiet and easygoing, a really nice guy, but he was killed in a plane crash when I was thirteen. I knew him as a father but I never had the chance to get to know him as a man. I still wonder why he permitted his wife and his father to gang up on him, to make him superfluous in his own home."

"I still wonder why my mother put up with my father and his drinking," Ashlynne said with a sigh. "Why didn't she leave him and move away from this town, taking us kids with her? In the end it was too late to do anything because Mom died just a year after Dad did."

"How old were you?"

"My mother died a month before my twentieth birthday."

"That's very young to be orphaned."

"My little sister was even younger. Kendra was an orphan at twelve."

"And you've raised her ever since?"

"She's lived with me," Ashlynne corrected. "I haven't really raised her. Shortly after Mom died, Maxie was born and then Daisy nineteen months later. Kendra helped me raise them." She gazed into Cord's eyes. "I couldn't ask for a better sister. She's always been reliable and loving with the children, and she's hard-working and uncomplaining. But she grew up too fast and I'm worried that she will—"

Ashlynne suddenly busied herself with the mess on Ethan's desk top. She was loath to end the unexpected, companionable warmth between her and Cord, but she knew what she was about to say would bring it to a crashing halt.

"That she will what?" prompted Cord at last.

"I wanted to talk to you," she hedged, not looking at him. "If you hadn't come into the office, I was going to write you a note. I—I didn't know how else to get in touch with you. The telephone number at OakWay is unlisted."

Cord reached into the pocket of his suit coat and pulled out a card. She watched him write on the back of it. "My business card for the Glacier Lodge," he explained. "I wrote two OakWay phone numbers on the back. Call there if you need me."

He handed the card to her, and their fingers touched. Cord would have sustained the contact; his thumb was already wrapping around hers. His stare, intent and sexual, made her feel weak.

Quickly, Ashlynne pulled her hand from his and moved away, steeling herself, and taking a deep breath. "I was telling you about my little sister Kendra."

"Oh, yes. I met her at your apartment, remember? I liked her. She's a very beautiful, very amusing young lady."

"She's also only eighteen years old. In just a couple of weeks, she'll graduate from high school. *High school,* Cord."

She was making a point, Cord noted. He just wasn't sure what it was. "She's almost a high-school graduate," he tried. Her impatient frown cleared his head, and he made another attempt. "She's eighteen, she's young."

"Yes, very young. Much too young for your brother," Ashlynne said bluntly.

"Huh?" Cord was genuinely baffled.

"I have reason to believe that your brother Wyatt is— is—" Ashlynne bit her lip, anxiety surging through her. How to phrase this? There was no easy way. "Interested in my little sister. Interested in seducing her, that is."

The words seemed to hang in the air between them for one endless moment.

"That's the most ridiculous thing I've ever heard!" Cord exploded the silence, his voice harsh. "Dammit, you've been working with that sleazeball Thorpe for too long if you believe that my brother would even think of such a thing!" He started to pace the floor, treading over the results of Holly's earlier fury. "He's not capable of it! Seducing a teenager? Wyatt? It would be laughable if it weren't so— so damn insulting! It's slanderous, that's what it is. Totally untrue!"

Ashlynne watched him uneasily, half expecting him to pick up the broken chair and heave it at the window—or at her.

"What in hell is this all about, Ashlynne?" He came to a halt in front of her, standing way too close for comfort, her comfort. "Are you and your buddy Thorpe trying to discredit my brother by spreading these rumors that he . . . as if he would ever—" Cord broke off.

Ashlynne tried to take a subtle step back but his big hands clamped over her shoulders, pinning her to the spot. She felt his fingers flexing, digging into her skin. If she tried to pull away from him, would he grab her in a choke hold?

"This has nothing to do with Ethan or the campaign," she said, wishing her voice were steadier. "I would never start any rumors about my own sister or let anyone else do it either. I'm trying to protect Kendra. That's why I want you to warn your brother away from her."

"Wyatt does *not* need to be warned to keep away from an eighteen-year-old, soon-to-be high school graduate!"

"But he does!" she cried. "You and I can see how detrimental, how disastrous, this would be for both of them, even if they can't. Or won't," she added gloomily.

Cord gazed down into her deep blue eyes, wide and shimmering with distress. However outrageous her claims, she clearly believed them. He dropped his hands and moved away from her, jamming his hands deep into the pockets of his trousers. "Why do you think that Wyatt—" He couldn't even dignify the accusation by repeating it. "Do you have any proof of your allegations?"

"Not proof," she admitted, ignoring his hiss of sarcasm. She told him about Wyatt's hasty departure last night, about the conversation she'd had with Kendra. "I just have this uneasy feeling about them."

"You call it an uneasy feeling, a psychiatrist would call it paranoia."

"I'm not crazy, Cord!"

"But you are overly suspicious when it comes to the Way brothers with your sisters."

"Like I don't have a right to be!" she snapped.

"I know you didn't approve of my relationship with Rayleen. In your eyes I'm a rat who abandoned her, even if she didn't see it that way herself. But you're wrong to suspect Wyatt of lusting after Kendra, Ashlynne. My brother is a kind, thoughtful, considerate person. He wouldn't use people for his own political gain and if Kendra believed that he had and was upset about it, he'd want to reassure her. That's just the kind of guy he is. I know my brother and—"

"I bet you'd claim you know your sister, too, even though you just found out today that she had a secret scorching-hot five-year affair with Ethan Thorpe."

"That analogy is not apt." Cord's lips tightened into a thin straight line.

"It seems right on target to me. If I'd've told you that Holly had been involved with Ethan before you saw those pictures, you would've turned blue denying it. Well, I'm not going to wait until there's photographic proof of your brother with my little sister."

"You're determined to be unreasonable about this, aren't you?"

"I'm determined not to let Kendra be used and discarded—"

"—the way I used and discarded Rayleen?" Cord finished, exasperated. "Well, if I did, it was a mutual thing, but you prefer not to see it that way." He paused, a light suddenly dawning in his eyes. "That's what this is really all about, isn't it, Ashlynne? You won't let yourself forget about me and Rayleen because—"

"There's a very good reason why I can't forget," Ashlynne cut in sharply. A living, breathing reason who was five years old and named Daisy.

"Why you *won't* let yourself forget," repeated Cord, correcting her. He started walking toward her. Automatically, she began to retreat, walking backward. "Damn, it's all so clear to me, I can't believe I didn't see it before. You have feelings for me and you're trying to fight them. So you dredge up an old affair to use as a shield and you dream up this Kendra-and-Wyatt nonsense as additional ammunition to—"

"Oh, I have feelings for you, all right," Ashlynne flared. "Disgust, contempt, nausea. Those are the top three but there are others. Distrust and—"

"It's like a reflex. Every time we start to get along with each other, every time you let down your guard and we begin getting close—bam! You pull back and start a fight.

It's happened every time we've been together. Think about it, Ashlynne."

"I am. And only someone with an ego the size of China could mistake genuine hostility—which is what I feel for you—for suppressed passion."

She tripped over Ethan's onyx block pen and pencil holder but when Cord reached out to help her regain her balance, she pushed his hands away, continuing her backward retreat.

"You won't give an inch, will you?" He continued his forward advance. "You're the most stubborn woman I've ever met—and the most maddening." His voice deepened. "And the most intriguing."

"Oh, please!" She gave a huff of indignation. "Next you'll be telling me I'm beautiful when I'm angry." She felt her back touch the wall. There was no way to go except sideways, but Cord anticipated that move and placed a hand on either side of her, effectively caging her between himself and the wall.

"You are." His eyes met and held hers. "I should know, you seem to be angry most of the time you're around me."

"And what does that tell you?" she challenged hotly.

He smiled. "That you want me as much as I want you, and it makes you madder than hell?"

CHAPTER EIGHT

HER gasp of surprise froze in her throat when he raised his hand and took a strand of her thick, curling hair between his fingers. He rubbed it slowly, sensuously, letting it sift through his fingers.

For a full moment, she stood still, mesmerized by his touch and his nearness. Acute pangs of longing and lust, so intermingled that she couldn't begin to separate one from the other, kindled and flamed within her. Being Ashlynne, she tried to steel herself against them, against him. "Don't touch me," she said huskily and tried to move away from him.

He halted her by closing one hand around her throat while the other spanned the curve of her hip. "Stop fighting, Ashlynne," he murmured.

"I have to," she whispered.

"No you don't." He pressed his lips against the graceful, sensitive curve of her throat. "Don't be afraid, honey. You can let yourself go with me."

His evocative words sent a streak of heat flashing through her. Touching his thumb to her lips, he traced their shape, parting them, and delving within to touch the tip of her tongue.

Ashlynne felt a wild primal urge to draw his thumb fully into her mouth. In her current disoriented state, she might have succumbed if he hadn't withdrawn his hand to slowly slide it along her collarbone, over her shoulder, and down her arm, to rest on the narrow curve of her waist.

Her breath came in shuddering small pants and she slumped bonelessly, letting his body and the wall support her. "Cord, please, we can't."

"Which is it, honey?" Cord's hand slipped under her sweater and closed over her breast, fondling her as he spoke. "Please? Or we can't?"

Her mind seemed to splinter. The warmth of his hand felt so good on her breast. His fingers dipped into the silky cup of her bra to knead the soft flesh there, his thumb found her nipple and gently teased it into a full, taut bud.

Ashlynne gave a startled little cry. The wild sensations rushing through her were both thrilling and alarming. She couldn't think, she couldn't move. And she could find neither the strength to push him away nor the words to order him to stop.

His lips nibbled at hers and her eyelids grew heavier, until she could no longer keep them open. Cord's mouth moved softly over hers in a gentle, coaxing kiss, the kind of kiss that reassured and didn't threaten. The kind of kiss that made a woman feel safe and in control until it was too late—her head was spinning and her body was burning with hungry need—and she didn't care that she wasn't in control and never had been.

Ashlynne's arms wound around his neck and she instinctively pressed herself even closer to him, savoring the long, hard feel of his body. Cord angled his hips forward, and lifted her higher and harder against him. She made a whimpering sound of need as she felt his erection rub the most intimate, vulnerable part of her. The erotic pressure was exquisitely pleasurable; her femininity felt swollen and hot and moist, yet aching with an emptiness she had never before experienced. For the first time in her life, she felt raw need.

To her disappointment, Cord lifted his mouth from hers, though his lips remained within touching distance, brushing hers as he spoke. "Have dinner with me on Saturday."

It was more a command than an invitation but was so unexpected that Ashlynne's head jerked up, and she stared at him as if he'd just asked her to hop aboard the space shuttle for a quick trip past the moon.

"What?" Her body pulsed with unsated arousal. She tried to regain her equilibrium but knew it was a lost cause with his body still throbbing against hers. She placed her hands on his chest to shove him away, but he surprised her again by releasing her before she gave a single push.

"I'm asking you for a dinner date," Cord said rather sheepishly. "I'm trying to do things the old-fashioned way. I'll even show up with the traditional candy and flowers."

Her fingers trembling, Ashlynne tried to smooth her hair into place and readjust her clothing. Her blue cotton sweater had been pushed up and her slim black skirt was twisted and askew. She was so flustered that nothing made sense to her. Her thoughts were clouded and inchoate. *A dinner date? Candy and flowers?*

"Are you making fun of me?"

"Absolutely not. I know I came on too strong that night in your apartment, and I never did get around to saying what I wanted to say. This time I want to make it clear that my intentions are honorable, that I'm not looking for a fast, cheap thrill."

"What are your intentions?" The conversation had a surreal feel to it, like one in a dream. But her body's aching frustration was all too real.

"To go out with you. To have dinner with you on Saturday night."

"You're joking, of course." She left Ethan's office, her legs still unsteady from their bout of unslaked passion. It was a relief to sink into her own chair, behind the protection of her desk. Her nerves were jangled and on edge; she felt wound tight as a spring. Hot, unshed tears burned her eyes.

Cord followed her. "Say yes, Ashlynne."

"Cord, no. I just can't."

"We'll take the kids," he said quickly. She shook her head but he didn't acknowledge her refusal. "Okay, forget dinner, we'll go to the zoo in DC Saturday afternoon," he improvised quickly. "We'll make a whole day of it. Have lunch, go to the zoo, then find some kid-friendly restaurant for dinner and finally take in a movie. G-rated. How about it?"

She wanted to say yes so badly! Maxie and Daisy would love the day he had just described to her, but it wasn't strictly for them that she longed to accept Cord's invitation. She wanted to be with him, Ashlynne admitted to herself.

She enjoyed his company when they weren't fighting. Oh, why not be totally honest with herself? She enjoyed it when they were fighting too.

Cord sensed her weakening resolve. "I'll pick you and the kids up at eleven on Saturday morning. Your sister Kendra is also invited. Nobody is going to be left behind." He intended to shoot down every excuse she could come up with. "You know you want to go, Ashlynne."

She ran her hand through her hair, tousling it even more. "Cord, what's the point?" she asked wearily. He was wearing her down, and that worried her. Usually, nothing or no one could break her will to prevail. It was both her greatest strength and her greatest weakness. "Why should the girls and I spend the day with you?"

"Why?" Her question took him aback. He wasn't given to probing analyses of his actions and motives. "Because we'll have fun, that's why."

"I don't do something just because it's fun," she said primly. "If I operated on that principle, God only knows where Kendra and Maxie and Daisy would've ended up by now. Rayleen was the fun-loving one in the family."

"You're doing it again and I'm not going to allow it." Cord held up his hand, as if to physically ward off her statement. "I got too close so you drag in the specter of Rayleen. Sorry, honey, it's not going to work. I'm on to you now."

He leaned down and planted an impulsive kiss on the top of her head. "See you Saturday. Eleven o'clock."

"Cord!" she called after him as he dashed out the door. "Cord, no! I won't go!" She picked up a pen, then threw it down on the desk. She'd finally managed to turn him down unequivocally. Too bad he wasn't around to hear her.

"Hi, Judge!" Kendra greeted Wyatt's black Lab like an old friend. The dog gave a joyous bark of welcome, then lay down on the floor and rolled over onto his back, wagging his tail and gazing up at her with adoring brown eyes.

"Well, I'm glad to see you too." Laughing, Kendra knelt down beside the dog and rubbed his soft belly. The dog's tail wagged harder and he made a yipping sound, overcome with happiness at the attention.

Wyatt observed the scene, his lips curved into a tense smile. That restless, on-edge feeling that had been plaguing him since he'd first laid eyes on Kendra Monroe kept growing stronger. Logic told him he should avoid her altogether. His thoughts were growing increasingly carnal, and not even sleep offered a respite. His dreams were even hotter and more erotic than his waking fantasies.

He watched her hungrily. She was wearing a loose-fitting floral print dress that was short and made of some crinkly material, teamed with a white tank top that she wore under the dress. The dress was cut low over the shoulders and in the front; the tank top was a necessary adjunct to decency. He didn't think she was wearing a bra. As she played with the dog, her breasts jiggled beneath the material.

A fiery current jolted through him. Her sensuality was as potent as a bolt of electricity. And a whole lot more dangerous. For if it was logical to avoid the object of his lust, he had taken the opposite, irrational course. He kept seeking Kendra out, and every encounter created more memories and fueled new fantasies.

Tonight he'd stopped by the coffee shop at closing time and brought her to his home—where they would be alone and free from the threat of any intrusions or interruptions. Heat flashed through him. Suddenly, the warm May evening was unbearably hot. He strode to the temperature controls mounted on the wall and switched on the air-conditioning.

Kendra stood up, brushing her palms over the skirt of her dress. "Where can I wash my hands?" she asked. "I have doggy fur all over them."

"In here. In the kitchen." Wyatt strode into the kitchen, waves of shame crashing over him. He had never in his life lusted over anyone before; he'd always considered himself too cerebral. Certainly nothing in his life had prepared him for his uncharacteristic yet enthralling obsession with Kendra Monroe.

Kendra went to the sink and washed her hands. "I like your house," she remarked, glancing around the kitchen. It was big and airy and held all the requisite appliances. "But I have to tell you, it looks pretty normal. Nice, but nothing like a zillionaire's place. You know, the kind you see in magazines."

"Well, maybe that's because I'm not—er—a zillionaire."

Kendra shook the excess water from her hands, then reached for a paper towel. "Just a billionaire, huh?" Her blue eyes teased him.

He shook his head. "Not even close."

"You have to make do with only a few million? Poor, poor Wyatt." Kendra walked toward him, smiling. "I love it when rich people try to pretend they're not really all that rich. That they're no different than anybody else, except for a few extra dollars here and there."

"Well, we're not, not really." Wyatt shifted uneasily, watching her. Her legs were shapely and uncommonly long for someone of her height. The light fabric of the dress clung to her thighs, outlining them as she walked. He gulped and tried to concentrate on something else. Her footwear. She was wearing short black boots that looked absurd with that particular dress. The women he knew teamed dresses with high heels or colorful little flats. Of course, the women he knew were older than Kendra. A good deal older. As he himself was.

Kendra stopped in front of him. "You hate talking about money, don't you?"

He'd forgotten what they'd been talking about. The closer she got, the more his brain cells seemed to short-circuit. He shrugged uncomfortably. "I simply feel that there are more important, more interesting things to discuss than money."

She tilted her head, laughing at him with those fantastic blue eyes. "Would you take a piece of advice, Wyatt?" Her smiled widened. "Don't ever say that when you're campaigning. Because money *is* the most important and most interesting thing to voters and they like to talk about it too. Dan Clarkston is always blabbering about how much money he's going to save people when he cuts taxes and brings in jobs to the area."

"Dan Clarkston is saying a lot of things that people want to hear. That doesn't mean it's the truth or what's best for the area," Wyatt said stiffly. "I want to convince the voters

that I am the right man for the job but I don't want to lie
to them about what I believe in or what I stand for."

Kendra boosted herself onto the kitchen counter, swinging
her legs below. "I think you're the right man, Wyatt," she
said, dimpling. Her lustrous black hair swung around her
shoulders.

Wyatt drew in a sharp breath, stunned once more by her
radiant beauty.

"Dan Clarkston gives me the creeps," Kendra continued,
fully aware of his dazed scrutiny. "All those great big teeth
he's always flashing—yuck! I bet they glow in the dark."

Wyatt laughed appreciatively. It seemed that most people
were charmed by Clarkston's perpetual grin. Kendra's view
was music to his ears.

Their laughter faded, and a charged silence settled over
the kitchen.

"Well, here we are," Kendra said dryly. She swung her
legs out further, so that the tips of her boots brushed Wyatt's
sides. She seemed to be daring him—or inviting him?—to
touch her. Wyatt fought an almost overwhelming urge to
do just that—grab her smooth, shapely legs and wrap them
around him.

"We should get started," he said heartily, opening the
door to the pantry storage area. "I have the boxes of candy
bars in here." He carried out three large cardboard boxes, marked "Milky Way," and set them on the counter
beside her.

"And here are the stickers." He let Kendra peek inside
the bag. There were hundreds of round white stickers with
the word "Vote" printed in blue and red letters. She glanced
from the bag of stickers to the boxes of candy bars and burst
into laughter.

"How about letting me in on the joke?"

"You really did bring me here to paste 'Vote' stickers on
the Milky Ways!" Kendra seemed to find the entire concept
hilarious.

Wyatt stared at her, bemused. "That's what we talked
about on the drive over here," he reminded her. "The staff
came up with a candy strategy to counter Dan Clarkston's
Clark bars. We blot out the word 'Milky' with a 'Vote'

sticker and there is the Way, in all its name-recognition glory. Then we pass out the bars to the new voters at the high schools."

"It's great campaign marketing," Kendra agreed. She reached out and grabbed the end of his tie. "But I didn't really expect you to have either the candy or the stickers around. I thought asking me to help out was just a ploy to get me over here. To be alone with me," she added with a sultry smile.

Wyatt attempted to breathe, without much success. It felt as if the air were trapped in his lungs.

Kendra tugged at his tie, drawing him closer. "I thought you brought me here to pick up where we left off last night."

Wyatt caught her hand, ostensibly to remove it. Instead, Kendra quickly linked her fingers with his, and used her other hand to reel him in by his tie.

"You almost kissed me last night," she murmured huskily, pulling him as close as the counter would allow. "You would've, if we hadn't heard my sister and the kids coming up the stairs."

"Kendra, I don't—"

She wrapped her legs around his waist, trapping him. "I wanted you to kiss me, Wyatt," she breathed, sliding her arms around his neck. "I haven't been able to think of anything else since."

She leaned into him, then touched her lips lightly to his. "Kiss me, Wyatt." She wriggled sensuously against him.

Anticipation and need flowed like lava through Wyatt as he wrapped his arms around her. She was so soft, he thought, dazed. He could feel the enticing thrust of her breasts against his chest and her squirming had notched the hot feminine core of her against the hard ridge of his shaft.

"Kendra." His voice was low and strained, as he tried one last time to stop himself from giving in to temptation. He was perspiring and his heart was pounding; his erection felt as hard as stone and throbbed thickly between her thighs.

"I want you, Wyatt," Kendra whispered. She looked into his eyes. A fire burned there and she stoked it, opening her mouth over his.

Wyatt groaned, then took over the kiss, penetrating her mouth with his tongue, kissing her deeply, intimately, with a fierce male hunger that grew hotter and wilder as passion flared and burned between them. His hands slipped under her skirt and skimmed along her bare thighs to cup the roundness of her bottom. She whimpered as his fingers kneaded and stroked the firm flesh, sensuously exploring the crevasse through the thin material of her bikini panties.

Her eyes shut tight, Kendra clung to him, stunned by the fire he'd ignited within her, pressing herself against him, as she gave in to his possessive mastery, wanting more and more. She felt his sex throbbing boldly against her soft moist folds, the barriers of clothing between them frustrating and yet heightening the excitement. Blindly, she clutched at his shoulders, her fingers digging into the muscled hardness.

She tried to pull off his jacket to no avail; they would have to separate and neither of them wanted to, not even for a second. The pleasure of his mouth, of his hands, was overwhelming. She heard herself moaning softly into his mouth as she squirmed against him. What had started as a daring experiment on her part had exploded into a force that made her feel both weak and strong, bold and scared all at the same time.

They were both gasping when he lifted his mouth from hers and pressed his lips hotly against the sensitive curve of her neck.

"Oh Wyatt, it feels so good," she breathed. "And you taste so good. Kiss me again."

He didn't need to be asked twice. Wyatt took her lips again and she yielded immediately, opening her mouth to him as her slender body twisted sinuously against his. She felt on fire, her entire body flushed and tight and swollen. She sought relief by rubbing her breasts against his chest and opening her legs wider to press herself closer and harder to him.

And then suddenly, shockingly, they were no longer alone. They had a canine chaperon who stood on his hind legs and placed his front paws on the counter, nuzzling them both with his cold nose, and whining insistently.

It was the equivalent of being doused with a bucket of cold water. Wyatt and Kendra broke apart as Judge began to bark.

Breathless, shaking with the force of passion expended and unfulfilled, Kendra slumped against Wyatt, laying her head on his shoulder, her arms draped around him. He held her, his eyes closed, his whole body wired and primed for sexual release. Which would not be forthcoming.

Judge jumped up, then down again, yapping, trying to engage their attention. They ignored him.

"Kendra, I'm sorry," Wyatt said. "This shouldn't have happened." He lifted Kendra from the countertop, letting her slide slowly down the length of his body until her feet touched the floor, turning the release into a caress itself.

"Don't apologize," Kendra murmured huskily, clinging to him. "But maybe you should think about enrolling him in obedience school or something."

Wyatt drew back a little to gaze down at her. She tipped her head and met his eyes. "I wasn't talking about the dog interrupting us," he began, "I mean that you and I—what we've done—"

"Stop." Kendra laid her fingers over his lips to silence him. "I wanted it to happen, Wyatt, I'm glad it did."

A small aftershock of passion made her shiver. The force of his desire, and her own, caught her by surprise. Who would've dreamed that Wyatt Way could kiss like that? . . . Passionately . . . masterfully, nothing at all like the high school boys she'd kissed, just to learn what kissing was all about.

And his hands . . . Kendra actually blushed. His hot caresses had excited her so much she'd forgotten everything—time, place, her plan!—except the wanton hunger he'd stirred inside her. "I've never felt this way before, Wyatt," she confessed softly. "I want it again. And—and more. Much more."

Her provocative words reverberated through his head, nearly shattering the tenuous control he'd managed to achieve. She was warm and soft and curvy in his arms, the scent of her dark silky hair filled his nostrils when he breathed. Wyatt knew he should put her away from him, explain why and how this kiss was a never-to-be-repeated mistake, and take her home immediately.

But even though he knew what he had to do, it was wrenching to actually do it. He'd always done what was expected of him, but never had he resented having to do the right thing more than he did at this moment. He crossed the kitchen, needing the physical distance to bolster his resolve. "Kendra, we can't. What happened between us isn't going to happen again. It's wrong, it's impossible, and—"

Judge would no longer be ignored. The dog ran to the front door, barking insistently, then raced back to the kitchen, wagging his tail and watching them expectantly. Just then, the doorbell rang.

"Yikes!" Kendra exclaimed.

"Judge must've heard the car pull up." Wyatt looked at Kendra, whose hair was tousled and lips were kiss-swollen. And now someone was at the door. "That's why he's been so antsy, he's been trying to tell us someone is coming."

"Want me to hide?" Kendra raced out of the kitchen before Wyatt had a chance to respond. The doorbell rang again, followed by three insistent raps on the brass knocker.

"Hey, Wyatt, open up! I know you're in there!" Cord's voice sounded loudly through the door. "Don't worry, it's only me, not an irate constituent or a persistent salesman or—"

Wyatt flung open the front door. "Cord." He cleared his throat. "This is a—surprise." A colossal shock was closer to the truth, but naturally Wyatt did not say that.

"I've been on the phone with Mary Beth at the lodge." Cord strode in, oblivious to Wyatt's attempt to bodily block the doorway. Ever obliging, Wyatt stepped out of his way and let him pass. "I drove by, hoping you were around and not stuck at some meeting or rally and saw your lights on and the car in the garage."

"Are you having trouble at the lodge?" Wyatt stood in the hallway, directly in front of his brother. "You mentioned your chef—"

"Jack, I mean Jacques, is still bent on becoming French, although I think I've come up with a plan to keep him at the lodge *and* let him pursue his destiny." Cord smiled wryly. "I told Jack to consider a three-month leave of absence next March, April, and May, which traditionally have been our slowest months. He could go to France then and we'll hire a temporary chef with the option of keeping him on, should Jack and the lodge find it mutually advantageous to part. That gives us some months to find a quality replacement, and hopefully Jack will think twice about throwing away his career at the lodge when his understudy is waiting right in the wings, so to speak."

"Good plan!" enthused Wyatt. "Excellent. Thanks for sharing it with me, Cord." He took his brother's arm and attempted to walk him back through the door.

Cord didn't budge. "But that isn't why I'm here."

"No?" Wyatt stifled a groan.

"I know you'll appreciate this." Cord grinned in anticipation. "Before I talked to Mary Beth, I spent an hour on the phone earlier with a travel agent who wants to book a small but very select group into our lodge." He chuckled. "Are you ready for this? It's the Society of M-E-D Watchers."

"Med watchers?" Wyatt cast an anxious glance toward the kitchen. Where was Kendra and what on earth was she doing?

"No, M-E-D." Cord corrected, his grin widening. "That stands for moose, elk, and deer. The society knows that Glacier Natural Park is rich in their favorite species and wants to plan a retreat, to study and hopefully see and photograph the animals. The travel agent recommended our lodge but she wanted to be sure that vegetarian dishes were available. Apparently at their last gathering, elk stew and venison were served and the group went berserk."

The brothers laughed.

"You miss being at the lodge, don't you, Cord?" Wyatt murmured. "I wish that I didn't require the entire family's assistance in this damn campaign. You and Holly—"

"We're here because we want to help, Wyatt. Nobody's forcing us." Cord deftly stepped around him and headed straight for the kitchen. "Got a cold beer? Hey, where's Judge?"

His last question was answered the moment he set foot in the kitchen. Judge sat on the floor next to the chair on which Kendra Monroe was kneeling while she . . . pasted stickers onto candy bars? Cord stared at her in bewilderment. Which was immediately followed by a sickening feeling of consternation.

Ashlynne's voice, concerned and accusing, seemed to ring in his ears, filling the silence. *"I want you to warn your brother away from my little sister . . . Your brother . . . interested in seducing my little sister . . ."* He glanced from Kendra to Wyatt, frowning. It just couldn't be true! he attempted to assure himself. But here was Kendra Monroe, too-young-for-Wyatt Kendra, right here in Wyatt's kitchen.

"Hi, Cord," Kendra greeted him blithely. She welcomed him with a dazzling smile. Although he considered her outfit slightly strange, she was neatly groomed, her hair shiny and well-brushed, her red lipstick artfully highlighting her beautifully shaped mouth.

Her lack of furtiveness or guilt did reassure him a bit. "What are you doing?" Cord walked over to the table for a closer look.

"I'm the student coordinator for Wyatt's campaign to register new voters," Kendra explained, working as she spoke. She peeled off the sticker and slapped it over the word "Milky" on the candy-bar wrapper. "See? There's 'Way,' right here to remind everybody who to vote for. It's our counterstrategy to Clarkston's Clark bar campaign." She knew she sounded convincing. Wyatt had talked so much about Clarkston's Clark bar gambit, she was beginning to forget she'd invented the whole thing.

"You're the student coordinator!" Cord's apprehension and confusion were demolished by a tidal wave of relief. He said a silent heartfelt prayer that he hadn't launched into an embarrassing tirade of accusations and warnings. Ashlynne had completely misinterpreted the relationship between his brother and her sister and nearly caused him to do the same.

"Kendra and her friend Josh told me about Clarkston and his candy ploy so we're countering it," Wyatt put in, joining them at the table. He stood at the other end, careful not to get too close to Kendra.

"Want to help, Cord?" Kendra asked sweetly.

"Sure." Cord sat down at the table and pulled one box and a pile of stickers in front of him. "My fee is a cold bottle of beer."

Wyatt went to the refrigerator like someone in a daze. Cord's appearance was a stunning twist to an already incredible evening. Now all three of them were going to sit around and work on a project together?

"I'll have root beer, if you have it," Kendra called.

"I'm glad you didn't ask for anything stronger," teased Cord. "Or your sister would have my head. Not to mention my spleen and liver too."

They both laughed.

Wyatt returned to the table with a beer for Cord and a root beer for Kendra. He'd gathered his wits enough to realize something. "You two know each other," he observed, astonished.

"Cord was a very good friend of my dead sister Rayleen's," Kendra said dryly. "And he'd like to be a very good friend of my live sister Ashlynne's."

She watched Wyatt's expression change from speculation to abject amazement. "That's right, Wyatt, your brother has had a Monroe in his past and would like to have one in his present." She turned to Cord. "You're going to have to work awfully hard for that, Cord. Ashlynne's already said you're toast."

"Don't write me off yet, kid." Cord grinned. "Ashlynne is spending Saturday with me."

"She's going out with you!" shrieked Kendra. "No way!"

"As a Way, it's my duty to inform you that we are not crazy about that particular bit of slang, having endured countless bad puns because of it," Cord told her, his dark eyes gleaming with humor.

"Especially since Clarkston began using it to stir up the crowds. A mass of people screaming 'No Way' is dispiriting, to say the least," Wyatt added wryly.

"Anyway, I invited Maxie and Daisy along on Saturday, for a fun-filled day at the DC Zoo," Cord told Kendra. "You're also included."

"You actually got Ashlynne to agree to a date, even if the kids are coming along!" Kendra's blue eyes were glowing. "I didn't think there was a man on the planet persistent enough to make her say yes."

Cord carefully placed a 'Vote' sticker on the candy wrapper. "There were at least two others she said yes to," he reminded her.

Kendra looked at him blankly.

"Maxie and Daisy didn't come from the cabbage patch," Cord reminded her. "Obviously, Ashlynne said yes to their fathers. The stuntman and the classic jerk," he added under his breath.

"Ohhh! Oh yes, Maxie's and Daisy's fathers! Of course!" Kendra laughed nervously. "The stuntman and the classic jerk? Is that how Ashlynne described them?"

Cord nodded, leaning forward. "But that's all she said. So if you'd care to share any additional information "

"Nope, nothing at all." Kendra took a long drink of her root beer, diligently working all the while.

"When do you hand these things out?" Cord asked, dumping the stickered bars back into the boxes.

"I'm supposed to address the senior class in a special assembly tomorrow afternoon," said Wyatt. "But first I'm to meet with a small group of students to discuss issues pertinent to the youth of Waysboro."

"Which students?" asked Kendra.

"Missy Marshall, Doug Winchester, Jessica Spencer, Alec Jefferies." Wyatt recited the names. He had very good recall. "And a few others."

"So you'll be discussing issues pertinent to the stuck-up youths of Waysboro." Kendra used such force to place the last sticker on the last candy bar that it was squashed flat. She tossed it into the box anyway. "One really big problem for that clique is that the student parking lot is too close to a grove of trees and the birds target their brand-new BMWs and Cabriolets and Miatas. Such trauma!"

She flashed one of her practiced charming smiles but inside she was seething with a familiar yet inchoate anger. "I really have to go home now. I told Ashlynne I'm at Susie McClanahan's working on a collage for art class, and if we were, we'd be done with it by now. Is there a bus stop nearby?"

"Kendra, you are not taking the bus home," Wyatt interjected firmly. "I'll give you a ride."

"No need for you to venture out again, Wyatt, I don't mind driving her. Anyway, I should be getting back to OakWay. I want to talk with Holly." Cord frowned, anticipating *that* conversation. He thought of those photos he'd seen—and the ones he hadn't—and winced.

"I said I'll take her home," Wyatt countered, waiting for Kendra to acquiesce. She had to know how much he wanted to be alone with her.

"Whoa, don't fight over me, guys." Kendra tossed her hair and it tumbled dramatically around her shoulders. Wyatt watched her, his eyes burning. She smiled sweetly at him. "Cord is right, Wyatt, no use dragging yourself out when he's leaving anyway. I'll get my stuff, I dumped it in the hall." She flounced out of the kitchen.

"Cool car, Cord," Kendra remarked as they drove along Applegate Lane, Wyatt's house receding in the distance.

"Oh yeah." Cord chuckled. "An aircraft carrier on four wheels. And such an *interesting* shade of beige."

She cast him a measuring glance. "You don't like it?"

"No, I don't like it much at all. It's an official company car, selected by my woefully unimaginative brother Stafford. Even my grandfather's taste in cars is a little more exciting than this. Back home in Montana, I drive a Jeep Cherokee."

"Now that really is cool," Kendra said approvingly. "I was just being polite before. I thought this was your own car and that you must've liked it if you bought it."

"You're not at all like Ashlynne, are you? She doesn't tell people what they want to hear, she's far too honest to pander like that."

"You think Ashlynne has been honest with you?" Kendra laughed. "Well, good for her."

They came to a traffic light and Cord braked to a stop. "I'm not sure what you're all about, Kendra, and that troubles me." He stared thoughtfully at her. "I consider myself a fairly shrewd judge of character but I keep getting thrown off track by you. You seem warm and open and artless and yet . . ."

"I might really be a conniving schemer?" Kendra exclaimed. "That's interesting, Cord. You really are a shrewd judge of character. Of course, you already proved that by having a fling with Rayleen."

Cord grimaced. Rayleen again. He didn't miss the censure in Kendra's tone. She was more like Ashlynne than he thought. "Why are you working on my brother's campaign, Kendra?" he asked bluntly. "We both know that Ashlynne works for Ethan Thorpe, who is Dan Clarkston's biggest cheerleader. And I know for a fact that Ashlynne doesn't want you around my brother."

Kendra raised her brows. "She thinks he'll have his wicked way with me, like you did with Rayleen," she said mockingly. "I tried to tell her not to worry, but you know Ashlynne."

"I'm certainly beginning to."

"And you want to know her better, a whole lot better." Kendra curled up on the seat, her expression eager. "Tell me more about your plans for Saturday, Cord. I hope I can come along but I might have to work at the coffee shop if Letty is short-handed that day."

Cord told her about his plans. She vetoed certain details, offered ideas of her own. By the time they reached her apartment building, they were joking and laughing together. And Cord didn't realize until he'd dropped her off and was heading back to OakWay that she'd never gotten around to telling him why and how she happened to become a volunteer for Wyatt's campaign.

"You want me to go to Waysboro High School this afternoon and help Dan Clarkston pass out Clark bars to the students?" Ashlynne repeated incredulously.

Ethan Thorpe nodded his head. "Clarkston's headquarters received a tip that Wyatt Way is addressing the senior class this afternoon in a drive to register eighteen-year-olds to vote. He is passing out Milky Way candy bars to them, and the tipster suggested that Dan pass out Clark bars to *all* the students. They're all potential voters eventually, not just those students who can vote in this November's election."

"Dueling name-recognition ploys," Ashlynne remarked. "Who was the tipster?"

"An anonymous student." Thorpe smiled. "The staff spent the morning buying up all the available Clark bars in the area. From what we've been told, Way will be sequestered for a meeting with some student leaders before he meets with the rest of the class, so I want to make our appeal to all the other students, a broad base, stressing diversity. I thought Dan could make a little informal speech about elitism and exclusion."

"The purpose of which is to make everybody not in the select group meeting with Wyatt Way feel excluded," Ashlynne surmised, "and to ally themselves with Dan who is a friend to all."

"Unlike Wyatt Way, who chooses to hobnob with the elite," finished Ethan. "An excellent strategy, and I wish I could personally thank our anonymous student benefactor who came up with the idea."

Ashlynne did not share his glee. The candy-bar campaign meant closing the office and driving with Ethan to Waysboro High, a place she had loathed during her four-year incarceration. As a Monroe, she'd automatically been branded a loser, consigned to the status of outcast. It was safe to bet that there would be no Monroes among the select group meeting with Wyatt Way.

At the high school, large crowds of students gathered on the grassy lawn in front of the building, and rock music was playing so loudly that Ashlynne could hear it through the closed windows of Ethan's air-conditioned car.

"Good, the DJ from WWEX is here," Ethan noted. "The radio-station manager owed me a favor and I called in the chips today," he added, smiling his satisfaction.

"How did you ever manage to pull this off in such a short time?" Ashlynne marveled, looking at the DJ, who was playing music and talking to the eager groups of teens gathered around him. Many of them were dancing. And in the middle of it all were Dan and Cindy Clarkston, smiling their brilliant signature smiles.

"Money and incentive, plus a touch of creativity," Ethan explained. "The DJ idea was mine. I remembered how much music meant to my brother and me when we were in our teens, so I figured these kids would go for the most popular DJ in the area. We needed to get everybody's attention and to keep it away from Wyatt Way."

"Well, I think you've succeeded. It looks like everybody in the whole school is out here on the lawn," Ashlynne said. "Oh, there's my little sister Kendra with her friends Josh and Susie and Taniqua."

"An Asian, a black, and two working-class whites. Perfect!" Ethan viewed the group, his smile calculating. "We'll put them to work distributing the candy and take pictures of them with Dan." Ethan swung the car into a parking space and quickly headed toward the center of the action. Ashlynne lagged behind, waving to Kendra and motioning her over.

"What are you doing here, Ash?" Kendra asked. She didn't wait for an answer. "Isn't this cool? They canceled the last two periods this afternoon. We're supposed to be learning all about civic responsibility."

"While the Crashman plays the sounds of today and gives away free CDs and tapes!" Josh chimed in jovially. "How'd they ever get the Crashman to come here? He never does gigs like this."

Ashlynne thought of Ethan's reference to WWEX's station manager owing him a favor and knew that the Crashman had been given no choice. One did not say no to Ethan Thorpe.

"I'm supposed to be handing out Clark bars," Ashlynne said. "You all can help me."

"Sure, we'll help," Kendra agreed. She cast a glance at the high school building where Wyatt was ensconced with the student elite, and the rage she'd felt last night at being excluded from that meeting stung her anew. She felt betrayed, though she knew as well as any Monroe that in Waysboro to be among the chosen elite had nothing to do with brains or even looks and everything to do with financial and social status. Why had she ever expected Wyatt Way to be different? She was almost as angry at her own uncharacteristic stupidity than she was at him.

"We'll be thrilled to help," she added balefully.

"Girl, you are such a wench," Taniqua said rather admiringly.

"And then some," muttered Josh.

"This is an outrage," Holly said through gritted teeth as she, Wyatt, and Cord stood on the sidelines, watching the giant party taking place in front of the high school.

Wyatt's meeting with the future movers and shakers of Waysboro had been quite brief as rock music blared outside, drawing and keeping the attention of the teen leaders. They had been as eager as the unselected masses to join the Crashman on the lawn—where Dan Clarkston had insinuated himself at the popular DJ's side, occasionally bantering with him and drawing laughs from the students.

"The chances of herding the entire senior class back into the auditorium to hear Wyatt extol the virtues of voting are slim to none," she said tightly.

"I think this is what the television industry calls counterprogramming," Wyatt said, sighing resignedly. His eyes narrowed as he saw Kendra Monroe laughing and throwing Clark bars into the crowd, much the same way she tossed dog biscuits to Judge.

Holly's gaze was fixed on Ethan Thorpe, who stood talking to a smiling Dan Clarkston. Cord stared at Ashlynne passing out candy bars. Unlike Kendra, who was clearly not taking the job seriously, Ashlynne was quite diligent, handing out one bar per student. Diligent and serious, that was Ashlynne, whatever the task. He frowned.

"Waterloo for the Ways," Cord muttered, glancing at his sister and brother and following their gazes.

"No. Armageddon." Holly balled her fingers into fists, her dark eyes never leaving Ethan Thorpe.

Suddenly, several young toughs muscled their way through the crowd and snatched the boxes of candy bars, hoisting them up and taking off in a run with them. At the same time a pair of pregnant identical twin girls, dressed alike in jeans and pink maternity shirts printed with the word "Baby" and an arrow pointing to their swollen bellies, scooped tapes and CDs from the Crashman's giveaway bin, filling shopping bags with their booty. A big fierce-looking young thug raised an enormous fist armored with old-fashioned brass knuckles to protect the thieves, whom nobody seemed inclined to stop anyway.

"Good grief, they're pulling a heist right in front of everybody," Cord exclaimed. They watched the larcenous gang depart with their cache of candy and music without any interference.

"I recognize three of them," Wyatt said. "Philly, Mitch, and Lonnie Joe Monroe. The twins must be Ben's sisters. Chances are the others are Monroes and their cohorts as well. I guess this sort of thing is expected of them."

"And your alleged student coordinator seems to be a double agent," Cord pointed out, glaring at Kendra. "What a sneaky little brat!"

The theft was causing consternation in the Clarkston camp. Ethan appeared downright irritated, Dan's smile almost wavered, and the Crashman was definitely annoyed. Ashlynne looked mortified; Kendra was howling with laughter.

"Here's our chance to play Wellington," Cord said, picking up a box of the Vote Way candy bars. He pushed his way through the crowd, tossing out bars the way Kendra had been doing. The students grabbed for them. Free candy was free candy no matter whose name was on the wrapper.

Wyatt followed suit. "Be sure to register to vote," he called out. "And don't forget to keep the name Way in mind when you're voting."

Holly scored a coup of her own. She snaked a path to the small stage where the Crashman was lamenting his loss of giveaways. She flashed a smile as dazzling as Dan's, murmured a few words to him, and the instantly smitten DJ turned his mike over to her.

"Crashman is going to continue drawing names for free tapes and CDs," Holly announced. "In fact, he's going to step it up and draw a different name every five minutes. You can redeem your prizes at local record stores, courtesy of WWEX."

There were cheers and applause and shrieks of approval. "Who's number one?" the Crashman shouted, and the crowd responded with a roar, "The Crashman!"

"He's not the one running for office," Dan Clarkston muttered crossly. "This is a disaster! All these kids will remember about this afternoon is Crashman, not Dan."

Ashlynne gaped at him. This was the first time she'd seen the candidate without his trademark grin, and he looked like a sullen little boy.

She turned to Ethan just in time to see him grab Holly's arm as she stepped from the platform.

"I told Crashman to bill the Clarkston campaign for all those tapes and CDs he will be giving away this afternoon," Holly announced. She moved closer to Ethan in what Ashlynne considered an act of suicidal folly. But Holly didn't appear to fear for her life. She lifted her face to Ethan, her dark eyes challenging. "I also told Crash if he wants payment even quicker to bill Ethan Thorpe directly."

Ashlynne held her breath as Ethan's hand tightened on Holly's arm and he jerked her even closer. The couple seemed completely oblivious to the noisy crowd and raucous music.

"That qualifies as a political dirty trick, Holly," Ethan said silkily. "And you were so ready to condemn me for the same thing."

"Where is the Federal Election Ethics Committee when you really need them, hmm?" Holly smiled nastily, making no attempt to pull out of Ethan's grip. "I learned all I know about dirty tricks from you, Ethan."

"You learned all sorts of things from me, darling," Ethan purred. "You were quite an adept little student and you loved every lesson I ever taught you. In fact, I think you want more. But you get what you give so you'll get nothing but misery from me, Holly."

Ethan released her so abruptly and so roughly that Holly stumbled backward. He turned to Ashlynne. "Are you ready to go back to the office?" he asked brusquely.

"I'll drive you back into town, Ashlynne." Cord had materialized in front of them. He was looking at Ashlynne with fiery dark eyes, his gaze possessive.

He was remembering their kiss in Ethan's wrecked office, Ashlynne was sure of it. A shudder of desire chased along her spine. The intensity of it scared her. If she were alone with Cord, he would take her in his arms again, he would kiss her, and she knew she would not resist. She couldn't pretend that she didn't want him, not even to herself. Especially not to herself. And she couldn't have him. He was as forbidden to her as that apple tree in the garden had been to Adam and Eve.

Ashlynne gulped. She cast a quick glance at Ethan, who immediately reacted to the apprehension in her eyes.

"I'm driving Ashlynne back to the office," Thorpe announced coldly.

Cord burned with frustration. What a day this had turned out to be! First, this morning's phone call from Mary Beth informing him that a particularly vitriolic travel-magazine writer had taken up residence in the lodge and was loudly criticizing everything, from the wood paneling in the bar to the brand of soap in the bathrooms, next this campaign fiasco, and now another round of Ashlynne's favorite game of approach-avoidance. She was a master player and he was sick and tired of it.

If only he would get sick and tired of *her*! But it didn't seem to be happening. He seemed to be as hooked on her as a trout on a fly-fisherman's lure in Glacier Lake. It was a disconcerting notion, one that sent him stalking off in the opposite direction without another word.

CHAPTER NINE ───────────

CORD was at Ashlynne's door promptly at eleven on Saturday morning. Her snub at the high school rally still rankled but he was willing to give her another chance to redeem herself with him. He didn't care to dwell on the ramifications of that.

Kendra opened the door. "Good morning." She managed to make the greeting sound both mocking and challenging.

"Well, if it isn't the little back-stabber." Cord scowled at her. "You know, after the other night I thought you were on our side, but then you turn up working for the opposition. What gives, Kendra?"

"I'm not on anyone's side."

"You were passing out candy for Clarkston, standing right up there with him and Thorpe and—"

"I also told my cousins to grab the free stuff 'cause I knew Clarkston and his people wouldn't do anything it." She shrugged. "I'm on my own side."

"I'm very disappointed in you, Kendra."

"I'm crushed." Kendra rolled her eyes. "What are you doing here, anyway? Didn't you get all those messages Ashlynne left on your answering machine saying she'd changed her mind and wouldn't go with you today?"

"I chose to ignore all of them." Since she had yet to invite him in, Cord brushed past her and stepped inside. "Are you ready to go?" It was a warm day, already nearing eighty degrees, and she was wearing jeans shorts and a cotton blue-gray vest. "Aren't you going to put a shirt on under that?"

Kendra ran her hands over her bare arms. "So now you're a fashion consultant?" She stared at his khaki slacks and short-sleeved madras sports shirt, the boat shoes without socks. "I'll give *you* some advice—lose the preppy look. It's so Waysboro, it makes me want to hurl."

"Just tell Ashlynne I'm here," Cord said tersely.

"She's in the basement doing laundry. Tell her yourself." Kendra drifted out of the room, leaving him to his own devices.

An inauspicious beginning to the day, Cord acknowledged. He sat down on the sofa to wait.

Maxie and Daisy came running inside a few minutes later, their small faces sweaty and streaked with dirt. "Hi, Uncle Cord," Maxie called as she dashed into the kitchen.

Cord stood and watched from a discreet distance as Maxie climbed nimbly onto the counter, removed a glass from the cabinet, turned on the taps, and filled the glass with water. "Do you want some water too?" she asked her sister.

Daisy nodded, and Maxie reached for another glass and filled it with water.

The ensuing scene seemed to unfold in slow motion before Cord's eyes. Maxie jumped down from the counter, holding a full glass of water in each hand. Weighted down and off balance, she was unable to control her landing and ended up falling on her knees on the kitchen floor. The glasses went flying, dousing both little girls with water, before crashing to the floor and breaking.

Maxie surveyed the scene—her sister and herself dripping wet, pieces of broken glass scattered around—then let out a piercing shriek that brought Kendra running. "Maxie, are you all right?" Kendra asked, checking for blood. Maxie wailed loudly.

"I think she's fine," Cord observed. "She didn't start crying till she saw the mess she'd made."

Ashlynne arrived at that precise moment, lugging a plastic basket filled with towels. "What happened?" she asked wearily, setting the heavy load down. She saw Cord standing in the kitchen and froze. "What are you doing here?"

"I was just asking myself that same question. I came to take you and the girls to the zoo, remember? Although I think I see why you tried to back out of going. This place is a zoo in itself."

Maxie's wails instantly ceased. "The zoo?"

"Are we going to a real zoo?" whispered Daisy, acknowl-edging Cord's presence for the first time. "With real ani-mals?"

"Cord, don't," warned Ashlynne.

Cord smiled smugly and turned to the children. "You bet we're going to the zoo. Why don't you two wash your faces and hands and get into some dry clothes, so we can be on our way?"

Squealing with joy, Maxie and Daisy tore out of the kitchen toward the bathroom.

"That was unconscionable!" spluttered Ashlynne. "I left word on your answering machine that we were *not* going with you today. How dare you come here and get the children all excited about a trip we won't be taking!"

"He plays dirty," Kendra pointed out.

"No, playing dirty is leaving messages on an answering machine to avoid speaking to the person you're canceling out on," said Cord. "It's also cowardly. The last thing I felt like doing was fighting with you over the phone, Ashlynne. I figured it was easier just to show up here today. So here I am." He raked his eyes critically over Ashlynne, who was wearing a baggy pair of faded cotton shorts and an equally ancient sleeveless blouse. "We'll leave as soon as you've changed out of your grunge clothes."

"I am not going anywhere with you," Ashlynne said through gritted teeth.

"We're ready!" Daisy and Maxie appeared, their faces scrubbed clean. They had changed their outfits, from their dirty play clothes into matching pink and white checked sundresses.

"Well, don't you two ladies look beautiful!" Cord effused. He was both amused and touched that the little girls had dressed up for their outing. What had been a game he was playing with Ashlynne suddenly became something else, something more. He was not going to disappoint these children, he vowed.

"Mommy has to stay here and wash some clothes, so you two and Kendra and me will be going to the zoo," he said, looking Ashlynne squarely in the eye.

She saw the challenge there and her jaw tightened with angry determination. She was not going to allow Cord Way to manipulate her this way. She would call his bluff. "That's right," she agreed. "It'll be the four of you at the zoo today."

"Sorry." Kendra heaved a regretful sigh. "I'd love to go to the zoo, but I'm working today from twelve to five."

Cord frowned. The situation was deteriorating rapidly, but he refused to throw in the towel. "No problem," he said with more élan than he was feeling. "Just the three of us will go then—Maxie, Daisy, and me." The very idea filled him with horror but he tried to seem upbeat about it.

Daisy looked at him, her dark eyes wide with apprehension. "I'm scared to go with you without Mommy or Kendra." Her lower lip quivered and she ran from the room.

"I'm not scared, Uncle Cord," Maxie said blithely. She walked over to Cord and slipped her small hand in his. "Let's go."

The sound of Daisy sobbing heartbrokenly in her bedroom could be heard throughout the small apartment. Cord, Ashlynne, and Kendra stood still and silent.

"Poor Daisy," Maxie sighed. "She really wanted to go."

Cord glanced imploringly at Kendra. She seemed his best shot out of this wretched dilemma. "Could you call the coffee shop and tell them you can't make it today? Look, I'll reimburse you for your lost wages—I'll double them—if you'll come with us."

"It's not only that. Letty is there by herself this afternoon," Kendra said glumly. "Nobody else can come in today, that's why she scheduled me in the first place. I can't let her down."

"Congratulations, Mr. Way." Ashlynne folded her arms in front of her and glared at him. "If you came here to cause trouble, you've been a smashing success." She stalked from the room, Kendra at her heels.

Ashlynne had won, Cord conceded grimly. He could not take Maxie to the zoo alone. Not only did a solo trip feel all wrong, he knew that Ashlynne would never permit it. "Er, Maxie," he began uneasily, bracing himself for the waterworks that were sure to follow when he told her the outing was not to be.

Maxie was dancing around the room, singing a happy little tune.

Cord sank down onto the sofa, groaning. Life was too short for the many complications created by Ashlynne Monroe. After he left this apartment today, the heartrending sobs of two disappointed tots doubtlessly ringing in his ears, he would not be back. Ever. And this time, there would be absolutely no more exceptions to his self-imposed rule.

Back in Daisy's room, Ashlynne and Kendra attempted to comfort her. "Maxie won't be going either, Daisy," Ashlynne promised, sitting on the edge of the bed where Daisy was crying her heart out.

Daisy was not consoled. "I wanted to go to the zoo," she wailed. "I wanted Maxie to go too. Everybody in my class goes to the zoo and the circus and the beach and lots of other places too. And me and Maxie don't go anywhere."

Ashlynne stood up, pain welling within her. It didn't help that lately she'd been thinking exactly what Daisy had just voiced, that the children's world was becoming too circumscribed for them. But all those places Daisy had mentioned required a car to get there, not to mention plenty of money. And after paying their living expenses, anything extra was socked away into their get-out-of-Waysboro fund.

"Daisy, if you want to go to the zoo today, you could go with Maxie and Cord," suggested Kendra. "He's not a stranger, you know him."

"I only know him if you or Mommy are there," Daisy said, looking scared and woebegone.

"Cord is Daisy's *father*, Ashlynne," Kendra murmured, pulling Ashlynne aside, out of earshot of Daisy. "It's, like, sad she's scared to be with her own father."

Kendra wasn't the only one bothered by Daisy's response to Cord. Though father and daughter, the two were strangers to one other, and Ashlynne was keenly aware whose fault that was. Guilt was a potent force, and she yielded to it.

"Stop crying, Daisy." She sighed. "I'm going to the zoo with you."

Daisy was jubilant. "Mommy's coming!" She raced into the living room to tell Cord and Maxie the good news. Her face was still streaked with tears and she wiped her cheeks with the back of her hand.

Cord felt weak-kneed with relief and profoundly grateful that there would be no more tears from sad little girls. It was ridiculous he'd been reduced to such straits, but it was all Ashlynne's fault for being so damn contrary.

Ashlynne joined them minutes later, having changed into old blue jeans, an oversized pea-green T-shirt—a truly hideous color, sized to fit Godzilla—and sneakers that had once been white. She'd pulled her thick, springy hair back into a loose ponytail and not bothered with makeup, not even clear lipstick.

She was not dressed like a woman hoping to attract a man, just the opposite, in fact. Cord got her nonverbal message, loud and clear. She didn't want to go, and her appearance reflected her antipathy toward him and their outing.

"I want you to know I think your tactics today are nothing but emotional blackmail and this is the last time I'll allow myself to be manipulated," Ashlynne told him, breaking the icy silence that had enveloped them since leaving the apartment. She kept her voice low so that Daisy and Maxie, who were in the backseat of the car, did not hear. "I won't stand for my children to be used this way. After today, I don't want to see you or hear from you."

"I can completely reassure you on that score, babe. I'm sick of the one-step-forward, five-steps-backward games you play. I'm only going through with this zoo farce because I don't want to disappoint the kids." Cord's hands gripped the steering wheel so tightly, his knuckles were white. "After today, I will definitely not bother you again."

He couldn't wait for the day to be over, to expunge her completely from his life.

"Good!" snapped Ashlynne. In just a few hours, her Cord-free existence would begin anew. She could hardly wait.

They didn't say another word to each other until Cord asked what she wanted for lunch as they walked into a McDonald's restaurant near the zoo. It was Maxie and Daisy's choice, and they each requested a Happy Meal, which included a toy along with the usual burger, fries, and soft drink.

"I saw the commercials on TV. There's little tiny Barbies for girls, with hair to comb," Maxie eagerly explained to Ashlynne, sounding a bit like a commercial herself. The three Monroes claimed a booth while Cord stood in line to order.

"And there's dumb cars for boys," Maxie added disdainfully. She and Daisy laughed at the hapless prize and the equally hapless boys doomed to receive it.

Cord ordered lunch for himself and the children. Ashlynne didn't want anything, no doubt because she couldn't bring herself to eat a morsel of food paid for by him, he thought irritably. This was truly going to be a very long day.

"I'm awfully sorry, we're all out of the miniature Barbie dolls," the contrite teen behind the counter informed him. "But we have plenty of the toy cars available."

"No problem," Cord said.

But there was a problem, a big one.

"A car!" Maxie exclaimed in horror, removing the toy from the brightly colored cardboard box. "Where's my Barbie?" She burst into tears. "I want a Barbie doll! Cars are stupid! They're for boys!"

She bawled loudly and inconsolably, drawing glances from other customers, some sympathetic, a few amused, the rest condemnatory. Ashlynne was aghast. Maxie had never behaved so badly in her life! But she was making up for lost time now, throwing a tantrum in a crowded restaurant, with Cord Way looking on. He looked embarrassed and totally disconcerted.

"I have an idea," Cord said, with far more enthusiasm than he felt. A long day? This one was going to last well into eternity. "We'll go to a different McDonald's where they aren't out of Barbies. We'll buy lunch there and get the dolls and—"

"Okay," Maxie sniffed, jumping to her feet. "Let's go."

"Throw away perfectly good food that no one has even touched so we can buy more food, just to get a doll?" Ashlynne gasped, incredulous.

"It's a small enough price to pay for some peace and quiet," Cord said flatly.

"Absolutely not!" Ashlynne decreed. She fixed the girls with a stern-eyed stare. "You two are going to sit here and eat this lunch."

"Noooo!" shrieked Maxie. "It's not fair!" She picked up the toy car and threw it onto the floor.

Daisy's eyes grew rounder. She grabbed her hamburger and began to eat.

Cord glanced around at the interested audience, which included virtually everyone in their field of vision. "I feel like the floor show at a dinner theater," he muttered. "Let's bring an end to Act One and go to the car."

"Fine." Ashlynne took Maxie's hand and led her, howling, from the restaurant.

Cord and Daisy exchanged glances, then followed them out. "I guess your sister doesn't like cars much," he remarked, for lack of anything else to say.

"No," Daisy agreed, glancing down at her own toy car, which she clutched in her hand. "Especially when she thinks she's getting a little Barbie like on TV. She's been wanting one ever since we saw the commercials. Only boys are supposed to get these cars." She looked uncertainly at the toy car again.

"I see," Cord said. He was actually beginning to.

"Could I keep this car, even though I'm a girl?" Daisy asked, a little worriedly.

"You certainly can. Girls play with cars too, you know. My sister Holly used to love to play with my cars and trucks. She thought her dolls were stupid and boring." He smiled, remembering Holly's fierce pronouncements every time she was gifted with another doll.

Daisy looked at him, shocked. "Dolls are not stupid and boring," she informed him, her inflection, her tone so like Ashlynne's he almost did a double take.

They reached the car where Ashlynne was scolding an unrepentant Maxie.

"Kids, get in the back, I want to talk to your mother for a minute," Cord ordered.

They obeyed at once, clambering into the car and closing the door.

"You can take us home now," Ashlynne said, averting her eyes from his. "I'm terribly sorry, I'm at a loss for Maxie's behavior. She's acting like a spoiled brat and I don't know how . . . I don't know why . . . Heaven knows, they aren't spoiled, they couldn't be. It's not like they get everything they want or ever have."

"It's no big deal, Ashlynne," Cord cut in briskly. "The kid is only six years old and she's acting like a six-year-old."

"She's acting like a little monster!"

"Try looking at the situation from Maxie's point of view. She sees all these commercials on TV and when she finally has the chance to go to the restaurant to get the toy with the meal as advertised—what happens? There is no doll, she's stuck with a car instead. A car that is marketed strictly for boys. She felt ripped off and she went ballistic. What kid wouldn't?"

"Daisy didn't have a tantrum," Ashlynne reminded him.

"Oh, Daisy." Cord shrugged. "RoboKid."

"What do you mean by that?" Ashlynne's temper flared. "Daisy is—"

"—just like you. Uptight, wary, controlled. I know you overvalue those qualities but don't punish Maxie because she is spontaneous and emotional. Instead of trying to suppress her, you should reward her for being so open with her feelings. Maxie is high-spirited like Rayleen was, and that just freaks you out because you didn't approve of her."

Ashlynne paled. "I loved my sister," she said fiercely. "And they'll be selling ice cream in hell before I take any child-rearing advice from you!" She jerked open the car door and climbed inside.

"Are we still going to the zoo, Mommy?" Daisy whispered, as Cord slid behind the wheel.

Cord took it upon himself to answer. "Of course we are! And after the zoo, we'll stop to eat and I promise that you girls will get those little dollies." It was difficult to sound jovial while clenching his teeth but he gave it his best shot.

Maxie began to wail again, as soon as they left the parking lot to pull into the lane of fast-flowing traffic. "I left my car back there!" She knelt on the backseat and pointed to the restaurant, already out of sight as they rounded a bend. "I want my little red car!"

Cord drew a sharp breath. Kids! He'd never dated a woman with children before. He reminded himself that he wasn't dating Ashlynne either. This was their first and last nondate, and thankfully so. Children were okay when they visited the Glacier Lodge and campgrounds with their parents who were paying guests. Otherwise . . .

Ashlynne bristled. Cord looked exasperated and disapproving. She was feeling both at the moment herself, except since the children were hers, she also felt defensive. "Maxie's being spontaneous and emotional," she muttered under her breath, just low enough for him to hear. "Don't you think she should be rewarded for being so open with her feelings?"

"Here, Maxie, you can have my car," Daisy soothed, handing her sister the toy.

Maxie stopped crying at once.

"That was very kind of you, Daisy," Ashlynne said, shooting Cord a cold look. RoboKid, indeed!

"Thanks, Daisy," Maxie exclaimed. "Now I have a little car for my new little Barbie to ride in when I get her."

Cord braced himself for another blast of wails, this time from the carless Daisy. But there wasn't a sound. He glanced at the children through the rearview mirror. Maxie was running the car over the seat, while a quiet and composed Daisy watched.

It occurred to him that twenty years ago, an equally controlled little Ashlynne had probably observed a free-spirited little Rayleen, much the same way that Daisy was watching Maxie today. The thought gave him pause.

Their first stop, the gift shop at the zoo, was a great hit with Maxie and Daisy. They were enthralled by the stuffed toys and coloring books and hundreds of other animal-related items.

"Get whatever you want, kids," Cord said indulgently, a veritable Santa Claus in May. "Uncle Cord is treating."

Ashlynne wanted to sink with humiliation. The children were snatching items with the frenzy of game-show contestants unloosed in a store with a grab-and-keep time limit. "This has to stop," she announced, cornering the girls by a magnet display. "Put all those things back where you got them right now."

"Uncle Cord said we could have—" Maxie began, but Ashlynne cut her off with a firm, "Put it back." Her voice brooked no argument. Daisy obediently began to return the merchandise to its rightful place.

But Maxie stood firm, clutching her loot, unwilling to give it up. "Uncle Cord, make her say yes!"

Cord's lips twitched. He liked Maxie's never-say-die spirit. She rather reminded him of himself as a child. "I wish I could, Maxie. But since she's your mom, I'm afraid it's her call."

"That's right, make me the heavy," Ashlynne said. "It's so much easier and so much more fun not to set any limits. And fun and easy is what your life is all about."

"Except when I've had to deal with you," Cord shot back. "You manage to make everything so complicated and tedious that you suck the joy right out of life. And you'd like nothing better than to turn your kids into junior replicas of yourself, a humorless drudge who's allergic to fun or pleasure of any kind. Well, it's working too well with Daisy, but Maxie has enough spirit not to buckle under to you."

He turned to Maxie, who was watching intently. "I'm going to buy you these things, sweetheart," he said, picking her up. "I said I would, and I'm keeping my promise."

Cord carried her to the register and set her on the counter as the salesclerk began to ring up the purchases. Short of dragging the child out of his arms and creating a scene to rival that at lunch, there was nothing Ashlynne could do, and he was counting on that. Maxie's spunk and verve should be rewarded, at least once, Cord decided righteously. This would be his only opportunity to show the little girl that standing up and fighting for what one wanted could reap positive results. Always bowing to authority simply caused one to—

"Grab that panda for Daisy, Uncle Cord," Maxie ordered expansively, pointing to a stuffed panda on a shelf.

As Cord automatically reached for it, his eyes connected with Daisy's. She was standing beside her mother, watching him and Maxie at the register. Following her mother's orders, she'd put everything away, and was now empty-handed.

Cord turned away from them. If looks could kill, Ashlynne's would've already put him on the embalming table. And Daisy's big black eyes haunted him. If Maxie had learned that refusing to give in to authority got her what she wanted, what had Daisy learned from all this? If you listened to your mother, you wound up with nothing? That her pretty blond sister could get a man to buy her anything she wanted, but there would be no such bonanza for a quiet girl who tried to do the right thing?

Maxie was triumphant as she clutched her filled-to-the-brim plastic shopping bag decorated with exotic animals. She clung to Cord's hand, chattering and smiling. Cord glanced from Maxie to Ashlynne, who was holding silent little Daisy's hand. He'd never felt so befuddled and out of his depth in his life. He had a sickening feeling that he'd made a ghastly mistake, but couldn't think how to remedy it.

Child-rearing was hell, he decided. It was a good thing he had no child to rear because he had no idea what to do.

After the gift-shop fiasco, they actually did tour the zoo, walking around to the various sections where the animals were housed in areas as closely resembling their natural habitats as possible. Unlike the old-fashioned cages where the animals were clearly visible to visitors at all times, the environmentally correct settings permitted the animals to hide under trees or rocks or whatever else was available.

"I didn't see any tigers or lions or pandas," Maxie complained, after they'd seen the natural habitats of said animals but not the animals themselves.

"The monkeys were fun to watch, though, weren't they?" Cord reminded her.

Maxie immediately launched into an imitation of the monkeys, complete with sound effects. Daisy watched her, laughing, her dark eyes bright. "Do it again," she urged, giggling. Maxie, loving an audience, repeated her performance, adding even more antics.

Daisy held the small stuffed panda bear Maxie had given her and didn't seem to begrudge her sister the bulging bag of souvenirs. But Ashlynne certainly held a grudge against him for buying them, Cord acknowledged grimly. She wouldn't look at him, wouldn't speak to him.

"Mommy, I have to go to the bathroom," Daisy whispered to her mother.

"I don't!" Maxie sang out, before she could even be asked. "I'll stay with Uncle Cord."

Cord had the feeling she was avoiding being alone with her mother—not that he could blame her. "Maxie and I will sit here and wait for you two," he said, pointing to a bench under a tall, shady tree. Ashlynne made no response and walked toward the women's restroom with Daisy.

Moments later, Maxie changed her mind. "I want to go to the bathroom too."

"It's right down there." He pointed to the compact building about fifty yards away. A winding cement path led directly to it.

"Would you watch my stuff, Uncle Cord?" Maxie asked, carefully placing the shopping bag on his lap. He promised to guard it with his life. She started down the path, her two blond ponytails swinging back and forth as she alternately skipped, hopped, and jumped her way to the restroom. Cord watched her, smiling.

Just as he saw her enter, three elderly women speaking in heavily accented English and waving a map of the zoo approached him to ask for directions. They were confused by the map and his directions seemed to confuse them even more. By the time Ashlynne and Daisy arrived back at the bench, several other passers-by had joined in the explanations, to no avail.

"Look, just follow me. I'll take you to see the elephants," a college student finally offered. The women went off with him, murmuring in their own language.

"Where's Maxie?" Daisy asked, glancing around.

Cord looked around too. And didn't see Maxie. "She went to the restroom a few minutes after you did." He looked at Ashlynne, whose blue eyes were already widening with apprehension. "Didn't you see her in there?"

"No," Ashlynne said tersely.

"I watched her walk down," Cord reassured her. "She must still be inside, you must've missed her."

"Daisy, stay here," Ashlynne said, gulping for breath. She broke into a run as she headed back to the restroom. Maxie had to be there; she simply hadn't seen her! "Maxie!" she shouted, unable to keep the ring of panic from her voice.

The restroom was uncrowded, with only a few stalls occupied. And none of them by a six-year-old wearing pink socks and white sneakers, she could see that for herself. "Maxie!" she cried again, and then began to ask the others inside if they'd seen a little blond girl in a pink and white sundress.

Nobody had.

Cord and Daisy were standing back at the bench together, their matching eye and hair color so apparent, their expressions of concern so identical, that Ashlynne blinked with astonishment. And then the terror of Maxie's disappearance slammed into her full force, making her gasp for breath. Already, her stomach was churning so furiously, she felt as if she were going to be sick.

"She wasn't there!" Ashlynne heard herself say, the words echoing in her head.

Daisy clasped her hands over her mouth. "Maxie is gone!"

Ashlynne's knees nearly buckled. Cord saw her sway and put a firm arm around her waist to steady her. "We'll find her. She probably took a wrong turn out of the restroom. I'll walk back down there and look all around the building. You two sit on the bench and wait for her here. Don't worry, Maxie will be back in a minute or two."

Ashlynne sank down onto the bench, her mind swirling, every dreadful story she'd ever heard about children suddenly disappearing, never to be found again, leaping to her consciousness. Nearly paralyzed with fright, she stared at Daisy, who was standing beside her on the bench, straining her neck to look in every direction.

"Mommy, what if an alligator ate Maxie?" she asked, her small voice choked with terror. The alligators basking in the sun had made an impression on Daisy. It hadn't helped that a ghoulish teenager standing next to them had related a gory story about an alligator devouring a child in Florida.

"That couldn't happen, Daisy." Ashlynne pulled herself together to reassure the little girl.

She wished she felt as certain as she sounded. What if Maxie did somehow wander into the wild animals' domains? Yet she knew that Maxie was in greater danger from human predators who viewed a defenseless small child as prey. Petrified by her dark imaginings, Ashlynne reached for Daisy and held her close.

Cord arrived back at the bench, his heart sinking when he did not see Maxie there.

"We'll go to the lost-and-found. There's no need to panic," he attempted to assure them. "Kids get lost every day. Last year, an eight-year-old boy wandered away from our campgrounds and was missing overnight. The entire town was out searching for him. He turned up alive and well in the woods, scared and scratched but none the worse for the experience."

Still talking, Cord scooped Daisy up in his arms, walking so fast that Ashlynne practically had to run to keep up with him. He stopped at the first information booth he saw and pushed his way to the front of the line, his urgency and intensity causing others to defer to him. "We're looking for a little girl . . ."

CHAPTER TEN

WYATT was exhausted. Earlier that morning, he'd met with the editorial board of *The Exton Evening Post* for a grueling two-hour question-and-answer session, then headed to the Exton Mall for a traditional meet-the-candidate appearance at the area's largest shopping center. He had not enjoyed either experience.

The editors' questions were either baiting or hostile, and many of them were prefaced with "Dan thinks" or "Dan says." It wasn't hard to figure out that Dan Clarkston was the candidate who was going to be endorsed by the paper. And Wyatt's own natural reserve prevented him from glad-handing the mall shoppers in the seemingly effortless way Dan Clarkston did.

A late afternoon stop was scheduled at his campaign headquarters in the square for a brief brainstorming session with his staff. The meeting was strictly perfunctory, mainly an effort to bolster the low-level staffers' and the volunteers' commitment to his candidacy. The actual campaign was mapped out by his top aides who had private offices elsewhere, but the staff and volunteers seemed to enjoy the exchange.

After the meeting, instead of heading home as he'd been longing to all day, a sudden yet irresistible impulse sent him down the street to the coffee shop instead.

His eyes met Kendra's the moment he set foot inside the door. She stared impassively at him for a moment, then turned her attention back to the pie she was slicing.

"Well, hello there, Mr. Way," Letty called out, moving from behind the counter to greet him. "And what can I get for you?" She was giving him the honor of waiting on him personally, escorting him to a booth in the back. "The pie is fresh and homemade today," she added.

"Well—uh—what kind of pie do you have, Letty?" he asked, though he wasn't at all hungry, at least not for pie.

"Today's special is strawberry. And there is a piece of chocolate pie left too."

Two of his least favorite pies. But he could think of nothing else to order, for he hadn't come here with the intention of eating anything. His eyes lingered on Kendra. Every time he thought about their passionate embrace, how her soft curves had pressed tantalizingly against him, the sexy little whimpers she made as he kissed her, when he touched her, his body grew hard with need.

"Strawberry," he said, hoping he looked enthusiastic.

"Kendra, honey, bring Mr. Way a great big slice of strawberry pie," Letty ordered, then slipped into the booth across from him. "I'd like to hear all about your campaign," she said chattily. "You know, that Ethan Thorpe is in here every morning and he keeps talking up this Dan Clarkston fellow. But I feel a loyalty to the Way family. Let's face it, the Ways *are* Waysboro and have always done a fine job of—"

"Here's your pie, Mr. Way." Kendra joined them, pie in hand.

She was showing a lot of skin in those shorts and vest, her bare arms and legs supple and smooth. Wyatt remembered how tightly she'd wrapped her limbs around him and suppressed a shudder of desire.

"Did you want whipped cream with it?" Kendra asked, setting the plate in front of him. Her arm grazed his as she leaned over, and her position gave him a clear view inside her vest, of the firm white breast filling the pale blue cup of her brassiere.

Wyatt quickly glanced away, at the thickly glutinous pie. "No, thanks." He could barely swallow.

"No? You'd be amazed at what I can do with a can of whipped cream." Kendra arched her dark brows, her tone unmistakably provocative. "Let your imagination run wild."

Wyatt's face colored. Letty laughed heartily. Kendra gazed at Wyatt, that come-hither smile of hers sending his blood pressure up too many notches.

"Oh, you are such a tease, Kendra!" the older woman admonished, still chuckling. "You made poor Mr. Way turn as red as this pie. Don't pay her any mind, Mr. Way, Kendra is always joking with the customers. My goodness, look who's here!" Without pausing to breathe, Letty rose to her feet. "Excuse me, there's my nephew and his wife coming through the door." Letty quickly departed to greet the young couple entering the coffee shop.

"You're still blushing, Wyatt," Kendra said, her voice low and husky, for his ears only. "What sorts of things are you imagining with that whipped cream?"

"Kendra, for heaven's sakes," Wyatt said hoarsely.

"Well, as they say on TV, *bon appetit*." Kendra turned to walk away.

"I've been invited to speak at the Waysboro High graduation," Wyatt called after her. He was unable to simply let her leave. "Apparently, Clarkston is too. We're each limited to five minutes of nonpartisan good wishes and advice to the graduates."

Kendra sauntered back to him. "That's cool. What are you going to talk about?"

"If I tell you, will you go running to the Clarkston campaign with the information?"

"Are you accusing me of being a spy or something?" But she was blushing and couldn't seem to stop.

"I know you were the one who told Clarkston that I was coming to the high school with the candy, Kendra," he said quietly. "The information enabled Ethan Thorpe to arrange for the DJ to show up and give away free CDs and tapes to—"

"Crashman ended up giving away five thousand dollars worth of stuff!" Kendra exclaimed, grinning. "And your sister Holly told him to bill Ethan Thorpe for all of it, including what the twins stole. Ashlynne said he turned purple when he found out how much he had to pay! You'd better tell your sister to hire a bodyguard 'cause Mr. Thorpe is out for blood. Hers!"

Wyatt smiled slightly. "Holly has always been able to take care of herself." His hand snaked out and caught her wrist, drawing her closer to the booth. "Kendra, I want to apologize to you."

"Apologize?" She stared at him, clearly taken aback. "Why?"

"I should have insisted that you be among the students chosen to meet with me at the high school. It was thoughtless of me not to have included you."

"Including me would have been a stupid move," she said coolly. "The Monroes are considered scum at that school. You wouldn't want to be accused of consorting with white trash, now would you?"

"You're not white trash, Kendra, and I'm sorry if I made you feel that way."

She felt flustered and out of her depth. Nobody had ever apologized to her for snubbing her. Being a Monroe, she was supposed to expect and accept it. She stared at his fingers locked around her wrist, revealing a firm male strength. His hand was tanned and strong around her delicate wristbone. She liked the dominant masculine power it implied.

"Am I forgiven?" His thumb moved slowly over the inside of her wrist in a secret caress.

The intensity burning in his eyes excited her. "Well, okay." She strove to sound nonchalant.

He held on to her, loath to let her go. "Since you're graduating very soon, have you given any thought to what you want to do in the future?"

"What are you all of a sudden, the guidance counselor?" Her blue eyes laughed at him.

"If you're interested, I could arrange a paid position for you on my campaign staff," Wyatt said, reluctantly dropping her hand. "And if—uh, *when*—I win the election, that might be parlayed into an office staff job."

"No, thanks," she said blithely. "I don't want to sit over there at your campaign headquarters and stuff envelopes and make phone calls. Anyway, I like working here at the coffee shop. The tips aren't bad and—"

"You could keep working here and work for me parttime." Wyatt cleared his throat, knowing he was plunging into risky, uncharted waters. Never in his thirty careful, plodding years had he considered breaking out until he'd met this daring, vibrant young beauty.

Kendra rested one hand on her hip and tilted her head, studying him.

"You wouldn't have to work at campaign headquarters," Wyatt continued. "You would be—with me as a sort of—uh—personal assistant. You're a talented young woman with a lot of ideas and a direct voice to the new voters. You could make some suggestions on what I should say at the graduation, for example, and—"

"I wouldn't be able to tell my sister that I was working for you," Kendra cut in. "Ethan Thorpe is her boss. He would freak if he knew I was with Dan Clarkston's rival."

"We could keep our arrangement confidential, if you'd prefer," Wyatt agreed, his neck reddening. The "arrangement" was beginning to take on wicked-sounding overtones, though he assured himself his offer was strictly aboveboard. He was giving a bright but rather directionless young woman a chance to establish a career for herself in the political arena. The flush spread to his face and he found himself loosening his collar and his tie.

Kendra wondered how cool she should play it. "I'll think it over," she said, tossing her long, lustrous hair.

"Perhaps we should discuss this some more," Wyatt suggested casually. "Over dinner tonight?"

Kendra paused, to give the illusion of considering it. "Okay." She didn't allow herself to jump up and down and squeal triumphantly. Such behavior was catastrophically uncool.

"Shall I pick you up at your apartment around seven?"

"Hey, little lady, do you plan to give me my check while it's still the twentieth century or wait until the next millennium?" a disgruntled customer called from across the shop. "I'm eighty-two years old and I don't want to spend what little time I have left waiting for you to give me my damn check!"

"Uh-oh, I'd better go before old Mr. Carter starts pitching the salt and pepper shakers at me. He does that when he doesn't get enough attention. And seven tonight is fine."

Kendra grinned at Wyatt, then headed over to the table of the displeased diner.

At first, the personnel at the zoo were encouraging, even making jokes about lost children, which were a daily occurrence. Cord tried to maintain the matter-of-fact attitude of the personnel. Of course Maxie would be found, it was just a matter of time. No child lost in the zoo had ever *not* been recovered.

Ashlynne didn't say a word. She sat numbly inside the lost-and-found office, her blue eyes huge with fright, her body rigid with tension. From the moment they had realized Maxie was gone, Ashlynne suspected the worst. She *expected* the worst, because in her experience, the worst was what usually occurred. Her father's drunken decline and death; her mother, killed by a hit-and-run driver while crossing the street; Rayleen, drowned in a boating accident. And now little Maxie, missing.

Ashlynne sat staring into space, thinking the unthinkable. Maxie was gone! Her eyes were burning but there were no tears, a lump of ground glass seemed to have lodged in her throat. She couldn't swallow, couldn't talk. She felt Daisy shift in the chair beside her, and automatically put her arm around the little girl. Daisy had been sitting quiet and still for over an hour. She gripped her new panda bear tightly. The bag of souvenirs from the zoo gift shop was on the floor near their feet. Neither Ashlynne nor Daisy touched it.

Cord paced back and forth. He noticed a lessening of jocularity in the atmosphere as one hour elapsed into two. Voices were becoming hushed, and an unsettling sense of urgency gripped the increasingly grim-faced personnel. All the usual haunts of lost children had been searched and Maxie hadn't turned up in any of them.

He watched Ashlynne stroke Daisy's dark silky hair as the child leaned against her mother, and finally had to look away from the pair. They looked so stricken, their pain and fear terrible to behold.

Cord felt sick. *If only he had taken Maxie by the hand and walked her to that damn restroom, she would be with them right now*. If only. But he hadn't, and it was his fault the little girl was missing.

Her lively friendliness, which had delighted him, became a source of terror to him. Maxie had accepted him so easily, talking to him, smiling at him, slipping her little hand in his. It was all too easy to picture Maxie smiling and chattering as she took a stranger's hand to go off on some proposed adventure . . .

Well into the third hour of Maxie's disappearance, a somber official announced that the zoo had been thoroughly searched, and it was time to call in the city police.

Ashlynne closed her eyes in despair. In her experience, the police delivered nothing but bad news. Her hope dimmed and flickered so weakly, it was more a source of sorrow than strength.

"Mommy, I'm thirsty," Daisy whispered, rubbing her eyes. "Can I get a drink from the fountain?"

Ashlynne nodded. She saw the fear in the five-year-old's expressive dark eyes and wanted to cry herself. She didn't, though. She didn't dare cry, not when Daisy was depending on her to be strong.

"I'll take her over to the fountain," offered Cord.

"No, I want my mommy to take me," Daisy piped up, clutching Ashlynne's hand. "She won't let me get lost."

Cord felt the implied accusation in that little voice impact like a body blow.

"Don't blame yourself," Ashlynne murmured to him raspily. Her throat was so dry she could hardly speak.

Cord ran his hand through his hair. "Ashlynne, I am so sorry." He took her hand in his. It was so cold, almost icy, despite the stuffy heat of the office. "I should have gone with Maxie—"

"It's not your fault." She could barely handle her own pain; having to deal with his was unbearable. It was easier to absolve him and withdraw further into herself. "Bad things happen, they just happen. No matter how hard you work to control things and try to make things different or better . . ." Ashlynne took a deep breath and removed her hand from his. Talking drained her of what precious little energy she had left.

The police arrived, and a search of the area surrounding the zoo was begun. The neighborhood was an affluent one, comprised of big old houses and wooded lawns separating them. Several blocks to the north were convention-sized hotels, with hundreds of rooms. Even more worrisome was the nearby Metro station. If someone had taken Maxie there, within minutes the subway train could have whisked them far from the area.

The zoo officials, though sympathetic, were clearly relieved when the police suggested that Ashlynne, Cord, and Daisy proceed to the precinct house for further questioning. Ashlynne and Daisy rode in a patrol car, while Cord drove his own car to the station.

Once they arrived they were surrounded. Local TV news crews were on hand at the station, bombarding them with questions. Ashlynne reluctantly gave them Maxie's school picture, taken last winter. Handing over the photo was like losing another link to her little girl, and she made them promise to return it. Unless Maxie was found in the interim, the stations intended to broadcast the story and picture on the six o'clock news, along with videotape of the searchers spanning the neighborhood and a plea to "anyone who has seen little Maxie" to please call the precinct house or the television station.

"I'll have to call Kendra," Ashlynne said, a whole new wave of dread crashing over her. Having to tell her sister made the nightmare even more real, tearing into the numbness that enshrouded her. "She can't hear about this on TV."

Cord nodded his head. "Is there anyone else you want to call? I want you to use my long-distance calling card to make as many calls as you need." He handed her the card. "Please feel free to call anyone, anywhere."

She accepted the card and walked to the pay phone, Daisy trotting along at her side. The little girl gripped her panda with one hand and a fistful of her mother's shirt with the other, holding on to both as if she would never let go.

Kendra was crying when the doorbell rang. Wyatt Way stood in the hallway, his face drawn and sober. "Kendra, my brother Cord called me from a DC police station." He stepped inside and closed the door behind him. "He told me about your niece."

"It can't be happening," she cried. "Not Maxie! Oh God, Maxie is missing!"

Wyatt took her in his arms. "They'll find her," he soothed. "She's a lost child, not a missing child. There is a difference, Kendra. They'll find her."

"Just like they found my mom, lying on the street. Just like they found Rayleen in the river." Kendra tried to pull away from him, fury momentarily replacing the savage grief. "They'll find her in time for us to bury her."

Wyatt held on to her, not letting her go, feeling her slender body shake with the violence of her sobs. "That isn't going to happen, Kendra," he soothed.

"Ashlynne told me to stay here so if Maxie calls I'll be here to answer the phone. Maxie knows her phone number and address, she's known them since she was four." Kendra drew back a little, her blue eyes fever-bright. "Oh Wyatt, what if she doesn't call? What if we never see her again?"

"My poor little girl." Wyatt scooped her up in his arms and carried her to the sofa. He sat down with her on his lap, cradling her against him as she cried and cried, her body wracked with great convulsive sobs.

"I know how hard this is for you, but everything is going to be all right," he whispered softly, holding her, stroking her, his lips nuzzling her hair. "Just hang on and don't give up hope." His arms tightened protectively. "Right now I want you to tell me all about Maxie. And I'd like to see some pictures of her too."

"We have lots of pictures." Kendra leaned against him, limp from her spent emotions. "Ashlynne puts them all in photo albums. In fact, she just put our Easter pictures in a couple weeks ago."

"I'd like to see them," Wyatt said quietly. "I'd like to see all your family pictures. Will you show them to me, Kendra?"

Kendra nodded, her blue eyes brimming, her mouth tremulous. She lay in his arms for a full five minutes before summoning the energy to fetch the photo albums. And when she returned, she sat back down on his lap, and he held her there, while they pored over the Monroe family pictures.

A kind of well-organized chaos prevailed throughout the hectic precinct house. Ashlynne, Cord, and Daisy stayed in a small waiting room, with police officers and various ancillary personnel coming and going with questions and updates. The updates were all the same—the search was continuing but Maxie had not yet been sighted by anyone. The TV news broadcast elicited some calls, none of which had panned into a lead. The reporters pressed for more interviews, but after a few minutes Ashlynne retreated, unwilling to talk to the eager press, whose questions were clearly slanted toward a doomed and hopeless outcome.

The police took over, making the facts and the photo available to the media, but not Maxie's family. Sandwiches were sent in at dinnertime, but Ashlynne didn't eat a bite. She tried to drink some coffee but her throat seemed to close after just one sip.

"Ashlynne, you have to eat something." Cord got down on his haunches in front of her chair and took both her hands in his. "You don't want to pass out again, like you did at the hospital blood drive."

Ashlynne shrugged. Being unconscious, if only for a few minutes, struck her as a worthy alternative to this hellish waking nightmare she was trapped in. She glanced over at Daisy, who was napping on two chairs that had been pushed together. She was grateful the little girl had been able to escape into sleep.

"We'll order in anything you want," Cord coaxed. "Just tell me what—"

"Ashlynne!" Ethan Thorpe's commanding tones filled the room. He strode toward them, wearing a bright green golf shirt and green and yellow plaid slacks that somehow did not distract from his air of authority.

Ashlynne blinked. She'd never seen her boss wearing anything but a dark suit. His leisure wear was shockingly colorful and very unlike him.

"My answering service paged me at the club with the news. I was on the golf course," he added unnecessarily.

So Ashlynne had called Thorpe? Cord grimaced. And with his calling card. As if the afternoon hadn't been bad enough. Scowling, Cord watched Thorpe take one of Ashlynne's hands in both of his.

"I want you to know that I'll do everything in my power to find little Maxie, Ashlynne," Ethan said urgently. "I've put up a ten-thousand-dollar reward—no questions asked—for any information involving her whereabouts. I've also paid for television time on all four local stations for Dan to announce the reward and urge someone to come forward with news of the child." He glanced at his watch. "We have two minutes in prime time, from eight twenty-eight to eight-thirty. We ought to watch. Is there a television set around here?"

"I don't think so," said Ashlynne. Not that she was up to watching Dan Clarkston's performance, even if there was a set. She had no doubt that the reward announcement was a showcase for Dan to be seen by voters in the district, as all four stations were carried by cable to homes in Waysboro and Exton.

"Reward money can really open up a case," a young rookie cop told them. "People who wouldn't bother to get involved otherwise become remarkably cooperative for the right price."

"I hope so," Ethan said, giving Ashlynne's hand a squeeze. "Ashlynne knows how fond I am of those little ones of hers."

Actually, Ashlynne didn't but she appreciated his gesture, whatever his motives. Ethan was an incorrigible manipulator, willing to work any angle, and any good deed he performed invariably benefited himself handsomely. But he was the most powerful man she knew, and she had called him in a desperate attempt to use his power to find Maxie.

Cord's dark eyes were burning, his face a taut mask of fury as he stared from Ashlynne to Ethan.

"Thorpe, can I have a word with you?" Cord growled.

Ethan's eyes flicked over him in contemptuous dismissal.

"I suppose I can spare a minute." He looked at his watch as he walked toward Cord. "Beginning now."

Ashlynne followed him, sensing disaster.

"What do you have to say for yourself, Way?" Ethan asked coldly.

"I was going to ask you the same thing," Cord countered, his tone as hotly intense as Thorpe's was coolly detached. "Using Maxie to promote that showboat candidate of yours is low, even for you, Thorpe."

"I want everybody to know that we intend to pull out all stops to find that little girl," Ethan replied. "Who better to deliver that message than Dan, a skilled and moving orator? Why should you mind? In fact, you should be thankful that others are willing to take over the mess you've made. But of course, you Ways expect that, don't you? You believe you're entitled to waltz into other people's lives, screw them up, and then take off without facing either consequences or responsibilities."

"What the hell is that supposed to mean, Thorpe?" Cord demanded.

"Ethan, please." Ashlynne tugged on the sleeve of his brilliant green golf shirt. "Don't—"

"I'm sorry, Ashlynne, but it has to be said. I talked to the police before I came in here to see you, I know that Way is the one who lost Maxie. He let her wander off by herself while he was otherwise occupied."

Cord felt the color drain from his face. He couldn't dispute Thorpe, though he longed to wipe the self-righteous smirk from the other man's face.

"It wasn't like that," Ashlynne whispered. "I don't blame Cord."

"Well, I do." Ethan's gray eyes flashed with icy, barely controlled rage. "I blame him for deciding to play at parenthood for a day—to the detriment of a defenseless, innocent child. Typical Way family behavior, of course. This cretin lost your child with the same careless ease that his slut of a sister had my child scraped out of her."

"What?" Cord gaped at him incredulously. His eyes briefly met Ashlynne's own wide shocked ones. "You're a damn liar, Thorpe. I—I ought to punch your lights out."

He clenched his hands into fists and started toward Thorpe. "And I'm going to."

Ashlynne quickly stepped between the two men. "This is not the Waterside Bar! If you start brawling in here, the police will arrest you both."

"You heard what he said about Holly," Cord said through gritted teeth. "I will not stand quietly by and listen to him—"

"—tell the truth?" Ethan cut in. "Because it is the truth. Ask your precious sister." He made an exclamation of disgust. "You Ways always have to have it your way. Perhaps you believe your name gives you that right?" His cold smile was without mirth. "Holly didn't want to be inconvenienced by my baby and the hell with what I might want, which was to raise my child. Compare her cold-blooded selfishness to a woman like Ashlynne who—"

"Ethan, stop!" cried Ashlynne. This was dangerous territory. Ethan knew too much and was in the mood to use his knowledge as a weapon to verbally bludgeon Cord. Unfortunately, she and Daisy would be the ultimate casualties. "Please don't say any more!"

Ethan gazed into her fearful blue eyes, then cast a loathing glance at Cord. "All right, I'm leaving now. I want to catch Dan's broadcast. Promise that you'll keep me informed, Ashlynne." She nodded. "And if you need anything at all, just ask."

He swept out of the room. Cord and Ashlynne silently watched his departure.

"I don't know what to say," Cord murmured at last. "Thorpe has a talent for leaving me speechless."

"At least he provided a momentary respite," Ashlynne said wearily. She had been so petrified that Ethan would reveal Daisy's parentage to Cord, she'd been spared a few moments of agonizing over Maxie. But the pain and the terror returned now in full force.

"What he said about Holly—" Cord began. Her white strained face stopped him. "Never mind, it doesn't matter now. All that matters is finding Maxie."

"Do you think we ever will?" She covered her face with her hands, her stoic front faltering.

Cord put his arms around her. "We'll find her," he promised, willing her to believe it. He willed himself to believe it too.

"You can't know that," Ashlynne whispered, her face buried in the still crisp cotton of his shirt. It was strange how holding on to someone bigger and stronger than yourself seemed to give you a kind of strength-by-proxy.

Cord rubbed his cheek against the pale silkiness of her hair. Her softness and her warmth made it easy for him to share his deepest secret thoughts. "You know, I'm not very spiritual but today I found myself asking my dad for help. I know how stupid that must sound. I mean, the man has been dead for years and I've certainly never tried to reach him in the great beyond before. I'm not even sure—"

"It doesn't sound stupid. Sometimes I pray to my mother—and sometimes I even ask Rayleen for help," Ashlynne confessed. "Not that Rayleen helped much when she was with us, but I thought maybe as a spirit she would feel more inclined to pitch in."

She closed her eyes, unconsciously leaning into him, allowing the warm strength of his body to support her. "But it's hard to have a relationship with someone who's dead. You never get any feedback."

"I suppose if you did, you'd be dealing with an entirely different problem," Cord said wryly. "Have . . . you asked your mother and Rayleen to help find Maxie?"

"I'm the one who screwed up." Ashlynne's voice quavered. "I can't expect them to bail me out." Pain slashed through her and she shuddered. "People have to help themselves, not depend on anyone else, from this world or the next."

"You didn't screw up," Cord said firmly. His big hands rubbed slowly over her back, pressing her even closer. He could feel every rib; her small breasts were crushed against his chest. "You don't expect anyone in this world or the next to ever help you, do you, Ashlynne?"

"No," she said softly. "I don't expect it." She drew back a little and met his intense dark eyes. "But I'll accept help from whoever offers, whether it's Dayland Way Junior or Rayleen or Ethan Thorpe and Dan Clarkston."

"Quite a collection of spirits and spooks there."

Ashlynne's lips curved into her first smile since Maxie's disappearance. It was fleeting and quickly turned sad, but it lifted Cord's spirits to soaring heights. His body surged with an emotion he couldn't identify but could not deny.

"We're going to find Maxie," he said, staring deeply into Ashlynne's tired blue eyes. This time he was sure of it.

CHAPTER ELEVEN

A HALF-hour after Dan Clarkston's dramatic plea for the public to "get involved and help find this precious little girl," Kendra was still outraged.

"That creep!" she stormed, jumping up to pace back and forth like a wild tigress. "That jerk! That smug, conceited prick! He practically came right out and said my sister wasn't a good mother!"

"That's not what he said, Kendra," Wyatt soothed. He was in the odd position of having to defend his rival—or at least try to explain him to an overwrought Kendra.

Kendra whirled to face him. "We all heard him blathering on about the importance of intact families and how fathers are a necessity, not a luxury. Like Maxie is missing because my sister doesn't have a husband!"

"He wasn't condemning your sister, he was accusing my brother. His point was that since Cord isn't Maxie's father, he didn't really care if she got lost or not. His own peculiar version of family values, I guess—that only married couples are capable of caring about their children's welfare. To accuse Cord of negligence was so unfair." Wyatt shook his head sadly.

"The way that cheesehead Clarkston kept bragging how he and his wife keep such a careful eye on their little Scotty!" Kendra fumed. "How the two of them would never let him get lost! As if my sister lost Maxie on purpose!"

"He wasn't intentionally denigrating Ashlynne, he was grabbing publicity for his campaign using the TV time as his forum. And not too subtly bashing Cord because he is my brother. He must have said the name Way ten times in two minutes—as if it were synonymous with 'irresponsible'."

"I didn't notice." Kendra flexed her fingers, as if practicing for a strangulation. "All I heard was that Maxie was missing because—"

"Lost," Wyatt corrected. "Temporarily lost. Come here." He reached out and caught Kendra's hand, pulling her back down on the sofa beside him. His hand curved around her nape and he began to massage the taut muscles with his fingers. "Kendra, Dan Clarkston did not cast any aspersions on your sister's mothering. He made no references at all to the Monroes. It was my brother that he blamed, because his last name is Way, and I am the opposing candidate."

"He did so cast . . . as-aspersions. And I'm going to get him for that. I'm going to get him good."

"To forget a wrong is the best revenge," Wyatt quoted quietly. "The Book of Ecclesiasticus."

"Oh well, of course the Bible would say something like that." Kendra scowled. "But Dan Clarkston is a politician. The rules in the Bible don't apply to him—except that one about an eye for an eye."

"And it's easier to be angry with Dan Clarkston than scared about Maxie." Wyatt's warm brown eyes were understanding. He drew her head down on his shoulder, and Kendra lay quietly against him, tears glistening in her eyes.

Cord, Ashlynne, and Daisy returned a short while later. Kendra sprang up and rushed to greet them at the door, Wyatt at her heels. Her gaze flicked quickly over Ashlynne, who was carrying a sleeping Daisy. Cord stood behind them holding a toy panda bear and a bulging shopping bag of zoo souvenirs.

Ashlynne and Kendra looked at each other, bereft.

"The police said to go home, there was nothing more we could do at the station tonight. They promised to call the second they hear anything," whispered Ashlynne. "Poor Daisy is exhausted."

"Ashlynne, have you met Cord's brother Wyatt?" Kendra asked tiredly. "He's been keeping me company."

Ashlynne and Wyatt nodded their recognition, but

Ashlynne was too weary to exchange greetings and Wyatt respected her silence.

"I'm going to put Daisy to bed now," Ashlynne said dispiritedly.

The two sisters walked back to the children's bedroom.

"Still nothing?" Wyatt asked Cord.

"Not a word. Not a clue. It's like she dropped off the face of the earth."

"Maybe the reward money will spur someone into coming forward."

"I should have been the one to offer that reward, Wyatt. But I never even thought of it, not until Thorpe blew in to announce that he was putting up ten thousand dollars. I couldn't think of anything but . . ." His voice trailed off in a groan of pain. "Wyatt, I'd give twenty years of my life to find that child."

"I know." Wyatt embraced his older brother.

Cord stiffened at first, then put his arms around Wyatt and held on tight.

Back in the bedroom, Ashlynne laid Daisy on her twin bed, and Kendra removed her small white sneakers. They didn't bother to undress her; both dreaded waking her.

"What is Daisy going to do without Maxie?" Kendra whispered tearfully as the two sisters stared down at the small sleeping body. "What are we going to do?"

"We can't think that way, we have to think positively, Kendra." Ashlynne put her arm around her younger sister. "Let's go into the kitchen and have some tea." She forced herself not to cast another glance at Maxie's empty bed. She didn't dare fall apart, not with Kendra so upset, not when Daisy needed her to be strong.

"I need something a lot stronger than tea," Kendra said bleakly. "I made some coffee earlier that makes you feel like you've been hit with a lightning bolt after a couple of gulps. I could use some of that now."

Cord and Wyatt were already seated at the kitchen table, drinking that bracing brew when the sisters joined them. Shortly after Ashlynne and Kendra poured cups for themselves, the telephone began to ring. For a moment, no one spoke or moved or even dared to breathe.

Then Ashlynne snatched the receiver from its cradle.

"Hi, Mommy," said Maxie.

For a split second, Ashlynne thought she was dreaming. "Maxie!"

Kendra squealed and flew to her sister's side. "Let me listen! I want to hear her voice."

"Maxie, where are you?" cried Ashlynne. Her knees felt so rubbery that she had to hold on to Kendra so she wouldn't collapse to the floor.

"I don't know," Maxie replied cheerfully.

"Are you all right, Maxie?" Kendra half shouted into the phone.

"Uh-huh," the small voice assured her. "I want to come home now."

"Maxie, is there anybody with you who can tell me where you are?" Ashlynne tried to keep her voice steady though tears were streaming from her eyes.

"Mommy wants to talk to you," they heard Maxie say to someone who was with her.

Ashlynne braced herself. She couldn't imagine who she was about to speak with or what they might say, but she steeled herself to stay strong and alert.

"This is Norma Brunner at the Safe Haven Home in Chilton, Virginia." The woman sounded as nervous as Ashlynne felt. "We're a shelter for abused women who are escaping domestic violence. They come here with their children and stay for an indefinite period, until they've resolved their crisis situation. We provide the necessary support, be it legal, financial, emotional." She paused, and then blurted out, "And—and we seem to have acquired your daughter Maxie. We found her asleep in the playroom during a routine check when the night staff came on duty. We recognized her at once from the TV news."

Ashlynne was floored. "Maxie is in an abused-women and children's center in Virginia?" she repeated incredulously, and watched Kendra and the Way brothers gape in mutual astonishment. "But how did she get there? We were at the zoo—"

"And so were we," Norma Brunner said grimly. "Some volunteers here at Safe Haven chartered a bus and took a group of the children on an outing to the zoo this afternoon. From what Maxie tells us, she met one of the little girls in the women's restroom. They struck up an instant friendship and the child invited Maxie over to play. The bus was leaving at that time to return to the shelter and Maxie came aboard with the group. Our weekend staff is minimal with volunteers picking up the slack and we're not an institution where there are regular head counts. Nobody noticed this extra little girl. Maxie spent the day here, playing with the other children. She had snacks and dinner with them and watched evening cartoons on our VCR in the playroom."

"It sounds like she had a wonderful time," Ashlynne breathed. The relief surging through her was as overwhelming as her earlier terror. Maxie was safe!

"Bedtimes are pretty chaotic around here, especially on weekends," Norma Brunner continued apologetically. "By the time all the children were finally in bed, it was nearly ten o'clock. Since she didn't have a room or a bed, Maxie curled up on the couch to sleep. We found her there after the shift change."

"Oh, I'm so thankful and so relieved to know that Maxie is safe!" A sob escaped from Ashlynne's throat. "Could you give me directions to Safe Haven so I can bring her home now?"

Norma Brunner provided directions and a thousand apologies for having unknowingly harbored Maxie.

"Chilton is about a half-hour drive from Waysboro," said Cord. "Kendra and Wyatt can stay here with Daisy while we go get Maxie. Come on, Ashlynne." He grabbed her hand.

Ashlynne followed him to the door, but paused to glance at Kendra and Wyatt. After she'd hung up the phone, she and Kendra had hugged for joy. Next Kendra had hugged Cord. And then Wyatt. She was still hugging Wyatt.

Cord gave Ashlynne's hand a tug, then half dragged her out the door, pulling her behind him. He ran down the flights of stairs, elation pumping through his veins like a drug. The exhaustion and soul-wearying worry had dissipated the moment he'd heard the marvelous news.

At the bottom of the staircase, he grabbed Ashlynne and

swung her high in a wide arc. "We're bringing Maxie home!" He set her back on her feet, but kept his hands around her waist. "God, Ashlynne, it's enough to make you believe in answered prayers."

"Your father and Rayleen teamed up and worked together on the other side to keep Maxie safe?" Ashlynne grinned.

"What a concept." Cord was smiling too, his dark eyes aglow. He drew her to him and hugged her hard for a moment, then took her hand and led her to the car.

Ashlynne stared up at the lights in her living room as they pulled away from the apartment building. "There's just one thing that has me worried."

"Daisy," guessed Cord. "That poor little kid was scared to death today! She's going to be in worse shape than Maxie, who doesn't even seem to know she was lost."

"Daisy will be fine as soon as she sees Maxie," Ashlynne said confidently. "Although she'll probably keep a strict eye on her for a while. Right now I'm concerned about leaving Kendra and your brother alone for the next hour or so, especially in the pumped-up state Kendra's in."

Cord reached over and patted her hand. "You know something? You get worried when you don't have anything to worry about." His tone was affectionately indulgent. "I give you full permission to just relax and enjoy this moment, Ashlynne. Maxie is safe and we're going to get her."

His smile broadened. "I admit that Kendra has a kind of kittenish, Lolita-type appeal, but Wyatt is the not the type to respond to her. He's always been guided by his head, not by—uh—any other organ."

"She was all over him like a rash, Cord. And he didn't look like he minded at all."

"They were both excited and happy that Maxie was found. Give them a break, Ashlynne. Give yourself a break. No more worrying about anything or anyone—at least until tomorrow morning." His fingers curled around hers. "Think you can do that?"

Ashlynne leaned back against the seat, a warm lethargy sweeping through her. She sighed deeply. "I think I'd like to try."

*   *   *

"I'll call the police and report that Maxie has been found," Wyatt announced.

Kendra went back to check on Daisy, who was still sleeping soundly, then returned to stand behind Wyatt's chair in the kitchen, listening to him talk to the police.

She leaned over the back of his chair and wrapped her arms around him, her hands fiddling with the knot of his tie. As she loosened it, she kissed the strong tanned column of his neck.

Her breath was warm and sweet against his skin, the touch of her lips electrifying. Gulping for air, Wyatt half rose from the chair, then sank back down on it.

"Yes, Officer. The Safe Haven Home in Chilton, Virginia."

Kendra was nibbling on his ear. She'd unfastened the top buttons of his shirt and slipped her nimble fingers between the material to stroke the wiry mat of hair covering his chest. The spicy, feminine scent of her perfume filled his nostrils. His head lolled back and encountered the soft pillowing comfort of her breasts.

Wyatt bolted upright. "Yes, Officer," he said hoarsely. "Maxie's mother is on her way to Chilton right now."

Kendra's hands continued their sensual wandering. His shirt was completely unbuttoned, his tie undone and hanging loosely around his neck. She kissed a trail along the curve of his neck, using her lips and her teeth and her tongue in erotic tandem.

"The—the media? Yes, Officer, we would appreciate it if you would notify them that the child is safe."

He was sitting ramrod straight but Kendra had draped herself over both him and the back of the chair. Her long dark hair tickled his bare chest as her thumb dipped beneath the waistband of his trousers to slowly circle his navel. Her other hand toyed with the buckle of his belt. And all the while, her mouth continued its lazy, sultry play.

"Yes, Officer. You can reach us at this number." Wyatt stifled a groan of pleasure. "We'll be here . . ." He managed to replace the receiver in its cradle. "Kendra, for God's sake!"

His hands felt heavy as he lifted them, trying not very successfully to disengage her arms from around him. "Kendra, I know what's happening here . . ."

She smiled, catching his earlobe between her teeth. "I figured you would."

"But I don't think you do," he said desperately. His hands were caressing the smooth length of her arms while her hands continued their sensual exploration. "You see, in a crisis situation, extra adrenaline is released into the bloodstream."

"I think I remember that from science class." Kendra laughed softly against his ear. "But science class was never like this." Moving with the slow, languid grace of a cat, she slipped from behind him onto his lap.

"And though tonight's crisis has been resolved, our adrenaline levels are still extraordinarily high," Wyatt continued. He rested his hands on her hips, the better to lift her to her feet and bring this interlude to an end. "There have been studies linking danger to sexual arousal." Somehow his hands had lost sight of their duty. Instead of ejecting her from his lap, he was caressing the curve of her hip. "That's why you have these . . . feelings."

Kendra's lips nuzzled his neck and the curve of his jaw. She was intensely aware of the hard strength of his thighs under her bottom, of the pulsing length of his erection. "I have these feelings 'cause you're hot, Wyatt," she whispered against his lips. "You are, you know. You are one hot guy."

Wyatt's hand slid along her thigh, his palm gliding over the denim of her shorts to the smooth, silky feel of her bare skin. "Hot," he repeated, dazedly. His hand moved slowly, inexorably over her thigh. "I know you make me burn."

"Do I?" she asked throatily. Her hands gripped his shoulders and she wriggled sensuously against him.

"You know you do."

"I'm glad you want me." Suddenly hot and breathless with unexpected tumultuous need, she opened her mouth softly under his.

Wyatt forgot the scientific studies, he forgot everything but the strange, wild desire that only Kendra evoked in him. His tongue tangled with hers and thrust deeply into her mouth.

They kissed hungrily, their mouths mating, clinging together as their bodies arched and twisted, pressing closer and closer. Wyatt deftly opened the few buttons of her vest and slipped his hand inside to cup the soft fullness of her breast. Kendra gasped and clutched him tighter. Her breast felt swollen and constricted by the confining material of her bra, and she pressed urgently against his hand, wanting to be freed from it, wanting to feel the rough warmth of his fingers on her skin. She sighed with sensual relief when he unfastened the front clasp of her bra, then palmed her breast, sliding his thumb over the delicate, sensitive peak.

"Yes," she murmured huskily. "Oh yes, please, Wyatt." She clenched her fingers in the springy thickness of his hair and kissed his neck. She loved the feel of him under her hands, loved the heady excitement sweeping through her. Loved the passion that blazed between them, every time they touched.

He shifted her on his lap, lifting her to him as he lowered his mouth to her breast.

"You are so beautiful," he breathed as his lips touched the tip of her nipple.

She felt the warm, wet tracing of his tongue, then an excruciatingly sensual suction as his mouth took her breast. Kendra whimpered as she cradled his head against her, wanting this heavenly pleasure to go on and on. The insistent hunger of his mouth was making her body throb in the most intimate, secret places. A tight, twisting tension gripped her and she moaned. How could this fullness and this deep ache feel both fantastic and unbearable at the same time?

And then shockingly, abruptly, Wyatt lifted his mouth and sat up straight. He drew her vest together, covering her, then gripped the arms of the chair, focusing his eyes on some fixed point in the distance. His breathing was shallow and erratic, and he tried to take some calming deep breaths.

Kendra, aroused and confused, held on to him, snuggling closer, deeper into him.

"Kendra, no." Wyatt groaned. He didn't have the will-power to push her off his lap, but he did restrain himself from holding her. He kept his hands grimly locked around the narrow arms of the chair. "Sweetheart, I can't take advantage of you at a time like this. It isn't right, it isn't fair."

Kendra stared into his tortured brown eyes. Apparently, he was entirely serious. She cast a glance at her arms, which were locked around his neck, her legs sprawled over him, his clothing askew. "You think that *you're* taking advantage of *me*?"

Wyatt sighed and permitted himself to release the chair to lightly fasten his arms around her. "Oh Lord, Kendra, what am I going to do with you?"

She arched her brows. "How about whatever you want? Because I want it too."

He laughed, a little desperately. "You're so sexy, Kendra. So alluring." He sighed heavily. "And so young. Too young for me. It's wrong."

"You believe you shouldn't be with me just because of what other people might think?" Kendra scowled. "Well, you have to make up your own mind."

Sitting up straight on his lap, she fastened the clasp of her bra and buttoned up her vest. Wyatt watched her, his eyes riveted as she completed the intimate acts with unselfconscious ease. There was an excruciating heat pooled in his groin and no relief in sight. And he had no one to blame but himself.

Kendra gazed at him as she combed her fingers through her hair, trying to restore some semblance of style to it. She succeeded in tousling it more, making herself look even sexier, as if she'd just crawled out of bed after a hot, steamy night of making love. Wyatt's mouth was dry.

She fixed him with an intense blue-eyed stare and then lay back against him. "If you were my age, you wouldn't interest me, Wyatt. High-school guys are immature geeks. That's why I avoid them."

"So you . . . don't have any boyfriends?" He scorned himself for the ridiculous streak of jealousy that ran through him at the thought of Kendra with any of the good-looking young men he'd met at the high school the other day.

"I tried the boyfriend thing," she said frankly. "I didn't want to be a virgin my entire life and I decided I'd better try sex at least once. So I got this boyfriend and we had sex— once." She shuddered. "It was awful! I decided Ashlynne had been right to warn me against it all these years. I couldn't figure out why Rayleen kept doing it—and with all different guys too! Gross!"

She gazed deeply into Wyatt's eyes. "I'm not a slut but you don't have to freak about taking my virginity, like I know you would've."

Wyatt stifled a groan. "I'm not sure how to deal with your honesty, Kendra. I've never met a girl—"

"—woman," she corrected promptly.

"—young woman like you. You surprise me, you delight me. Sometimes you scare the hell out of me."

"I turn you on," she added. She carefully pressed her thigh against his still hard male heat.

"That too, of course." He covered her knee with his hand. "You know I want you, Kendra, but it's more than that. I . . . care about you. Too much to rush things when the time isn't right."

Kendra was dizzied by the rush of euphoria sweeping over her. Hearing Wyatt say he cared for her was almost as thrilling as learning that Maxie was safe. She paid no attention to the rest of what he'd said. "I want you, Wyatt."

Their lips met and they kissed with lingering tenderness. Which quickly flared into something more, something hotter and wilder and deeply intimate.

"No more, not now." Groaning with mingled pleasure and unfulfilled desire, Wyatt finally lifted his mouth from hers.

Kendra gazed at him with passion-drugged eyes. "I want more," she cried breathlessly. "Wyatt, you can't stop now!" She thrust her fingers through his hair to hold his head as she began to nibble on his lips, using her teeth and tongue to entice him.

Wyatt breathed deeply, fighting for control. Finally, he cupped her face with his hand and kissed her hard. "It's too soon for what I want," he rasped, his lips brushing hers.

"But I won't end it like this. It isn't fair to you."

Kendra felt his fingers on the metal button of her jeans shorts and sucked in her breath. The sound of the zipper being lowered seemed to echo in her ears. She felt his hand glide along her belly, pausing to explore the shape of her navel with his thumb.

She squeezed her eyes shut as his hand moved lower, slipping inside her silky bikini panties. She felt his fingers skim through the soft thatch of curls before probing deeper, gently nudging her thighs apart. She was embarrassed by the wetness he found there, but her aroused body blocked all inhibitions and she arched helplessly against his hand.

"So wet and tight and hot," Wyatt growled thickly. "I'm going to give you what you need, my baby."

He stroked her until she was twisting with urgency, then carefully opened her and entered her. She cried his name and clung to him as his mouth took hers.

He withdrew his fingers slowly and then thrust them deeply inside her, again and again, teasing her, pleasing her, making her moan with pleasure. His thumb found the throbbing little hidden bud, which was swollen and aching for his touch.

Her head fell back and her lips parted, her breasts rose and fell as she gulped for breath. An unbearable tightness gripped her lower body as it curled with heat. Instinctively, she clenched herself around him.

"Oh, Wyatt!" Her small choked cry rose to a scream that he quickly swallowed by covering her mouth with his. And then she went rigid as the small erotic convulsions began, and went on and on until she was whimpering and pliant in his arms.

A few minutes later Kendra stirred drowsily. A glowing warmth radiated from deep inside her belly to every nerve and muscle in her body. She felt wonderful, energetic and relaxed at the same time. She opened her eyes and found Wyatt staring down at her, his gaze intimate.

Kendra blushed. His hand was still inside her panties, his fingers gently caressing. She watched as he slowly withdrew his hand, then adjusted her clothes. She found the bulge, still hard and stiff in his trousers, and pressed it. "But Wyatt, don't you want to—"

With a half laugh, half groan, Wyatt removed her hand. "Yes, I most certainly want to, but I already told you it's not the right time." He kissed her palm and her skin tingled excitingly all over. "Now, no more making out. We're going to talk."

"We could talk about making out," Kendra suggested mischievously.

He carried her to the sofa and sat her on the cushion beside him. "We'll talk about something completely nonsexual. Like my campaign. Nothing could be less arousing than that."

Kendra rolled her eyes heavenward. "Why don't we talk about why you're running for Congress when you hate being a politician, you hate campaigning, and you hate politics?"

He glanced at her askance. "What makes you say that?"

"Because I know you better than you think I do." She leaned over and playfully rubbed her nose to his, Eskimo-style. "But not as well as I'm going to."

They smiled at each other. They were so completely absorbed in each other that the time waiting for Maxie's return flew by.

Cord walked into the apartment, carrying a sleeping Maxie. Ashlynne trailed behind them. She looked exhausted, great dark circles shadowing her blue eyes.

"This day has lasted at least a hundred years," she whispered wearily as she led Cord to the children's bedroom. Daisy was sound asleep, her panda tucked under her arm. Cord laid Maxie in her bed, Kendra removed her shoes, and Ashlynne covered her with a sheet and light blanket.

Outside the girls' bedroom, Kendra gazed assessingly at her older sister. "You look ready to pass out, Ash. Go to bed right now before you fall over." Her blue eyes gleamed. "And since the butler has retired for the night, I'll show the Way brothers to the door."

"Jokes at this hour. I like your spirit, kid." Cord chuckled appreciatively. He was charged with energy. Retrieving Maxie had infused him with adrenaline-fueled vim and vigor.

His eyes sought Ashlynne's. Though she looked worn and drawn, she managed to maintain her aura of tense watchfulness, her gaze flickering tiredly from Cord to Wyatt to Kendra.

Cord's smile began to fade. Unlike himself, Ashlynne had not successfully banned the terror of the day. He felt his elation ebb. She disappeared into her room, without a good-bye.

His lips tightened and he made himself remember what Ashlynne undoubtedly had not forgotten for a minute—that before Maxie embarked on her great adventure, they'd barely been on speaking terms. Just because they'd temporarily shelved their hostilities during those traumatic hours that Maxie had been missing, did not mean the truce would extend beyond them. The realization depressed him and the depression made him angry. Lately, all his highs and lows seemed to be Ashlynne-induced.

In the living room, at the front door, Cord saw Wyatt lift Kendra's hand to his mouth and brush her fingers with his lips.

"I'll talk to you tomorrow," Wyatt said huskily.

Kendra gave him a smile so warm and so intimate that even if Cord hadn't seen the hand-kissing, alarm bells would've gone off.

"Wyatt, I want to warn you that Ashlynne is already harboring suspicions about you and that little sister of hers," Cord said to his brother as they walked to their cars, parked in front of the apartment building. "I know it's ridiculous but when you act so—er—chummy with Kendra, Ashlynne is bound to misinterpret and freak out."

"Cord, you don't know how—" Wyatt began. Then he sighed and shook his head. "Never mind. Just go home and get some rest. You need it, after what you've been through today." He reached out to affectionately cuff his brother's shoulder. "I'm so glad that little girl is home safe and sound."

"So am I, Wyatt." Cord grinned. "You wouldn't have believed the scene at Safe Haven. There were camera crews and reporters from all the TV stations, plus reporters and photographers from the area newspapers. Maxie faced them like a pro. Told her story, smiled, and hugged her mom for the cameras. She's quite a little performer. I guess it's in her genes. Her father was a movie stuntman who was injured in the line of duty and then became a stunt coordinator."

"I know. I saw pictures of him tonight. Kendra showed me their family albums while we waited for news."

"You saw his picture?"

Wyatt nodded. "Tall, blond, athletic guy, well built enough to be a recruiting ad for one of those fitness programs. Looked like a movie star himself."

Ashlynne hadn't mentioned the movie-star looks and body-builder physique when she'd spoken of Maxie's father. Cord frowned. "Were there any pictures of Daisy's father?"

"Not a one."

"That doesn't surprise me. Ashlynne described him as a classic jerk. I suppose she feels a certain lingering fondness for Mathison, but not Daisy's daddy."

"Maybe." Wyatt shrugged. "But my guess is that Rayleen didn't even know who Daisy's father was. Kendra clammed up at the mention of him. Seemed very uneasy and defensive about Rayleen's—er—activities back then."

"Rayleen? You mean Ashlynne. She is the children's mother."

"Well, she certainly is their mother in every way that counts. But Rayleen was definitely the biological mother. I saw pictures of her, pregnant with each child."

"Wyatt, you must be mistaken. Ashlynne is the mother of those children," Cord insisted. Though the night air was warm and balmy, he felt a chill rip through him. "She—she's raising them. They call her Mommy," he added lamely.

"From what Kendra told me—and what I saw in those pictures—Ashlynne has been Mommy ever since they were born. Taking care of them, supporting them. Rayleen was never around for those kids. Her death, however untimely, didn't change their lives a bit."

Wyatt shook his head, frowning with disapproval. "Rayleen's sole maternal contribution was to act as an incubator for nine months, give birth and then dump the babies on her sisters."

"Are you sure?" Cord's voice was little more than a hoarse croak. "Rayleen is the mother?"

"I saw pictures of a very pregnant Rayleen Monroe, and the pictures had captions." Wyatt gazed curiously at his brother. "Why are you getting so bent out of shape? The police won't care. Maxie has been found. It doesn't matter if Ashlynne is the birth mother or legal guardian. The case is officially closed."

It doesn't matter if Ashlynne is the birth mother or legal guardian. Wyatt's words tumbled through Cord's mind. Oh, it mattered, it mattered a great deal to him. For if Rayleen, not Ashlynne, had given birth . . . Cord felt his throat close. Six years ago he'd had a fling with Rayleen Monroe, then he had left Waysboro for Montana. His hands were beginning to shake. Time enough for the length of a pregnancy that had produced a little girl, just Daisy's age.

No, he was using faulty logic to jump to the wrong conclusions, Cord quickly assured himself. Daisy couldn't be his daughter. It wasn't as if he were the first and only man to have slept with Rayleen Monroe.

But still . . . Rayleen was Maxie and Daisy's mother! Cord was reeling. Rayleen, not Ashlynne, had been the one to have the affair with the married stunt coordinator who was Maxie's father.

And Daisy's father? "A classic jerk," Ashlynne had said cryptically. Cord's insides churned with apprehension. Had she been talking about *him*? He closed his eyes, swaying a little, reaching out to place his hand on the hood of Wyatt's car to steady himself.

"Are you okay?" Wyatt asked with concern. "You don't look it. How about letting me drive you home and we'll pick up your car here tomorrow?"

"No, I'm fine. You go on, Wyatt. I'll drive myself back to OakWay."

He had to be alone, to try to make some sense out of the words and images whirling maniacally through his mind. Daisy. The thick, dark hair and thoughtful dark eyes. The bright, wary, and cautious little girl who was quick to obey her mother and kept protective watch over her impulsive, adventurous sister. He'd called her RoboKid because she lacked Maxie's spontaneity and sparkle. He remembered the infamous scene in the zoo gift shop; he'd loaded Maxie with toys and presents while Daisy stood quietly by and watched.

Cord climbed into his car, despite Wyatt's frown of concern, and pulled away from the curb at a rate of speed too high for the quiet suburban street. He had to get away from this place! He wished he could escape his thoughts as easily. But they continued to haunt him as he drove through the deserted streets of Waysboro.

He couldn't be Daisy's father. Cord repeated it like a mantra.

Why, the child didn't even like him very much. She certainly didn't trust him. She had flatly refused to go to the zoo with him without the reassuring presence of her mother; she'd even balked at accompanying him to the water fountain just a room away.

Cord's neck reddened. Daisy viewed him as an unreliable incompetent who'd lost her beloved sister. It was humiliating to be judged by a five-year-old, but if he thought for one minute that the disapproving little girl was his own daughter . . .

Cord shook his head. No, it just couldn't be true.

Chapter Twelve

"GET up! Get up, boy! Do you plan to sleep all day?" Dayland Way Senior's booming voice echoed throughout OakWay as he pounded on Cord's bedroom door with the brass handle of his walking stick. "Your mother wants me to remind you that the Oak Ridge School's Ice Cream Sunday benefit is today and you're supposed to be there to help scoop up. Camilla, did I get that right?" he bellowed. "Camilla?"

"Mother says 'Yes, that's right,' Grandfather," Holly shouted from downstairs, her mother's spokesperson. Camilla Way would never raise her voice to such decibels.

Cord moaned and tried to put his pillow over his head, but his grandfather kept up the infernal rapping on his door. Stuporously, he sat up and glanced at the bedside clock. Eight o'clock. An intolerably late hour for the early-rising Ways but intolerably early to Cord, who had lain awake and tense for hours after he'd finally climbed into bed. He had heard the giant grandfather clock in the hall chime six before he'd finally fallen into a restless sleep. Which had lasted less than two hours.

He groggily recalled that his mother had mentioned the Ice Cream Sunday benefit for the Oak Ridge School, a residential treatment center and school for troubled children located in the lush countryside between Waysboro and Exton.

Camilla had been on its board for years, holding every office at one time or another. All the Ways were expected to be present at the annual event, but this year Wyatt's appearance there took on added importance. While scooping up ice cream and taking part in the games, he would be rubbing shoulders with the corporate sponsors and local media assigned to cover the benefit. The price of admission was steep, limiting participation to the monied classes of Waysboro and Exton.

Cord gripped his head. It was throbbing monstrously, as if a jackhammer were inside trying to drill through his skull. And his family expected him to show up and shine at an ice-cream social? The appeal of Waysboro society had always eluded him, but never more so than right now. Surely the past twenty-four tense, frenzied hours he had spent excused him from any social obligations!

"I'm not going to be able to make it today, sir," Cord called to his grandfather. "I think I might be coming down with—"

"The only thing you might be coming down with is a guilty conscience, Cord Way." His mother's voice sounded through the door.

Cord heard the doorknob rattle, heard the key turn in the lock. Heard Holly's voice.

"Mother, you can't barge into Cord's room," Holly exclaimed indignantly. "Mother, for heaven's sakes, he is a grown man, you have to respect his privacy."

"This is my home, and I am entitled to enter any room I choose," Camilla said, her well-modulated voice steely but still finishing-school soft. "And if your brother has smuggled his young lady friend into his bed, then we shall all meet her right now, won't we?"

"Mother, this is inexcusable!" cried Holly.

Just before the door to the bedroom opened, Cord adjusted the top sheet to cover himself to his waist. A moment later, Camilla and Holly stood at the threshold, Grandfather Way behind them. Camilla's eyes darted from the bed, throughout the empty room, and finally came to rest on the open door to the adjoining bathroom.

"I didn't bring a lady friend home last night, Mother," Cord said dryly. "I don't know why you would suspect that I had. I've never smuggled women into my room here in the past, and it's unlikely I would start now."

"You never made the front page of the newspaper before

either, but there you were this morning in *The Exton Sunday Post* with a Monroe girl and that child of hers who was lost and then found." Camilla sniffed delicately with distaste. "I expect *The Waysboro Weekly* will follow up with their own version of your misadventure in their issue this Tuesday."

"The paper?" Cord would've leaped from the bed, except he was nude and didn't dare risk scandalizing his mother and sister.

"Right here, boy." Old Dayland, leaning on his walking stick, dropped a section of the Sunday paper onto the bed. "There you are carrying the brat, with her mama hanging on to your arm. You're a damn fool, Cord! I can see she's a pretty piece, but to get mixed up with any Monroe—and one with a kid yet! . . . Why, it's the height of folly. Next thing you know she'll be claiming it's yours."

In light of yesterday's stunning revelations about Rayleen, Cord felt himself grow pale, then flush with heat. Fortunately, his family didn't notice. They weren't even looking at him. Their collective attention was fixed on the newspaper article.

"I saw the TV newscasts yesterday, when the little girl was still missing," Holly said. "I also saw Dan Clarkston's nauseating plea and offer of a bribe to return her."

"The reward was offered by your friend Thorpe," Cord said casually, and watched the flush suffuse Holly's cheeks. He remembered Thorpe's fury as he'd uttered his scathing accusation: *"Your slut of a sister had my child scraped out of her."*

Holly's eyes narrowed to slits. "Don't use the words 'friend' and 'Thorpe' together, even in jest."

"Do you mean this—incident—was on television?" Camilla was horrified.

"Since Mother never watches television, she didn't learn about the—uh—incident until this morning's paper arrived," explained Holly.

"Cord, I'm so disappointed in you," Camilla said, her voice heavy with maternal grief. It was a tone Cord had been hearing all his life. He seemed to have a special talent when it came to disappointing his mother.

"Cavorting with a Monroe! And then having your affair splashed over the front page of the paper! It's disgraceful!" growled old Dayland.

"Grandfather, I was *not* cavorting. And the focus of the article is the child being found, not my alleged affair."

"I simply do not understand how you could put yourself in such a position, particularly now, at this crucial time during Wyatt's campaign." Camilla heaved a long-suffering, woeful sigh. "But if you care at all about your brother, you will attempt to make amends and attend today's benefit. You have already been signed up to scoop ice cream with Eliza Jarrett's daughter Sloane for the Ice Cream Olympics."

Cord caught Holly's eye. She was trying to hold back a laugh.

"Well, come along, Camilla. The boy needs to shower and shave, make himself presentable for the crowd. And for the lovely Miss Jarrett." Old Dayland guffawed, clearly amused by the sentence imposed on his grandson. He held out one arm, which Camilla took. They left together with the elegant grandeur of royalty departing a coronation ball.

Alone in the room, Holly and Cord faced each other. "Mother will never give up matchmaking until we're all stuck in marriages from hell," Holly said, grinning. "You and Sloane Jarrett? She has all the warmth and charm of Cinderella's stepsisters. What if she's set her sights on you and—"

Cord shrugged. "No sweat. I can scare off any Waysboro woman by mentioning the lodge in Glacier. My eligibility is automatically canceled out by my inappropriate address and occupation."

"Does Ashlynne Monroe consider you ineligible because you live in Montana?" Holly's dark eyes searched his.

Cord laughed harshly. "She considers me ineligible for entirely different reasons."

"Cord, I want you to be honest with me. I already know about your fling with a Monroe a few years back. It was Ashlynne, wasn't it?" Holly smoothed an invisible wrinkle from her amber silk dress. "And her child, the one who got lost yesterday . . . Cord, are you the father of that little girl?"

"Good grief, Holly, what was it Grandfather said? Get mixed up with a Monroe who has a child, and everybody will assume it's yours?" Cord cleared his throat and tried to block out the roaring in his ears. "Well, just for the record, I am not mixed up with Ashlynne Monroe, and I am *not* Maxie's father."

But Holly was not diverted. "If there is nothing between you and Ashlynne Monroe, what were you doing at the zoo with her and her children?"

"Good question. Wish I had the answer." Cord was glib. "By the way, did I mention that Ethan Thorpe arrived at the police station in a state of highly righteous indignation?"

Holly stiffened, her face becoming a cool, expressionless mask. "I don't want to talk about Ethan Thorpe, Cord."

"He certainly talks enough about you. I mean, for someone who supposedly only knows you casually. That's what you told me you and he were, right? Just casual acquaintances?"

"I'll leave you to get ready for the benefit." Holly walked to the door.

"Holly, Ethan Thorpe said you'd had an abortion." Cord's words stopped her in her tracks. "Except he put it a bit more graphically."

Holly uttered a cry and covered her face with her hands.

"Holly, I'm not condemning you!" Her distress was very real. Cord wished he was dressed and could go to her side to offer comfort. But he was trapped in bed beneath the sheet, so he tried to make her smile. "Frankly, I wouldn't want to have Thorpe's kid for a nephew or a niece. It would probably have horns and a tail and yellow eyes that glowed in the dark."

His attempt at humor backfired. Holly's eyes filled with tears. "Cord, I didn't have an abortion, although I know that's what Ethan thinks. I—I let him think it."

"You and Ethan were a lot more than casual acquaintances."

Holly nodded, taking a shaky breath. "I met him in Columbus, shortly after I arrived there. He was ten years older than me and was so sophisticated, so exciting. I fell hard for him—he made sure that I did. I—I didn't think I was capable of feeling the way he made me feel. It was crazy and wild and romantic. I was totally out of control."

She stared blindly at the carpet. "It's been over three years and sometimes I still want him so badly I . . ." Her voice trailed off, then rallied fiercely. "But I hate him, too, and my hatred is as out of control as my love for him was. When I hear his name, when I look at him . . . I want to hurt him. I want to make him bleed."

Her emotional intensity was unsettling. Cord wasn't sure what to say to her. "I—saw what you did to his office."

Holly smiled ruefully. "You should've seen what he did to my apartment, just before I moved from Columbus to Atlanta." Her smile faded. "You should've seen what he did to me!"

Cord was aghast. And outraged. "God, Holly, *I'll* make him bleed!"

"No, Cord, you don't understand." She blushed to the roots of her auburn hair. "We had a very complicated relationship. I won't go into detail but I was a very willing participant."

"Complicated? Try sick! Holly, how did you get involved with—in—"

"I was crazy about him. When he wasn't making me crazy, that is." Holly shook her head. "But it lasted five years, and when it ended, I thought I would die. My life is flat compared to what it was with Ethan; I live on a very even keel now, no highs or lows, and I know it's better this way. But with Ethan, the highs were so high—"

"Forget the highs." Her dreamy-eyed stare alarmed him. "With a man like Thorpe, the lows must've been pure hell."

Holly pulled herself together. "You're right, of course. But if I hadn't gotten pregnant and—and lost the baby, I'm afraid I would still be in thrall to him. The baby was the catalyst for our final breakup and my move to a different city, away from him."

"You were pregnant and lost the baby," Cord repeated softly. "I'm so sorry, Holly. I wish I'd've known. I would have—"

"There was nothing you or anyone could have done to keep me away from Ethan," Holly said, sighing. "I wouldn't have listened, I couldn't have. It was as if we were . . . destined to come together."

"Oh no! Not that hocus-pocus drivel!"

Holly actually laughed. "I know how you feel about fate, destiny, kismet, and karma, and all that. But in the case of Ethan and I—the Thorpes and the Ways—"

"So he moved here to Waysboro and is set on defeating Wyatt for Congress because he's still furious with you?" Cord tried to divert her from the mystical angle.

"Partly. But he hated the Ways before he ever met me, Cord. In fact, he deliberately sought me out in Columbus to . . . settle the score." Holly took a deep breath. "Ethan holds Way Communications and our family personally responsible for his younger brother's suicide."

"What?"

"Ethan's brother Elliott was the restaurant critic for the Way paper in Philadelphia. He was extroverted and charming and funny, and in addition to his newspaper column, he landed himself a TV cooking show on one of the local television stations. He was very popular in the city, a part of the social scene."

"Until?" Cord prompted ominously.

"Until he got caught selling good reviews for the paper. Apparently, a three- or four-star review from Elliott Thorpe brought an incredible increase in popularity for the restaurant, and Elliott was not averse to taking bribes from restaurant owners to get them. Elliott had expensive tastes and lots of bills to pay. He escalated from taking the bribes offered to threatening restaurant owners with bad reviews if they didn't pay up. Eventually, some of the owners got tired of the shakedown and went to the district attorney to tell all. There was a sting set up, with a new restaurant owner wearing a wire when Elliott came in to make his demands."

"So they got him on tape? Ouch."

Holly nodded. "Since he also plugged restaurants on his TV show, there were all kinds of charges filed by the FCC, in addition to those filed by the district attorney.

Elliott was facing serious prison time and thousands of dollars in fines. Plus he was deeply in debt, with a slew of unsavory characters breathing down his neck, demanding repayment."

"So why didn't he go to see his brother Ethan for a loan? And for a good lawyer? We all know he's got the bucks."

"I guess Elliott was too proud to do that. Or maybe he felt that nothing or no one could help him."

"So he killed himself," Cord finished. "But why blame Way Communications?"

"The moment the news about the charges surfaced, the paper fired Elliott and took great pains to disavow him. They wouldn't even let him back inside the building to clean out his desk. Elliott was despondent about his reputation and the way he was suddenly a pariah. His old colleagues wouldn't return his phone calls, on the orders of management—who took *their* orders from Dayland and Stafford Way. The TV station followed their lead. Stafford even made a special trip to Philadelphia to do some damage control and totally repudiated Elliott, to save the credibility of the paper. Ethan claimed it was Stafford's attack that finally drove Elliott over the edge, but who really knows for sure? There wasn't a suicide note."

"How did Elliott kill himself?"

"Carbon monoxide in his garage." Holly's eyes misted with tears once more. "Ethan was distraught. He adored his younger brother. Whenever he talked about Elliott, his face would take on this whole different cast. Not hard and cynical and calculating. 'Elliott could always make me laugh,' he would say. He loved that Elliott was so outgoing, so social and popular. So different from Ethan himself. And their parents . . . well, they've never gotten over the shock."

Cord suddenly pictured Maxie and Daisy together at the zoo, when Maxie had been imitating the monkeys and Daisy had laughed and laughed, as if her sister were the funniest, most talented entertainer alive. With that came a surge of empathy for cool, steely Ethan Thorpe, who'd so enjoyed his lively younger brother. He frowned.

"Okay, you felt sorry for Thorpe," he said rather sternly to Holly. He was not about to be suckered by sympathy for the man—or allow it to happen to Holly again. "But knowing what had happened to Elliott, why did you ever get involved with his brother?"

"I didn't know the whole story," Holly countered quickly. "Ethan told me his younger brother was dead but nothing else. I didn't know all the facts until I got pregnant." She gulped. "It was unplanned, though Ethan accused me of deliberately trying to trap him into marriage. I won't deny I wanted to marry him—we'd been together for five years! True, we'd broken up a few hundred times and he cheated on me whenever he pleased, but I loved him and I wanted to marry him."

Cord's head was spinning. His sister's life had been more tortured than any soap-opera heroine's and he'd been completely in the dark about all of it. "Did you get pregnant accidentally on purpose, Holly?"

"I don't know. Maybe subconsciously I did." Her lower lip trembled. "I was always the one responsible for birth control, Ethan didn't want to be bothered. I was careful, but there were a few times when I wasn't." She shook her head sadly. "Ethan was furious about the pregnancy. That's when he told me everything, including his plan of using me for revenge. He'd deliberately introduced himself to me, made me fall for him, and planned to break my heart whenever it suited him. He said he would never marry me, that my family had murdered his brother and he would never desecrate Elliott's memory by marrying a Way."

"You must have been devastated," Cord said quietly.

"I was. And enraged too. I couldn't believe I'd spent five years of my life with a man who claimed he'd never loved me. I told Ethan I'd never have his baby, that I was going to have it scraped out of me." She flinched at the imagery. "It was the most bitter, cruel fight we'd ever had." A tear trickled down her cheek. "I hated him but I still loved him. I planned to have the baby. I even thought about naming it Elliott, if it were a boy."

"Oh, Holly!" Cord groaned.

"Ethan never called me and he refused to take my calls, but I kept hoping when the baby was born he'd come around. I was in my fourth month when I began to hemorrhage and was rushed to the hospital. I had to have surgery because my Fallopian tube had ruptured. The fetus was developing in the tube, not the uterus, an ectopic pregnancy, the doctor said. The baby was a boy, too small to survive," she added sadly. "I spent almost a week at the university hospital and kept it a secret from everybody. And then, a few weeks later, Ethan arrived at my door with a huge bouquet of flowers and a teddy bear."

Holly's voice choked on a sob. "He'd been doing a lot of soul-searching, he said. He realized that it was wrong to penalize me for what had happened to his brother. Oh, he still hated the Ways but he'd exempted me from the charges. He said he loved me and wanted to marry me. He wanted our baby."

"And you told him there was no baby."

"Ethan didn't give me a chance to explain. He immediately assumed I'd had an abortion, like I'd threatened, and he just went berserk. Accused me of murdering his child, like my family had murdered his brother. Said that now the Ways had the blood of two Thorpes on their souls."

"And he swore more revenge," Cord added.

"Yes. He wants to make life miserable for the Ways and he can do it. Look at the direct hit he scored with that condo development. The fabric of the town really has changed, and our relatives and friends are very unhappy about it. I know they're insular and snobbish, but is having Ethan Thorpe and his minions running the town any improvement?"

"At least the Ways have a certain *noblesse oblige* and recognize the need to give something back," Cord remarked dryly.

"Not Ethan. He's the human equivalent of strip-mining. When I heard he'd moved to Waysboro, I panicked and deliberately stayed away these past years. Ethan will do whatever he can to hurt or humiliate, or even simply annoy or irritate any Way. I think he actually enjoys his vendetta."

"It doesn't seem likely he'll let up or go away," Cord agreed.

"I don't want Wyatt to get hurt," Holly whispered. "Or you either, Cord. I think everybody else can fend for themselves."

"So can Wyatt and I," Cord assured her. "Holly, you would never consider getting back together with Thorpe, would you? If his revenge should take a charming bent, would you fall for him again?"

"No," she said decisively. "When Ethan and I are together, something bad happens to both of us. I don't ever want to live that way again, no matter how dull or colorless my life sometimes seems now. I was sorry about losing the baby, but Ethan and I as parents would've been more toxic than any in those self-help books that proliferate the best-seller list. Don't worry, Cord. He and I are finished forever."

The Ice Cream Sunday benefit was in full swing on the spacious grounds of the Oak Ridge School. There were clowns, pony rides, elaborate box luncheons, lemonade with peppermint sticks, and music from an old-fashioned brass band. The guests were given straw hats and parasols, in keeping with the turn-of-the-century atmosphere. And, of course, there were countless vats of ice cream, great tubs of toppings—from fruits to marshmallow creme to butterscotch and hot fudge—and a surfeit of whipping cream in nozzled cans.

The Ice Cream Olympics included ice-cream eating contests, ice-cream sculpting, ice-cream painting, and creative combination desserts. Cord scooped on demand. He was so busy supplying ice cream to the artistic and competitive Olympic participants, he hardly had time to talk to Sloane Jarrett, who spent most of her assigned scooping time socializing with her circle, therefore leaving Cord to pick up the slack at their end of the table.

"We want six scoops of gray ice cream," demanded a laughing, feminine voice. "We're going to make a shark, right, Scotty?"

Cord glanced up from a vat of strawberry ice cream into the gleaming blue eyes of Kendra Monroe.

"Gray ice cream?" Cord asked dryly. Kendra was holding the hand of a small, dark-haired boy in a white Eton suit. Maxie and Daisy stood beside her, both dressed in yellow shorts and white T-shirts, printed with pink, blue, and white daisies.

"Hi, Uncle Cord!" Maxie cried, all smiles and delighted to see him. "Look, we have on daisies!" She pointed to her outfit, then to her sister. "Daisy in daisies." She laughed merrily at her own wit.

"Well, hello!" Cord felt his heart begin to pound, and it had nothing to do with the sun and the continuous bending and scooping. His eyes were inexorably drawn to Daisy, who was holding tightly to Maxie's hand.

He smiled at her, staring at her, seeing her as if for the first time. The color of her hair, the shape and color of her eyes . . . didn't they match his own? And unless his imagination was playing tricks on him, Daisy's small face, her very expression, matched Holly's in a portrait of her at about the same age. It still hung in the small sitting room off the kitchen in OakWay.

Cord felt his eyes sting with a burning moisture and was appalled. He quickly tried to calm himself. He was seeing things, feeling peculiarly emotional due to his lack of sleep.

Daisy gave him a small smile, her innate reserve preventing her from bestowing an exuberant Maxie-like grin. "What does gray ice cream taste like?" she asked. "Pink is strawberry, brown is chocolate, white is vanilla, yellow is lemon. What is gray?"

"Disgusting!" Cord joked, an odd joy pulsing through him. Daisy hadn't snubbed him, she'd smiled at him, actually made conversation! Even as he mocked himself for craving a five-year-old's goodwill, he still savored it.

"Anyway, we don't have any gray, you'll have to make your own somehow by mixing flavors. I didn't expect to see you ladies here today," he added, glancing from Daisy to Kendra.

"And gentleman," Kendra added, picking up the little dark-haired boy. "This is Scotty Clarkston. We came with his parents and Ethan Thorpe. Scotty wants to make a gray shark, but I guess we'll have to use some other color of ice cream. Okay, Scotty?"

Scotty looked ready to cry. "I wanna go home," he whimpered. "See Maria."

"Maria is his nanny and he loves her sooo much," Kendra explained. "Although why a so-called devoted, stay-at-home mother like Cindy Clarkston needs a full-time nanny for her kids is a bit of a mystery, hmm?" She turned her most dazzling smile on the little boy. "Come on, Scotty, we're going to have fun. We'll make a rainbow shark and win a prize. Start scooping, Cord," she ordered. "We want at least three scoops of every single color ice cream you have."

"Can I help scoop?" Maxie asked.

"Sure, come on back," invited Cord. Maxie came around to the back of the table, Daisy clutching her hand, as if they were cuffed together. He gave Maxie a metal scooper. "Would you like to scoop too, Daisy?"

Daisy nodded. "Kendra is baby-sitting Scotty," she said seriously.

Cord looked across the table at Kendra, who was still holding Scotty. She was talking to him and he listened, nodding his head, his lips still quivering.

"Scotty didn't want to come here but his mommy and daddy made him." Daisy's big dark eyes were wide with concern. "He cried and yelled, and they yelled and were going to make him sit in the car but Kendra said she would take him with us."

"Well, that was nice of her," said Cord. He recalled the incessant references to little Scotty that Dan and Cindy Clarkston never seemed to tire of making. And here they were at a family extravaganza, and they'd dumped the kid on Kendra Monroe.

He squinted his eyes and scanned the horizon. Sure enough, Dan and Cindy were far across the lawn, working the crowd. "Is your mom here?" he asked the girls, his voice most casual.

"Yeah, she's with Mr. Thorpe," said Maxie. "We came in his car and guess what, Uncle Cord? We stopped at McDonald's and got lunch and they had those little Barbies we wanted! Mr. Thorpe bought them for us."

"Mr. Thorpe wants to take us to the zoo," Daisy said, shivering a little. Perhaps it was because she was leaning over a vat of ice cream, but Cord doubted it. "I don't want to go back there," she added succinctly.

"I do!" Maxie sang out. "The zoo is fun."

Cord's eyes met Daisy's. He felt a telepathic link between them, and he didn't even believe in telepathy. But he knew that she knew it would be a long time before either of them could set foot in a zoo without reliving yesterday's terrible scare. What if Thorpe should insist on the outing? Would Ashlynne make the children go? They were here today on his command, weren't they?

Cord was not prepared for the waves of anger that swept through him, surging and cresting as the children's voices swirled around his head. A strange nimbus surrounded the scene before him, blurring his vision, yet his thoughts fell in place with perfect clarity. It was as if he were fitting pieces of a puzzle together, seeing the full picture at last . . .

Mr. Thorpe bought Daisy and Maxie the little dolls Cord Way had been unable to, *Mr. Thorpe* wanted to take the children to the zoo, where they had all too recently spent a disastrous afternoon.

Cord's eyes darted to Daisy. Suddenly there was no more rationalization and self-deception. Daisy was his daughter. He would seek and obtain confirmation, of course, but in that staggering moment of truth, he knew Daisy was a Way—and he knew that Ethan Thorpe knew it too. Knew it and had begun to use it against him, thus the lunch, the dolls, the promised outing to the zoo. What sweeter revenge than to usurp a child's affections from her own father?

A darker motive occurred to him too. Though Daisy was only a child, what if she were on Thorpe's Way hit list too? Did he have some invidious scheme in mind to damage her too?

It was an alarming—but plausible—possibility. Ethan Thorpe's revenge against the Ways already included playing sex-and-mind games with Holly for five years, wounding her so thoroughly that, even three years later, she was still alone, unable to love or trust a man. He'd disrupted

Wyatt's campaign and was willing to spend a fortune to change the town of Waysboro simply because most of the Ways lived there. And Ethan Thorpe was Ashlynne's boss, to whom he'd made certain she felt beholden . . .

"Hi, Wyatt!" Kendra's voice drew Cord from his disturbing reverie.

Wyatt joined them, smiling at Cord, then fixing his eyes on Kendra. "Hello, Kendra."

"Daisy, Maxie, this is your uncle Wyatt." Kendra made the introductions. "You met him last night except you were both sleeping so you don't remember. But I'm sure he remembers you."

"I'm not likely ever to forget last night," Wyatt agreed, moving closer to her.

"Me either. Hey, don't you ever wear anything but a suit?" Kendra teased playfully, reaching out to give his tie a yank. She was wearing curve-fitting blue jeans and a burgundy-colored blouse knotted at the midriff, revealing the smooth white skin of her waist and stomach.

"Not since I became a candidate," Wyatt said rather wistfully.

"We're going to have to get you out of those suits," Kendra purred. "The sooner the better. We'll start with the coat. Take it off, ditch the tie, open the top button of your shirt and roll up the sleeves."

To Cord's astonishment, Wyatt proceeded to follow Kendra's instructions to the letter. "I'll save on dry-cleaning bills," Wyatt said, with a sheepish glance at his brother.

"Yeah, you've always been concerned about the high cost of dry cleaning," Cord said dryly.

There was no way Cord could misinterpret the desire shining in his brother's eyes as he gazed at Kendra. Nor the caressive tone of his voice when he spoke to her.

"Wyatt, did I introduce you to little Scotty Clarkston?" Kendra asked, ever so casually.

Wyatt's eyes widened. "Kendra!" This time he sounded alarmed.

"Next time I go to the zoo, I'm going to see the tigers and the panda," Maxie announced. "Mr. Thorpe said so.

He said he'll make them come out to see me. He said the animals listen to him."

Once again, Cord and Daisy exchanged glances. "Animals in the zoo don't listen to Mr. Thorpe," Daisy whispered. "But Maxie thinks they do."

Cord felt a rush of pride as he gazed down at his small skeptical daughter. "You're right not to believe everything you hear a grown-up say," he murmured. "Sometimes kids do, and it's a big mistake."

Daisy nodded her agreement. "I believe Mommy and my teacher."

Cord wondered if someday he would ever qualify for that hallowed list and was surprised by how very much he wanted to.

Sensing an ally, Daisy met his dark eyes with her own. "I don't want Mr. Thorpe to take Maxie to the zoo. She could get lost again. And I don't want to go either. Not till I'm ten."

"Don't worry, Daisy," he said, daring to reach out to touch the top of the child's head. Her dark hair felt soft and silky. "You don't have to go to the zoo again until you're a grandmother, if you don't want to." He felt protective, he felt paternal. Nobody was going to hurt this little girl. *His daughter!*

He tossed his scooper into a vat of pistachio ice cream. "Wyatt, take over here for me."

Without giving his brother time to either agree or refuse, he stalked off. To find Ms. Ashlynne Monroe, the mother of his child.

CHAPTER THIRTEEN ─────────────

ASHLYNNE moved unobtrusively through the crowd looking for Kendra, Maxie, and Daisy. Ethan was nowhere to be seen, either, whereas Dan and Cindy Clarkston were being seen and heard everywhere. The music from the brass band filled the air and flocks of beautifully dressed children raced around, laughing and clutching helium-filled balloons.

The young inmates of the residential school were not present. Ashlynne wondered if they were watching the festivities from behind the barred windows of the red-brick buildings.

In jeans and a blue chambray shirt, opened over a white cotton T-shirt, she was dressed all wrong for this event, Ashlynne noted ruefully. So were the equally casually attired Kendra, Maxie, and Daisy. Everyone else was dressed in their Sunday designer best. Dressing up to participate in what was billed as the Ice Cream Olympics and to ride ponies struck her as insane, but then, what did a Monroe know about the Waysboro social scene?

Ethan had insisted that she and the girls come today, much to her dismay. As if being surrounded by Waysboro socialites wasn't daunting enough, she was still jittery from Maxie's escapade yesterday. Her restless, mostly sleepless night left her feeling weak and depleted.

The unpleasant scene staged by the Clarkstons in the parking lot earlier had been an additional strain. Watching Dan, Cindy, and little Scotty throw nearly identical tantrums would have been hard to stomach, even on a day when her biorhythms were in perfect sync.

In the midst of it all, Kendra had impulsively scooped up Scotty and spirited the little boy away, bringing the warfare to a halt. Maxie and Daisy had taken off with her.

Ethan had stayed her own flight, enlisting her to help calm Dan and Cindy and bolster them for their crowd-pleasing duties. From the looks of the smiling, hand-shaking, baby-kissing candidate and his wife, now enjoying their usual fix of voter and media attention, the couple had recovered from their fit of pique.

Her eyes flickered to a clown who was making balloon animals for a crowd of children gathered around him. She scanned the group for Maxie and Daisy.

"I want to talk to you, Ashlynne."

Cord Way stood before her. His face was hard, his dark eyes narrowed and intent behind his glasses. He was pure Waysboro establishment in cream-colored slacks and a pale yellow sport shirt with pencil-thin blue stripes running through it.

Ashlynne jerked backward with a gasp, startled by his looming presence and the rough demand in his voice.

Cord scowled. "No wonder you're so jumpy all the time." The look in his black eyes made her shiver. "Anyone harboring as many secrets as you has to be hypervigilant. But it's all over, Ashlynne." His hand fastened like a manacle around her wrist. "You're coming with me."

"No I'm not." The day when she would mindlessly follow anyone on a threat had yet to arrive. She gazed pointedly at her wrist, frowning her disapproval. Cord either didn't get her point or he ignored it because he did not remove his hand. "I'm looking for Kendra and the children and I won't—"

"I just left them scooping ice cream with Wyatt. They're fine. Now come on." His fingers tightened around her.

Ashlynne balked and pulled back. "No."

"So we're enacting the old physics principle—the immovable object meets the irresistible force?" His expression was cool and sardonic. "Want to take bets on who prevails?"

"You're even more overbearing than usual today. And if you don't let me go, I—I'll—"

"You'll what? Go running to your friend Thorpe?"

"Maybe!" It was the wrong thing to say. Ashlynne knew it the moment she said it.

Cord's face was a taut mask of fury, his dark eyes burning into her. Abruptly, he turned and headed toward a small grove of trees, several hundred yards away from the party site. As he'd retained an iron grip on her wrist, Ashlynne was forced to go with him, although certainly not quietly or willingly. She tripped and stumbled along after him, complaining mightily, while trying to pull herself free.

When they were finally alone in the thickness of the grove, Cord stopped and turned to face her, though he still did not release her. Ashlynne's stomach tightened anxiously, but she lifted her chin and met his eyes haughtily. She was determined to brazen it out, although not knowing the reason for his rage was definitely a handicap.

"Maybe this macho act works for you in your role as the big boss of Glacier Lodge and Campground, but it leaves me cold, Cord Way. If you have something to say to me, you—"

"Oh, I have something to say!" A primitive, possessive fury lashed at him, making him lash out at her. He caught her upper arms, his fingers completely encircling them. "I have so much to say, I hardly know where to begin." For just a moment, he was distracted by her softness, her slender fragility. His fingers wanted to linger and stroke, not restrain her.

But Ashlynne began to struggle, her blue eyes reflecting her fury. "Well, I'm not interested in hearing any of it."

"You'll listen, honey." Her anger stoked his own, dissolving his momentary tender lapse. His voice was soft and deep and more threatening than if he'd shouted at her. "You will certainly listen to this." His eyes met hers. "From now on, I do not want my daughter anywhere near Ethan Thorpe."

Shock froze Ashlynne in place and drained the color from her cheeks. For a moment she felt almost disoriented. *His daughter?* She had to have heard him wrong.

"I don't understand," she whispered.

"What don't you understand? That I know Daisy is my daughter? Well, I know she is, Ashlynne. What else isn't clear? Why I don't want her around Thorpe? That's easy. He's sworn vengeance on the entire Way family. He's already gone after my sister and my brother. I'll be damned if I'll let him have a crack at my child."

Panic and fury took the place of shock, reviving her. "I— I don't know what you've been drinking or—or—"

"So you're going to deny it?" Cord dropped his hands from her arms. "Well, it doesn't matter. I intend to obtain a copy of the birth certificate, and odds are a million to one that Rayleen listed me as Daisy's father on it. I just don't see her filling 'unknown' in that space, she was too street-smart for that. She'd've figured that someday Daisy might want to claim her heritage."

Ashlynne wanted to run away, but horror kept her rooted to the spot. Cord had read Rayleen exactly right. Though her sister had adamantly refused to inform the Ways about Daisy, she had listed Cord's name on the baby's birth certificate.

"When the kid's older, she might want to cash in on being a Way and she'll need proof." Ashlynne remembered Rayleen's glib explanation, made a few hours after Daisy's birth as she lay in her hospital bed, so blithe about the future. Ashlynne, who had been cuddling newborn Daisy in the chair beside Rayleen's bed, had felt a cold chill at the news.

"There will also be blood tests, of course, DNA testing, the works, for both Daisy and me," Cord continued, his voice becoming even softer and deeper and more intense. "I intend to present my family with irrefutable evidence that I am Daisy's father so there can be no opposition to accepting her. And we both know those tests will provide conclusive proof that Daisy is mine."

"Daisy is mine!" Ashlynne cried. "I'm her mother and you're a selfish, irresponsible—"

"Classic jerk?" Cord suggested sharply. He hadn't forgotten her description of Daisy's father. "Well, if I'm selfish and irresponsible for not being a part of my child's life, it's because I didn't know I was a father. No one bothered to inform me of my own daughter's existence. I'm curious as to how many others are involved in this conspiracy to keep me in the dark. Who else knows the truth about Daisy?"

Ashlynne swallowed the lump of fear blocking her throat. "There is no conspiracy. Besides me, only Kendra knows and she just recently figured it out. Rayleen and I never told anybody else in the family who Daisy's father is."

"Ethan Thorpe knows," Cord added flatly.

"He—he knows, too, but not about Rayleen." She flushed. "He thinks that Daisy is our child, yours and mine. Was he the one who told you?"

"I'm sure nothing would've pleased him more than to throw my negligence in my face again, but no, Thorpe didn't tell me. Nobody told me. Certain facts came to light, and I put them all together."

Somehow he managed to look both condemning and hurt at the same time. Ashlynne could've stood firm against the condemnation but the raw pain in his face struck her deeply.

"At first I wanted to tell you, I even tried to, though Rayleen warned me against it," she blurted out. "I knew Max Mathison had refused all responsibility when she told him she was pregnant with Maxie, but I thought the circumstances were different with you. For one thing, you weren't married. You actually seemed to like Rayleen and—" Ashlynne threw up her hands in a gesture of futility. "This is pointless. Why rehash this now?"

"It may be a rehash to you but I'm hearing this story for the first time. Exactly when did you try to tell me about the baby?" Cord's tone was patently disbelieving.

"I waited for you one night outside the Waterside Bar. But before I could mention the baby, you said you were leaving Waysboro for good. I figured it was hopeless then. Since you'd already decided to leave, you wouldn't change your plans because of Rayleen. You made it very clear that night you considered your relationship with her to be just a temporary one."

Cord swallowed. "I . . . think I remember that night."

"You probably don't," she countered scornfully. "You'd been drinking. At first you weren't even sure who I was. It happened a few weeks after Rayleen found out she was pregnant. She knew it was your baby. In spite of what everybody said about Rayleen, as long as she considered herself to be a man's girlfriend, she slept only with him."

"And she considered herself to be my girlfriend?" Cord was guilt-stricken. He had never for one moment considered Rayleen his girlfriend. She had given birth to his child, but he still could not imagine her as anything but a short-term fling. A short-term fling with lifelong consequences, he amended grimly.

"Rayleen didn't go in for romantic daydreams," Ashlynne said coolly. "You don't have to worry that she spent any time fantasizing about the two of you living happily ever after. But she liked you. You treated her well, better than most of her loser boyfriends. She thought you were a gentleman, even though you fancied yourself the tough lone rebel."

Cord stared at her without speaking, remembering how he'd been back then. The tough lone rebel . . . *fool*!

"Now you've decided to play another role, the devoted daddy charging to protect your child from the evil Ethan Thorpe," Ashlynne said angrily. Remembering Rayleen's lusty fling with Cord always irritated her in a way that the memory of Rayleen's affair with Max Mathison did not. "Well, thanks to my job with him, Ethan has done more for Daisy than you ever have. He pays me a good salary and health benefits that enable us to have a decent life and—"

"That man made a mess of my sister's life and I won't give him the chance to ruin my daughter's, using you as the means to do it," Cord exploded. She'd hit him square in the male ego with that remark, temporarily sidelining all thoughts of regret and remorse. "I don't want him anywhere near my child, not even peripherally, and if that means you quitting that damn job of yours, so be it!"

"You're joking!" Ashlynne's voice rose on a note of fury. "That's impossible!"

"Do I look like I'm telling a joke?" His jaw was clenched, his dark eyes glittered with anger. He was definitely not the image of a jolly jokester. "Leaving Thorpe's employ is very possible, Ashlynne. It's downright simple. Just hand in your resignation the first thing Monday morning."

"And then what? Apply for welfare?" Ashlynne burned with white-hot rage. "No, I can support my family and I intend to."

"My sentiments exactly. From now on, *I'll* support you and the girls."

"Take charity from a Way? I'll never stoop to that!"

"It wouldn't be charity, damn it!" Cord said fiercely. "Rayleen gave birth, but you're the real mother of my child, Ashlynne. You've loved her and taken care of her and worked hard to give her a good life. You've done it all alone, but not any longer. From now on I want to help, I want to be part of Daisy's life and—"

"*You* want," Ashlynne cried, her fists clenching at her sides. "It's always about what *you* want, isn't it? Whatever Cord Way wants, he gets. Well, not this time, mister. I don't want your help, I don't want you in our lives. I don't want you!"

A flush darkened his cheekbones. "I can cite a few recent occasions when you wanted me very much, Ashlynne."

"Don't you dare talk to me like I'm some cheap Waterside Bar tramp!"

"I was talking to you the way a man talks to the woman he wants to—" He stopped in mid-sentence, his face suddenly taut. "But you wouldn't know about that, would you?"

He shook his head, as if to clear it. "I should have figured it out as soon as I learned that Rayleen was the one who gave birth to Maxie and Daisy. You've never talked sex with any man, let alone actually had sex. No wonder you get so nervous and edgy when the sexual tension starts to rise. You're a virgin, Ashlynne."

Ashlynne's whole body was one hot scarlet blush. The silence between them was charged with sexual tension, the very kind that Cord claimed made her edgy and nervous. Much to her annoyance, he was right. The way he was looking at her—his gaze sliding slowly over her body, lingering on her lips, her breasts, the long length of her legs—made her nervous and edgy, indeed. And excited. And aroused.

She fought against it, against him. "Don't try to confuse the issue!"

"And what issue is that?" Cord asked huskily. "I'm starting to get confused myself."

Even his voice held seductive power over her. She was determined to defuse that power and regain the upper hand. "That—I—I won't let you take Daisy from me!" The very thought of a custody fight galvanized her rage in the most effective way. "I'll do whatever it takes to keep her."

Cord reached out to cup her chin and tilted her head upward, forcing her to meet his gaze. "Do you really think I'd try to take a little girl away from the only mother she's ever known?"

His voice was calm now, which, oddly, made things all the more difficult for her. She could meet his fury and scorn with her own, multiplied a thousandfold, but she was at a loss against his equable reason. Not to mention his touch. His hand slid to her throat and his idly stroking fingers sent disturbing tremors through her. Ashlynne was acutely aware of his body heat and strength as he stood so closely to her, holding her by just one hand.

For a moment, she longed to sway forward and lean into the hard frame of his body. She'd been held in his arms before, pressed tight against that warm muscled strength that both beckoned and tempted her now. Her traitorous body ached to feel it again, to taste his mouth, hot and hungry . . .

An alarm bell seemed to sound in her head and she quickly pulled away from him. Her skin felt hot, as if his handprint had been burned into it like a brand. "I—I don't know what you're capable of doing! You drag me down here and make all kinds of accusations and demands! Who knows what you'll do next?"

"Yeah, who knows?" But Cord knew exactly what he was going to do. He couldn't stop himself.

Before Ashlynne had time to figure out his intentions, he acted, yanking her into his arms and covering her mouth in a hard kiss. She reacted wildly, struggling against him, but Cord had the element of surprise in his favor and wrapped his arms tightly around her, pinning her arms between them, rendering them useless as weapons against him.

When she tried to twist her head free, he wouldn't let her, keeping her mouth trapped beneath his own. She bucked and strained against him, but each movement only increased the seductive pressure of her breasts against the wall of his chest, of the burgeoning heat of his thighs against her own quivering limbs.

Within a few moments, she crossed the invisible line that separated anger from passion, or perhaps transformed it. Her movements were no longer inspired by the desire to fight him, only by desire. She was moving against him because it felt too wonderful not to.

With a sigh of surrender, Ashlynne finally let her emotions rule her. She relaxed in his arms, opening her mouth hungrily for the insistent thrust of his tongue and meeting it with her own. Her hands were freed now, but there was no thought of her using them to push him away. Instead, she wound her arms around his neck, smoothing her palms over his shoulders, his back, caressing him, savoring the strong, masculine feel of him.

He continued to kiss her deeply, possessively, his hands moving boldly over her soft curves. Her breasts swelled, the tiny hardened points pressing sensuously, and she rubbed them against his chest, seeking relief from the exquisite ache. Cord gripped her buttocks hard and lifted her, fitting her against the driving force of his masculinity. Instinctively, she began to rotate her hips in erotic rhythm. She was whimpering against his mouth and moist with need. All sense of time and place was abolished by the stark emotional and sexual hunger raging through her.

Ashlynne writhed in his arms, consumed with the need to get closer. She couldn't get enough of him. She'd finally broken through all her self-imposed restraints and was experiencing the primitive, deeply feminine need to envelop a man, to absorb him into her very being.

Cord cupped the soft fullness of her breasts, finding her taut, aching nipples and caressing them. "Ashlynne." He lifted his mouth from her and groaned her name.

The sounds of young voices broke the sensually charged silence enshrouding them. A group of children were tramping through the grove, laughing and talking, enjoying a not-very-quiet game of hide-and-seek.

Cord and Ashlynne broke apart before they could be observed. Breathless and trembling, she gazed at him, frightened by her incendiary response to him. It was as if she were being conditioned to his touch. Each time he took her into his arms, she grew wilder and hungrier, totally governed by the passion he so easily roused in her. She shivered, her nerves tingling. No one had ever had such power over her.

Cord stared back at her, equally shaken. His dark eyes shifted from her flushed face to the tempting roundness of her breasts. He could still feel the shape and weight of them in his hands; he wanted to see them, to taste them . . .

A taut, unsated sexual tension pulsated between them.

"Let's get out of here," he said at last, his voice raspy and thick. "Just the two of us."

Ashlynne allowed herself to imagine the two of them alone in her apartment, kissing, touching, uninterrupted in complete privacy. She visualized herself lying on her bed, with Cord's long, lean body stretched out beside her . . .

It was as far as she dared to take her fantasy. She was a realist who knew that fantasies and reality had a nasty way of clashing. "No," she said firmly. "I won't go to bed with you."

"I feel like I'm going out of my mind." He was thwarted and frustrated and aching. And perilously close to pleading with her. "I don't think I've ever wanted a woman more than I want you, Ashlynne."

"You don't *think?*" she repeated sarcastically. "Don't you *know?*"

"Ashlynne, I'm trying to be honest with you. I'm thirty-four years old and I have wanted other women—"

"Oh, don't I know it! My sister was one of them."

He clutched his head. It was throbbing along with every one of his erogenous zones. "Talking about this is getting us nowhere," he said tersely. "There is only one solution, only one way to get past Rayleen and to keep Ethan Thorpe away, one way for me to be a part of my daughter's life and to—to meet my obligations to both her and you." He drew an uneasy breath and then simply blurted it out. "I— you—we have to get married, Ashlynne."

She stared at him, dumbstruck.

He stared back at her, more than a little embarrassed. Impassioned declarations were not his style, and the one he'd just made certainly lacked any trace of finesse. But the words were out. And they were true enough. He wouldn't recall them, even if he could.

"The dreaded M-word. Marriage." He sounded both dazed and ironic. "I've avoided it for years. I've never been even remotely tempted to buy a ring and sample wedded bliss. It's as if I were waiting, as if some part of me knew . . . God, I used to make fun of Holly when she spouted all that nonsense about fate and destiny, but—"

A small reckless smile played about his mouth. "This does seem almost fated, doesn't it? I return from Montana and find you raising my child. Well, I'm through fighting it, Ashlynne. It's time for Daisy's daddy to be married to her mommy."

Ashlynne found her voice at last. "I think it's time for Daisy's daddy to be committed to a mental institution. Hmm, that's an M-word too."

Cord actually laughed. "An interesting response to the first marriage proposal I've ever made. But we are going to be married, Ashlynne. It's inevitable."

"Inevitable? No. Inevitable is when you eat undercooked meat and get sick. Marrying you is unthinkable."

"Why is that?" he demanded, his voice, his expression aggressive and resolute. He was all masculine pride and imperious Way, resenting her refusal.

"Do you have a few hours to spare while I list the reasons? Well, I don't, so I'll start and end with the number one reason why you and I should not get married. We don't love each other."

"Oh, that." Cord shrugged. "Don't tell me you really believe all that romantic nonsense about falling in love?"

"Maybe not." She glared at him. "But most people marry at least *thinking* they're in love."

"And you believe that gives them an edge?" Cord laughed. "They're deluding themselves, Ashlynne. Most people confuse sexual attraction and passion for love. We won't be foolish enough to make that mistake. We know the sex will be good, but we don't have all the expectations and disappointments of romantic love to muddy the waters."

She felt a sharp thrust of pain deep inside her. Hatred, she decided. Though she occasionally lost sight of the fact from time to time, she really did hate him. Especially right now. Her eyes flashed with it. "I've never heard anything so cynical and cold-blooded in my life!"

"I'm being honest, Ashlynne. If I were really cynical and cold-blooded, I'd spin some fairy tale about falling in love with you, all the while deliberately concealing my ulterior motives." He scowled. "Like Ethan Thorpe did to Holly."

She did not want to discuss Ethan Thorpe, a subject guaranteed to inflame any Way. "Since you're using reason to get me to agree to this harebrained scheme of yours, let me appeal to *your* reason, Cord. You're in an overemotional state today; you just found out you're a father. Most men have nine months to get used to the idea and then they're presented with a little baby. You got hit with the whole thing at once—and instead of a baby, you have a five-year-old. You're not thinking clearly."

"My mind is perfectly clear. *And* it's made up," he added firmly.

"Have you really thought about what this marriage would be like, Cord?" She rose to the challenge in his dark eyes. "You would acquire an instant family. Remember the scene at our apartment yesterday, remember the lunch and the zoo? That would be your life if you married me, Cord. Maxie and Daisy and Kendra and me, all the time."

Cord felt a creeping panic. She'd painted a daunting picture. Yesterday flashed to mind in a series of hair-raising vignettes. Maxie's brattiness. Daisy, withdrawn and disapproving. Kendra's teenage machinations, leading to God-knows-what. Ashlynne's coldness. Ashlynne, quarrelsome and hostile. His own guilt and anger, the suffocating feeling of being trapped.

Ashlynne watched him. He looked like a deer stunned by the glare of blinding headlights. "Could you really live that way, Cord? Every single day?" Any minute now, his brain would clear and he would run for his life. And out of hers. She was counting on that.

"Ashlynne!" The forceful and instantly recognizable voice of Ethan Thorpe echoed through the grove. "Ashlynne, are you here?"

The sound snapped Cord to attention. Ashlynne tensed, wishing she could run for her life. Ethan's timing was terrible, his appearance instantly bolstering Cord's flagging resolve. And now, she was about to be stuck in the middle of another skirmish in the Thorpe–Way war.

"Yes, Ethan. I'm over here," she said resignedly.

Ethan Thorpe was upon them, his steel-gray eyes taking in every detail, from the flushed, tousled Ashlynne to Cord's aggressive stance and challenging scowl.

"Leigh Harrison told me she saw Cord Way dragging a young woman down here," Ethan said briskly. "I knew from her description that it was you, Ashlynne."

Ashlynne could imagine the way Leigh Harrison, Ethan's irate spy, undoubtedly had described her. She shrugged slightly and tried to smile.

"Are you all right?" Ethan asked, in a manner so solicitous, it set Cord's teeth on edge.

"Of course she's all right," Cord answered for her. "She's with me. And I might as well tell you the news right now, Thorpe. Ashlynne and I are going to be married."

"Cord!" Ashlynne was horror-struck. "I didn't say that I would—"

"As your soon-to-be-former employer, Thorpe needs to begin searching for your replacement," Cord cut in, then turned to Thorpe. "Consider this announcement as Ashlynne's official notice of resignation."

Ethan ignored him. "I can see he's attempting to bully you, Ashlynne." His voice was warmly reassuring. "Don't worry, I intend to disregard everything he's said. You know your job with me is secure."

"She doesn't need her job with you," Cord snapped. He put his arm around Ashlynne, anchoring her to his side, his eyes, his tone, his actions fiercely possessive. "From now on, I will be supporting my—"

"He knows about Daisy, Ethan," Ashlynne inserted quickly, pulling away from him. "He's upset and—"

"I am not upset!" Cord cut in. "I'm thrilled that I have a child."

"So you know about your daughter?" Ethan was coldly amused. "Were you told or did you finally manage to figure it out on your own? I don't know what took you so long, Way. The child's resemblance to you and your sister is startling. I had no trouble working out her identity. But then, you weren't eager to acknowledge your paternity, were you?"

Thorpe's casual reference to Holly made him want to grab the man by the throat and strangle him. Cord thought of his talk with Holly that morning, remembered the way her eyes had filled with tears, the choked sadness of her voice as she described her five tumultuous years with this condescending creep. Cord's temper flared to flash point.

"I wish I'd've known about Daisy from the start, but I wasn't informed of the pregnancy or the birth. If I had been, I would have acknowledged her as my child and my role as her father. You can't make a similar claim, Thorpe. You knew about Holly's pregnancy, she told you herself. Your paternal response was to walk out on her. She was four months along in what turned out to be an ectopic pregnancy when she began to hemorrhage and was rushed to the hospital for surgery. The baby was a boy that Holly called Elliott."

Cord saw Ethan's face turn ashen and was momentarily ashamed for dealing that low blow. But only momentarily. Thorpe wasn't the only one with a bent for avenging his family. As Holly's older brother, emotionally decking the man who'd hurt her was marvelously satisfying revenge.

"No, I'm not lying," he added, before Ethan could think to hurl that charge. "Check the records at the university hospital back in Columbus yourself. Holly was a patient there. She was still recovering from the loss of your child when you showed up to savage her again. Yeah, you're a real role model of paternity, Thorpe."

Cord reached for Ashlynne's hand. "Let's go," he ordered. "We'll round up the kids and I'll take you home."

Ashlynne kept her hands at her sides. She glanced from Cord's unsmiling face to Ethan's shocked one. She had always considered her boss the epitome of formidable cool. Now he appeared devastated, as if a mask had been ripped from him, revealing the terrible anguish disguised beneath.

"I said we're leaving, Ashlynne!" Cord's voice boomed. "Do you want me to pick you up and carry you out of here?"

"Ethan, are you all right?" Ashlynne asked hesitantly. A moot question. He looked terrible.

Cord came toward her, clearly ready to make good on his threat.

"I can't leave Ethan like this!" she cried, ready to fend Cord off. "He's in shock!" Three years of loyalty kept her rooted at Ethan Thorpe's side. He had seen an intelligence and promise in her that nobody else had, he'd hired her and paid a top salary, had always treated her with courtesy and respect.

"You feel sorry for that—that sociopath?" Cord was outraged. He glared at the pair of them. "Fine. You tend to Thorpe's psychic wounds. I'm going to get my daughter!" He stalked off.

Was he threatening to take Daisy from her? Ashlynne uttered a cry, maternal instinct urging her to chase after Cord and claim Daisy.

"You'd better go get Daisy," Ethan said, as if reading her mind. "There's no telling what a self-righteous hothead like Cord Way will do."

"You'll be okay?"

"Of course." Color was returning to his pale cheeks, though his gray eyes glittered strangely. "Ashlynne, just one thing. Is what he said about Holly . . . true?"

"I don't know. It's the first I've heard of it. I—I guess you'll know for sure when you send for the hospital records." She had no doubts that he would do so.

"Yes, then I'll know." He used his plan-in-the-works voice but Ashlynne had no inclination to stick around and hear whatever he was plotting.

"I'll go get the children now." She hurried off, her heart pounding. Cord wouldn't simply grab Daisy and forcibly take her to OakWay, would he? She imagined Daisy's terror in such circumstances, and a sob rose in her throat.

Yesterday, she'd agonized over losing Maxie, today she faced the possibility of losing Daisy. She felt as if her life—the life she'd worked so hard to make for herself and the girls—were falling apart. It was exactly what she had feared when she'd heard that Cord Way was back in town. And there was nothing she could do to stop him.

CHAPTER FOURTEEN

CORD strode through the crowds, past the band playing a startlingly lively rendition of "Danny Boy" while Dan and Cindy Clarkston smiled and chatted and shook hands with prospective voters. They had definitely politicized this charity fund-raiser. Unfortunately, they did it so well.

He arrived back at the table where Wyatt was still scooping for a crowd of children who enthusiastically sculpted ice cream with their hands or used wide brushes to make ice-cream paintings.

Little Scotty Clarkston sat on Kendra's lap. Maxie bounced around the table chattering, sampling flavors of ice cream, and launching into spontaneous cartwheels. Daisy was busy at work on her picture, displaying a multiflavored impressionistic flair. She applied some whipped cream to a strategic area, studied it thoughtfully, and added much more. When the nozzle spluttered, she reached for another can, shaking it vigorously.

"Giving small children unrestrained use of whipping cream is on a par with giving them explosives," Wyatt remarked, catching his brother's eye. "Everyone in the immediate area should be evacuated."

Cord smiled, watching his daughter with pride. While the other kids zoomed around like Siamese cats on speed, Daisy worked diligently on her project.

"Our ice-cream shark won the prize, Uncle Cord!" shrieked Maxie, running up to him. "Then we ate him."

"What was the prize?" asked Cord.

"A blue ribbon," Daisy replied. She reached into the pocket of her shorts and pulled out a piece of royal-blue ribbon she had carefully folded. "First prize" was printed on it in gold letters. Cord was touched that she'd saved it.

"Yes, they won first prize with a shark that resembled a rainbow-colored submarine," Wyatt said dryly. "It definitely didn't hurt that Holly was one of the judges."

Cord stared at his brother, surrounded by ice-cream-stained kids, far removed from the frenetic campaigning/socializing being practiced by the Clarkstons. He looked happier than Cord had ever remembered seeing him.

"Wyatt threatened to drown Holly in a vat of hot fudge if she didn't declare our shark the winner," Kendra added, flashing Wyatt a teasing, unmistakably flirtatious look.

Wyatt gazed at her raptly. Kendra stuck her finger in a glob of melting chocolate ice cream and reached over to touch his nose. He wiped it off with a handkerchief, then leaned down and murmured something in her ear. The two of them shared a private laugh.

Cord watched them uneasily, relieved that Ashlynne wasn't around to claim that her suspicions about them had been confirmed. He himself was beginning to worry that she might be right about Kendra and Wyatt. He had to talk to his brother, as soon as possible. Now?

Before he could make a move, they were suddenly in the midst of a media blitz. Revolving around the Clarkstons, of course.

"Oh, look, Cindy, there is your precious little Scotty!" The voice belonged to an elegantly dressed woman about Cindy Clarkston's age, who was leading the Clarkstons and a group of reporters, armed with still cameras and video cams, toward the table.

The crowd surged around them, knocking aside some of the children painting and sculpting at the table. Cord pulled Maxie safely out of the path of an oblivious member of the press.

"Scotty, you're going for a pony ride," Cindy said in a voice so cloyingly sweet that Cord feared for any diabetics within hearing distance.

"We're going to ride the pony and get our picture taken, Scotty," Dan added, smiling boyishly while his picture was snapped.

Scotty took one look at them and began to howl. "No! No!" he wailed, clutching Kendra around the neck and holding on for dear life.

The Clarkstons looked at all the interested reporters and other observers surrounding them. "Kids!" Dan said with a forced chuckle.

"I don't want to go with them!" Scotty howled, clinging to Kendra. "Let me stay with you. Please!"

A cameraman with a sadistic smile began to let the tape roll.

"Scotty, I wish you could but you have to go where your mother and father want you to go," Kendra told him gently.

"No, no!" Scotty was distraught. "I don't want to! I'm scared!"

"Stop it, Scott!" Cindy snapped. "You are not being given a choice, you are coming with us now!"

Scotty cried harder, as if his little heart were breaking. Kendra rocked him in her arms. "He gets very attached to his baby-sitters," she confided to a reporter who leaned down to listen to her. "He isn't comfortable with his parents because they're never around and when they are—"

A whole flock of people were listening now. Kendra gazed earnestly at them, a beautiful teenaged madonna consoling a pitiful little waif. "They threaten him," Kendra said with a masterful combination of sorrow and righteous indignation. "They told him they were going to lock him up alone in the car this afternoon, just because he was scared of all the crowds here."

"That's emotional abuse!" gasped the society reporter for *The Waysboro Weekly.*

"I think charges can be filed if an animal is locked in a car in hot weather," mused another reporter. "Wonder if that applies to kids too?"

"It ought to," Kendra said. Were her blue eyes filled with compassionate tears? "Poor little Scotty."

"I'm scared, I'm scared!" cried Scotty.

The group was mesmerized by her and the unfolding drama of the helpless child and his cruel parental tormentors.

Dan Clarkston tried to make a joke, but the crowd had turned against him. His attempt at humor seemed coldhearted and was met with hostile silence. Clutching sobbing little Scotty, Kendra had never looked sweeter. Cindy Clarkston's face grew redder. "Dan, do something!" she ordered frantically.

Dan, correctly gauging that he'd lost the crowd, did an about-face. "If Scotty doesn't want to ride a pony, he doesn't have to." His perpetual smile was still in place, though noticeably forced. "I don't blame him for wanting to stay with the pretty young lady. If he prefers women to horses, what red-blooded American male can blame him?"

"I will not be humiliated this way," Cindy hissed through clenched teeth. "You get him away from her this minute, dammit!" Though her orders were for her husband's ears only, Cord and other bystanders heard.

Dan looked mutinous for a moment, then leaned down and jerked Scotty from Kendra's arms. "Come on, son, we've had enough ice cream for the day."

Scotty kicked and screamed and called pitifully for Kendra as the Clarkstons hurriedly departed from the scene. Several members of the press followed them, others lingered around the table, gazing speculatively at Kendra.

"Is that man really Scotty's daddy or is he a stranger?" Daisy asked suspiciously, breaking the momentary silence following their departure.

There was a burst of cynical adult laughter. "It does make you wonder," remarked a feature writer for *The Exton Evening Post.*

"Scotty's mother said a bad word," Maxie piped up.

"Sweet Cindy actually cursed in front of little kids." One of the reporters grinned. "An interesting development."

"How come they were smiling when they were so mad?" a little boy wanted to know.

Another child performed a dead-on imitation of Dan Clarkston's phony, fixed smile. More laughter. A few reporters were still taking notes.

Wyatt and Kendra exchanged glances. She smiled at him, then turned her attention to the members of the press.

"At last. A crack in the picture-perfect family." Kendra's eyes narrowed to slits. "Danny Boy's smile is so phony that even little kids can see through it, and the Sweetheart of Central Maryland has no patience with her own child. She doesn't even seem to like him very much."

"First time there's been a chink in the armor," agreed a photographer. "I kept waiting for their dark side to emerge. Knew there had to be one."

"This guy here, Wyatt Way." Kendra pointed to Wyatt with her thumb. For the first time, the assembled members of the press noticed that the other candidate was present. "He doesn't flash those big grins but he's been around all afternoon scooping ice cream for all these kids. And none of them are even his!"

She waited for that to sink in, then continued. "You should get a picture of Mr. Way with the kids and put it next to a picture of the Clarkstons terrorizing poor little Scotty." Kendra smiled invitingly at a reporter who couldn't seem to take his eyes off her. "That would be so cool."

"I—um—no pictures, please." Wyatt was embarrassed. "This is a charity event, not a political photo opportunity."

"Tell that to the Clarkstons," cracked one of the photographers.

"You've got the instincts of a real cutthroat media consultant, kid," an admiring photographer told Kendra. He began to snap pictures of Wyatt with the children.

The crowd finally dispersed and Wyatt sat down next to Kendra. "You couldn't have planned that awful scene with the Clarkstons," he murmured. He could not forget her rage at Dan Clarkston's veiled criticism of her sister and her fierce vow to "get him good." "But you certainly succeeded in paying him back in kind."

"In spades!" Kendra looked as satisfied as a blue-eyed cat who had just finished snacking on her prey. "My brother Shane says you have to play the hand you're dealt. I guess I'm getting pretty good at it," she added demurely.

"You certainly are. It won't be long before you're dealing your own hand."

Kendra stretched, her movements sultry and sensuous. "Josh said that too."

Wyatt watched her, entranced.

Cord watched the two of them, glad the press was gone. Wyatt had been dubbed the good guy of the day, but if any astute reporter had seen the way Wyatt looked at Kendra, the unmasked hunger in his eyes . . .

Cord didn't allow himself to think of the scandal that could ensue. He had enough on his mind already, keeping a watchful eye on Maxie and Daisy, and wondering what in the hell Ashlynne was doing with Ethan Thorpe all this time.

He regretted not heaving her over his shoulder and carrying her out of the grove, as he'd threatened. Ashlynne and Thorpe. The thought of the two of them together made him crazy. She'd punished him by choosing Thorpe's company over his, and all he could do was to stand here watching his daughter, knowing that he didn't dare make a move without her mother's consent. He'd never felt so powerless in his life.

He was seething when Ashlynne joined him a few minutes later.

"You're still here!" she cried breathlessly.

Where else would he be? Cord thought sourly. Having been separated from his daughter for the past five years, he would hardly take off and leave her right after learning of her existence. It galled him that Ms. Monroe was flaunting his helplessness. "Yes, I'm still here."

Ashlynne drew a sharp breath that was closer to a sob. Cord looked at her more closely. She was shaking and on the verge of tears.

"What did Thorpe do to you?" he demanded. His dark eyes flashed with fury. "What did he say to you?"

"Ethan?" Ashlynne was confused. "Nothing."

"You were with him long enough," snapped Cord. "And he said nothing all that time?"

"I haven't been with Ethan, I left him right after you did. I've been running all over this place looking for the children. There was a crush of people, there were mobs chasing after the Clarkstons, and I couldn't get through or see anyone." This time a sob did escape. "I—I thought you'd left with Daisy."

"As if I would do that!" Cord glanced at her sharply. "Are you going to cry?"

"I—I—don't know." A tear seeped from the corner of her eye and she quickly brushed it away. Her defenses were down, her emotional state as volatile as the former Soviet Union. "I just know I—we can't go on this way, Cord. You've only known about Daisy a short while and already everything is different. The uncertainty is—it's too much, Cord. I can't handle not knowing when you're going to—if you will . . ."

Her voice trailed off. This was no time to become weepy and incoherent; she had to pull herself together and fight. But to her horror, she couldn't do it. The strain of the past two days was finally taking its toll, and the control she'd so rigidly maintained was being dissolved in a stream of hot tears.

Cord watched her. Astonishingly enough, she didn't seem to perceive that she held the winning hand and it was hers to play. Which meant another round and another chance for him to prevail!

"I agree with you, something has to give," he said coolly. She looked so young, so miserable and exhausted. She was completely vulnerable, and he was about to take full advantage. He was behaving like a rat of Thorpe-like proportions, Cord acknowledged, then pushed the guilt aside. Politics aside, there were certain situations when the end really did justify the means!

"We need to go to a place where we can work this out, where we won't be disturbed." He reached into his pocket and handed her a handkerchief to wipe her eyes. "Will you come with me?"

She nodded mutely. What choice did she have? He was calling all the shots now.

"Wyatt, can you drive Kendra and the children home when they're ready to leave?" Cord called to his brother. "I'm taking Ashlynne to your house. Uh, if it's okay with you," he thought to add.

"It's okay with us," Kendra replied eagerly.

Clearly bemused, Wyatt stared from Cord to Ashlynne, then tossed his brother the keys to his house. "Judge makes a beeline for the door the moment it's opened. Be careful not to let him escape," was all Wyatt said.

Cord took Ashlynne's arm. "Let's go." It was a command, not a suggestion.

"I have to say good-bye to the kids," Ashlynne protested as Cord increased the pressure on her arm in an attempt to lead her away.

"Right. The kids," Cord repeated. It was disconcerting to realize that in his haste to get Ashlynne alone, he hadn't remembered to say good-bye to his own daughter. Ashlynne never forgot the children, he noted, not even for a moment. As a parent, he had a long, long way to go.

They made their good-byes and Cord held out his hand for Ashlynne to take.

She didn't take it. "I agreed to go with you. You don't have to drag me along like a—a manacled criminal."

"I'm not going to manacle you. I simply want to walk to the car holding hands with my brand-new fiancée, Ashlynne."

She did not appreciate the teasing note in his voice. "I am not your fiancée. Why, you can't even say the word with a straight face!" Ashlynne stalked past him.

"If I'm smiling, it's because I'm relieved we've called a ceasefire in our war of nerves and we're going to come to a resolution." Cord caught up with her, and this time determinedly took her hand, his fingers fastening around hers.

" 'Ceasefire.' 'Resolution.' You use more doublespeak than a politician. With that talent, you're the one who should be running for office, not Wyatt." Ashlynne's heart was pounding, her thoughts swirled in a manic jumble. "Why not be honest and call it what it really is?"

"And that would be?"

"Blackmail. Sexual blackmail. You're taking me to your brother's place and if—if I go to bed with you, you won't threaten me with a custody suit."

Cord saw her pale and immediately came to a halt. "Before we take another step, I want you to know that I am not going to threaten you with a custody suit, Ashlynne. I told you I would never take a child away from her mother, but I guess you didn't believe me."

She shook her head. All those warning voices in her head—Rayleen's, Ethan's, her own!—made it impossible for her to dismiss the danger the powerful Ways presented in a family court hearing.

"Believe me, Ashlynne." It was an order. He gazed down at her, his intense dark eyes demanding her to trust his word. "I have no intention of taking Daisy from you. But I want to be a part of my daughter's life and I don't mean just as a support check mailed from Montana. I'm not some tomcat who casually fathers offspring and then goes off on my merry way, Ashlynne. Do you think I can forget about my child now that I finally know I have one?"

He scowled. "Given your low opinion of me, you probably do. So let me enlighten you, Ashlynne. I am not going to take Daisy but I'm not giving her up either."

He sounded so convincing. Ashlynne stared at him, searching his dark, dark eyes.

"Which brings us to your charge of sexual blackmail." Cord's tone was mocking, but the expression on his face was nothing less than dangerous. "Not only do I not rip little children from their mothers' arms, I also do not resort to sexual blackmail in my dealings with women. So if you think I'm taking you to Wyatt's place to have my wicked way with you, you're reading me all wrong."

He gave a short, cool laugh. "I said we needed to talk where we won't be continually interrupted. Wyatt's house is the only place I can think of that offers us that kind of privacy."

"Talk," Ashlynne repeated dubiously. The sickening fear of losing Daisy receded, to be replaced by a nerve-tingling tension rising in her and spreading from her toes to her fingertips until she was trembling with it.

"That strikes you as an alien concept?"

"Between you and me it is." Ashlynne blurted out. "If we're alone in your brother's house, we'll end up in bed and you know it!"

A slow smile spread from one corner of Cord's mouth to the other. "No, I didn't know that but you certainly seem convinced of it. Why, Ashlynne? Because you want me as much as I want you, and you know that unless some outside force intervenes, you won't stop me from making love to you?"

Ashlynne blushed scarlet, aghast at her own rash statement and his arrogant interpretation of it. "You—you're twisting everything I say!"

"What's to twist? You're the one who said if we're alone in Wyatt's house, we'll end up in bed." He laughed rather wickedly.

She seemed bogged down in verbal quicksand and everything she said to get herself out only caused her to sink deeper. "We will not!"

It was hardly the devastating comeback needed to put him firmly in his place, but whatever was lacking in originality was made up for in fierceness.

Cord merely shrugged. "You seem to be having some trouble making up your mind, Ashlynne."

"My mind is perfectly clear!"

"If you say so." He flashed a smile as irritating as any of Dan Clarkston's. "But I can assure you that nothing is going to happen unless you want it to happen. I'm not going to play games with a nervous little virgin who says no when she really means yes, please!"

Ashlynne was so incensed she didn't speak to him once during the half-hour drive to Wyatt's house.

Judge was pleased to see them. He retrieved an assortment of his doggy toys and dropped them at Ashlynne's feet, then rolled over on his back and gazed up at her adoringly.

"Is he always this welcoming to someone he's never met before?" Ashlynne asked, amused despite the nervousness that had overtaken her the moment she'd set foot inside the house. "What if I were a burglar?"

"Judge never quite got the hang of the watchdog routine." Cord patted the dog's big head. "His philosophy is more like 'my house is your house.'"

"And yours seems to be 'my brother's house is at my disposal.' You didn't ask Wyatt if we could come here, you told him we were."

His own high-handedness did not disturb Cord in the slightest. "Wyatt could've said no," he said reasonably.

Ashlynne tossed one of Judge's toys, a bright yellow rubber cat, and the dog scrambled to fetch it, delighted with the game. She and Judge played several rounds of toss-and-fetch while Cord watched.

He just stood there, his hands in his pockets, watching her, grinning as the dog jumped and leaped and ran for the toy in a frenzy of excitement. He was acting as if the sole reason he'd brought her here was to watch her play with Judge. Ashlynne, who'd initiated the game with the dog to cover a sudden attack of paralyzing shyness, kept on playing. She wasn't sure how to stop or what would happen if she did.

Judge was the one who finally made the decision to quit. After running and fetching his cat at least fifty times in a row, he dropped it at Ashlynne's feet, then ambled into the living room where he climbed up on the sofa. Ashlynne tried to entice him into another game by tossing a red ball his way, but Judge had had enough. He closed his big brown eyes and promptly dozed off.

"Poor Judge is down for the count." Cord's dark eyes gleamed. "Guess you wore him out."

"We were having fun," Ashlynne said defensively. The house was so very quiet. She glanced at her watch. "I—I really should be going home. Sunday evenings are always hectic. I have to make dinner and give the kids a bath and shampoo and get their things laid out for school tomorrow. I usually try to do some ironing and make up menus for the week and—"

"You're murder on a man's ego," Cord complained mildly. "Choosing that list of mundane chores over my scintillating company . . . Ouch!"

"I've never pandered to any man's ego and I'm not about to start now."

"I realize that." He smiled grimly. "Look, there is no sense in postponing this any longer. Why don't we have a glass of wine and—talk? You do agree that we have a lot to talk about?"

Ashlynne closed her eyes against his hard stare and shivered, even though she was burning with anxiety—and something else that she didn't dare acknowledge. "Yes, we do have to talk," she said stiffly.

"And I see no reason why we can't discuss our—er—situation like the two rational, mature, civilized adults we are," Cord continued. He handed her a glass of cool wine, which he'd poured from a bottle in the refrigerator and led the way into Wyatt's wood-paneled den.

He sat down in the middle of the dark brown leather sofa. A large octagonal-shaped coffee table separated the couch from the oversized recliner, halfway across the room. Sitting over there seemed as awkward as choosing the chair behind the big cherry desk in the corner. Ashlynne gingerly sat down on the edge of the couch.

She took several nervous gulps of wine, her fingers clenched tightly around the stem of the goblet. She felt as if a trap were closing on her. Worse, she was more curious than afraid, thus robbing her of the elemental instinct to escape.

Cord watched her every move. He couldn't remember ever being so aware of anyone. It was disconcerting to find her so fascinating when she was regarding him with the wary suspicion of a crime victim viewing an assailant in a police lineup.

He cleared his throat. "Have you thought about marrying me?" Might as well come straight to the point.

Her stomach lurched at the same moment her heart seemed to somersault in her chest, but the wild internal upheaval was nothing compared to the riot in her mind.

"Cord, it's . . . generous of you to offer but you know it just wouldn't work." Her hands were shaking. She drank some more wine to keep it from sloshing over the rim of the glass.

"Why wouldn't it work?" Cord demanded.

Strange, but the more she resisted, the more determined he was to prove her wrong. Reverse psychology? Whatever, his determination was now absolute. "We can make it work if we want to. You told me you don't believe in those falling-in-love fairy tales any more than I do," he reminded her.

"But how can we possibly make it work when we don't even have anything in common?" she cried. "And don't say we have Daisy and that's enough, because it isn't. Look how many marriages break up, regardless of the children involved."

"We have things in common," muttered Cord.

"Name two," she challenged. "Not that you'll be able to come up with even one."

He paused to think. "Passion!" he announced triumphantly. "I want you, Ashlynne. I can't stay away from you no matter how many times I vowed that I would. And you want me too. Every time I touch you, you show me how much."

"A marriage based on sex doesn't last! Anybody who's turned on a TV talk show knows that. Anyway, having two little kids and a teenager living with us wouldn't give us a whole lot of time for sex."

"Believe me, we'll find plenty of time," Cord promised. The glittering intent in his eyes immobilized her. "And I've just thought of something else we have in common. We both know how it feels to be on the outside. We've learned to cope and it's actually made us stronger. See, there are two things. If I keep thinking, I'll come up with more."

"Hopefully, none will be as preposterous as the notion of you and me as fellow misfits. A Way in Waysboro is not an outsider," Ashlynne assured him. "That's like saying the Pope is an outsider in the Vatican."

"I meant we're both outsiders in our families. Think about it, Ashlynne. It's true. You're the good-girl achiever in a notoriously—uh—underachieving family, and I'm the bad-boy disappointment in a distinguished corporate family. My own mother describes me as 'some kind of forest ranger out West,' which to her is akin to being an alien on a distant planet. Grandfather calls me 'the innkeeper' and is grateful that such a dim bulb is far away from Way company headquarters."

"You're not a dim bulb." She looked into his eyes and something intangible yet very strong flickered between them. "But you are definitely a bad boy." She hardly recognized that husky, flirtatious voice as her own.

"A reformed bad boy," Cord amended. "Don't go throwing my stint at the Waterside Bar in my face again."

Ashlynne felt his warm breath fan her cheek. His fingers were lightly stroking her hair. How had they come to be sitting so close? she wondered dizzily. She couldn't seem to remember him moving across the couch.

It seemed imperative to keep the conversation going. "If not for your stint at the Waterside Bar, we never would've met." He was so close she could feel the heat emanating from his hard frame. She breathed in his heady male scent and her thoughts grew even more scattered. "I—I think I've had too much wine," she murmured.

"No you haven't." He touched her cheek with his fingertips. "It's not the wine making you feel this way." Carefully, he removed the glass from her hand and set it on the table, then skimmed his knuckles along the smooth, firm line of her jaw.

"No," she agreed softly. Something swift and liquid and hot was surging through her, melting her. Paradoxically, she felt both languid and charged with energy at the same time.

Cord dropped one hand to her stomach and traced light concentric circles across it. "It's me, isn't it, Ashlynne? I make you feel . . ." His voice trailed off. No description of her breathless arousal was necessary.

Ashlynne gave a shaky nod. She couldn't have denied it, she didn't want to.

Cord continued his rhythmic caresses, tracing one wide circle to briefly brush the undersides of her breasts. On another, his fingers skimmed the tops of her thighs. A burning ember of desire flared deep inside the core of her and a piercing, glowing warmth spread through her body.

"Say yes, Ashlynne," Cord demanded softly. While still caressing her with one hand, his other hand curved around her nape, exerting a slow, inexorable pressure to draw her head closer to his.

"Say yes to what?" she murmured tremulously. His lips were almost touching hers, and his nearness obliterated her remaining vestige of resistance. She wanted him to kiss her so much she ached. Just one kiss. Where was the harm in that?

Her hands crept slowly to his shoulders and she felt the muscled strength beneath her fingers. Her breath caught as he touched his mouth to hers.

"To me," he whispered against her lips. "To everything."

The sexy rasp of his voice was an added stimulant to her already pulsing senses. She was swamped in a sea of sensation, sinking under each warm, seductive wave. Without a word, she moved fluidly against him.

His strong arms encircled her and her eyelids closed heavily over her passion-cloudy eyes. She opened her mouth eagerly to him and his tongue plunged into the moist warmth, probing and stroking, seeking the response she so willingly gave. Ashlynne clung to him as the kiss grew deeper and hotter, the first kiss blending into a second, then a third in ever-increasing intimacy.

Ashlynne's mind, always so disciplined and controlled, seemed to splinter and spin off, letting her body take over. And her body's impassioned urges were quite different from her mind's orderly agenda. Moaning, she arched against him in insistent invitation, exerting sensual demands all her own. Her breasts were swollen and aching, the tips pointed and throbbing. She wanted him to touch her there so much she almost took his hands and placed them there.

But she was too reserved, too sexually shy to make such a move. Instead, she whimpered a strangled little sound of frustration and arousal as his big hands continued to caress her with maddeningly slow precision, gliding over her waist and hips and around to her back, avoiding the very places that burned for his touch.

They fell back into the sofa cushions, his hips pressing against hers, letting her feel the hard strength of his masculine arousal. His mouth left hers to burn a trail of fiery kisses along the sensitive curve of her neck.

"I want to make love to you, Ashlynne," Cord said huskily. He was dazed by the force of his own passionate urgency and intensity. "Tell me that you want it too."

She gazed into his eyes. Oh, how she wanted him! All these years, she'd never had any trouble leading her chaste life. She'd never been tempted to sample sexual pleasure, not after watching Rayleen and numerous other Monroe women crash and burn from sampling too much.

But Cord Way had broken through her defenses to sexually awaken her. Now she had to deal with needs she hadn't known she possessed, with emotions that were both exhilarating—and scary.

Ashlynne gulped. "Part of me wants to," she confessed.

"This part," Cord said knowledgeably. He placed his hand over her heart. "And this part too." He expanded his fingers to cup her breast, his thumb seeking and finding the almost painfully sensitive nipple.

"And this part of you wants me," he added, sliding his hand slowly, tantalizingly to the apex of her thighs.

Gasping a little, she instinctively parted her legs and his fingers slipped lower, between them, to cup her possessively. He stroked her there, applying a deep, gentle pressure.

Ashlynne drew a deep, shuddering breath. She felt desirable, aroused, and so very feminine, lured into this swirling vortex of sensuality. "Cord." She whispered his name, her senses reeling. A searing heat radiated from where he was touching her to every nerve ending, making her whole body throb with a pulsating hunger.

"Is there still a part of you that is uncertain?" Cord asked hoarsely.

"Yes. No. I don't know." She sighed and pulled his head back down to hers, slipping her tongue into his mouth. She'd never felt less like talking in her whole life.

Cord pulled back a little. "I have to know that you're sure about this, Ashlynne." His primal instincts urged him to physically sweep away any lingering doubt she might have and possess her, here and now. She was so ready for him.

But he held back. This was not just an impulsive fling; he'd had enough of those to know the difference. There was so much at stake . . . "I don't want to blow this." He mumbled his thoughts aloud. "I don't want to rush you."

"You don't?" An exciting, most uncharacteristic wildness welled up in her. She felt daring, yet inexplicably safe at the same time. But she didn't bother to ponder the odd paradox. She didn't want to think, she didn't want to analyze. Instead, she stirred sensually in his arms, letting him feel her every soft curve press against him. "Then what are we doing here?"

He gave a soft laugh. "Maybe, just maybe, you want to be rushed." He stood up, taking both her hands and pulling her to her feet. "You can trust me, Ashlynne." Cord was suddenly serious. "I promise that you're safe with me."

Somehow she'd known that even before he'd said it, but his attempt to assure her touched her.

She took a tentative step toward him.

It was the sign Cord seemed to be waiting for. He scooped her up in his arms and strode from the room.

Ashlynne wrapped her arms around his neck and hung on, caught up in the novel experience of being carried. His arms were so strong, his chest broad and hard. He took long, swift strides through the hallway into a gray and blue-green bedroom.

Her eyes widened at the sight of the big bed. A gray and blue-green geometric-patterned quilt covered it along with piles of pillows in matching shams. "Is—is this Wyatt's bedroom?"

"This is his guest room. I've camped out here occasionally over the years, when I needed a break from OakWay. Back then, I resented the fact that Wyatt had been gifted with a house of his own while he was still in law school and only in town during breaks. Meanwhile, Grandfather and Stafford pulled out all stops to keep me from even *buying* a place for myself in town. I was not to be trusted and therefore must be kept under watch at OakWay." While Cord was talking he slipped her blue chambray shirt over her shoulders, then pulled her white T-shirt free from her belt.

"And being a Way, of course, you never considered renting an apartment," Ashlynne said dryly. "It was either buy a building or suffer living under supervision at the family mansion. Not that they supervised you very well," she added, recalling his activities back then.

"Ouch." Cord grinned. "I had that one coming, though. You're right, I never considered renting."

Before she could blink, he'd slipped the shirt over her head, then lowered her down onto the soft, thick comforter. He stared at her breasts, which filled the cups of her modest white bra. "I want to see you," he said huskily, reaching for the front clasp.

Ashlynne closed her eyes and a surge of hot color pinked her cheeks as he removed her bra, exposing her to him. But she made no attempts to stop him. She wanted him to see her, she admitted achingly to herself. She wanted him to touch her . . .

"Don't be afraid," Cord soothed. "Don't be embarrassed, Ashlynne. You're beautiful." He gazed at her raptly. "So beautiful. Soft and white here." He fondled her plump, rounded breasts, which were warm and full and aching for his touch.

"So tight and pink here." His thumbs caressed the taut nipples.

Ashlynne held her breath as his mouth replaced his hands on her breasts. She felt the moist warmth against her sensitive skin and cried out with pleasure. It was more wonderful than anything she could have imagined, so good she felt a shudder of fear. In Ashlynne's experience, nothing good ever came easy. And it was so easy to lie here and be pleasured by Cord's lips and hands and words.

"You're so sexy, baby." Cord began to kiss her again, her lips, her neck, then back to her breasts. "So strong and beautiful. Bright and sweet. I want you so much."

The rough passion in his voice affected her as potently as his caresses, like an inhibition-shattering aphrodisiac. She'd never felt so desirable, nor had she ever imagined herself feeling such desire for a man.

Her fingers fumbled with the buttons of his shirt, but he didn't rush her, waiting until she had finished the small task before he assisted her by shrugging out of the shirt. Shyly, tentatively, Ashlynne allowed herself to touch him, her excitement building at the contrasting feel of him.

She cast a quick glance at the burgeoning distension beneath his trousers but felt no fear. Just a deep feminine curiosity that made her lightly run her fingertips along the hard bulge.

Cord reacted as if she'd struck him with an electric prod. He gasped and jerked, pulling her hand away from him.

Ashlynne swallowed. "Did—I do something wrong?"

"Wrong?" Cord laughed weakly. "Not unless you think that almost shooting my control to hell is wrong." Still clutching her hand, he carried it to his mouth, kissing the center of her palm. "It's been a long, long time since I've gone off like a rocket when a woman touched me, Ashlynne. I don't want it to happen now. I don't want to be knocked out in the first round." He traced the shape of her mouth with his finger. "Let me rephrase that a bit more . . . romantically? I know this is your first time, Ashlynne, and I want to make it good for you. *I* want to be good for you."

He smiled wryly. "And while speed is of the essence in certain situations, this certainly isn't one of them."

His consideration warmed her. She hadn't known what to expect, but knowing that he cared about her own pleasure and comfort was a sweet gift. She stroked her hands over the broad expanse of his back, then daringly moved lower to explore the muscular tautness of his buttocks. A heady feminine thrill of power swept through her as he shuddered with desire.

His mouth closed hungrily over hers again, his tongue thrusting deeply inside to tease her with a tantalizing simulation. His lips were ardent, his hands firm and insistent, exciting her, making her respond to him with a demanding hunger of her own. Ashlynne clung to him, moving beneath him as she reveled in his satisfying masculine weight pressing her sensuously into the mattress.

She was hot, burning with a need she knew must be satisfied, and she twisted with an urgency she couldn't control. When Cord took off her jeans and divested himself of his clothes, she was relieved. Their clothing was annoying, restricting and confining.

When his big, warm hand slipped inside her white cotton panties, she obeyed the wanton urge to arch her hips and open her thighs to him. His long fingers brushed the thatch of downy curls. When he lightly touched the swollen, achy nub hidden within, she gasped his name.

Her eyes locked with his, and she felt the searing heat inside her grow even hotter. "Please," she whispered, not sure why or what she was pleading for. The words were as instinctive as her body's response to his erotic caresses.

Cord's eyes continued to hold hers as he stripped her panties from her with one deft movement. "Yes, sweetheart," he murmured, his voice deep and low. "I will please you."

His fingers stroked her warm, wet heat, gently finding the most exquisite pleasure points, evoking waves of radiant spiraling sensation. She panted and moaned and clamped her thighs around that provocative, masterful hand. She was dizzy as the pleasure intensified to a wild frenzy. It was too much; she tried to pull away from him.

"Don't fight it, honey. Let go," Cord urged her, his mouth against her ear, his hand continuing its wonderful wicked work. "Come for me, sweetheart. I want you to."

Ashlynne squeezed her eyes shut and surrendered herself to the tumultuous sweet fire. The remaining threads of her control dissolved and she exploded into ecstasy.

He didn't give her time to come down. While her body still pulsated intimately, she heard a drawer open and she languidly opened her eyes a slit to see him tearing open a foil packet.

Her eyes snapped open wide at the sight. The lovely, dreamy sensual mist lifted. Suddenly, she was painfully alert. "Your breaks from OakWay are for sex! You can't or won't bring a woman there, so you bring her here. That's why you keep a ready supply handy right in that drawer."

She admonished herself for being shocked. Cord was a practiced veteran in the world of adult sexuality and knew all the rules. Being a first-time, and rather late, entry into that world, she had much to learn.

She felt so very vulnerable. What was new and wondrous to her was simply another notch in the proverbial bedpost for Cord. Or, more literally, another packet from the box.

"I haven't used this bedroom in over six years, Ashlynne," Cord said quietly. "But I told you that I'm no tomcat who indiscriminately fathers children. My—my slipup with Rayleen was an aberration."

"Your slipup is Daisy." Ashlynne's eyes watered. "And I love her so much, it hurts to hear her referred to as—"

"I'm sorry. It was tactless of me." He sounded genuinely remorseful. "I—I'm proud to have a daughter like Daisy."

Ashlynne stared at him, her gaze lingering on his handsome face, his strong muscled body. She swiftly averted her eyes from the full, throbbing shaft that looked enormous and dangerous and not at all affected by this passion-killing detour their lovemaking had taken.

She swallowed hard. "Did you bring Rayleen here too?"

"No!" Cord shook his head. "I swear I didn't, Ashlynne."

"Then I guess it was the backseat of a car or a room down at good old Motel Six on the highway. Those were Rayleen's usual haunts," Ashlynne added bleakly.

"You are so different from her." Cord's voice was husky. "I wish—I wish I'd been smart enough or mature enough to have appreciated you back then, Ashlynne."

"You didn't know I was alive back then," Ashlynne said, her blue eyes wistful. "It's like that old song in my daddy's 45-record collection—something about 'I was just a kid who you wouldn't date'."

"Any records in that collection about stupid fools?"

"Plenty. They sung a lot about fools in those days."

"Well, I might've been too big a fool to date you back then, but I've wised up, Ashlynne. Now I'm going to marry you."

She arched her brows. "So you say."

"And I mean what I say." He glanced at the condom. "I was going to use this for your protection because I don't want to make you pregnant unless you want to be. But we're going to be married and if you want a baby right away, I'll get rid of this now."

"I—I've never had to consider pregnancy before," Ashlynne said, a little shakily. "Except Rayleen's, of course."

"You had no choice in either of those. This time you do."

"Thanks to you." She gulped. "I—hadn't given a thought to—"

"You weren't thinking at all." Cord smiled, his eyes gleaming, his gaze possessive.

She flushed and reached for the edge of the quilt to try to cover herself. "I'm not really up to listening to you joke about my—"

"I'm not joking." He gently pried the quilt from her hands. "I think I was bragging." He eased her back down on the mattress, leaning over her, his dark eyes intense. "You're so responsive, so passionate. Do you know how it made me feel to watch you come apart in my arms?"

She shook her head mutely.

"Like the sexiest, most powerful man alive," he whispered, brushing her lips softly with his. "You make me lose my head, Ashlynne. When I'm with you—"

"Don't," she cut in, draping her arms around his neck and gazing earnestly at him. "I don't want to hear that I'm the most exciting woman you've ever been with or any of the other well-meaning lies you think I need to hear."

"Ashlynne—"

"I've always dealt better with reality, Cord, you don't have to indulge me with romantic fantasy. What's real is that I know you want me right now." She moved beneath him, and his hard body supplied undeniable evidence of that. "And—and I want you."

How strange that he wanted to say things to her that he'd never said to any other woman—and she didn't want to hear them, wouldn't believe them even if he did. Cord felt frustration surge through him, and it wasn't strictly physical. He wanted to give and she wouldn't take. It was a most peculiar role reversal for him.

"You're making it very clear that you want me strictly for sex," he said, striving for a light note.

He instinctively knew that if he were to get intense and possessive and demand certain words and promises, she would bolt. And the reason he knew was because he had been in the position he'd put her in right now. A *most* peculiar role reversal. If he hadn't been so incredibly aroused, he would be totally flummoxed.

But nature took over, replacing painful analyses with a need so fierce, it could not be denied. He kissed her deeply, intimately, and she responded with an ardent urgency of her own.

"Considering the—um—rocky status of our relationship, I think we should postpone the chance for a baby," Ashlynne murmured, as she felt the hot, hard thrust of his manhood against her.

"I agree, except our relationship is not rocky, it's on solid ground. We're going to be married." His voice was slurred with passion. He was governed by a primal need to possess his woman and he did so, lifting her hips to accept him, surging into her slowly, inexorably, not stopping until he was deeply inside her.

Finally, locked together, they lay still while her body accommodated itself to the size and strength of his. "I hope I didn't hurt you too much," he said through gritted teeth. He'd never taken a virgin, not until now. He'd always considered a woman's virginity to be a burden he didn't care to assume.

But he liked the idea of being Ashlynne's first lover; he felt as old-fashioned and possessive as any Victorian bridegroom. And being tightly sheathed in her sweet, wet heat felt more wonderful than anything he could remember.

Ashlynne closed her eyes, feeling her body melt and flow like hot honey around his. He filled the aching void inside her in the most thrilling, satisfying way. "It's good, Cord," she breathed. She banished from her mind the sharp stab of pain she'd experienced as he had penetrated her. Why dwell on that when it felt so natural and so right to lie with him this way?

He began to move, slowly at first, and Ashlynne trembled as hot waves of pleasure rippled through her. His strokes grew deeper and longer and quickened in pace. She arched and clung to him, moaning her need, matching her movements to his and complementing his masculine rhythm with her own enticing feminine motion.

His desire, his need, spurred hers, and hers incited his. They were sublimely attuned to each other, united in an erotic intimacy that was both universal and distinctly their own.

Finally, their passion flared to flash point and burst into an intense, shattering climax, thrusting them both to the heights of rapture where they lingered blissfully before slowly drifting down into the warm seas of satisfaction.

Chapter Fifteen ─────

WORDS did not seem necessary as Ashlynne lay drowsy and sated in Cord's arms. A sweet, drugging lethargy claimed her as he petted her with long, lazy strokes, and she could not summon the strength to open her eyes. Her cheek was pillowed on his chest and his musky, masculine scent filled her nostrils.

She felt limp and languid, drifting in a sweet private world. A small sigh escaped from her throat.

Cord was instantly solicitous. "Are you all right?"

"I'm better than all right. I never knew I could feel so . . . relaxed." Ashlynne's eyes slitted open and met his. "I think that's the word I'm looking for."

Cord smiled. "There are more descriptive ones. 'Orgasmic' comes to mind." His dark-eyed gaze was so very intimate and possessive that she blushed.

"You don't have to be shy with me," Cord whispered, leaning down to kiss her lips with a reassuring tenderness. He heaved a deep sigh of contentment. "I wish we could stay here forever. Just lie here and fall asleep . . ." His voice trailed off and Ashlynne watched his eyelids close. His chest rose and fell beneath her head, his breathing deep and even.

She knew what he meant, how he was feeling. Right now, she felt closer to him than she'd ever felt to anyone. Cord was her lover, her first lover.

A glowing thrill coursed through her and her lips curved into a joyous smile. It had been so much more than she had ever dreamed of! How could she have imagined that anything could be so shatteringly intimate, such shared bliss?

The physical pleasure had been intense but there was much more. She had felt an intertwining of their very beings, a convergence of souls. He was her first lover and she knew that he would be her only lover, the only man she would ever . . . She drifted into a deep, exhausted sleep and almost immediately began to dream . . .

She was holding the infant Daisy, giving her a bottle of formula while the baby gazed up at her intently with her big dark eyes. Her daddy's eyes. Toddler Maxie played at her feet, tossing a ball and then running to fetch it, climbing onto the sofa to touch her baby sister, then scrambling off. Rayleen was combing her hair, talking and laughing as she watched herself in the mirror. She was wearing the high-cut skimpy hot-pink shorts and low-cut matching tank top that she'd worn to go boating with friends on the Seneca Creek River on the last day of her life.

"You finally get laid and now you get all mystical and believe that you and Cord are joined body and soul, heart and spirit!" Rayleen hooted with laughter. "That's priceless, Ashlynne! Exactly the kind of sappy sentiment I'd expect from you! But whatever you do, keep your girlish fantasies of from-here-to-eternity to yourself. Don't tell Cord! Sure, he had a good time in bed with you. He's a man and men love sex. He loved sex with me. And if he's eternally linked with anyone, it would be with me because of Daisy." Rayleen glanced at the baby as she headed out the door. "Thanks for taking care of the kids, Ashlynne. You're a good sister, the best."

Ashlynne felt a cold terror grip her. Those were the last words Rayleen had spoken before leaving for the accident. They'd been unusual at the time for Rayleen seldom expressed thanks or appreciation. She expected things to be done for her. The timing had haunted Ashlynne ever since. Surely Rayleen couldn't have known . . .

"Rayleen, wait!" Ashlynne tried to call her sister, tried to stop her from leaving the apartment, knowing that if she did, she would never return. But Rayleen left laughing. The phone began to ring and Ashlynne knew it was the police, telling them that there had been an accident and they were dragging the river for her sister's body.

"Hello?" Cord was jerked awake by the incessant ringing of the telephone. He had been sleeping so deeply he was still somewhat disoriented when he awoke.

It took his mind a few moments to assimilate the facts: he was in Wyatt's guest bedroom and Ashlynne was lying nude in his arms. She, too, had been startled awake. And the wary guardedness was back. She clutched the sheet to cover her nakedness and sat up, withdrawing from his arms. Cord knew the distance was more than physical; she was withdrawing emotionally from him as well.

Cursing softly, he found the phone, fumbling with it before finally answering it.

"Cord, I am so sorry to bother you." Mary Beth Macauley's voice sounded both shaken and apologetic. "I called OakWay and your grandfather gave me the number of some school where you were supposed to be, but your brother Wyatt said—"

"What's happened, Mary Beth?" Cord cut in, knowing that since she'd gone to so much trouble to track him down, something was very wrong, indeed.

"There's been a fire at the lodge," Mary Beth said and hastened to add, "Not too much damage, thank God. The firemen were terrific and put out the blaze before it really spread, but six rooms in the south wing have smoke and water damage and, of course, the room where the fire started is destroyed."

"How did it start?" Cord asked tersely.

"A guest was taking a nap, smoking in bed, and he fell asleep with the cigarette still lit. He's in the hospital with first-and second-degree burns and is damn lucky to be alive. The idiot!" Mary Beth's tone was scathing. "Fortunately, there were no other injuries but we had to temporarily evacuate the place and I—well, I knew you'd want to know."

"Yes, of course. Where are the guests now?"

"Back in their rooms. Everything else is business as usual. We were lucky that only three of the smoke-damaged rooms were occupied at the time. We've put those guests in other rooms and sent their clothing to the dry cleaners, on our tab, of course."

"Good. They will not be charged for their stay, make sure they know that. I'll take a plane out tonight." Cord hung up and took a deep breath. "Damn!"

"I—couldn't help but overhear your end of the conversation," Ashlynne said tentatively. Working for Ethan Thorpe had instilled an innate caution about phone calls. "You're leaving tonight?"

Cord nodded grimly. "There was a fire at the lodge. It sounds relatively minor, thank God, but I've got to get out there."

"Yes." Ashlynne slipped from the bed and snatched up her clothes, taking them into the bathroom and locking the door behind her.

Cord frowned. The timing couldn't be worse. He knew instinctively that the closeness they shared would no longer exist when he returned. Already it was beginning to dissipate, though he didn't know why. Perhaps Ashlynne had some virginal misgivings. He knew she was sexually shy, despite the wellstorm of passion within her; she needed him to be both reassuring and aggressive to break through her reserve.

He pulled on his clothes, then knocked lightly on the bathroom door. "Let me in, Ashlynne."

To his surprise, she opened the door at once. She was completely dressed and was attempting to tame her blond mane by pulling it back into a thick ponytail. "I—um—I can take the bus home. I know you want to get to OakWay and begin packing."

"I'll take you home," Cord said firmly, drawing her into his arms. She let him but stood stiff and tense and did not embrace him in return. Frustration lanced him. "Ashlynne, I wish I had time to cuddle you and tell you what you need to hear, but right now I've got an emergency situation and—"

"I don't expect anything from you!" Ashlynne exclaimed indignantly, pulling away from him. "You don't have to worry about wasting valuable time on me."

She was thankful that Rayleen had set her straight, even if only in a dream. Dispirited, she brushed past Cord, out of the bedroom. Even the phantom Rayleen knew more about men than her living, breathing sister. Judge appeared and followed her to the front door, nuzzling her hand with his cold, wet nose.

Cord took her arm and walked her to the car, his expression grim. "I do not consider time spent with you as wasted, Ashlynne," he said tightly. "And I am not going to leave you."

"You have to go, I understand that."

"Ashlynne, I am not hopping a plane to Montana leaving you here to build a wall against me so impenetrable that I'll never breach it. Not after—" he paused—"the gains we've made today."

"We went to bed," Ashlynne flared. "It's no big deal." There, she'd spared him her sappy sentiment! Rayleen would definitely approve.

But Cord didn't. "I'll ignore that since I know you're upset. When a twenty-six-year-old woman finally loses her virginity, it's a very big deal to her. Which is why I'm making allowances for your slightly hysterical behavior. And why I'm not leaving you behind to stew over whatever it is you're stewing over. I'm taking you with me, Ashlynne. You're coming to Glacier with me tonight."

"Have you lost your mind? I can't just up and go halfway across the country! I have a family and a job and—"

"We'll only be gone a few days. I fully intend to return to Waysboro to help some more with Wyatt's campaign, but if I should have to remain at the lodge longer, I'll arrange for you to fly back alone. We need this time together, Ashlynne."

"You sleep with me once and now you expect me to—to come running whenever you snap your fingers. To be at your beck and call, even if you're in Montana?"

She would not acknowledge the hopeless longing deep inside her, to go with Cord, to never be separated from him again. Oh, how Rayleen would laugh herself silly over that one! And Cord would either be appalled at her dependency or use it against her.

"You can have your own room at the lodge if you're nervous about having to satisfy my insatiable demands," Cord drawled. "Look on this as a free vacation."

"There is no such thing as a free vacation!"

"I thought that only applied to free lunches. Free vacations are an entirely different matter."

They were still arguing when they arrived at her apartment. That is, Ashlynne was arguing with Cord. While she insisted she could not possibly leave Waysboro, citing the children, Kendra, her job, et al, Cord merely reiterated calmly, "You're coming with me."

An eager Kendra greeted them at the door, her blue eyes sparkling with speculation as she gazed from her sister to Cord. Ashlynne immediately tried to enlist her opposition against Cord's preposterous plan. "You know I can't leave the kids, Kendra. It would be too much responsibility for you to have to take over completely. And I just can't not show up for work!"

Cord rebutted her every argument. "Kendra is more than capable of watching Maxie and Daisy for a few days. She can adjust her coffee shop schedule with Letty to fit the children's hours. And she can phone Thorpe and tell him you won't be in. If he doesn't like it—tough!" His eyes met Kendra's over the top of Ashlynne's head. He sensed an ally and gazed beseechingly at her.

Kendra smiled enigmatically. "Can I talk to you alone, Ash?" She took her older sister's arm and the two went back into their bedroom.

"You know you can trust me with the kids, Ashlynne. And you also know that Ethan Thorpe isn't going to fire you. Who else would put up with working for him? So what's the real reason you won't go with Cord? Are you scared of him? Did he do something to hurt you?"

"No!" Ashlynne cried. "And I'm not afraid of him, but I just can't go traipsing off—"

"I think you ought to be afraid of him," Kendra broke in, her blue eyes glittering. "You used to be, remember? You were scared to death he would take Daisy from us. Well, he still can, you know. Nothing's changed, he's still a Way and rich and we're still Monroes who couldn't afford a lawyer in a custody trial."

"He promised he wouldn't do that, Kendra," Ashlynne said nervously.

"Well, *I* certainly wouldn't want to cross him, not from the looks of him out there."

Ashlynne's eyes widened. "What do you mean?"

"I mean, he doesn't look like the kind of man you'd want to cross. He's really pissed, Ashlynne, maybe enough to try to take Daisy if you don't"—she paused and shrugged expressively—"do what he wants. That means going to Minnesota with him."

"Montana," Ashlynne corrected in a whisper.

Kendra joined Cord in the living room moments later. "Ashlynne's packing a suitcase," she announced. "She'll be ready to go in a few minutes."

Cord stared at her. "How did you ever talk her in to it?"

"It was easy." Kendra smiled. "I just told her you'd take her to court and get custody of Daisy if she didn't do what you wanted."

"And she believed you?" He groaned. "*Kendra!*"

Kendra was unrepentant. "I have my own reasons for wanting a little more freedom around here. Have a nice trip!"

They were on the plane en route to Salt Lake City, the first leg of their journey to Glacier, when Cord broached the subject of Kendra's scheme. "How many times do I have to tell you that I am not going to take Daisy from you?" he asked, laying his hand over hers. "Will you ever trust me enough to believe me?"

Ashlynne glanced down at his big tanned hand covering hers. The plane was darkened with small soft lights casting shadows throughout the cabin. Everything seemed unreal. It was as if she had passed from normal, everyday reality into some other zone where she was leading someone else's life. Someone whose lover was Cord Way, someone who was flying—first class yet!—to Montana, taking a break from all responsibilities for this unplanned and fully paid-for trip across the country.

"Kendra told me what she'd said to you." Cord lifted her hand to his lips and kissed her fingertips, one by one. "I wanted you with me, Ashlynne, but I didn't want you to feel threatened into coming."

"I—I don't think I did." Ashlynne swallowed. The aura of unreality swirled around her, enabling her to drop her guard. She gazed at him, her clear blue eyes troubled but earnest. "I think I used that threat as an excuse to come. Because even when Kendra was saying it, even while I was packing, I—I felt like you wouldn't do it. That sounds crazy, doesn't it?" She smiled slightly. "Maybe I've finally gone over the edge."

"You had to find a reason to give yourself permission to come with me." Cord leaned closer, his lips against her ear. "Because you wanted to be with me, Ashlynne. That doesn't sound crazy at all to me." He sounded extraordinarily pleased. There was a touch of pure male smugness in his tone too.

Ashlynne's cheeks pinked and she looked away from him, fixing her eyes on the seat ahead. She wondered if she'd said too much. Would it have been wiser to let him think he'd bullied her into taking this trip? He wanted her along for sex, that much was obvious. The blush on her cheeks spread throughout her whole body.

She thought of the things they had done only a few hours earlier, the intimate, impassioned, torrid, and downright carnal things they had done! Her body was still slightly sore, tingling in certain erogenous zones that now raced and pulsed with the erotic memories. And she wanted to experience it all again, she wanted him again, over and over.

She was shameless, she decided, and wondered why it didn't seem to matter so very much to her. Maybe it was because right now she was a different Ashlynne, high in the sky, hundreds of miles away from Waysboro where she struggled constantly to be a role model to the girls in a town that had already condemned them as trash. A town without pity. Her father had played that song so much she could never think of the lyrics and music without remembering the places where the old worn-out record had crackled and hissed.

This was the first time she'd left Waysboro since moving there all those years ago. It seemed the farther she got from the town, the more she began to feel like her old self—the spontaneous and brave "Army brat" who had traveled all over the world before being exiled to Planet Waysboro to live in shame and fear.

"I'd offer a penny for your thoughts but the expression on your face tells me they're worth a helluva lot more than that." Cord smiled at her. "I hope you're not having second thoughts about coming with me."

He lifted the armrest between them and put his arm around her shoulders, pulling her close to him. Ashlynne rested her head on his shoulder, and he laid his other hand in her lap. She felt surrounded by him, protected and safe.

She closed her eyes. It felt so wonderful to be held this way, to feel the strength of his arms around her, to lie against his muscled warmth, as if she belonged there. As if she belonged to him. Which she did, Ashlynne acknowledged achingly. But she didn't dare tell him that. She must keep her girlish from-here-to-eternity fantasies to herself.

She knew Cord did not feel that he belonged to her. She was raising his child and she'd gone to bed with him. Obligation and sexual desire, that was what he felt toward her.

"I've already had second thoughts, I'm on at least twenty-second thoughts by now," she said lightly.

"I'm glad you're here," Cord murmured, raising his hand to cup her chin. He lifted her face to his.

She saw the hunger in his dark eyes as he looked at her and it made her pulse beat faster and her mouth go dry. She thought about making love with him again and knew that if he asked her to share his bedroom at the lodge, she was not going to demand a room of her own.

He kissed her bottom lip, then the upper one, and the tip of his tongue traced along the sensual curve of her mouth. Ashlynne leaned into him, her arms going around his neck to pull his head closer and deepen the kiss. She acted without thinking, responding only to her hungry need to kiss him and dismissing every other thought and concern. Desire flooded her and she clutched him, trembling with the force of it.

When they finally broke apart, they gazed at each other, their eyes dilated with passion, their lips moist and slightly swollen. "We'd better stop or you're likely to find yourself an official member of the mile-high club," Cord said raspily.

She'd heard of that; it was a staple in soap operas, movies, and even sitcoms. But she was not yet ready to join. "I think we should try to get some rest," she said huskily. "We have a long trip ahead and we didn't get much sleep last night."

"Last night seems like a million years ago," Cord murmured, leaning back in his seat. He reached for her, settling her comfortably in his arms again. "Twenty-four hours ago, we were in the police station, desperate for news of Maxie. And now we're here together." He found himself almost glad about the careless smoker who had caused the problems that were bringing him home to Montana. Because he was taking Ashlynne with him and, for the first time ever, he would have her completely to himself.

"Phone call for you, Kendra," Letty called, motioning the girl to the telephone in the back of the coffee shop. "Deep voice. Sounds like a guy," she added in a conspiratorial whisper.

Kendra took the receiver. "It is a guy," Wyatt confirmed. "I feel like I ought to be asking you to the prom or something."

"I don't do proms." Kendra smiled. "You're lucky you called when you did, I'll be leaving here soon. I'm waiting for Maxie and Daisy to be dropped off after soccer practice and then we're taking the bus home."

"They play soccer?"

"Those kids do everything. Ashlynne has them in this cool after-school day-care program, and there's a different activity every day of the week." She paused to breathe, then lowered her voice. "The kids and I are on our own for a few days. Ashlynne isn't in town, she went with your brother."

"Ashlynne is with Cord, and you're home alone," Wyatt said slowly. "Except for the children, of course."

"Who go to bed by eight o'clock. I guess I have some long, boring nights ahead of me. Hope something good is on TV." She laughed wickedly.

Wyatt cleared his throat. "I have to give a speech in Exton tonight." He paused. "But I should be out of there

around ten. I—could be at your apartment by ten-thirty if—
uh—you feel like having company."

"I feel like having company," Kendra said sexily, her
tone giving tingling innuendo to that bland statement.

Wyatt caught his breath and held the phone tighter. "Then
I'll see you around ten-thirty tonight."

"Well, don't you look just like the cat who ate the canary
and polished off the cream," Letty observed as Kendra
sauntered back to the counter.

"Mmm-hmm," Kendra murmured enigmatically and
began to ladle soup into two bowls for the customers
in the booth by the window.

Cord spent part of the morning closeted in his office with
Mary Beth, going over insurance forms and police and fire
reports. "We may as well close the south wing while the
repairs are being made," he said, studying the reservation
and guest lists. "We're lucky this happened in May when
we weren't at full occupancy. We will be within a few
weeks, but with any luck the work will be done by then."

"Spoken like a man who has never faced the horrors of
redecorating." Mary Beth shook her head. "Not only do we
have to order new furniture, we also need new wallpaper
and rugs and bedspreads. All that takes time, especially
when—"

"We'll take whatever is in stock," Cord said firmly. "I'm
not going to mess around with special orders and color
schemes. For those seven rooms, we'll use neutral colors
that match with anything. Nothing hideous, mind you, but
we're going with what is immediately available, and that
includes furniture. I don't mind forgoing discounts and paying more in this instance, because right now time is money.
I'll drive into town and visit Bobby's shop today."

"You mean Roberto," Mary Beth corrected him, her eyes
twinkling. "He feels Roberto is a more fitting name for an
interior decorator than plain old Bobby."

Cord uttered a derisive hoot. "Bobby is Roberto, Jack is
Jacques. How come everybody is turning continental?"

"We all feel the need for change, now and again. Including you, Cord."

"Mary Beth, I promise you I am not going to begin calling myself Cordello or Cordolfo or Corday."

"Glad to hear it." Mary Beth laughed. "But I was talking about you getting married. That is certainly a change for a confirmed bachelor. And so sudden too! When you left here, as far as anyone knew, you were the most eligible man in the town of Glacier, with no plans for settling down. And now you're acquiring not only a wife but two little girls. An instant family."

Cord nodded. He'd introduced Ashlynne as his fiancée to Mary Beth this morning and mentioned that Ashlynne had two small daughters. He hadn't gotten around to adding that one of them was his. The time wasn't right to share that particular information.

He glanced at his watch. "I'm going to find Ashlynne now. I told her to have a look around the lodge while I was in my office."

"She seems like a very sweet young woman," Mary Beth said. "Very pretty too. I wish you much happiness, Cord."

"Thanks." He grinned. "Let's hope the KOA inspector shares your goodwill toward me."

"He's here?"

Cord nodded. "Apparently, he's been in the campground for the past three days. His name is Yoder."

"Mr. Yoder!" Mary Beth exclaimed in recognition. "A quiet, unassuming type."

"I'm meeting with him at one. I don't anticipate any problems, do you?"

"Not a one. While you show your bride-to-be around, I'll call the travel agent and go over the details for the M-E-D retreat. Jacques has promised them a full vegetarian menu that will put this place on the veggie circuit."

"Great." Cord heaved a mock groan. "Then we'll be invaded by granola bars clamoring to turn the area into yuppieville. Maybe we should tell Jack to serve mooseburgers."

He found Ashlynne standing outside on the wooden sun deck, gazing at the spectacular view of the valley and the towering mountains beyond. Maples, aspens, and giant pines framed the deep blue pond that seemed to blend into the vast, cloudless blue of the sky.

He came behind her and wrapped his arms around her waist, dropping a kiss on the side of her neck. Ashlynne didn't gasp or jump. Her usual hypervigilance was absent, she was feeling downright mellow. She tilted her neck to give him greater access and allowed herself to melt against him.

"I understand why they call it Big Sky country," she breathed, staring raptly at the scenery. "The sky seems immense, so much bigger and closer than back home. You feel as if you could almost reach up and touch it. It's so beautiful here, Cord. No wonder you didn't want to move back to Waysboro."

"I love it out here," Cord affirmed. "And you and the kids will too."

Ashlynne stiffened a little. She didn't want to spoil this peaceful moment with talk of the future, a future she wasn't yet sure would come to pass.

"The lodge is fabulous too," she said instead, placing her hands over Cord's. He laced his fingers with hers. "I was in the gift shop and the lady working there—"

"Donna." Cord supplied the name.

"Donna showed me all the T-shirts and sweatshirts with Great Northern designs. And the mountain-craft jewelry and baskets and wood carvings, the caps and adorable stuffed animals and Indian dolls. I'd like to buy everything in the shop!"

"We'll have to bring the kids back lots of souvenirs. And I'm going to take you in there and insist that you pick out some things for yourself too. Whatever you want."

"Uncle Cord is treating?" Ashlynne teased, remembering the tumultuous zoo gift-shop spree. It seemed almost funny, in retrospect.

"Definitely. And we'll have to bring something special back for Kendra, that little trickster who let you con yourself into coming with me."

"I wonder how they're all doing?" Ashlynne mused.

She was surprised that she wasn't overwhelmed with the grief of leaving them behind. She felt a little guilty that she wasn't. But she loved being alone with Cord, whether just standing here talking to him or having breakfast with him in the sunny breakfast room with its wall of windows or spending the night in his bed, as she'd done last night. As she was going to do tonight . . .

Desire sliced through her, sharp and hot and delicious. She turned in his arms and pressed herself closer to Cord. He responded at once, tightening his grip on her and taking her mouth, deepening the kiss into soaring intimacy.

"Do you want to go back to the room?" he asked huskily. "I have two hours before I meet with the KOA inspector and get his report, then I have a meeting with the fire marshal." He smiled into her eyes. "I don't think I can wait that long to be alone with you."

"I can't wait either," Ashlynne said, wriggling provocatively against him. She felt sensual, she felt free. "Let's put those two free hours to good use."

Ashlynne was with Cord constantly for the next three days. They slept together, they ate together, they played together. He acted as her own personal tour guide around Glacier, taking her to ride the high-speed quad chair lift to the top of the grassy mountain, which in winter was a snow-covered skiers' paradise. They took a half-day whitewater rafting trip, which was thrilling as the raft raced along the water, wild and high due to the spring runoff of melted snow. They moved so fast, bouncing over the rapids, that the acres of wildflowers seemed to fly by. She watched the wild white water in fascination, keeping her eyes on the speeding, splashing current, and forgot to look for the wildlife that populated the surrounding forest.

"Next time you'll see elk and bear and mountain goats," Cord promised. "We'll go in the late summer when the water is calm and the raft floats down the river instead of flying like a stunt plane. We'll bring the kids along, they'll love it."

He talked about her return and their marriage as if the license were already signed, sealed, and delivered. Ashlynne knew it wasn't. A different side of her had emerged here in Glacier—relaxed, sexy, and fun-loving—but every evening when she talked to Kendra, Maxie, and Daisy on the telephone, she was reminded that this new Ashlynne didn't fit into their world. The real world, where she had to live when she left this fantasy she was living here with Cord in Montana.

Cord wanted her with him, and even kept her by his side as he worked. She accompanied him on his tours of the kitchen and watched him convince Jack the chef to take off three months during the off season next year so they could come up with a temporary replacement. She secretly chuckled as she watched Jack's discomfiture. It seemed he was quite possessive of the lodge kitchen—"his kitchen"—and did not care for the idea of turning it over to another. She wondered if he would decide against being Jacques after all, with the specter of another chef ready and waiting eagerly to replace him. She congratulated Cord on his handling of the situation. He had been tactful and unthreatening yet made his point, quite different tactics from Ethan's bludgeoning ones.

She also went with Cord to the newly named Roberto's House of Interior Design, where she picked out curtains, rugs, and wallpaper for the seven damaged rooms. Roberto admiringly told her that she'd chosen the best of the immediately available stock and complimented her on her taste, which he claimed was simpatico with his own. He was less pleased with Cord, who called him Bobby and bluntly rejected his more avant-garde decorating ideas.

She enjoyed her tour of the offices in the lodge and listened avidly as Cord explained the workings of the place. It was fascinating to see him in his role as head of the Glacier resort. He was not the rich rebel she'd known during his Rayleen interlude or the aristocratic Way scion she knew from his return to Waysboro. He was a different man, a hardworking one, a man she could respect. A man she could love.

She didn't let herself dwell on that because Cord never mentioned the word "love" to her, not even in the most heated and intimate moments. And there were plenty of them during this Western idyll. As Ashlynne lay in his arms, deliciously languid and replete from making love, she wondered how she was going to be able to fall asleep when Cord wasn't in bed with her. She pictured waking up alone in her small bed back in Waysboro and flinched with the pain of loss. It was almost as if they were honeymooning here, a couple beginning their life together.

Except they weren't. They would return to their separate beds and separate residences and separate lives as soon as they returned to Waysboro.

It ended all too soon. On her fourth evening away from home, Maxie wailed piteously over the telephone because she missed her mommy so much, and Daisy kept asking plaintively, "When are you coming home, Mommy?" Only Kendra encouraged her to "stay as long as you want, things are great here," although she did concede that "the kids miss you like crazy."

"I have to go home," Ashlynne told Cord after the call. "The kids miss me, they need me." She missed them, too, of course, but felt a sharp pang of guilt that she ought to miss them more. That she shouldn't feel so sad because her time alone with Cord had to come to an end.

The guilt intensified when she thought of how Rayleen had left the children in her care to run off with her man of the moment. Hadn't she done the same thing? She'd dumped the kids on Kendra to fly out to Montana and have a perfectly wonderful time with Cord, *her* man of the moment.

"Just stay till the end of the week and we'll fly out on Sunday," Cord coaxed, reaching for her.

"I can't! I have to leave tomorrow. I told Maxie and Daisy I'd be home to tuck them in bed tomorrow night." She moved away from him, out of his reach. He was frowning at her, and she was shocked at how much his disapproval upset her. It wasn't so long ago that she'd actively encouraged his hostility! Not anymore. She was in love with him and his displeasure with her hurt.

She loved him. Ashlynne finally admitted the truth to herself. She was not only Maxie and Daisy's mom and Kendra's big sister, she was also a woman in love. With Cord Way. Who'd offered to marry her but didn't love her.

He had already gone on the record as believing love to be romantic nonsense, the stuff of fairy tales.

He thought good sex and a sense of responsibility could sustain a marriage, that love played no part. Ashlynne knew he was wrong but how to tell him? Rayleen had always considered her beliefs on love and marriage to be comical; Ashlynne was certain that Cord would too. He'd already admitted that he and Rayleen had had a good laugh over her naïve romantic ideals six years ago.

Ashlynne's face burned. She wasn't about to set herself up as his comic foil this time around. And she couldn't face a loveless marriage, not even with Cord. Especially not with Cord.

Cord stared at the mutinous set of her jaw and knew that extending their stay was a lost cause. That mulish expression of hers meant that no earthly force could change her mind—and probably an unearthly one would strike out too. Ashlynne could be maddeningly stubborn; he might as well call the desk and ask the clerk to make the airline reservations.

He did not want to return to Waysboro. Being back here, he felt truly himself again, working and planning and running the lodge and campground. He had a purpose here, something he'd always seemed to lack as the Ways' second-born son.

"You don't have to come back with me," Ashlynne said softly. She was watching him, her light blue eyes shimmering with unshed tears. "Why don't you stay? Your family can carry on Wyatt's campaign without you."

Cord had been considering that very course, booking Ashlynne on a flight out tomorrow but postponing his own departure. He'd already convinced himself that Wyatt's campaign could proceed without him; there were plenty of other Ways around to help. But hearing Ashlynne urge him to stay irked him.

"And you can manage without me just as easily, can't you, Ashlynne?" The acknowledgment stung. He wanted her to need him, to demand that he come back with her. That realization was even more disturbing.

"I was just trying to point out that—that you're free to do whatever you want." Ashlynne gulped. Instead of looking relieved, Cord was glowering.

"We're engaged. That does not spell freedom to me, Ashlynne."

She understood his anger now. He felt trapped. "We're not really engaged," she said quickly. "We're still . . . thinking about it."

"Maybe you are, but as far as I'm concerned, we *are* engaged and we're getting married, dammit! And I am going back to Waysboro with you tomorrow, so stop trying to talk me out of it."

CHAPTER SIXTEEN ────────────

THE phone was ringing when Ashlynne arrived at the office Monday morning. Ethan's inner office had been completely renovated in record time by a highly paid crew. There was not a single remaining sign of Holly Way's rampage of revenge.

Ashlynne spent the next hour fielding a barrage of calls, each labeled "urgent" by the testy, impatient voices on the other end of the line. The messages they left were terse and obscure, and when Ethan still hadn't arrived by mid-morning, she guessed that something must be quite wrong. Not a particularly difficult assumption to make. Ethan's life seemed filled with the potential for wrongdoing.

It was nearly noon when Thorpe came careening into the office like a rabid dog. All that was missing was the foam around his mouth. Ashlynne eyed him with trepidation as she handed over the stack of phone messages. "You're supposed to get back to each and every one of these callers—at least two hours ago." She tried to make a small joke.

Ethan did not crack a smile. "I wasn't sure if you would be coming in today, given your abrupt leave of absence last week. I had a different temp in here every day, each one more stupid than the last. I didn't even bother calling for one today." He glared at her. "Since you deigned to show up this morning, shall I assume that you haven't yet given your erstwhile lover an answer to his proposal?" His icy tone left no doubt as to his low opinion of said erstwhile lover or the proposal.

Ashlynne, who was still mulling over that proposal and therefore still needed to be gainfully employed, ignored his sarcasm. "I bet you never got around to picking up your chocolate donuts from Letty's," she said with determined perkiness, noticing the telltale lack of bag. "Would you like me to run up there and get you some?"

"I've been gulping antacids for a week and you expect my stomach to handle those grease-laden gobs of fat?" Ethan glared at her, as if she'd just confessed to trying to poison him. "Do you know where I've been all morning?"

"At the hospital?" she guessed. Had his longtime donut habit finally wreaked havoc on his gastrointestinal system?

"No!" He did not add "you imbecile" but his tone and his furious gray eyes certainly implied it. "Let me describe to you in detail just what kind of a chaotic morning I've had. First, there was a meeting at *The Exton Evening Post*. I'd been tipped off to a negative article about Dan, complete with an unflattering series of pictures, that those jackals planned to run in this evening's moronic Lifestyle section."

Ashlynne recalled her boss's usual raves for *The Exton Evening Post* and their favorable-to-the-point-of-fawning coverage of the Clarkstons. The staff he had formerly praised as "astute" and "insightful" had now been reduced to moronic jackals?

She stared at him inquisitively.

"Don't play dumb with me, Ashlynne." Ethan glowered accusingly at her. "You know damn well what a disaster that goddamn ice-cream benefit last week turned out to be. I've been doing damage control all last week while you played cowgirl out West. Maybe that's why you felt the sudden urge to get out of town? Because you know your conniving little sister was the one who lit the fuse that blew Dan's temper!"

"Kendra?"

"Yes, cunning little Kendra." Ethan snapped. "She sabotaged Dan and Cindy as neatly as a submarine torpedoes its target."

"But how?" Ashlynne was baffled. Kendra hadn't mentioned a thing about sabotage or the Clarkstons during any of their phone calls last week, nor had she said anything since Ashlynne's return.

"You know exactly what Kendra did to the Clarkstons!

What I want to know is why she did it. Did the Ways put her up to it? A few days ago the *Post* had a nauseating photo of Wyatt Way playing Good Humor Man to a group of children at the benefit. Did his campaign staff—"

"I truly don't know what you're talking about," Ashlynne cut in boldly. When her little sister's honor was at stake, she wasn't afraid to take on anyone, including the snarling Ethan Thorpe. "But I do know that Kendra would not allow herself to be used by anyone. What she does, she does for her own reasons."

"Then kindly explain her reasons for inciting that little brat Scott Clarkston to humiliate his parents in full view of the county-wide media!"

From his outraged rantings, Ashlynne eventually pieced together what had happened among Kendra, little Scotty, and his parents at last week's Ice Cream Olympics. In full view of the county-wide media.

"Kendra loves children and was concerned for Scotty." Ashlynne defended her sister. "We all saw how abysmally the Clarkstons treated poor little Scotty that afternoon in the parking lot. They were going to lock him up alone in their car!"

"They wouldn't have done that," muttered Ethan. "They were just letting off steam. But that spoiled brat of theirs takes full advantage of the tension between Dan and Cindy and plays it for all it's worth. After that scene with Kendra, when they carried him off screaming, both Dan and Cindy were so guilt-ridden they made separate trips to Toys 'R' Us and spent four hundred bucks on toys and video games. The little monster made out like a bandit. Too bad he didn't cut Kendra in on a piece of the action. But then, maybe he did. Maybe she's in collusion with that nanny of theirs who actually seems to encourage his tantrums."

"Ethan, little Scotty is not quite five years old! No child that young is devious enough to—"

"You don't know the kid or his parents as well as I do," Ethan interrupted, with a contemptuous glare at her. "When I tapped Dan to run for the nomination last fall, I thought I had made a sound investment, but it turns out I might as well have backed—well—one of the Monroes!"

Ashlynne's eyes widened. Ethan had never trashed her relatives so unsubtly. She knew he was high in the stratospheres of rage to do so now.

"I thought the Clarkstons were perfect." Curiosity edged her anger aside. "What happened?"

She wasn't sure if it was arrogance or anger that prompted the usually closemouthed Thorpe to spill, but talk he did.

"Cindy is furious she had to give up her career as a real-estate agent, which she did when Dan began his run for office last fall. She was in the agency's multimillion-dollar selling circle—you know, a real competitive barracuda— the kind we could *not* have as the wife of the candidate who was peddling the 'old-fashioned family togetherness' spiel. Even worse, Cindy was the major breadwinner in the family, and since she isn't bringing in big bucks like she used to, the Clarkstons are now having financial problems."

"Dan should've thought of that before he made her quit her job," Ashlynne murmured.

"As if Dan Clarkston has the balls to stand up to Cindy, let alone make his edict stick!" Ethan laughed unpleasantly. "*I* was the one who made her quit. We needed a stay-at-home wife and mother for Dan's image as Mr. Family Man. I found it an effective contrast to Wyatt Way's self-centered, shallow bachelorhood. And Cindy is an excellent campaigner. I wanted her available whenever we needed her for public appearances."

"And Cindy agreed to do what you told her?" Ashlynne was awed. "She quit her job because you said she had to?"

"Of course. The woman is a barracuda but she's not stupid," Ethan said darkly.

"And how does conniving little Scotty fit into the picture?" Ashlynne dared to ask. The World According to Ethan Thorpe was a strange place, indeed.

"Let me explain it all to you," he said with condescending patience. "Cindy loved her career and hasn't exactly—well, flourished in the full-time wife-and-mother role, not that she is exactly that what with the demands of the campaign. The nanny has always done most of the child care in that house, but Cindy and the kids didn't seem to mind—until now.

Since last fall, Cindy has turned into a frustrated shrew, flying off the handle with the children, with Dan, with everyone. Dan is still floundering, trying to sidestep her as if she were a minefield, but manipulative little Scotty figured out how to turn the situation to his advantage. Pit the parents against the nanny. His poor-little-lost-boy act works like a charm every time."

"Maybe it's not an act. He sounds like a mixed-up little boy," Ashlynne said thoughtfully. "It's too bad Cindy didn't keep her job. It certainly wouldn't've hurt Dan politically; there's nothing wrong with a woman working, especially in these times. If she had, the Clarkstons wouldn't be having money and marriage problems, their children wouldn't be screwed up, and—"

"If, if, if. There is nothing more useless than Monday-morning quarterbacking," Ethan interjected, annoyed.

Considering it was Ethan's decree that Cindy quit her job that had plunged the Clarkstons into dysfunctional familyhood, Ashlynne decided not to comment further. The facts spoke for themselves.

"I convinced the *Post* not to run those pictures or anything else negative about the Clarkstons," Ethan said in a tone that made Ashlynne shiver.

Not for the first time, she wondered at his methods of persuading others to do his bidding. Did he make them certain godfather-style offers they couldn't refuse?

"Which brings me to my second meeting of the morning, which was a complete waste of time." He sneered. "I met with those battle-axes from the Safe Haven Home for the domestically beat-up. They drove in from Chilton at my request."

Ashlynne cringed at his flippancy. His scorn spoke volumes.

"They'd already begun to hound Dan Clarkston for the ten thousand dollars offered as a reward for information on your daughter Maxie," Ethan exclaimed indignantly. "Imagine the nerve of those broads! Claiming a reward for their own incompetence! They were the ones responsible for taking the kid, they harbored her all those hours. It was all their fault and now they expect to be paid?" Thorpe laughed at the very notion. "Dan was all in a dither so I told him I'd handle the situation personally. They left empty-handed and they will *not* be hounding us again."

Ashlynne gulped, mortified. "The reward money was promised and Maxie was found, thanks to their information," she pointed out quietly.

"I made the offer in good faith, Ashlynne," Ethan defended himself. "But that was when I thought Maxie had been kidnapped by some psycho. However, to expect me to pick up the tab for Cord Way's negligence—he let the kid wander off—and Safe Haven's incompetence—they carried her off and didn't even notice . . . Well, forget it. I am not one to be suckered."

"No, you aren't," Ashlynne agreed. When it came to suckering, Ethan Thorpe was the perpetrator, not the victim.

She thought of her indescribable relief at finding Maxie safe and well cared for at Safe Haven. It seemed Ethan would've found it preferable had the little girl been grabbed by some demented psychopath. At least he would've considered it worth paying for. She thought of the dilapidated but cheerful rooms in Safe Haven where abused and terrified women and their children were safely housed and cared for, and how much ten thousand dollars would mean to their already overextended budget.

She gazed at Ethan Thorpe, seeing him, really seeing him in a whole new light. What else could she have expected from a man who had walked out on his pregnant girlfriend, then self-righteously turned the facts around to favor himself? And having heard his scathing take on young Scotty Clarkston, she decided that Thorpe's baby had been lucky not to have been born. Empathy was certainly not his strong suit, and being a parent herself, she knew how very necessary it was.

Cord might not have had much experience with children but he was blessed with empathy and good instincts, and he would try his best to be a good father. But Cord Way as a husband, her husband . . .

Uncertainty mixed with pain streaked through her. Cord didn't love her. That thought was never far from her mind.

He thought falling in love was self-deceptive foolishness, but Ashlynne found herself wondering if it was the idea of falling in love with *her* that struck him as absurd.

"I can tell by the look in your eyes that you're in some other world, one where the Clarkstons and I are but minor players." Ethan sounded impatient but amused. "And Cord Way is your leading man. Terrible casting, I'd say, but then some would find my own choice of leading lady to be . . . questionable, in light of past events."

Ashlynne looked up to see Ethan Thorpe contemplating her. She was embarrassed by her transparency—and by the turn her thoughts had taken. She seemed unable to keep her mind from constantly conjuring up Cord.

At that moment, the door to the office opened, and a uniformed delivery boy from Wilshire's Florist entered, carrying a long white box. Ashlynne knew him, he was Randy Monroe, a cousin a year older than Kendra. The pair had sometimes played together as children. Randy was a cut above many of the Monroe teens. Though he'd dropped out of high school, he was working on a GED, and he held down a steady job at Wilshire's Florist.

"Mr. Ethan Thorpe?" Randy asked. He did not make eye contact and his voice was sullen and oddly pitched.

"This is Mr. Thorpe, Randy." Ashlynne spoke quickly and sharply. She was too well versed in the nuances of Monroe behavior not to recognize a potential problem. "What are you doing here?"

The younger Monroe cousins were scared of Ashlynne from force of habit. At the sight and sound of her, Randy's shoulders slumped and he lost the slight aura of menace Ashlynne had detected in him. "I don't know what I'm supposed to do now," he said nervously. Balancing the box, he reached into his pocket and pulled out a bill. "Look, Ashlynne, it's fifty dollars. A tip for me."

He glanced glumly from the box to Ethan. "Miss Holly Way gave it to me when I delivered these roses to her house. She gave me *fifty dollars* to take the roses and throw them right in Mr. Ethan Thorpe's face. But if I don't do it, do I still get to keep the tip?"

Ethan muttered a curse.

"You shouldn't throw the roses, Randy," Ashlynne assured her cousin. "Mr. Wilshire would be furious if his flowers were used as assault weapons. And I'm sure Ms. Way would want you to keep the tip. You did—uh—deliver her message loud and clear."

"Cool!" Randy smiled happily. "Hey, what do I do with the roses?"

"Take them back to OakWay," Ethan ordered at once. "Just leave them on the doorstep—with this message. Wait a moment while I write it." He scribbled something down on a piece of paper and slipped it into the box.

Randy continued to stand there expectantly. With an impatient huff, Ethan pulled a bill from his pocket and handed it to the boy. "It's not a fifty," he said caustically, before Randy had a chance to check the denomination.

"That's okay," Randy said, smiling affably. "I never got a fifty-dollar tip before today, anyway. Hell, I never even seen a fifty-dollar bill till today. Them Ways are cool."

"Them Ways are cool," Ethan repeated acidly as Randy left the office. Then his tone changed. "Are you going to accept Cord Way's proposal or simply hit him up for a monstrous sum of retroactive and ongoing child support?" Ethan asked suddenly.

She resented the question. The very idea of talking about Cord with Ethan offended her now. "I haven't decided what to do. But I definitely won't hit him up for money," she added coolly.

"Well, you should. He owes you and your daughter plenty of cold, hard cash." He smiled slyly. "Do you realize that if you do decide to marry him, you and I will be related, Ashlynne?"

Related to Ethan Thorpe? Ashlynne realized how very much she did not want to be. "How?" She wondered if she sounded as appalled as she felt.

"I intend to get Holly back," Ethan announced. "Now that I know she didn't betray me, I've decided to marry her."

Ashlynne felt real sympathy for Holly Way. Excluding the prison population, there might be worse husband material than Ethan, but at the moment she couldn't come up with any examples.

"I take it you got a copy of her hospital record," she murmured. Poor Holly! Being the object of Ethan Thorpe's romantic pursuit struck Ashlynne as unappealing as serving as a target for his revenge.

"It was faxed to me." For a moment, he looked genuinely unhappy. "I made a terrible mistake back then."

Ashlynne agreed with a silent nod.

Ethan's cool arrogance instantly returned. "I rarely make mistakes and I intend to make that one up to Holly. I know her very well and I also know how to win her back. So if you say yes to Cord Way—and I believe you will because you are too practical not to—you will be my sister-in-law."

Ashlynne tried hard not to look pained. She already had a host of people she wished she weren't related to. She did not care to include Ethan Thorpe among them.

"It is with our future relationship in mind that I'm not going to fire you," Ethan continued grandly. "You can continue to work here and draw your salary while you toy with Cord Way."

"You were going to fire me?"

He nodded. "I didn't appreciate your totally irresponsible jaunt to Montana, leaving me in the lurch. And I don't trust that devious little sister of yours. She deliberately set Dan up. I want you to warn her that I'm on to her tricks and I will—"

He didn't have the chance to voice his threat or warning or whatever he was promising. Cord entered the office, looking none too pleased.

"I didn't expect to find you here." Cord cast an accusing glance at Ashlynne. "When I called your apartment this morning, I expected to find you there."

She tensed. He was wearing a light gray suit and looked formal and aristocratic, the kind of handsome man-out-of-reach who should have never become her lover. Who wouldn't have unless the circumstances were extremely extenuating. Which, of course, they were.

His dark eyes were cold, his voice angry. It seemed almost impossible that he was the same man that she'd shared those long sensuous nights with, lying together, their bodies intimately joined, a cool mountain breeze blowing through the open window of their bedroom in the lodge. And it seemed like such a long time since she'd done so! Since their return on Friday afternoon, they hadn't made love once, due to the ever-present Daisy and Maxie.

"It's a Monday morning. Where else would I be, but at work?" she asked lightly. "I have to earn a living and support my family."

Ethan smiled. Cord scowled.

"You're going to marry me, Ashlynne." Cord's voice was hard, not the loverlike tone of a man addressing his wife-to-be. "There is no reason for you to be here."

"He sounds like one of those chauvinistic tyrants who doesn't approve of women working outside the home." Thorpe turned to Ashlynne, his gray eyes gleaming. "I think you're wise not to allow yourself to be bullied into anything you're unsure of, Ashlynne. Start as you mean to go on, for in the immortal words of Euripides, 'A bad beginning makes a bad ending.' "

"The perfect opening sentence for your life story, Thorpe." Cord tried hard to hang on to his temper. Having to hear Ethan Thorpe warn Ashlynne against being bullied after the way Thorpe had treated Holly was enough to drive a concerned older brother to the brink of homicide.

But forcing himself to maintain his cool gave his mind a chance to clear. And when it did, Cord realized that Ethan Thorpe was taking great pleasure in driving a wedge between him and Ashlynne and would continue to do so as long as they remained in his verbal range. He looked at the strained expression on Ashlynne's face. Her tension was all too apparent in her rigid posture.

He stifled a sigh. This was going all wrong. It was certainly not the way he'd planned to greet her, after another long, lonely night away from her. They hadn't made love since they'd left Montana and the weekend abstinence was taking its toll on his nerves!

"I didn't come here to argue," Cord said tightly. "Ashlynne, have you had lunch yet? And if not, may I take you out to eat?" He couldn't resist slanting Thorpe a disdainful glare. "I assume you permit your employees to take a lunch break? Or will you dock her pay for daring to leave the premises?"

Ethan actually laughed. Sparring with Cord Way had transformed his mood from ugly to downright jovial. "Go on to lunch, Ashlynne." He waved her away. "Hit him up for the most expensive place in town—that would be the Waysboro Hotel's Empire Room, I believe. And take a full hour. I have a lot of calls to return." He went into the inner office, closing the door behind him.

"Talk about being caught between a rock and a hard place," Ashlynne muttered, reaching for her purse. "I'm only going because the thought of staying with Ethan right now is worse than the idea of having lunch with you."

"How flattering," Cord said dryly. "But then, you did warn me that you don't make a practice of pandering to male egos."

He took her arm as they walked along the sidewalk. Ashlynne carefully removed it from his grasp. Cord sighed. "Okay, I won't push it. I guess I should consider myself lucky that this time you chose my company over Thorpe's."

"You should consider yourself arrogant and overbearing!" Ashlynne snapped. "Because that's how you were acting at the office."

"I plead guilty." Cord's mouth twisted into a rueful smile. "Blame it on Thorpe, he brings out the worst in me. I hate the guy."

"Well, you'd better get used to him," Ashlynne warned succinctly. "He intends to be your brother-in-law."

"What?"

"Ethan's decided to give Holly another chance with him. He kicked off his campaign this morning with a big box of long-stemmed red roses." She did not add that it had boomeranged.

"Holly won't take him back! She swore to me that she's through with him."

Ashlynne shrugged. "Rayleen always said that about Max Mathison, but I often wondered what she would've done if he'd decided that he wanted her back and then pulled out all stops to win her."

"The situations are nothing alike," Cord muttered. Would

he ever feel anything but miserably guilty at the mention of Rayleen? Mathison's shabby treatment of the girl naturally led to thoughts of his own fling with her. And of course, the results of that fling, his little daughter Daisy.

"Except for the fact that Max Mathison was married, the situations were not all that different," mused Ashlynne. "Both Ethan and Max deliberately ran out on their pregnant girlfriends, leaving them to face the consequences alone."

"Ethan Thorpe did a lot more than that to Holly, and his motives were vile and vengeful and—" Cord cut himself off, not bothering to elaborate further. "Can we change the subject? I'm tired of talking about the man."

Ashlynne held her head high and strode on.

Cord watched as she walked, slightly ahead of him and nearly an arm's length away. Her mass of thick blond hair was anchored with two tortoiseshell barrettes and fanned over her shoulders like a bright, glorious mane.

He had a sensual flashback to their nights together at the lodge, when he'd taken handfuls of that beautiful hair and buried his face in it, smelling the sweet, clean scent, caressing the soft silkiness with his lips. There was no question the pale blond color was natural and not from a bottle; the positive physical proof was the dark golden thatch between her thighs.

The provocative memories winded him and he tried to concentrate on other things: the bright "Congratulations, Graduates" display in the card-shop window as they passed, the travel posters heralding the excitement of a "trip of a lifetime to China."

But nothing captured his interest except Ashlynne. He turned his attention exclusively to her, his eyes riveted.

She moved fluidly, tall and slender with a natural grace. Her ivory-colored pleated skirt, though only a few modest inches above her knees, swirled sexily as she walked, giving him a tantalizing glance of her long, shapely thighs. He remembered the strong, smooth feel of those legs wrapped around him and heat jolted through him like a bolt of lightning. Her cotton blouse, demure and ironed to starched crispness, was a soft periwinkle blue that heightened the blueness of her eyes.

Perspiration beaded on his forehead. He felt himself becoming fully aroused, right in the middle of the square in downtown Waysboro!

Ashlynne reached Letty's Coffee Shop and started to push open the door. He caught her round the waist and steered her away. "I thought we'd have lunch at the Waysboro Hotel."

"Contrary to Ethan's advice, I don't intend to 'hit you up' for an expensive lunch in the Empire Room. The coffee shop is fine."

"Actually, I'd planned to go to the Waysboro Hotel even before Thorpe mentioned it." Cord fastened his hand around her elbow. "But I'm not particularly in the mood for the Empire Room either. I had room service in mind." Cord slanted her an assessing glance. "In fact, I've already reserved a room there."

A rosy blush stained her cheeks. Suddenly, she couldn't seem to catch her breath. To be alone with Cord again. Alone in a bedroom, her suddenly fevered mind amended. "Well, I—I—" She faltered, too weak to speak.

"I haven't been able to stop thinking about you, to stop wanting to be alone with you again, Ashlynne," Cord said huskily. "We had fun with the kids this weekend but I need time alone with you." He slid his hand down the length of her arm and linked his fingers with hers. "After I finally escaped from that tedious meeting with the campaign honchos this morning, I went to your apartment, planning to take you to the hotel for a very special lunch. I was so pumped up, it was a crashing letdown when you weren't there."

"So you barged into Ethan's office and started yelling at me."

There was an edge in her voice but it was more baiting than condemning. Cord's lips twitched. "Once again, guilty as charged. Am I forgiven?"

"Are you apologizing?"

This time he treated her to a roguish smile, his dark eyes alight with a teasing gleam. "I think I am. Do you think you'll accept?"

"I'll think about it." She smiled up at him.

Cord stared at her, blindsided by the pounding surge of hunger, desire, and need rising within him. Her alluring smile primed him for much, much more.

He had to have her again! And he knew he was going to, for she was willingly accompanying him to a room at the Waysboro Hotel. But he also knew that taking her to bed and satisfying his physical urges wasn't going to be enough for him. He wanted more than sex from her.

The realization struck him as forcefully as her irresistible smile. He wanted all that she was, all her warmth and loyalty, her strength and her humor and her temper too. He wanted her to confide in him, to need him.

He'd never had these feelings before. The thought of a woman depending on him and demanding his time and attention had previously filled him at best with alarm, at worst with horror. But a heady mix of pleasure and pride suffused him when he pictured Ashlynne doing the depending and the demanding.

Was he in love with her? Suddenly unnerved, he slanted a quick covert glance at her. They'd discussed love and dismissed it. He was not about to go sailing into those uncharted waters—*alone!*

Ashlynne wanted him sexually, he knew that. For now that would have to be enough.

He led her through the hotel lobby to the old-fashioned elevator that, unlike the self-service freight elevators, was still run by a uniformed operator who'd held the job for the past forty years.

"Hello there, honey." The white-haired bellman recognized Ashlynne from her days as the night clerk. "Haven't seen you for a while." He glanced from her to Cord. "Eighth floor, you said, sir?"

Ashlynne blushed. It was embarrassing that old Jack Vickers thought she was headed upstairs for a hot lunch-hour tryst. Which she was, she supposed.

Cord felt compelled to protectively cloak her in an aura of respectability. "Did you tell your friend here that we're getting married, sweetheart?" He addressed Ashlynne, though his remark was for the old man's benefit. "Very soon," he added.

"No kidding?" Jack Vickers evinced mild interest. "Well, congratulations to both the bride and the groom." The elevator doors snapped on the eighth floor.

"The elevator operator is a witness. Now we have to go through with the wedding," Cord teased as he led Ashlynne into the big, tastefully decorated room.

A table was set up, covered with a snowy white tablecloth and a centerpiece of fresh cut flowers. Two crystal goblets and a bottle of champagne, cooling in a bucket of ice, were placed on the sideboard.

"I thought we could order lunch . . ." Cord's voice, oddly hesitant, trailed off. He reached into the inside pocket of his suit jacket and removed a small velvet box. "This is for you," he said, almost shoving it into her hands.

Her fingers trembling, Ashlynne lifted open the lid. There was a diamond ring inside. She knew a little about jewels and stones from Rayleen's passionate interest in that area; Kendra had recently begun her own study.

This stone was a marquise-cut diamond, a big one, maybe three carats? It looked like an engagement ring, the likes of which no Monroe had ever been gifted with. She quickly snapped the lid shut, as if she'd been caught sneaking a peek at something forbidden.

She was speechless. He'd bought her an engagement ring? And from the quick look she'd allowed herself, it was the most beautiful ring she'd ever seen.

Cord was as undaunted as she was dazed. He took the box from her, removed the ring and slid it on her third finger, left hand. It was a perfect fit. "It's official," he said, drawing her into his arms. "Now all we have to do is set the wedding date. We'll make it soon, Ashlynne."

Ashlynne glanced down at the ring on her hand. Light sparkled and shone through the facets of the diamond. "Why rush?" she asked nervously.

"Why wait? We know we're going to do—what needs to be done. And I want to be back at the lodge before our peak summer season." He kissed her forehead, then walked over to the sideboard to pop the cork on the champagne. She watched him fill the two goblets with the pale bubbly liquid.

"How about a traditional but highly unoriginal toast?" Grinning rakishly, Cord handed her one glass, then clinked his to the side of it. "To us."

"Champagne in the middle of the afternoon?" Ashlynne recovered enough to say. She glanced from the ring to the champagne to Cord's handsome, smiling face.

"This is a celebration, honey. And needless to say, you are not returning to work in an hour. Thorpe can fend for himself in that garish office of his for the rest of the day."

"Ethan will have a fit! I just got back from—"

"Maybe he'll fire you. Good!"

"He already said he won't fire me, since he fully expects to become my brother-in-law."

"He is *not* going to be either your brother-in-law or mine," Cord assured her.

"I'm depending on Ethan's goodwill this week because I need to make special arrangements for Maxie and Daisy during the day," Ashlynne continued. "Tomorrow is the last day of school, and the kids only go in the morning. Their day camp doesn't start until next week so I have to—"

"I'll stay with the girls," Cord volunteered promptly.

"You're offering to baby-sit? For the rest of the week?"

He nodded. "Do you think Daisy will feel safe with me? If we're at your apartment she won't have to worry that I'll lose her or Maxie," he added quietly.

Ashlynne gazed at him. His sensitivity to Daisy's feelings thrilled her far more than the diamond ring, the champagne, and the lavish room. And his offer to baby-sit during the hard-to-fill week between the end of school and the beginning of camp was something out of every working mother's wildest dreams.

"I'll talk with Daisy," she promised. "I'll make sure she's all right with it."

"I want my daughter to trust me. I don't know if it's possible to make up for five lost years but I don't want Daisy and I to always be strangers to each other." He smiled wryly. "Of course, my mother and I have remained strangers, and I was born into that house and shared it with her for years. Which leads me to believe that closeness involves other factors than mere proximity."

"I agree," she said quietly.

"And do you also agree to spend the afternoon here with me? I've arranged for Wyatt and Kendra to pick up the kids."

"You've gone to so much trouble." Ashlynne was so overwhelmed, she was having trouble comprehending it all.

"You once said you preferred reality, that you didn't need romantic fantasy." Cord cupped her cheek with his big hand and stroked the smooth, soft skin with his thumb. "It occurred to me that there's no reason why we can't combine both. An engagement *requires* some romantic fantasy, Ashlynne."

Her eyes filled with sudden emotional tears. "Cord, I don't know what to say."

"You'd better say 'yes, I'll marry you.' You're not leaving this room until you do. But take your time, honey, I don't mind being locked up here with you for as long as it takes." He drained his glass. "Drink up. I have something to show you."

Ashlynne sipped the champagne. It was cold and surprisingly sweet and the bubbles tickled her nose. Cord led her into the huge tiled bathroom where a dark burgundy-colored whirlpool tub stood against the length of the wall. He turned on the taps. "Remember how much you enjoyed the Jacuzzi at the lodge?" His eyes gleamed and he smiled a wicked satyr's grin.

Ashlynne finished her champagne in a gulp. Cord was already unbuttoning her blouse.

"Yes?" he asked as he slipped it from her shoulders.

Her fingers were already at work, divesting him of his coat and tie. "Yes," she said softly.

CHAPTER SEVENTEEN ────────────

WYATT Way's speech to the Waysboro High School graduating class was not particularly memorable, but it was clear and concise and ran slightly under the five allotted minutes. The audience gave him a warm response, possibly as thanks for his brevity. Dan Clarkston took the podium next, his great white smile visible even to those in the stadium's far-off upper bleachers.

Ashlynne, Cord, and the children were seated in the first row with a close-up view of the football field where the speakers and the graduates sat on folding chairs, and the band and chorus were separately corralled for their respective performances. Ashlynne had insisted on arriving nearly an hour early in order to claim the best seats to watch Kendra's graduation.

Maxie was sitting on Cord's lap, carefully removing the purple cap and gown from her new Graduate Barbie doll. Underneath, Barbie wore a brief hot-pink spandex minidress and impossibly high-heeled pumps. "Kendra's graduation dress doesn't look anything like that," Cord observed in a whisper.

Since Kendra's graduation dress was a demure white cotton frock, even Maxie and Daisy got the joke. They both giggled.

Cord had purchased each girl the doll of her choice on their trip to Toys "R" Us earlier in the afternoon. The day before he'd taken both children miniature-golfing in Exton. They'd enjoyed an excursion to the park on another day, another visit to Chuck E. Cheese too. His temporary run as baby-sitter was a huge success. Daisy hadn't expressed a single doubt about his competence to ferry her and Maxie to the places they wanted to go. She even chatted with him, though the voluble Maxie tended to dominate any conversation.

Thirty seconds into Dan Clarkston's rousing speech, a series of firecrackers went off as startling and loud as a volley of gunshots. The crowd tittered nervously.

Dan paused, smiling, and waited for the noise to subside.

The moment it did, he began to speak. And the moment he began to speak, the firecrackers exploded once again. The crowd laughed loudly this time. Dan gripped the podium, his smile frozen into place. The principal of the high school and the district superintendent of schools exchanged grim glances.

An ear-splitting blast from a car horn sounded, nearly drowning out the noise from the firecrackers. When it blared again, long and loud, the crowd began to stir and talk among themselves. The scowling principal rose to his feet, walked to the podium, and demanded that the noise cease immediately. To everyone's surprise, it did. But when Dan Clarkston tried to resume his speech, the firecrackers and the car horn sounded again in raucous tandem.

Clarkston was no longer smiling. He tried to shout above the noise, but his efforts netted even more firecracker explosions and longer and louder blasts of the car horn. Maxie and Daisy covered their ears with their hands, as did most other children in the stands; several adults did too. A few babies, alarmed by the noises, began to cry, adding to the din.

"Clarkston isn't having a very good night," Cord murmured to Ashlynne. He couldn't pretend to mind. He'd never thought he would actually enjoy listening to a barrage of firecrackers and incessant horn-blowing, but this wasn't bad at all.

"Dan isn't having a good week," Ashlynne whispered back.

The Exton Evening Post had not heeded Ethan Thorpe's warning against publishing the negative article about Dan along with the unflattering pictures of the Clarkstons carrying their screaming son from the Ice Cream Olympics benefit. Worse, the paper had responded with a scathing editorial reprimanding "Ethan Thorpe, a major Clarkston supporter" for attempting to "manage the news."

Since then, the paper's coverage of Wyatt Way had been noticeably more favorable, much to the outrage of both Dan and Cindy Clarkston. Ethan tried to bolster his candidate's endurance to the unaccustomed criticism; Ashlynne had overheard Ethan's pep talk to Dan through the closed office door.

"Pull yourself together, Dan. Politics is a cycle of ups and downs and you're hitting a downswing for the first time. No big deal." It had been a singularly loud and emphatic pep talk but apparently ineffective because Dan had stormed from the office as incensed as when he'd entered.

Ethan appeared to be taking Dan's downswing in stride, but was not as sanguine about the downswing in his own personal campaign to win back Holly Way. Ashlynne had heard that the roses he'd re-sent Holly had come back to the office via Randy with pieces of the torn-up note scattered amidst the petals.

"Get Holly on the phone" he tersely ordered Ashlynne every day.

Ashlynne tried but was foiled at every turn. "I think it would be easier to call the White House and get the President on the line than to reach Holly by phone," she informed Ethan. He hadn't taken the news well.

And now this, sabotage by sound at the Waysboro High graduation. The superintendent took the podium and silence descended. He made his plea for "respect and order" without incident, then turned the podium back to Dan Clarkston.

Dan got out one word, and the cacophony started all over again—the firecrackers, the car horn, and a new sound—the deafening clang of cowbells. It was becoming clear to the crowd that the noise accompanied Dan only. "Get him off and let's get on with it," bellowed a voice from the stands. A swell of voices seconded him.

"This was definitely planned," Cord murmured to Ashlynne. He glanced down at his ring on her finger, then possessively laid his hand over hers. "A salvo in the Holly–Thorpe war with the hapless Dan Clarkston serving as the battlefield."

Ashlynne felt the warm weight of his hand on her lap as his thumb idly caressed her palm. The heat spread from her thighs to pool in her quivering, aching center. It was hard to concentrate on Ethan or Holly or hapless Dan Clarkston when her body seemed to have taken over her mind. She could think of nothing but how good it felt to sit close to him, to lean against his hard frame while he played arousing little games with his fingers.

From somewhere under the stands, an enormous inflatable beach ball was tossed onto the platform and landed in the middle of the graduating class. Amidst much laughter, the center guard on the basketball team, a towering six feet five, seized the ball and sent it flying. Whether intentionally or merely coincidentally, the beach ball slam-dunked Dan Clarkston, right on the top of his head.

Clarkston jumped, and the entire crowd howled with laughter. Even the principal's lips quirked into a reluctant smile, which he quickly hid behind his hand.

Dan Clarkston glanced around, glaring at the graduates in the folding chairs and the proud relatives and friends in the stands, at the beach ball rolling toward the minister who'd given the invocation. The firecrackers were popping, the car horn blaring, and the cowbells clanging.

Dan's signature smile was conspicuously absent as his temper flared to flash point. He gave the ball a fierce kick, sending it flying into the stands, and then began to shout. His face was flushed, his teeth bared, and his arms flailed disjointedly as he pounded the podium with his fists.

The background noise abruptly ceased, allowing his venom-spewed diatribe to be clearly carried over the public-address system. When the school superintendent raced to claim the microphone, Clarkston let loose a string of obscenities that shocked the crowd and drew a mixture of boos and sarcastic jeers from the graduating class.

"Mr. Clarkston, watch your language! There are children present!" the superintendent reprimanded sharply. He quickly apologized to all present and announced that the graduation ceremony would resume with an inspirational song sung by the high school chorus.

As Dan Clarkston was being ushered off the stage by the muscle-bound high school vice principal, the chorus burst into "You'll Never Walk Alone."

"I can't believe it!" Cord shook his head. "Clarkston lost it right in front of everybody, including *The Waysboro Weekly* and *The Exton Evening Post*. They always send a reporter apiece to cover the graduation."

He glanced at Ashlynne, who was dispensing Life Savers candy to bored and restless Maxie and Daisy. "Do you think Holly really is behind all this?" he asked, more than a little concerned.

"If she is, I don't even want to imagine how Ethan will retaliate." Ashlynne felt a shiver of apprehension.

"You're not going into that office tomorrow," Cord decreed. "You're close enough to being a Way for Thorpe to include you in his vendetta."

"Ethan knows I haven't made any final decisions." And she hadn't, Ashlynne assured herself. She was still considering Cord's proposal.

"You're wearing my ring, you're making love with me every day." Cord's words were deep and low and for her ears only. "Face it, honey, your decision has been made."

"I lost my Barbie shoe!" yelped Maxie. "Help me find it, Daisy." The two little girls scrambled around the bleachers looking for the missing shoe.

Ashlynne joined in the search. It was a welcome diversion from Cord's proclamation, which was still ringing in her ears. Though she was indeed wearing his ring and making love with him, though he'd spent every day this week looking after Daisy and Maxie while she worked, the actuality of her marrying Cord still seemed preposterous. A kind of cruel, surreal satire.

She'd been living with the town's assertion that the Monroes were trash since moving to Waysboro at the age of twelve, and too many of her relatives had substantiated those charges for her to disregard them. Though she worked hard to prove otherwise, though she tried to be more upstanding than any non-Monroe, the label pinned on her family had seeped into her very being and she'd absorbed it, despite her best efforts to disprove it. How could someone like her be worthy of an exalted Way?

Basically, deep down inside, she believed she was undeserving and unsuitable. And the moment she officially accepted Cord's proposal and dared to anticipate a life with him, the punch line of this cosmic joke would be delivered. Ashlynne knew she wouldn't find it funny.

"Mr. Way, over here, sir!" Byron, the Ways' uniformed chauffeur, called out to Wyatt as he finally reached the sidelines of the bustling crowd of graduates, families, and well-wishers. Way Communications' corporate limousine, a sleek black double stretch limo, was parked on the far end of the school grounds.

CEO-brother Stafford had insisted that Wyatt use the company limo tonight. "The last thing you'll need is to cope with traffic, after hobnobbing with that crowd," he'd said with a disdainful sniff. "Let Byron do the driving while you relax."

Stafford, a proud alumnus of private schools, considered attending a public-school graduation a grim political necessity to be endured, fortunately by Wyatt and not himself. "Anyway, you've been seen driving your own car often enough to be thought one of the people," Stafford had added imperiously. "Use the limo tonight."

Right now, Wyatt was grateful for the convenience. He wanted to pour himself a stiff drink from the limo's fully stocked bar while Byron drove him home. For if he were behind the wheel himself, Wyatt knew his destination would be Kendra Monroe.

And he couldn't go to her; he'd spent the past days talking himself out of contacting her. He had to face the fact that the interlude they'd shared while Ashlynne and Cord were out of town was over. He was a dozen years older than Kendra, and though she reached him on a level that no other woman ever had, though he felt connected to her in a way he'd never thought possible, it was his obligation to stay away from her. Tonight Kendra would undoubtedly be out celebrating with her classmates, exactly what she ought to be doing, and he had no right to try to take her away from that. He had no right to her whatsoever.

But the very thought of her made his pulses roar in his head. The last time he'd seen her was the afternoon Cord had asked him and Kendra to pick up little Daisy and Maxie after their dancing lesson in Exton. Kendra had told him the wrong time, and he'd arrived an hour early, leaving the two of them alone until they had to fetch the children. And in that hour alone . . .

His body began to throb. Kendra had found a sensually memorable way to pass the time, and it had taken every ounce of willpower he possessed to keep from taking her right there and then. He'd been both relieved and disappointed when it was time to go get the little girls. Daisy and Maxie were effective chaperons, and he knew he needed to be chaperoned or he would find himself involved in a full-fledged affair with the sexiest teenager this side of Amy Fisher. A beautiful one, without homicidal tendencies. But the consequences of such an affair could only be disastrous, both personally and politically.

Byron opened the door for him, and Wyatt climbed into the darkened interior.

"Hello, Wyatt." The teasing feminine voice sent his heartbeat into overdrive.

Kendra sat far back on the seat, still wearing her flowing graduation robe. The traditional mortarboard, complete with red and gold tassel, the school's colors, was on the floor.

Wyatt swallowed, his throat suddenly quite dry. "How— did you get here?" he heard himself ask. His voice seemed to echo peculiarly within his head.

"Byron let me in." Before Wyatt could ask her how she had pulled that off, she moved closer to him on the seat. "I liked your speech tonight, Wyatt."

He wondered how she could manage to sound sweet, sincere, and sultry all at the same time. She inched closer still, and he inhaled the sexy, spicy scent of her.

"It—uh—went over better than most of my speeches, probably because it was so short." It was hard to even remember his speech to the graduation crowd with her so near. They were alone in a darkened limousine, and the way she was looking at him aroused every cell in his body.

He straightened in his seat and tried to concentrate on his political career instead of alluring, luscious Kendra. "Dan Clarkston certainly unraveled right in front of the crowd. Well, those sound effects were maddening. I guess I'm lucky they didn't start until Dan took the podium."

"Oh, you didn't have to worry about that." Smiling, Kendra handed him a drink. "Scotch on the rocks. Byron said it was the official Way family drink." A sexy, smoky saxophone rift was playing on the jazz CD. Obviously she'd familiarized herself with the limo's amenities. She sipped a drink of her own.

Wyatt returned his Scotch to the bar. "My grandfather and my brother Stafford like Scotch on the rocks, I don't." He took the glass from Kendra's hand. "And I don't want you getting drunk."

"Jeez, are you in a bad mood!" Kendra complained. "I thought you'd be happy 'cause your speech went so well and Danny Boy's didn't." Her blue eyes sparkled. "Did you hear some of the words that came out of his mouth? After all his talk about 'offensive language polluting the airwaves,'—she imitated Clarkston's pompous tone and inflection—"he spits it out like toxic waste! And then he got hollered at by the superintendent and hauled away by the vice principal!"

"Clarkston didn't handle himself well," Wyatt agreed stiffly. He sipped the liquid he'd taken from Kendra. Rum and Coke? He frowned. "But I hesitate to gloat—"

"Why?" Kendra was perplexed. "You should be gloating, I'm gloating! We got him good!"

The car began to move, so smoothly that the liquid in the glasses didn't even ripple. "I told Byron to take us for a little ride," Kendra said, tucking her legs under her and settling back in the thick, soft seat. "I've never been in a limousine before. It's so cool!"

Wyatt fixed her with a hard stare. "What do you mean, 'we got him good'? Kendra, do you know anything about the disruption at the graduation tonight?"

"Sure. It was my idea." Kendra smiled with satisfaction. "And I'm so proud of my cousins. They followed my directions to the letter. I was worried they'd screw up because they're not exactly known for their comprehension skills, but they were perfect!"

"Your cousins were the ones setting off firecrackers and the car horn—"

"—and the cowbells. And only when Dan Clarkston tried to speak," Kendra said proudly. "That was the part I was afraid the cousins would mess up, that once they started, they'd keep the noise up. It was crucial that they only drown out Dan. And they got it right!"

"I can't believe this." Wyatt was aghast. "Kendra, you interfered with—with Clarkston's free speech, you disrupted a public ceremony, you—"

"The beach ball wasn't my idea," Kendra interjected. "I don't know who came up with that." She grinned. "But it was so cool when Jamal sent it flying right at Clarkston's head. Can he aim or what? No wonder he won that basketball scholarship to the University of Kentucky!"

"This is unconscionable!" exclaimed Wyatt. "Kendra, how could you do such a thing? You—"

"You're mad?" Kendra stared at him incredulously. "But I did it for you. Well, sort of. I wanted you to look excellent in comparison to Clarkston. And you did!"

"Kendra, I don't want or need any dirty tricks on my behalf. It's—unfair and unethical and downright insulting. If I can't make myself appear *excellent* without resorting to—"

"I said, *sort of*," Kendra cut in, her voice rising with temper. "I also wanted to pay Dan back for what he said when Maxie was missing and for being such a phony creep and for dragging Scotty off when the poor little kid wanted to stay with me."

She grabbed for her drink and took a defiant swallow, then set the glass back in the bar with a forceful thud. "And *I* didn't screw things up for Danny Boy, *he* did it all by himself. He didn't have to totally freak, he could've been cool and laughed or done something to get the crowd on his side. But he showed what a—a piece of hurl he really is behind that great big phony smile of his!"

She glowered at Wyatt, staring defiantly until he finally

looked away. He cleared his throat. "Piece of hurl?" he repeated faintly.

"And that's paying him a compliment," Kendra snapped.

"Ohhh, Kendra!" Wyatt reached for the Scotch and gulped it down.

Kendra watched him. "When I told my cousins they'd be helping you tonight, they wanted to do it. You're kind of a Monroe family hero, you know."

"No, I wasn't aware of that."

"Well, you are. Remember my cousin Ben who you got into the rehab program at the state hospital? And his mother, Aunt Debbie?"

Wyatt closed his eyes. "I remember them well. Did Ben escape, armed with a boxful of firecrackers and cowbells?"

Kendra laughed. "Ben wasn't involved tonight, he's still at the hospital and he's doing great. Turns out he loves it there! He's sworn off liquor, he's a whole new Ben. He's made dozens of ashtrays in occupational therapy— the uncles are using them at the Waterside Bar—and he's into this physical-fitness program run by an ex-marine volunteer. Ben decided he wants to go into the Marines and the volunteer guy is going to help him do it."

"That's wonderful." Wyatt felt slightly guilty at his own astonishment. Expecting a Monroe to fail had become something of a reflex. Certainly he hadn't considered that the boy would thrive if given a chance.

"And there's good news about Aunt Debbie too," Kendra continued. "She got involved in volunteer work at the state hospital while she was visiting Ben. She's really good with the patients there and has been hired as an aide. And her twins, who are pregnant? Well, some hospital personnel connected them with two couples who want to adopt their babies after they're born. They're paying the twins' medical expenses, plus a little extra. Best of all, the twins have decided to finish high school so they can work at the hospital as aides when they graduate. They love it there too."

"Well." Wyatt was at a loss for words. "Well, well."

"Who'd have dreamed it, huh?" Kendra's blue eyes gleamed. "That that particular branch of the family would find true happiness at the state mental hospital?"

Wyatt was having a hard time suppressing a smile. Her sly humor struck a too-responsive chord in him. He should be furious with her for her antics tonight, he reminded himself.

"Since you're the one responsible for Aunt Debbie and her kids' good fortune, the Monroe clan feels beholden to you." Kendra, sensing his ambivalence, scooted even closer to him, until her knees were touching his thigh. She tilted her head and gazed at him under her lashes. "Don't be mad at me, Wyatt," she said softly.

He drew a deep breath. "Kendra, I will not tolerate—"

"Of course, *I* should be mad at *you*," Kendra cut in. "After all, you offered me a job as your personal assistant or something, and you haven't called me about starting. What kind of an employer are you? Or was the job offer bogus?"

He was distracted by the abrupt change of subject. And by the subject itself. He remembered making that job offer in a fever of desire. When she reached over to loosen the knot of his tie, a lusty recurrence of that fever swept through him.

"Kendra, I—you know I—I want to protect you and—"

"I don't want you to protect me from you." Kendra smiled mischievously. "Anyway, I've taken care of the protection. Hmm, now where did I put it?" She leaned across the seat and retrieved a neon-bright orange bag.

"Look inside," she invited.

Wyatt did. And burst into startled, shocked laughter.

"Josh drove me over to Condom Nation on the outskirts of Exton," she said, grinning. "It's so cool, you have to go see it. Too bad we don't have a store like that here in Waysboro, but it's hard to picture it right in the middle of the town square."

"The town fathers would expire at the thought," Wyatt murmured.

"The town mothers too," Kendra added cheerfully.

Wyatt tried to imagine his mother and aunts and their friends walking into Waysboro's own Condom Nation shop. He couldn't. Such a scene was unimaginable.

"Well, what's your pleasure, Mr. Way?" Kendra removed five condoms from the bag, each a different brilliant color. Red, aqua, purple, jade-green, and gold.

Wyatt had not yet collected himself from the sight of the crayon-colored condoms when she proceeded to stun him again. Her graduation robe had a long front zipper and she slowly began to lower it. Wyatt's eyes grew wider and rounder as it became apparent that she was not wearing her brand-new graduation dress under the gown. She was not wearing any dress at all!

"Kendra!" He leaned forward to stop her, but Kendra was already wriggling out of the robe. Wyatt gaped at her. The snow-white camisole she wore somehow both covered and revealed her firm, round breasts. Her nipples were already erect and jutting against the silky fabric.

Like one in a trance, he watched her discard the graduation robe with a toss. It drifted down over the opposite seat, where he spied a swathe of white cloth. "My dress," Kendra told him, following his gaze. "It's incredibly dweebish, but Ashlynne picked it out for me and I didn't want to hurt her feelings so I wore it to the graduation. I couldn't wait to take it off."

He saw two sheer white stockings on top of the dress before his eyes returned compulsively to Kendra. Her white bikini panties were merely a scrap, giving him a full view of the smooth ivory skin of her stomach. His eyes followed the length of her shapely legs from thigh to ankle. It was then he noticed that she'd kept on her white high-heeled strappy sandals.

He gasped as she sensuously slithered onto his lap. This couldn't be happening! He waited for himself to wake up in a sweat-drenched bed, the usual ending of his dreams of Kendra.

But she stirred, warm and soft and very real in his arms.

"I'm tired of waiting, Wyatt." A teasing wanton desire shone in her eyes as she began to undress him. Her warm, sweet breath fanned his neck as she worked. "I think you are too."

Without pausing to think, he slipped out of his jacket and assisted her efforts to remove his tie and shirt. The limo braked to a stop as she opened his belt buckle, momentarily jolting Wyatt back into the real world. "Where are we?" he asked, like one dazed.

"I told Byron to take us down by the creek." Kendra slipped her hand inside his trousers to cup him intimately. Her smile was deliciously wicked and daring. "I gave him directions to this clearing deep in the woods near the place where the creek runs into the river."

"I've never been there," Wyatt managed to say. Leaning back against the seat, he groaned with pleasure as she slowly, gently kneaded his erection.

"Most people haven't. It's way off the road and you have to know where you're going to be able to find it. It's Monroe country," she added playfully.

She felt him shudder with desire as she bent to trail soft kisses from the base of his throat to his navel. Her dark hair brushed his bare skin as her lips caressed him.

"Kendra." He caught her face between his hands and gazed deeply at her. Her eyes, glassy and hot, locked with his. "I want you so much," he said hoarsely. "But it shouldn't be here, not in a car in the woods. Kendra, I—"

"Do you really want to stop?" Kendra asked, provocatively gliding the tip of her tongue over her lips. She slipped the camisole over her head, exposing her creamy breasts to him. He stared at her dusky-rose nipples, high and tautly pointed.

"No, baby, no," he panted. He fondled her breasts, massaging them as he kissed an urgent path along her neck. His mouth lowered to her nipples and he laved first one and then the other with his tongue. She moaned, her body twisting with need, as he took one distended nipple in his mouth and suckled her gently.

He was pulsing and hard in her hands, and when she reached for his zipper, he sucked in his breath.

"God help me, I can't stop." The excitement and need coursing through him were more powerful than anything he had ever experienced.

"Me neither," Kendra whispered. She closed her eyes as he lowered her down to the seat, wrapping her arms around him to hold him tightly.

Wyatt clenched her round, firm bottom and arched her against him. "I feel as if I've been waiting my whole life for you," he confessed shakily. His lips took hers in a fiercely possessive kiss, his tongue invading the sweet, moist warmth of her mouth.

Kendra clung to him, moaning deeply as she sank her nails into the muscled hardness of his shoulders. Scorching flames of sensual heat licked through her body, rendering her soft and pliant.

"I've never felt this way before," she whispered, both awed and scared by the intensity of the emotions surging through her. A long, long time ago the girl she'd once been had conceived a plan, had started a game and been an eager player. But she was not playing at anything now, her feelings were deep and real and intense. She'd fallen in love with him.

She felt both tearful and exultant. *Kendra Monroe in love with Wyatt Way?* It was ridiculous, it was hopeless, but right now she'd never felt happier in her life.

"Kiss me, Wyatt," she pleaded, lifting her mouth to him.

Wyatt obliged at once. His mouth opened over hers in a deep, drugging kiss that went on and on, building in passion and intensity, until they were both engulfed in a firestorm of sensual need.

He removed her panties and helped her tug off his briefs and they lay together, savoring their nakedness, exploring with their hands and lips. He tested her readiness with firm, loving fingers that parted and caressed her as she moved restlessly, wantonly against him. She was wet and hot and aching for his possession.

And then he was there, surging inside her, hot and hard, filling her, uniting them. With a wild little cry, Kendra held him inside and out, rocking her body to match the fierce rhythm of his.

"Wyatt, please!" She couldn't stop the words, they tumbled out as he moved deeply within her, taking her to the brink of excruciating pleasure, only to retreat and send her soaring back up to the heights. "Please don't leave me."

"No, baby, never."

Sighing his name softly in wonder and surrender, Kendra gave herself up to the magnificent spiraling heat. Moments later, in the intimate shimmering darkness, she heard Wyatt's deep male sounds of release.

He lay sprawled atop her, spent and enraptured by the sexual ecstasy they had just shared. He felt a completion with her that he'd never known, a bond that he'd never expected to feel with any woman. Who would have guessed that after years of dating, disappointment, and disconnection, he would finally find love? His life, always so ordered and predictable—and dull!—was suddenly bursting with spirit and excitement, with endless possibilities.

Content in the warm afterglow, he kissed her with a lingering tenderness.

Kendra lay beneath him, her arms and legs still wrapped around him, her body still tingling from the explosive mutual climax. She sighed, feeling contentment mingled with an aching sadness. "I wish it could always be like this. You on top of me. You inside me."

"Oh, I think you'll want some variety after a while. For example, you on top of me while I'm inside you." Elation swelled within him, unleashing a playful teasing side of himself that he'd never suspected existed. He felt powerful, invincible, able to conquer the world. He laughed his delight. "Ah, Kendra, you're the best thing that's ever happened to me."

Her heart melted with love for him. At this moment, he seemed so young and hopeful, practically boyish. She felt a maternal urge to protect him from himself. "Wyatt, I'm probably the worst thing that's ever happened to you. The biggest mistake you'll ever make. Anybody would agree."

"I don't. And you don't either." He raised himself up on his elbows and gazed into her deep blue eyes. "When we were making love, you begged me not to leave you and I promised I wouldn't. That was no mistake, Kendra."

Her face flamed. She'd hoped he hadn't heard her when she'd blurted out that nonsensical request. Instantly, she tried to save face. "People say all kinds of things when they're all hot and passionate, everybody knows that."

Wyatt knew she intended to sound blithe and carefree; she probably would've, to someone else. But not him. He was too closely attuned to her not to detect the masked tension in her. The fear.

Their bodies were still joined, and the intimacy was so compelling that Kendra tried to look away from his probing, assessing gaze. To focus her attention on externals like the unfamiliar but strangely arousing music playing on the compact-disc player, the feel of the sinfully luxurious upholstery against her bare skin.

"Don't withdraw from me, Kendra. Talk to me. You can tell me anything."

She worried her lower lip between her teeth. It was awfully easy to talk to Wyatt. And perhaps setting the record straight would enable her to keep her self-respect.

She met his eyes again. "When I said 'don't leave me,' I didn't mean I expected you to stick around." The words tumbled out in a rush. "I don't want you thinking that I don't know how it is."

His eyes narrowed. "And how is it?"

"Everybody leaves everybody, it's like a rule. You don't have to pretend to be any different."

"It must seem like everybody leaves you," he said, suddenly understanding. His heart went out to her. "Your parents and Rayleen were careless with their lives and died as a result, leaving you when you were just a child. Your brother Shane went into the Navy and, except for a couple of days a year, is essentially out of your life."

"Max Mathison took off. And Cord." Kendra thought of their departures, the babies they'd left behind. "Only Ashlynne stays, but she has more staying power than anybody in the world."

"And you think Ashlynne is the only exception to your rule that everybody leaves? Well, what about yourself,

Kendra? You stayed around to help Ashlynne with your little nieces, and you didn't have to. You could've run off and left them if you felt like it. With your looks and your brains, you wouldn't have had any trouble getting anywhere you wanted to go."

"I couldn't leave Ashlynne to take care of Maxie and Daisy all by herself!" Kendra exclaimed, offended by the very suggestion. "I love them."

"And I love you, Kendra." Wyatt's brown eyes glowed with conviction. "You're mine, and I'm not going to leave you."

He was making her nervous. Kendra wriggled beneath him, trying to get free. Wyatt remained where he was, on top of her, inside her.

"Wyatt, it's pure sex, you don't love me." She hoped she didn't sound pathetic. She certainly felt pathetic, wanting desperately to believe him when everybody knew that girls like her were not loved by the Wyatt Ways of the world.

"It's not sex," Wyatt refuted stubbornly.

Kendra had to smile at that. "Wyatt, we're naked. You're inside me. Believe me, that's sex."

He nibbled her lips. "I concede that point. Now let me prove mine." He carefully disengaged his body from hers and sat up. "Hmm, I'll never be able to listen to Deep Purple again without thinking of this night. What color do you want to use next?"

"Red." Kendra reached into the bag.

Wyatt stayed her hand. "Not now. Later. Right now I want to prove to you that I love you and I'm proud of it. I'm proud of you. So no more sneaking around or hiding the way we feel. Get dressed, honey. I'm going to take you out to celebrate your graduation tonight." He began to pull on his clothes as he spoke. "Where would you like to go? I'll take you anywhere you want."

"Wyatt, the only place we can be seen together is the Waterside Bar, and even that's a risk. Sometimes reporters show up there to cover a knifing or a shooting, but if they saw us, we'd be the news. And just think what Dan Clarkston would do if he knew about us! Your career in politics would be over before it even gets started."

"Hardly a catastrophe." Wyatt looked thoughtful. "A catastrophe would be losing you, now that I've finally found you." He handed her her panties, which he'd retrieved from the plush carpeted floor. "Do you want me to dress you? It might not be as fun as undressing you, but I'll definitely enjoy myself."

"You don't know what you're saying! You don't know what you're doing!" Kendra dressed herself in record haste as Wyatt watched with interest.

He slid his hand under her skirt and ran his fingers around the lacy tops of her sheer thigh-high white stockings. "How do these things stay up without—"

Kendra pushed his hand away. "Wyatt, I didn't want to tell you this, but I—I guess I have to. I have to make you understand." She twined a lock of her dark hair around her finger and twirled it nervously. "I can't let you throw away your political career because you think you love me. You're one of the good guys, Wyatt." Her voice lowered and she stared blindly at the tinted window of the limousine. "And I'm not."

"You're not a guy at all," Wyatt agreed, sliding his hand over her slim shoulders and down her arms.

She looked young and sweet and innocent in the demure white dress, with its capped sleeves and modest neckline and gently flaring skirt. He thought of what was under that dress, and the provocative contrast stirred his blood anew.

"Wyatt, you're missing the point. Deliberately, I think."

"Quite deliberately."

"You can't. You have to listen to me," Kendra choked out. Tears of shame flooded her eyes. "I'm no good, Wyatt."

Wyatt cupped her chin with his hand and tilted her head. "I hope this isn't going to be a discourse on the lowliness of the Monroes, Kendra. Because if it is, I'm not going to pay any attention, so you may as well save your breath."

"It's about me!" Kendra cried. "And my plan to make you want me so I could blackmail you!"

She scrambled across him and pulled open the car door in an effort to escape. A stiff breeze gusted outside and a smattering of cool raindrops blew inside. Quick as a pouncing cat, Wyatt closed his hand over hers and pulled the door shut, drawing her back into the limo and onto his lap.

"It's raining," he said calmly. "I'm not letting you out to run around the woods at night in the rain while I chase after you. That's a bit too melodramatic."

"You should throw me out into the woods and let me get drenched." Kendra was distraught. "Didn't you get what I just told you?"

"I got it. What were you going to blackmail me for?"

"Money, of course! Enough so that Ashlynne and the kids and I could leave town for good."

"I see." He nodded. "I figured all along that you had to be up to something, but I wasn't exactly sure what it was, what your motives were. Let's face it, a beautiful young woman like you does not pursue a man like me unless she has some sort of—er—purposeful agenda."

"A man like you," Kendra repeated softly. "You're a wonderful man, Wyatt. The very best. And you must hate me, I deserve it." Kendra struggled against his arms, which had fastened like iron bands around her, keeping her firmly on his lap.

"I told you I love you, Kendra. I meant it."

She was exasperated at his apparent denseness, but valiantly tried again. "Wyatt, I was going to blackmail you!"

"But you didn't. You could've sicced the press on me a number of times and you didn't. You didn't even have to have pictures of us together, you could've achieved the same scandalous effect with a word to Ethan Thorpe."

"I just couldn't go through with it," she whispered. "And after a while I stopped thinking about . . . my plan."

"And do you know why?" Wyatt's voice rumbled deep and soft against her ear.

"Yes." She touched her forehead to his, squeezing back tears. "I love you, Wyatt. I love you and I hate what I planned to do to you. It's awful. I'm awful."

"You're certainly conniving," Wyatt observed, grinning. He felt idiotically happy. "And alarmingly clever. I'd hate to be on your enemies list because you not only get mad, you get even. I offer the ill-fated graduation speech of Dan

Clarkston as proof of your vengeful prowess."

He kissed her, long and hard. They were both breathless when he lifted his mouth from hers. "But you're also fiercely loyal and loving and devoted to those who love you. Since I intend to be among that lucky number, I'll brave your serpent streak."

"Oh, Wyatt." Her blue eyes were shining. "I don't deserve you. And I don't want to wreck things for you."

"The subject of who deserves what is permanently tabled," Wyatt decreed. "The issue at hand is where you want me to take you tonight."

"Your place. I can stay all night," Kendra said eagerly. "I told Ashlynne I was going to a bunch of graduation parties and would be spending the night with Susie McClanahan. She's too shell-shocked by Cord's proposal to even think about how bogus that sounds."

"We'll go to my place later. Where would you like to go right now?"

"Nowhere in Waysboro. Or Exton either. Let's go someplace where we can just be a couple. Not a Way and a Monroe, not a candidate and his—"

"—love," Wyatt interjected. "Because you are my love, Kendra. And I agree that what we want can't be found in Waysboro or Exton or anywhere in this district." He smiled at her. "But I have a plan. Will you come with me?"

The gleam in his eyes intrigued her, the warmth of his smile enchanted her. "I'll go anywhere with you, Wyatt Way."

CHAPTER EIGHTEEN ———————

"I JUST finished talking with Mary Beth," Cord told Ashlynne. He was lying on his bed in his room at OakWay. He wished he were lying in bed with Ashlynne in his spacious bedroom at Glacier Lodge. "The building crew is making good progress on the repairs in the south wing. And Bobby called me to report that he has the furniture and all the other stuff ready to go as soon as the workmen are through."

"You mean Roberto," Ashlynne corrected drolly.

"He'll always be Bobby to me." Cord paused. "I'd like to return permanently to Glacier within a couple of weeks, Ashlynne. And I want you and the kids with me."

Ashlynne tensed. The more he pressured her, the more she felt she had to resist. But Cord changed the subject. "I'm kind of at loose ends since you took over my baby-sitting job today. How are my two young charges?"

"Your charges are fine. They were invited over to play with their friend Steffi Dixon. She lives across the street and—"

"I know Steffi, I met her the other day. Her cat had six kittens last month and Daisy and Maxie are desperately hoping you'll let them have one. Or better yet, two kittens. I should warn you that I've been enlisted to talk you into it."

"We can't afford two cats." Ashlynne's reply was sheer reflex.

"Honey, we can afford an entire cattery, and then some," Cord said quietly.

Her cheeks grew warm. Cord was not subtle in letting her know how greatly her financial status would change when she married him. *If* she married him, she silently amended.

"Actually, I think it would be a nice idea to let the girls each have a kitten. Could ease the transition from Waysboro to Montana, not that I think either one is going to have any trouble adjusting to life at the lodge. The place is a paradise for kids."

"Cord, I think it's—"

"Of course, if you'd rather live in a house in town, that's fine with me. Maybe it would be better for the kids to be able to walk to school and be near their friends. There's lots of little kids in Glacier, so they'll have lots of friends. We don't have to decide now, we can stay in the lodge so there'll be no pressure to buy just any house. We can look around for what we really want or even build—"

"No pressure? Cord, you're pressuring me like a—a used-car salesman!"

He laughed. "Am I going to make a sale?"

"Cord!"

"Okay, I'll ease up a bit. Sweetheart?" His voice deepened.

Ashlynne shivered in response. He sounded like that when they were making love, his voice husky and low as he murmured exciting, sensual things that made her blush as she stood here remembering them.

"I'm glad you didn't go in to the office today," Cord continued. "Word has it that Clarkston's staff has gone ballistic over his temper tantrum at the graduation last night. *The Exton Evening Post* plans to feature the story and pictures on the front page of this afternoon's edition."

"How do you know that?"

"Campaign spies. The *Post* also plans an in-depth article detailing Clarkston's radical change of behavior and the speculation circulating that he can't handle the stress of politics and is buckling under the strain. Thorpe must be chewing nails, and I don't want you within his spitting range."

Ashlynne gulped. After the debacle at the graduation, she wasn't keen to be around Ethan either. But she still didn't approve of what she'd done. "I was a chicken to call in sick today. I'm not sick."

"The thought of having to face Thorpe every morning would be enough to make me sick." Cord's voice deepened and warmed. "I bet the kids were thrilled to have Mommy home with them today."

"Yes, they were." She stared down at the diamond ring on her finger. Its presence still startled her but she was slowly becoming accustomed to seeing it there. When she removed it at night, her finger felt oddly bare. "But they were disappointed that you weren't coming over. They said something about making cookies. You weren't really going to bake with them, were you?"

"They were going to do the baking. I was going to eat the cookies. Tell the kids our cookie-a-thon is still on. I'll be over later, after I—"

"I'm back!" Kendra burst into the apartment, her voice ringing with glee.

Overhearing, Cord chuckled on the other end of the line. "I'll let you go for now. I know you want to hear all about Kendra's graduation-night revelry. Good-bye, sweetheart, I'll see you later." Again, his voice lowered on a note of intimacy.

A wild, wicked thrill surged through her. Taking a deep, steadying breath, she turned to greet her little sister with a smile.

Her eyes widened with surprise. Kendra was wearing a short, trendy empire-waist dress of blue silk, the color exactly matching the beautiful shade of her eyes. Ashlynne had never seen the dress before but she knew at a glance that it was expensive, in a price range unaffordable to them.

And then she noticed four bulging shopping bags on the floor at Kendra's feet. Confusion and apprehension rose like bile in her throat. "Kendra, what are those—"

"Ashlynne, guess what?" Kendra threw her arms around her sister and hugged her. "I'm married!"

It was lucky they were in the kitchen, and a chair was handy, because Ashlynne's knees buckled. She sat down hard.

"See?" Kendra shoved her hand close to Ashlynne's face. A thick gold band encircled her ring finger.

Ashlynne felt as if she'd been hit in the chest with a bowling ball traveling at the speed of light. She couldn't speak, couldn't breathe.

Kendra didn't seem to require any verbal feedback, however. She supplied her own. "Kendra Way. How do you like my new name, Ashlynne?" Her cheeks were flushed, her eyes sparkling. She looked radiant. "Mrs. Wyatt Way. That's me!"

"Wyatt Way?" Ashlynne found her voice but wondered if she was losing her mind. "You married Wyatt Way?"

"Last night," Kendra exclaimed, thrilled. "Oh, Ashlynne, I'm so happy!" She plunked down onto Ashlynne's lap, the way she'd done when she had been a very little girl, the way Maxie and Daisy still did, and gave her a ferocious hug.

Still too stunned to move, Ashlynne watched Kendra hop to her feet, then boost herself up onto the counter.

"Want to hear the whole story?" Kendra asked, then proceeded to tell it without waiting for an answer. "Wyatt took me into DC last night to celebrate my graduation and our love." She picked up a glass and set it down, her legs swinging back and forth, her movements constant and kinetic.

"Celebrate your love?" Ashlynne repeated ominously. "Is that what he told you?" She envisioned the scene in her mind: an older, experienced man spouting words of love to lure an innocent girl into the big city. Then her mind went blank. Those clichéd tales did not end in marriage!

"We checked into this ultracool hotel, I mean it looked like something out of a movie, Ashlynne." Kendra sighed happily. "There was this expensive restaurant and a bar and dancing, and right in the middle of everything, Wyatt asked me to marry him."

Ashlynne winced. "Oh, Kendra, you're so young, too young! Wyatt Way is—"

"He's the best thing that ever happened to me, Ashlynne." Kendra sobered for a moment. "I love him. And he loves me. We're forever."

"Oh God, Kendra." Ashlynne leaned her elbows on the table and covered her face with her hands. A terrible thought struck. "Are you pregnant?"

"No! Don't you think I learned anything from Rayleen? I decided a long time ago that I wasn't having kids until I had a husband who would help me take care of them." Kendra frowned, but her spirits were too high to be dampened for more than a second or two. Her lips curved into an irrepressible smile. "Well, now I have the husband but we're going to wait a while for the kids. There's plenty of time for that."

"Why didn't you wait to get married? There's plenty of time for that too."

"Wyatt didn't want to wait and neither did I, so he made some phone calls and found out about this place in Virginia that condenses the usual three-day waiting period for a blood test and license into just a few hours. And it's open twenty-four hours a day! So we drove right over there and got married. See my ring!" Kendra held out her hand to proudly show off her wedding band again. "We didn't have a ring last night so Wyatt used his daddy's old school ring that he always wears. He bought me this one this morning."

Kendra stared dreamily at the thick gold band. "Anyway, after we were married, we went back to the hotel and—"

"Kendra, are you sure this marriage is real?" Ashlynne interrupted, not caring to hear what happened next. She *knew* what had gone on in that hotel room during the alleged wedding night. "The whole thing sounds fishy, an all-night marriage mill, a quickie ceremony—"

"Wyatt did not trick me into bed with a faux marriage!" Kendra was insulted. "I'll get our marriage license." She ran to pull it from one of the overstuffed bags. "See, according to the laws of the state of Virginia, we're officially married." Kendra showed Ashlynne the notarized license, running her finger over the crucial lines.

The document certainly looked real. Ashlynne swallowed a huge lump in her throat. Her baby sister was married!

Kendra dropped to her knees to rummage through one of the bags. "Ashlynne, I couldn't believe it but the hotel where we were staying was connected to a mall! We went shopping this morning. Wyatt bought me my ring and this new dress I'm wearing and all this stuff . . ." She began to unload the packages, gleefully showing Ashlynne the new clothes and lingerie Wyatt had bought for her.

Ashlynne felt sick. Wyatt Way was a rich man who'd bought Kendra as easily as Cord had bought those dolls for Maxie and Daisy.

"I brought you a present, Ash." Kendra pulled a sky-blue silk teddy from the bag and handed it to Ashlynne. "The color is perfect for you. Cord's eyes will pop out of his head when he sees you in it!"

Ashlynne blushed scarlet. Sex was not a topic she'd ever discussed with Kendra, except in terms of Rayleen's misadventures. And now little Kendra was married and having sex with Wyatt Way! Buying provocative lingerie for herself to wear for him, and for Ashlynne to wear for Cord Way! How had they come to this?

But she knew how it had happened. A searing guilt swept through her. Their downfall was all her fault. If she hadn't succumbed to temptation and slept with Cord, she would've somehow been able to prevent Kendra from doing the same with Wyatt. Instead, by her own behavior, she'd given her stamp of approval.

Kendra was determinedly oblivious to Ashlynne's distress. "I bought these outfits for Maxie and Daisy in Gap Kids. Aren't they adorable? Hey, where are the kids, anyway?"

"Playing at Steffi Dixon's," Ashlynne said distractedly. How could she pry her little sister from the clutches of Wyatt Way? She hadn't felt such panicky desperation since the day Rayleen had announced her last pregnancy.

Ashlynne gazed at her sister's bright, beautiful face. Kendra *Way*. "Where is he now?" She couldn't bring herself to say the name of her new brother-in-law.

"Wyatt? He's at his house. I wanted to tell you the news by myself so he dropped me off here." Kendra's face suddenly registered concern. "I stopped by Ethan's office first but there was a temp who said you'd called in sick. Oh wow, Ashlynne, I'm sorry. I should've asked right away. Are you really sick or did you just ditch work?"

"I'm sick about this marriage of yours," Ashlynne said tersely.

Kendra merely laughed. "I don't remember you ever faking sick before. You and Cord must've had a pretty wild time of your own last night, huh?"

"My calling in sick had nothing to do with—with that." Ashlynne's face flamed and she stalked from the kitchen. Her eyes went compulsively to the sofa where she and Cord had indeed had a "pretty wild time" after ascertaining the children were asleep. She was corrupt, Ashlynne thought miserably. Her true nature had surfaced at last. Worse, her example had led to the corruption of Kendra as well.

Kendra followed her into the living room. "Ashlynne, you're not taking this too well," she observed. "I knew you'd be surprised but I hoped you would be happy for me. Wyatt is kind and generous and rich and we love each other. Who could ask for anything more?"

"I'd say his generosity is awfully self-serving," Ashlynne said primly. "He buys sexy clothes to dress you in, for his own—"

"That's not fair!" Kendra cried. "I picked out the stuff I wanted. If I'd've wanted sweatsuits and granny gowns, he would've bought them for me. He really is generous, Ashlynne. And thoughtful too. Driving home this morning we saw a sign for Chilton and then I remembered how Ethan Thorpe refused to pay the reward money to the Safe Haven for finding Maxie. I told Wyatt how bad we felt about that and how you were too shy to tell Cord. Wyatt picked up his car phone right then and there and arranged for ten thousand dollars to be sent to Safe Haven in Maxie's name. He didn't even want his own name used. He did it for us, for Maxie and for Safe Haven. He said the company's charitable arm would handle everything." She looked puzzled. "Exactly what is a charitable arm, anyway?"

Ashlynne was floored by the information. "You mentioned the reward and he paid it?"

Kendra nodded. "I can tell Wyatt anything. You should try being more open with Cord, Ashlynne. I mean, it's not always easy to tell—certain things—but keeping secrets isn't—"

She was interrupted by a sudden pounding on the door. "Ashlynne, open up!" commanded a furious voice on the other side of the door. "I know you're in there and I know you're not sick!" The doorknob rattled as it was turned and jiggled too roughly.

Kendra and Ashlynne exchanged glances. "It's Ethan," Ashlynne murmured.

"I'm well aware you called in sick this morning because of the Clarkston disaster at that goddamn graduation last night! Now let me in, I have to talk to you!"

"Don't open it!" Kendra squealed, clutching at Ashlynne to hold her back. "What if he has a gun?"

Ethan heard her through the door. "I don't have a gun, you idiotic little twit," he bellowed. The pounding continued, the doorknob rattling. "Ashlynne, open the door!"

"Or he'll huff and he'll puff and he'll blow it in?" Kendra giggled nervously.

"Something like that," Ashlynne murmured. She knew her boss well enough to know that he was not going to quietly go away. For the sake of her neighbors' peace and quiet, she opened the door. Ethan pushed past her and strode inside.

"See, no gun!" he snapped at Kendra. "You've been watching too much violence on television," he added disapprovingly, then spun around to glare at Ashlynne. "If you were afraid to come to work this morning because you knew I'd be furious about Dan, you were right." He flexed and clenched his fingers.

Ashlynne watched, remembering Holly in the choke hold. She swallowed hard.

"You can't blame Ashlynne 'cause Dan Clarkston freaked out at graduation," Kendra inserted, looking scared. "It's not her fault."

"But she is engaged to Cord Way, who happens to be the brother of that scheming witch Holly—and it *is* Holly's fault." Ethan dismissed Kendra with a cold glance, turning his attention back to Ashlynne. "Oh, I understand—I even appreciate—Holly's need for revenge but she went too far, sabotaging Dan that way."

"Holly?" Kendra looked confused. "Holly Way?"

"The Mistress of Dirty Tricks." Ethan was seething. "The Princess of Treachery. Do you know where I've just been?"

"The psycho ward?" guessed Kendra. "Too bad you left before you were cured."

"Will you kindly send that little brat away so we can talk?" Ethan demanded of Ashlynne. "This is extremely important."

Ashlynne motioned for Kendra to leave the room and the girl sauntered out, looking quite pleased with herself.

"I've just come from Dan's house," Ethan said. His cold gray eyes were tense and piercing. "That place is like a— a psycho ward! I told you a bit about the strain Dan's been under lately. Well, Holly's nasty little symphony of noise last night pushed him over the edge. After he disgraced himself at the graduation, he went home and had a huge fight with that viper Cindy. The battle resumed this morning. Cindy insists that she is resuming her career as of this afternoon and she's also refusing to make any more campaign appearances."

"Well, maybe it'll help their marriage." Ashlynne tried to sound optimistic.

"Cindy threatened to throw Dan out of the house." Ethan gave a scathing, scornful laugh. "How helpful is *that* to their marriage? And Dan is one of those whiny wimps with no backbone. He has no idea how to control a woman. Do you know what he did after Cindy made her threat?"

Ashlynne shivered and shook her head.

"He locked himself in the basement!" Ethan shouted, his face wild with frustration. "Took his guitar with him and began playing protest-movement songs, but his own insipid versions of them. Like 'Dan shall overcome.' He kept singing it over and over."

"Oh my," Ashlynne murmured.

"But that isn't the worst of it, oh no!" Ethan raged on. "Two nosy reporters showed up this morning to question Dan about his unfortunate performance at the graduation last night, and that wretched little monster Scotty let them in the house. They witnessed Cindy's threats and Dan's flight to the basement, they heard him singing down there like a lunatic! I tried to evict them. A—er—fight broke out and I decked them both, and then that insufferable nanny called the police. I left before they arrived, of course. I came straight here to get you. You have to come with me to OakWay right now, Ashlynne. I must see Holly, but I can't get past their damn security system. As Cord's fiancée, you'll be admitted to the hallowed grounds of OakWay and I'll be in the car with you. It's time to stop the insanity," he added dramatically.

" 'Dan shall overcome'?" Kendra was back, laughing. She made no pretense of not having eavesdropped. "Wow, he's really wigged out! Cool!"

Ashlynne stared at the gold wedding band on her sister's finger. It occurred to her at that moment that Kendra was the *wife* of Dan Clarkston's political opponent. And in Kendra's current triumphant mood, she would probably begin to boast of that fact to Ethan anytime now.

Ashlynne glanced nervously at Ethan, who was pacing the small room like an enraged, caged beast. Like one of the man-eating tigers they hadn't seen at the zoo. Right now his fury was focused on Holly, but if he were to learn that Wyatt Way had married teenaged Kendra Monroe . . .

He would use the information as ammunition to destroy Wyatt and, in the process, Kendra would be hurt too. Maybe badly hurt. Ashlynne gazed at Kendra, so beautiful and vibrant and brimming with joy. All her life she'd been protecting her baby sister, she was not about to stop now. She had to get Ethan out of here, away from Kendra, before he learned that she was Wyatt Way's wife.

Ethan wanted to go to OakWay to see Holly? Then she would take him there. From what she'd seen of Holly, the lady could hold her own with Thorpe.

"I'll go to OakWay with you, Ethan," Ashlynne said. "But not inside the house," she added quickly.

She glanced down at her white denim shorts and blue bandana-print halter top, Rayleen's clothes, which she'd kept for both sentimental and practical reasons. They were loose on her, her figure would never be as ripely voluptuous as her sister's, but the clothes were comfortable and still looked good as new. Her hair was pulled back in a high ponytail.

"You can see I'm not exactly dressed for a visit there," she said.

Ethan's eyes flicked over her. "You can wait in the car while I go inside. Once we get through the gates, we're all set."

"Kendra, the kids are due back within the hour. Will you stay with them?" Ashlynne asked.

"Sure," Kendra agreed. "Maybe I'll go over to the Dixons' now and see the kittens."

"Good idea." Ashlynne fairly pushed the younger girl out the door.

Ethan insisted that she drive his jet-black Jaguar Sedan, all part of his plan to get past the estate security system. He seemed to know a lot about it. Ashlynne knew nothing. She'd never been to OakWay.

"You mean you're engaged to that jerk and he's never taken you to visit the old family mansion?" Ethan was offended on her behalf.

"No." She guessed that Cord probably dreaded introducing her to his family as much as she dreaded having to meet them. Ashlynne stared down at the ring on her finger. She felt as if she were slowly waking from a very muddled dream.

"You've never met his mother, his grandfather, and the rest of the dragons?" Ethan wanted to know. "Have they refused to meet you?"

"Cord hasn't told them about me," Ashlynne confessed. "I didn't want him to."

"I'm sure he agreed to that in a hurry. Hell, Ashlynne, if he can't bring himself to even mention you, how on earth will he ever explain your little Daisy to them?"

A profound depression descended upon her. How, indeed? At a traffic light, she removed the ring and slipped it into the pocket of her white denim shorts. Her finger felt strange without the ring's now familiar weight. "If Cord wants to spare himself the humiliation, it's okay with me," she murmured. "It's not like we're officially engaged."

"From what I'm hearing, it seems to get less official by the minute," Ethan observed irritably.

They were stopped at the gates of the tall iron fence surrounding the grounds of OakWay. Ashlynne spoke her name into a metal box that demanded her identity, and they sat in the car waiting while her name was relayed to some command center within the perimeters.

She was surprised that her name allowed them to pass. Having been admitted to the grounds, they drove along the private road leading to another checkpoint, this one at the gate of the huge stone wall surrounding the house. A guard was in a small booth, watching a portable television. Iron gates, stone walls, armed guards, and an electronic monitoring system; Ashlynne was truly intimidated. She felt as if she'd entered a different country—under false pretenses. She stared into the unsmiling face of the guard.

"Give the guard your name," Ethan prompted, and she did.

The guard requested ID, proof that she was not an imposter, and she handed him her driver's license and library card.

After scrutinizing both items, and taking a long look at her face, the guard let her drive through the gates and up the tree-lined driveway, leading to the grand old house.

"I bet it was easier to pass behind the old Iron Curtain than get into OakWay." Ethan was irked. "Then again, their vaunted security system rates an F in my book. Nobody seemed to notice or care that I was in the car. Sure, you're Ashlynne Monroe, Cord's fiancée, but for all they know, I could be a paid assassin. Stupid." He shook his head, his lips twisted in disgust. "I loathe incompetence."

Ashlynne pulled the car in front of the big brick-and-frame house and turned off the engine. "Well, good luck."

"You're coming in with me," Ethan decreed. "Holly will come down to greet you. She'll undoubtedly parachute out a back window if she's told I'm here to see her," he added grimly.

"I can't go in there looking like this!" Ashlynne was horrified. "I told you I'd wait in the car and you agreed."

"Well, I changed my mind." Thorpe opened the door and dragged her across the seat and out of the car.

"No, no!" She looked down at her bare legs and old sandals as Ethan pulled her along after him. The halter top bared her midriff, exposed her navel. "I—I look like a character out of *Li'l Abner*. I can't—"

"Stop being ridiculous!" Ethan snapped. "You've had Cord's baby, he's got to marry you unless he wants to be slapped with a costly paternity suit. So what do you care if his snobbish relatives don't like your clothes? Flaunt it! They're stuck with you!"

Her breath seemed to burn her lungs as he dragged her after him. He had succinctly and contemptuously summed up exactly why Cord was marrying her, the true facts of Daisy's birth slightly altered, of course. But as the sister of the woman who'd given birth to Cord's child, as the guardian who was raising an illegitimate Way, she could indeed slap him with that costly, highly embarrassing paternity suit.

Did he worry that she would? Was that the real reason for his proposal to a woman he'd admitted not loving? All these years she'd feared the Ways in a custody suit, never realizing that they would fear the scandal and exposure she could bring down on them even more. And there were two very good reasons to suspect her of such sleazy actions: she was a Monroe and she worked for Ethan Thorpe.

Just how long would it take Cord to resent sacrificing his freedom for the family reputation? Not very long at all, Ashlynne guessed.

Trust Ethan Thorpe to put the cold, cruel facts all in perspective for her. Pain and anger tore through her, so intermingled that she couldn't define one from the other.

A white-haired uniformed butler opened the door the moment they stepped onto the porch. "Good grief, the old family retainer! How positively gothic," Ethan muttered to Ashlynne.

She knew by his uncharacteristic hesitance that the servant's aristocratic bearing had momentarily intimidated even Thorpe.

But only momentarily. "We want to see Holly Way," Ethan announced. "And—Cord. This is his fiancée."

The butler was unable to maintain his superior, slightly bored demeanor when he heard that. He gaped openly at Ashlynne. But before anyone could say another word, Cord hurried out to join them. "Security contacted me and said you were here."

Ashlynne's heart sank when she saw him. His suit, his shirt, his silk tie—he was pure, wealthy, high-class Way. And standing on the porch of the Way mansion, he had never seemed more inaccessible to her. She touched the pocket of her shorts, feeling the lump that was the ring inside. She had to give it back. It didn't belong to her and the handsome son of Waysboro's own royal family didn't either. There were fairy tales and there was real life, and in reality, Cinderella did not land the prince.

"This is a surprise, Ashlynne." Cord stared from her to Ethan.

"And one would have to guess not a particularly pleasant one, judging by your tone of voice and that pit-bull expression on your face," Ethan taunted. "Not exactly a warm welcome for the woman you're engaged to marry, Cord."

Ashlynne expected he'd said that to get another rise out of the butler. It worked.

"Sir, is it true?" the butler asked, astounded. "Are you really engaged to"—his incredulous gaze traveled over Ashlynne, from her ponytail to her halter top to her painted toes—"the young lady?"

"No," Ashlynne said quickly.

Cord cleared his throat. "Yes, Madison, we are engaged."

Ashlynne and Cord stared at each other. She was the first to look away.

"I want to see Holly," Ethan told the butler. "I'm going to marry her, although I'm sure you haven't been informed of that either."

If his intention was to totally flummox the old man, Thorpe succeeded masterfully. "I shall tell her you are here," Madison said, looking thoroughly befuddled. He hurried inside, Ethan at his heels.

Ashlynne watched with a feeling of relief. "Since I'm of no further use, I'll wait in the car." She started down the wide porch steps.

"Wait a minute." Cord caught her arm. "What's going on, Ashlynne?"

"Please take your hands off me. I've been manhandled enough for one day."

"Why are you here with Thorpe?" Cord demanded. He glanced anxiously toward the house. "Holly will—"

"I think what you really mean is, why am I here at all?" Ashlynne cut in. "Well, you don't have to worry, I'm not going to stay. Tell Ethan to call himself a taxi, I'm driving his car home."

"This is no time for you to get into a snit," Cord said sharply, still holding her arm, too hard and too tight. Ashlynne grimaced. "If I seem—distracted—it's because we're in the midst of a family crisis. Stafford is here, and my mother and grandfather. It seems that Wyatt eloped last night. He called with the news but not the identity of the bride. He—"

"Has the world gone mad?" Old Dayland Way appeared on the porch, flanked by Camilla and Stafford. None of them looked happy. "Cord, who is that man who just came charging into the house demanding to see Holly? Madison claims it is her fiancé!"

"I didn't get a clear look at him but he resembled that underhanded scoundrel Ethan Thorpe," Stafford said through gritted teeth. "I must be mistaken. Holly would never associate with the likes of him!"

"Holly never mentioned a fiancé," Camilla said, frowning. "Then again, Wyatt never mentioned a fiancée either, yet now he supposedly has a wife!"

"And no prenuptial agreement." Dayland removed a handkerchief from his pocket and wiped his brow. He seemed to notice Ashlynne for the first time. His piercing dark eyes settled on Cord's hand, fastened around her forearm. "Who is this?" he demanded imperiously.

"I'm selling magazine subscriptions," Ashlynne replied. "But it seems no one here wants to buy any." She jerked her arm out of Cord's grasp. "I'm leaving, you don't have to forcibly evict me."

"We do not permit salespeople on the premises." Stafford scowled forbiddingly at her. "I don't know how you got past security but—"

Ashlynne tried to make a mad dash to the car but Cord was too quick for her. He caught her hand and pulled her toward him. "Ashlynne, stop it!" he ordered sternly. "She isn't selling magazines." He turned to his family, bringing her along with him. "We're engaged."

The three shocked pairs of eyes stared at her as if she were a fly that had landed in their soup. Ashlynne cringed. She'd been humiliated during her years in Waysboro, she'd been made painfully aware of her low status time and again, but nothing matched what she was feeling now. And when she was revealed to be a Monroe . . .

"Engaged?" Camilla repeated faintly.

"*Another* secret engagement?" Old Dayland thundered. "Cord, Wyatt, Holly—all three are secretly engaged?"

"Wyatt has progressed beyond being secretly engaged, Grandfather," Stafford reminded him. "According to him, he is married!"

"Without a prenuptial agreement!" Dayland howled.

Holly and Ethan walked through the door, past the group on the porch. They were side by side but not touching. Compulsively, curiously, Ashlynne studied Holly Way. She wore a simple copper-colored dress that flowed fluidly over her, flattering her auburn hair, her creamy complexion, her shapely figure. Holly was so refined and elegant. Ashlynne felt a self-conscious thirteen again, back in the soda shop as the teen princess of Waysboro swept in with her entourage.

Except now Holly was with Ethan, who watched her with his steely gray eyes. Even in her own hapless circumstances, Ashlynne decided she wouldn't trade places with Holly Way in this or any lifetime.

Stafford, Camilla, and Dayland turned their attention from Ashlynne and Cord to Ethan and Holly.

"You really are Ethan Thorpe!" Stafford gasped, clearly not pleased with that knowledge.

"You really are Stafford Way," Ethan mocked. His eyes swept over the group, then lingered on Ashlynne. "So he finally got up the nerve to introduce you to the clan, eh, Ashlynne? Has he told them about little Daisy yet?"

"Shut up, Thorpe!" warned Cord.

"May I be among the first to congratulate you on your adorable granddaughter, Mrs. Way?" Ethan smiled at Camilla, his manner quite courtly. "Cord's own angelic little daughter. She's a sweet, bright child, I'm sure you'll positively dote on her. And wasn't it thoughtful of Ashlynne to continue the garden names for another generation—Camilla, Holly, Daisy. How charming."

"What is he talking about, Cord?" Camilla asked, her jaw so tightly clenched she barely moved her lips as she spoke.

"Get into the car, Ethan," Holly commanded tartly. "Or I'll change my mind about talking to you."

Ethan shrugged and smiled. "Whatever you say, darling."

Cord glanced worriedly from Ashlynne to his sister, walking away with Ethan Thorpe. "Holly, don't go with him," he called to her.

Holly walked on silently, Ethan at her side.

"This is a nightmare," Stafford moaned. "Holly with our avowed enemy, Wyatt married without a prenuptial agreement, and Cord . . ." He glared balefully at his brother. "Tell me that Thorpe was lying. Tell me that you don't have a child!"

CHAPTER NINETEEN

"IT'S true." Cord met his eldest brother's eyes. "I have a five-year-old daughter named Daisy Marie."

"And this young woman is the mother?" Old Dayland studied Ashlynne, his rigorous scrutiny mortifying her. "The child is five years old and you just got around to getting yourself engaged?"

"I feel faint," Camilla murmured.

"I'm going to contact our attorneys immediately." Stafford turned and rushed inside.

"I'm ashamed of you, boy!" Cord's grandfather pointed an accusing finger at him. "You are not married, you have a child, and you still haven't made an honest woman out of the mother. You're a disgrace to the proud, upstanding name of Way."

For a wild moment, Ashlynne forgot that it wasn't she who'd given birth to a Way out of wedlock. Since Rayleen no longer existed, since she was the one raising little Daisy, she became the tramp Dayland Way condemned. The one whom Cord had yet to make an "honest woman."

But wasn't she doing exactly what Rayleen had done, sleeping with Cord Way? And enjoying it. Ashlynne's face flushed scarlet with shame. The only difference was that he hadn't made her pregnant. Odd, how that pierced her heart. She wanted Cord's baby; she wished that Daisy really was her and Cord's child.

She'd always wished that.

Ashlynne finally allowed herself to admit the truth. All through Rayleen's pregnancy, from the moment of Daisy's birth and during the five years since, she had wanted the child to be her own because Cord was the father. Because she'd been attracted to Cord from the moment she met him.

She had wanted him for herself. And now she had fallen so deeply in love with him, it hurt to be near him, it even hurt to look at him, knowing that he didn't love her and never would.

Ashlynne reached into the pocket of her shorts, grabbed the ring and pressed it into Cord's hand. "I can't do it," she cried. "It'll never work."

"Ashlynne, you're being overemotional," Cord snapped. "Take this ring and—"

"I can't!" Maybe if she didn't love him so much she could endure a marriage of convenience for the children's sake. But to be with him, knowing he had only married her to give his child a name—or worse, to avoid an embarrassing, costly paternity suit—when she loved him and desperately wanted him to love her in return . . . It would be pure torture. Days and nights of it.

She couldn't take it!

It occurred to her that she didn't have to. She'd been remarkably passive lately, letting herself be dragged around by both Cord and Ethan, allowing Cord to pressure her into a pseudoengagement. It was only since Cord's return to Waysboro that she'd become so unassertive, letting things happen to her, rather than making them happen.

It was time to stop reacting and take action herself.

She turned and ran toward Ethan's car, adrenaline pumping through her veins, giving her speed and nerve that she normally wouldn't possess.

She heard Cord call her name, heard his footsteps. Was he coming after her? Probably. After all, his grandfather had practically ordered him to marry her. If Cord caught her, she would have to go back to the porch where old Dayland and Camilla stood lamenting the foibles of the younger generation.

She actually felt sorry for the pair. It had been a nasty way for them to learn about Daisy, but that was typically Ethan—a viper whose nature was to strike and hurt.

"Ashlynne, come here!" Cord was closing in on her.

She ran faster. She wasn't going to hang around and watch the Ways' reaction when Cord introduced her as a Monroe. Nor did she want to be within screaming distance of any of them when they learned that Wyatt had married teenaged Kendra Monroe.

Ethan's car was moving slowly around the circular drive and Ashlynne grabbed the door handle and pulled open the car door, catapulting herself inside.

She caught a glimpse of Cord through the window before she pulled the door closed. "Quick!" she cried. "Let's get out of here!"

Ethan floored the gas pedal and the car zoomed off at top speed.

Holly turned and stared at Ashlynne with cool, assessing brown eyes. "If you want Cord to follow you, we'll have to pull over and wait. It'll take time for him to go to the garage and get one of the cars."

"I don't want him to follow me!" Ashlynne was panting with exertion. "Ethan, could you take me—" She paused. She did not want him anywhere near Kendra, who might artlessly blurt out the news of her marriage. "To the nearest bus stop. I have some errands to run before I go home."

"Of course." Ethan nodded, smiling. Having dropped a bombshell on the Ways and made off with Holly had clearly turned his mood from foul to splendid.

"Cord has a little girl and you're the mother," Holly stated impassively, still staring at Ashlynne.

Ashlynne nodded. She could explain about Rayleen, but really, what was the point? Let Cord do that, if he wanted. She suspected he wouldn't. It would only complicate matters.

Holly turned her gaze to Ethan. "You certainly got a kick out of breaking the news to the family."

"I felt they had a right to know," Ethan said righteously. "I've changed, Holly. I don't believe in keeping secrets or holding things back. People should be open and honest, the truth must be told." He cleared his throat. "If we had followed that course in Columbus, think how differently things would have turned out for us."

Holly said nothing, but she was listening.

So was Ashlynne, and the longer she listened to Ethan Thorpe expound on the virtues of truth and honesty and trustworthiness—qualities that he claimed to possess in full measure these days—the more rebellious she became.

Her anger simmered, her mind a logjam of images and memories, of words of advice and warning. Ethan's smooth voice cut in and out of her reverie. He was extolling candor and integrity as prerequisites for successful living and loving.

Maybe if he hadn't begun a sentimental narrative detailing his great love of children, she would've simply kept her mouth shut and got out of the car when Ethan braked at the bus stop.

But his words were a flame that heated her anger to the boiling point. She'd listened to him demonize little Scotty Clarkston, heard his coldhearted refusal to honor the reward for Safe Haven where children were sheltered, watched him use Daisy's existence as a weapon to wound the Ways. This was not a man who loved children.

And she was no longer a passive observer, she was a woman of action.

"Before I go . . ." Ashlynne opened the car door so she could make a speedy exit. "I want to say that after listening to what you said about being honest and trustworthy and candid, I decided that starting right now, I'm making it my policy to tell everything to everybody."

"Good. Fine. Now run along and wait for your bus," Ethan said impatiently.

"First, I want to be open with Holly and share some truths with her. I want to tell her about your plan for the discount strip mall by Seneca Creek River, the one that will require the district congressman's intervention with the Corp of Engineers. I'm sure you'll fill in the details for her, then she can be candid and open with her brother Wyatt. And he can share the truth with the voters. Candor and honesty sure are contagious, aren't they? And here's my bus! Bye."

She scurried out of the car and onto the bus. It wasn't until she'd paid her fare that she realized it was heading to the Exton Mall. She decided to walk around inside the mall for a while before heading home, allowing herself a brief respite before the full force of the Way fury descended upon them.

*   *   *

Cord watched Ethan's car speed down the long driveway, carrying both Ashlynne and Holly. He glanced down at the ring in his hand and was filled with gloom.

"We can have security stop them at the gates," his grandfather said, squinting into the distance.

Cord shook his head. "If I'd treated Ashlynne like a fiancée instead of a trespasser, she wouldn't have run. Dragging her back like a fugitive will only make matters worse. As for Holly, we can't rescue her from Ethan Thorpe if she doesn't want to be rescued."

They walked into the house. Dayland disappeared into his study.

"Cord, what does my . . . granddaughter look like?" Camilla asked quietly.

An image of Daisy flashed before his mind's eye. "She's the cutest little girl I've ever seen." His voice was warm with pride. "She resembles Holly as a child. In fact, there's a picture of Holly in the sitting room off the kitchen that's practically a dead ringer for Daisy. Except her hair is the same color as mine."

Cord saw the pain in his mother's eyes. He knew he had annoyed her down through the years, he had disappointed and angered her too. But this was the first time he had really hurt her. "Mother, I'm sorry," he said softly.

"Does she have dark eyes?" Camilla pressed.

Cord nodded. "Just like mine. And she's the smartest little kid! She started kindergarten a whole year early because she'd already learned everything that preschool could teach her."

"I have always wanted a granddaughter. I hope to meet her soon. Perhaps you will invite her and her mother to dinner this week?"

Cord was grateful for her diehard etiquette and for everything she didn't say. "I will, Mother. But first, I want to tell you some things about Ashlynne."

"You really don't have to, what's done is done," Camilla said quickly. She drew in a deep breath. "I recognized her as the girl in the newspapers, the one whose child was lost. Oh, you will have to bring that other little girl to dinner as well. Are there any more children?" she asked bravely.

"Mother, you really need to hear this," Cord insisted. He backed her into a side parlor. And began to explain. Everything.

Less than an hour later, he was knocking on Ashlynne's apartment door. The cast-off engagement ring was tucked into the pocket of his white T-shirt, his arms were filled with flowers. Daisies. He thought them symbolic.

Kendra opened the door. "Flowers for Rayleen's grave?" she asked jovially and laughed at her own joke. "Remember that day, Cord? It was the first time I met you and now we're—"

"Uncle Cord, we played with the kittens today!" Daisy came running over to him.

Her warm welcome thrilled him. He was finally becoming friends with his daughter. The hours he'd spent as the girls' baby-sitter had been invaluable in gaining her trust. Cord longed to pick her up and hug her but he held back. Knowing Daisy as he was beginning to, he was aware that any physical gestures would have to be initiated by her.

"You like the black kitten best," he said, remembering. "And Maxie likes the gray and white striped one."

"No, now I like the all-gray one best," Maxie called from across the room. She was standing on top of the back of the sofa and jumped off, hurling herself through the air, her blond pigtails flying. "Watch me, watch me!"

Cord and Daisy turned to look. And then, quick as a flash, he was striding across the room to catch Maxie as she somersaulted through the air. His heart was pounding as he set her on her feet.

"You almost landed on your head." Cord frowned sternly at her.

Maxie pouted. "I was doing a flip."

"You could've broken your neck, Maxie. No gymnastic stunts except in the gym, do you understand?"

Daisy joined them. "If you break your head or your neck, they have to give you a great big needle to make you better," she told her sister. "Right, Uncle Cord?"

Cord nodded. "That's right. The needle is this big." His hands spanned the length of a butcher knife.

"Maxie hates needles," Daisy explained rather needlessly, for Maxie gawked in horror at Cord's imaginary giant needle.

"I don't like them much either," said Cord. "Do we have a deal, Maxie? No more flips off the furniture?"

Maxie nodded. "Can I keep the gray kitty?" she asked.

"We'll see." Cord offered the time-honored adult stall.

"Can we have some peanut-butter crackers?" Maxie pressed. Cord knew that the requests wouldn't stop until she received a "yes" answer to one of them. He okayed the crackers, and the children skipped off to the kitchen.

"You sound just like a dad, Cord."

Cord noticed Wyatt for the first time, standing by the window. He stared at his brother in surprise.

"You act like a dad too," Wyatt continued. "You moved faster than Maxie and she moves at the speed of light."

"That she does. I'm looking forward to being their full-time father." Cord glanced toward the kitchen and lowered his voice. "Wyatt, there's something I want you to know about Daisy. She is my—"

"I already know, Cord," Wyatt said quietly. "Kendra filled me in on everything."

Kendra was suddenly at Wyatt's side. She slipped her arms around him and cuddled against him. Wyatt gazed adoringly at her.

And then Cord recalled the shocking news of the day, the phone call precipitating the family war council: the announcement of Wyatt's surprise elopement. Staring at Kendra and Wyatt, he finally put the pieces together. "You married *Kendra*? My God, Wyatt, have you lost your mind? She's—she's—"

"—my wife," Wyatt finished for him. "And I'm in full possession of all my faculties, thank you very much." Kendra rewarded him with a quick kiss and a dazzling smile.

Cord stared at them, at a loss for words.

"Ashlynne is thrilled for us," Kendra said breezily, then gazed thoughtfully at Cord. "Where is Ashlynne, anyway? Ethan Thorpe hustled her out of here to go to OakWay a while ago. Weren't you there? Didn't you see her?"

"I saw her. She gave me this." Cord pulled the ring from his pocket. "Then she left with Holly and Thorpe. I thought she'd be back here."

Kendra frowned, but before she could comment, the telephone rang and she hurried off to answer it.

Cord faced his brother. "What about the campaign, Wyatt?"

"I'm going to resign as candidate." Wyatt smiled. "It's a profound relief, Cord. I'm not a politician, I was playing a role I was all wrong for. Kendra is moving into my place today but we're leaving Waysboro as soon as possible," he added. "She has always wanted to go and, let's face it, we can't have a life together here."

"It's a lot to take in," Cord murmured. His mind was reeling. *Wyatt with a teenaged bride? Was it an early mid-life crisis or pure lust?*

"I love her, Cord. Marrying her is the best thing I've ever done," Wyatt said decisively, as if reading his brother's reeling mind.

Kendra joined the brothers a few minutes later. "That was Ashlynne. She said she won't be back for a while and asked if I'd stay with the kids." She frowned, her expression troubled. "It was a . . . strange call."

Cord felt a twinge of alarm. "What do you mean by strange?"

"Well, I heard Ethan Thorpe's voice and when I asked Ashlynne if she was at the office, she said yes. But the noise in the background didn't sound"—she paused—"like an office."

"I'll call her at Thorpe's office right now." Cord went into the kitchen to place the call only to be told by the temp that Ethan Thorpe was out of the office and not expected back. She had no idea where Ashlynne Monroe was either.

Maxie and Daisy asked for juice and he poured it for them before returning to the living room. Kendra and Wyatt, in the middle of a hushed conversation, immediately fell silent.

"You're holding something back," Cord guessed. "What gives, Kendra? What else did Ashlynne say to you?"

"I think she should tell you herself," Kendra said loftily.

"Well, she's not here to tell me, is she? Wyatt, kindly assert your husbandly authority and order your wife to tell me what my fiancée had to say."

"She's not your fiancée anymore, remember?" Kendra blurted out. "Ashlynne said that she's not going to marry you. She said she doesn't want a marriage of convenience. That's what she told me over the phone when I asked why she'd given you back your ring."

"Damn!" Cord sat down on the sofa.

"I have an idea," Wyatt suggested calmly. "Kendra and I will take the children home with us. I'm sure you and Ashlynne will have a lot to talk over and you'll need privacy."

Cord accepted the offer at once. Privacy was certainly essential for the conversation he had in mind. And the sweet aftermath.

"A little advice," Kendra offered on her way out the door. "Try to come up with another reason why she should marry you besides *convenience*. That is so uncool, not to mention totally unromantic."

"Bye, Uncle Cord," Maxie called, waving as she ran out the door.

"Uncle Wyatt has a VCR and he is going to rent some cartoons. Maxie loves cartoons," Daisy said, explaining her sister's haste. She looked up at Cord. "Want to come with us?" she asked shyly.

Cord felt a peculiar tightness in his chest. "I'd love to, Daisy. But I have to wait here for your mom." He laid his hand on top of her head. Her hair was smooth and silky. "See you later, okay?"

"Okay." Daisy flashed him a quick smile, then ran down the stairs to catch Maxie.

"Well, here we are. Home sweet home." Ethan pulled the Jaguar sedan into his garage, then triggered the automatic door to close.

Ashlynne sat beside him in the bucket seat, trying to maintain an air of calm. She'd worked for this man for three years, she told herself. He was a snake at times, but she was not afraid of him.

"You've never been to my house before, have you, Ashlynne?" Ethan asked, his tone that of the genial host. "How remiss of me not to have invited you before."

"You didn't exactly invite me here today," Ashlynne reminded him. "You grabbed me at the bus stop in front of the Exton Mall and forced me into your car."

She got out of the car while he was coming around to open the door for her. Having no other option, she had to follow him inside the house.

"Would you like something to eat? Something cold to drink?" Ethan asked politely. "Or perhaps you'd prefer something hot? Coffee or tea?"

"I don't want anything." Ashlynne declined the hospitality, if that's what it was. "I just want to go home."

"Not yet. Not enough time has passed to incriminate you." He smiled coldly. "Your foolish little sister must first tell Cord Way that she heard soft music playing in the background while she was talking to you and that she heard me call you darling. She has to tell him that I told you how much I've always admired you, that I long to be with you."

Ashlynne thought of that convoluted conversation she'd had with Kendra over Ethan's car phone. She'd called to make sure Kendra would stay with the children, but before she could hang up, her inquisitive little sister had demanded to know why she'd returned Cord's ring.

She might have been confused by Ethan's unexpected romantic utterings had she not been sitting next to him and seen with her own eyes that he didn't mean a word of it. His expression had been so sardonic, she'd thought he was making fun of her. Now she realized those words had been meant for Kendra to overhear. So she would tell them to Cord.

"You can't be trying to make Cord jealous?" Ashlynne asked incredulously.

"My goal is to make him miserable. Having the mother of his child in bed with his sister's lover surely won't be pleasing to him."

"I'm not going to bed with you!" Ashlynne cried. There was no use kidding herself now. He was a poisonous reptile and she was afraid of him.

"I don't want you enough to bother seducing you," Ethan said, shrugging. "But Cord Way will believe that you slept with me. I intend to make sure of that."

"You want to punish Cord and—and me because Holly turned you down?" Ashlynne glanced nervously around the large combination living-dining room. It was all chrome and leather with a black tile floor, black furniture, and black wallpaper striped thinly with white. The place reminded her of a bat cave, and a shiver ran along her spine.

"If you hadn't mouthed off about the strip mall, Holly would be here with me right now," Ethan said tightly.

"No she wouldn't. Holly told Cord she was through with you before I said a word about the strip mall." Ashlynne glared at him, unwilling to allow him his delusion. "You walked out on her when she was pregnant. No woman can forgive or forget that. Then you condemned her for having an abortion and decided to seek revenge against her whole family. How can you possibly believe that she would ever want anything to do with you again? You've been hateful to her and you made her hate you."

"It's far more complex than that. I made Holly admit the truth to me today and she did. She has deep sexual feelings for me that terrify her because she refuses to allow herself to lose control again. Does that sound like hate to you?"

"Well, it doesn't sound like love either," Ashlynne retorted.

"I have to win her trust back," Ethan muttered. "When she demanded that I let her out of the car, I did, instead of bringing her here."

"So you went looking for me and brought me here instead," Ashlynne said glumly. If only she'd put up a fight when she saw him at the bus stop. But she hadn't expected him to grab her into the car and he'd moved so quickly, she was inside before she could marshal a defense.

He nodded. "I noticed you'd taken the bus to the Exton Mall. I decided to see if I could find you there so I parked near the bus stop and waited for you to come out."

"And now you're going to make Cord think we're having a fling or something?" Ashlynne swallowed hard. "Ethan, that is not going to make you more desirable to Holly, trust me on that."

"Holly has always been most forgiving about other women," Ethan said with an arrogant smirk. "But I don't think her brother will be equally forgiving when the woman he is about to marry beds down with her boss. He might even brand you an unfit mother and go after his kid in court. It's no less than what you deserve." His voice turned menacing. "You made a big mistake crossing me, Ashlynne."

"Obviously." Ashlynne tried to keep her cool. She knew how much Ethan enjoyed threats and intimidation. "After all, you wrote the book on revenge." She folded her arms in front of her and hoped she looked fearless. "Now what?"

"Now we wait for Cord Way to figure out that his lovely fiancée is getting laid by her boss." He caught her arm. "Come with me."

She immediately began to fight, kicking and hitting and scratching. "I won't let you do this, Ethan! I'm sick of being dragged around like a rag doll. I'll fight you until you have to kill me, and don't think you'll get away with it either. Kendra knows you were with me, you'll be arrested, you'll get the death penalty—"

"Will you knock off the dramatics?" Ethan released her, rubbing his cheek that she'd scratched and wincing as she landed a swift kick to his shin. "I'm not going to rape you. I'm just going to lock you in my bedroom for a while. Now you can either walk there quietly or fight me the entire way, but keep in mind I know karate. I can render you unconscious with one blow."

"Then you'll have to do it because I'm not going to let you lock me up!"

Ethan looked at her for a long moment, then sighed. "This is your own choice, you know. I'm sorry, Ashlynne."

Ashlynne didn't even see it coming. Suddenly everything went black.

When she opened her eyes, she was aware of a dull ache in her neck. And then she saw the black wallpaper with tiny white dots, the black chair and ottoman, and the thick black coverlet that she was lying upon. She knew instantly where she was. Ethan Thorpe's bedroom. The decor was as sepulchral as the rest of his house.

She sat up gingerly, half expecting to feel a rush of dizziness. Happily, she did not, and she looked around the room. There was a set of handcuffs on the end table and an unopened bottle of bourbon. She shuddered, wondering what kind of weird scene Ethan planned to stage for Cord.

One thing was certain. She was not going to hang around to see.

Moving slowly and cautiously to the window, she glanced outside. The room was on the first floor; she wouldn't even have to jump. She opened the window, removed the screen, and climbed out. It was almost insultingly easy.

Then it occurred to her that she'd had a lucky break, that Ethan had undoubtedly intended to handcuff her to the brass headboard but hadn't gotten around to it yet. If he had, the ground window would've been of no use to her.

She began to run.

To distract himself, Cord used his calling card to place a series of calls from Ashlynne's apartment. He talked to Mary Beth about occupancy rates, the reconstruction progress on the south wing, and Jack Townsend's daily diminishing desire to leave Glacier. Next he called a wholesale food supplier and a new Washington State winery that was offering a special rate on their latest and supposedly best-ever vintage. He talked to three different travel agencies about the family vacation package he and Mary Beth had worked up for the lodge, based on their already-in-place, highly successful one for the campground.

Still charged with energy, he paced the small apartment, wandering from room to room as he rehearsed what he would say to Ashlynne when she walked through the door. Gradually, his intensity level began to diminish, and he reached for the phone again.

He called OakWay and asked for Holly, not expecting her to be there, worrying that she'd been mesmerized again by Ethan Thorpe. He was surprised when she came to the phone.

"I told Ethan it was over between us forever," Holly said. She sounded as if she'd been crying but Cord didn't press her on that. "He took it very well, like a gentleman. But he—he seemed so sad."

"You did the right thing, Holly," Cord assured her. "Don't undermine yourself with misplaced sympathy for the guy. Holly, where did Ashlynne go after the three of you left OakWay?"

"Ethan left her off at a bus stop, before he and I had our final talk." Holly sounded tearful again.

"Did you happen to see if she got on a bus?"

Holly paused, trying to remember. "I think she did. Yes, I'm almost sure she did," she added with a bit more certainty but not much interest.

"And did you happen to notice the destination of the bus?" Cord stifled a sigh of impatience. He was not surprised when Holly replied with a distracted, "No."

Where was Ashlynne?

She had taken the bus somewhere and then called Kendra to report that she was in Thorpe's office. But she hadn't been there, and neither had Thorpe. Cord frowned.

It was boring here in the apartment with nothing to do, no one to talk to. He switched on the television set. Soap operas were on every channel, and he watched the perfect people suffering and tried to interest himself in their problems. He decided his own situation was far more compelling.

After the soaps came the talk shows. The guests were eager to discuss all sorts of personal traumas, some so bizarre he found himself slack-jawed with astonishment. He had to admit that his own situation didn't hold a candle to theirs.

Still no Ashlynne. It was time for the evening news. Cord watched as he ate a bowl of cereal, obviously a brand favored by the children. The orange, red, yellow, green, and purple pieces of toasted oats turned the milk a very peculiar shade so he ate without looking into the bowl.

"An unusual twist in a Maryland congressional race." The newscaster's voice, rather slyly pleased, caught Cord's attention. He leaned forward to listen.

"Both candidates running for the House seat currently held by longtime Representative Archer Way have taken themselves out of the race." The anchorman smirked. "Wyatt Way, Congressman Way's great-nephew, and his opponent, Daniel Clarkston, have both cited personal reasons for their respective withdrawals. New candidates will be chosen either by party officials or in a special runoff election—"

The phone rang and Cord sprang to answer it. He desperately wanted it to be Ashlynne. More likely it was Kendra checking anxiously on her sister for at least the fortieth time.

It was neither. Ethan Thorpe was on the line. "I think you should know that your *fiancée* is on her way home after spending the afternoon with me." Thorpe's voice was cool and smooth and condescendingly amused. "Tell her that she forgot her hair band, at least I think that's what you'd call it. It's elastic and about the size of a bracelet and she uses it to pull her hair up in a ponytail. It's a blue print that matches the halter top she's wearing, so she'll undoubtedly want it back. Tell her that it's right here in the bedroom where she left it."

"Where is Ashlynne?" Cord asked roughly. "If you've done anything to her—"

"I did nothing to her that she didn't specifically ask me to do." Thorpe chuckled. "And she was gracious enough to return the favor. You're a lucky man, Way. Who would've dreamed that sweet, proper little Ashlynne is dynamite in the sack? Of course you already know that, don't you?"

"You're a liar, Thorpe! Ashlynne wouldn't touch you unless you held a loaded gun to her head. And maybe not even then."

"Oh, there was no gunplay. Just plenty of foreplay. And afterplay, following the main event, if you get my drift. And never underestimate the passion of a vengeful woman, Cord. Ashlynne feels very wronged by you and this time she's determined to get her own back. She might have been using me as an instrument of revenge but I didn't mind. My . . . instrument is at her disposal whenever she says the word."

Cord slammed the receiver down in the cradle.

Ashlynne and Thorpe? No, it was impossible! When Kendra phoned in again, he told her about the outrageous call. To his astonishment, Kendra burst into tears and hung up on him. When he called back, she refused to talk to him.

But Wyatt didn't. And Kendra had confided the details to him of that peculiar phone call with Ashlynne. "There was mood music playing," Wyatt said tersely. "And Kendra overheard Thorpe call Ashlynne darling. She heard him telling Ashlynne how much he'd admired her, how long he'd wanted her."

And Ashlynne had lied about her whereabouts, claiming to be at the office. But neither she nor Thorpe had been there; the temp had been clear on that fact.

"Ashlynne feels wronged by you." Thorpe's voice seemed to echo in Cord's head. And Thorpe had been rejected by Holly.

Cord pictured Ashlynne and her boss getting together for a little Way-bashing, Thorpe smooth and attentive, a hurt and angry Ashlynne vulnerable to his charms.

He closed his eyes. The thought of her with Ethan Thorpe or any other man was devastating. Pain richocheted through him, so deep and searing that he felt it viscerally, in his chest, in his gut.

He loved her. He really loved her. Cord acknowledged the truth he'd been dodging. He'd scornfully dismissed the act of falling in love as an exercise in self-deception, but he saw now that he had it backward. He was in love with Ashlynne and had deceived himself that he was not.

His timing was abysmal, there could be no denial of that. On the day he'd finally admitted his love for her, Ashlynne had disappeared with the devious Ethan Thorpe.

If he were to finally tell her that he loved her, would she even care?

Nobody knew better than he that Ashlynne was no casual bedhopper. If she'd allowed Thorpe to make love to her, it was not for revenge as Thorpe claimed but because she had deep feelings for him. Cord imagined the scene in sickening sequence: Ashlynne commiserating with her boss, then realizing that she loved him in a revelation as profound as the one he'd had about his love for her.

He was so preoccupied with his dreary reverie that he didn't hear the footsteps on the stairs or the key in the lock.

CHAPTER TWENTY

ASHLYNNE walked into the apartment. She was hot and sweaty and her feet were swollen and dusty from her long trek. And there was Cord, sitting on her sofa, staring mindlessly at the television screen.

Her heart took off at a ferocious rate. He was wearing jeans and a T-shirt and looked more like the rebellious alter ego of his Waterside Bar days. Minus his scandalously un-Way-like ponytail, of course. Perhaps it was his attire or maybe the fact that he was in her own apartment that made him seem approachable, unlike the aristocratic scion of OakWay.

She wanted to run to him and fling herself into his arms, safe at last from her frightening encounter with Ethan and her long, hot walk home. Being Ashlynne, she waited cautiously for a sign that he might welcome such a greeting.

Cord stood up. She looked hot and tired. It was very obvious that she'd been engaged in some kind of strenuous activity. In Ethan Thorpe's bedroom?

"Where have you been?" he asked, congratulating himself on his even tones. It wouldn't do to fly off the handle and hurl accusations like a man wronged.

The small glimmer of hope within Ashlynne died. He was as inaccessible as ever, cool and indifferent. She was not about to throw herself at him like a pathetic fool.

"Where are the girls?" She countered his question with one of her own. She was pleased that she'd managed to sound as laconic as he.

"At Wyatt's." Cord walked toward her. This wasn't going to be easy. Every hot-blooded male instinct he possessed urged him to grab her and show her who she belonged to and always would. But he didn't dare, not when she was regarding him with the detached air of a stranger.

"What are they doing there?"

"He's got a lot of room over there, a big yard for them to play in. He has a dog and a VCR, plus it's air-conditioned. We figured it was better than keeping them cooped up here all afternoon."

The implicit criticism stung. "I've never heard them complain about having to live here. This place may seem like a dump next to your exalted standards at OakWay but—"

"I didn't mean it that way!" Cord's voice rose. "Look, I'm not here to argue with you." He squared his shoulders and looked directly into her eyes. "Where have you been, Ashlynne? I—was worried about you."

"I was walking," Ashlynne said at last. She had no desire to fan the flames of the Thorpe–Way feud using herself as fuel. Therefore she wouldn't mention Ethan's depraved plan and her frantic flight. She'd kept watch over her shoulder every step of the way, terrified that Ethan would pop up like some perilous jack-in-the-box.

Instead, she glanced down at her feet in the old sandals. "These definitely aren't the shoes for a crosstown trek. I feel like soaking my feet in Epsom salts for a week."

"You've been walking," Cord repeated flatly.

"I had to pass by the cemetery so I stopped by the graves. The plant you bought for Rayleen is doing nicely," she added nervously.

Cord could no longer maintain the charade. Ashlynne's evasiveness served to confirm Thorpe's claim. But instead of rage, he felt only sorrow. He loved her. He couldn't lose her to a villain like Thorpe, a man who would only use and hurt her.

"Ashlynne, Ethan Thorpe called," Cord said quietly. "He said you left your hair band at his house."

Ashlynne instinctively touched her hair. "We call them scrunchies, not hair bands," she said. She wasn't sure where she'd lost the blue bandana-print one she'd worn earlier; she'd wished for it on the hot walk home, to pull her hair off her neck. So Ethan was in possession of it?

She gulped. "Did he say anything else?" It seemed highly unlikely that he would call to report her lost scrunchy without gleefully implementing his heinous plan.

Cord found he could not confront her. If he was to have any chance with her at all, she had to trust him enough to confide the truth to him. "Ashlynne, I—don't like Ethan Thorpe, I guess I've made no secret of that." He tried to smile encouragingly. "However, I realize that he must have a—a certain something—"

"He's got something all right," Ashlynne said. "It's called a personality disorder."

Cord felt a flash of hope. If Ashlynne had already figured out she'd been used by Thorpe, his own chances with her would improve greatly. But he had to be very careful not to put her on the defensive. "You sound angry with him," Cord remarked blandly. "Are you?"

Considering the dreadful afternoon she'd spent, the question struck her as so astoundingly stupid that Ashlynne reverted to Kendra-slang to answer it. "Does the word 'duh' have any meaning for you?"

Cord walked toward her, his dark eyes glittering. "Ashlynne, I just want you to know that I understand. I—I—I'm not happy about it, of course, but I promise never to bring it up again. From this moment on, we'll put it behind us."

"Put what behind us?" Ashlynne was disconcerted by the intensity of his eyes. The last time she'd seen a similar concentration and drive, she'd been karate-chopped and locked in a bedroom.

"Ashlynne, you don't have to pretend. I know. Thorpe told me. I hate him for using you, I hate the idea of you with him, but I know you're not to blame. I know you were hurt and confused and he took advantage of you."

"Exactly what did Ethan tell you?"

"Where you've been this afternoon, what you were doing. That you left your—er—scrunchy in his—his bedroom." Cord fought back the jealousy surging through him. "Sweetheart, I swear I'll never hold it against you. We—we can even find something positive in this whole unfortunate—incident. You see, I figure that this puts us on a more even footing. You've had to cope with the specter of my past with Rayleen and now I—"

"—have to cope with the specter of me and Ethan?" Ashlynne gaped at him, as comprehension dawned. Cord thought she'd spent the day in bed with Ethan Thorpe! Ethan had spewed those disgusting lies and Cord had believed him!

"And you're noble enough to forgive me?" Her voice rose to an indignant squeak. The more she considered it, the worse it got. "Well, how big of you!"

Her temper exploded hot and fast as a neutron bomb. She snatched Kendra's copy of *Cosmopolitan*, rolled it up, and began to swat at Cord. "Get out! Get out of my apartment right now! As if today hasn't been bad enough, now I have to endure your long-suffering forgiveness for something I haven't even done! Well, I won't, I've had it! I won't be a—a pawn for you and Ethan to use in your stupid family feud. I quit!"

Her attack caught Cord completely off guard. He'd been prepared for tears of remorse or the sad and disillusioned confession of a sadder-but-wiser girl.

But not for her unrestrained fury. He tried to dodge her blows as she drove him toward the door. He certainly hadn't expected to be beaten by a magazine reeking of perfume ads.

When they got to the door, Ashlynne caught him unawares again and gave him a hard push, forceful enough to get him across the threshold. She didn't waste a moment in slamming the door behind him.

He rang the bell and pounded on the door. Ashlynne did not respond. Her concern for her neighbors' peace and quiet had led her to open the door to that serpent Ethan Thorpe, but she was not going to fall into that trap again. If her neighbors were disturbed by the racket, let them call the police!

The phone rang and she hurried to answer it. A worried Kendra cried tears of relief when she heard Ashlynne's voice.

"Ashlynne, when I heard that sexy music, when I heard the things Ethan Thorpe said, I thought—"

"You thought exactly what that fiend wanted you to think," Ashlynne cut in. "Honestly, Kendra, you've known me your whole life. Give me some credit. The day Ethan Thorpe sweet-talks me into bed will be the day the lost continent of Atlantis rises from the sea."

"Does Cord think—" Kendra began, but Ashlynne cut her off immediately.

"I don't care what he thinks. He may be Daisy's father and your brother-in-law but he is nothing to me."

"Uh-oh."

"I'd like you to bring Maxie and Daisy home now, Kendra. I appreciate you and Wyatt taking care of them at his house. After all, it's so much bigger and cooler and more fun there than here."

"Yikes," said Kendra.

The ringing and pounding and demands for her to open the door had ceased by the time Ashlynne hung up the phone. She grudgingly credited Cord for having the good sense to know when to give up. Thorpe probably would've lobbed canisters of tear gas through the window. She shuddered, reliving her narrow escape from him.

She would never go back to that office. He could mail her the few personal items from her desk or she would send in some of her most unsavory relatives to collect her things—armed.

Trudging back to the bathroom, Ashlynne turned on the shower, lowered the temperature to lukewarm, peeled off Rayleen's clothes, and gratefully stepped under the cool, cleansing spray.

It was only then that she allowed the tears to fall, and they streaked down her cheeks, mingling with the water from the showers head.

Kendra and Wyatt arrived half an hour later with Daisy and Maxie in tow. The couple didn't stay, they were openly eager to return to the quiet privacy of Wyatt's house. Ashlynne gladly turned her attention to the two little girls. They were bubbling with the news of their day—the big black dog Judge, the cartoons they'd seen, the tree they'd climbed in the backyard.

They were also intrigued that Kendra would be spending the night with Uncle Wyatt.

"Uncle Wyatt is Kendra's husband," Maxie explained importantly. "That's like a boyfriend, except you can sleep over at his house."

"Do wish you had a husband, Mommy?" Daisy asked, watching her mother closely.

"Because Kendra has one, you mean?" Ashlynne pasted a bright smile on her face. "Well, I have you two girls, and I feel very, very lucky."

Someday, she would have to tackle the issue of the children's fathers, she'd always known that. Maxie and Daisy knew Rayleen had given birth to them but never referred to the fact. They never mentioned a father or the lack of one either. Perhaps they unconsciously realized it was a not a subject open for discussion.

But Ashlynne didn't want them to grow up in an atmosphere of secrecy and subterfuge. The day was coming for a heart-to-heart, fact-filled chat; she owed them that. She also knew it was not going to be today.

"Time for bed," she ordered, mustering up maternal cheer.

She tucked both little girls in their beds and kissed them good-night.

"Mommy, if you married Uncle Cord, he would be your husband, right?" Maxie called as she started out of the room.

Ashlynne paused. Maxie frequently came up with ploys to delay the inevitable lights-out. Ashlynne wished she'd stuck to her usual claims of unbearable thirst or demands for food.

"Uh-huh." Daisy answered her sister's question. "And he would be our daddy too. Uncle Cord wants to be our daddy. He said so."

He would! Ashlynne burned. Simply hearing Cord "I-won't-hold-it-against-you-now-we're-on-even-footing" Way's name infuriated her.

But the five-year-old's remark highlighted the predicament ahead—when and how to tell Daisy that Cord was her daddy, regardless of their marital status. She worried and wondered how both Daisy and Maxie would react to the news.

Her shoulders drooped tiredly. "Go to sleep," was all she said.

She said it again after bringing Maxie a glass of water.

Thankfully, there was no more talk of husbands or daddies for the rest of the night.

Ashlynne awakened shortly past dawn feeling charged as a high-voltage wire. The idea of spending the day in this apartment, dreading the appearance of Cord—or God forbid, Ethan Thorpe—activated a rebellious streak within her worthy of the most recalcitrant Monroe.

She woke Maxie and Daisy and dressed them in the new outfits Kendra had purchased for them.

"We're going on a trip," Ashlynne announced as the girls sleepily shoveled cereal in their mouths. "Just the three of us."

She almost called Kendra, so ingrained was the habit of keeping tabs on her little sister, but Ashlynne refrained. Kendra was married now, living under her husband's roof. Constant sisterly surveillance was no longer a necessity.

She packed a small suitcase and the three of them took the bus to the area bus station in Exton. Ashlynne boldly pulled out her charge card, which she'd obtained strictly for emergencies so dire she had yet to use it, and charged three bus tickets to the beach.

"We're going to Ocean City," she told the two excited little girls. "We're going to stay overnight in a hotel and go to the beach and swim in the ocean. We're going to walk on the boardwalk and ride some rides."

She thought of how much she'd enjoyed those days in Montana as a break from the routine of everyday life. Now she and the children would do it together, escape to an entirely different setting. She tried convincing herself that Cord's presence wasn't why she'd been so happy in Glacier, that it was the vacation and the getting away from it all that made those days so memorable. She knew she was kidding herself, and her spirits began to sag.

But Maxie and Daisy were thrilled with this adventure, and their enthusiasm was catching. By the time the bus finally pulled into Ocean City, Ashlynne was excited too.

She didn't let herself think about the credit-card bill arriving next month, she didn't worry how she would pay it.

She knew she would. Today was all about enjoying their time together at the seashore.

Maxie and Daisy loved the motel so much they were reluctant to leave it. They were delighted with their room, with the swimming pool, and with the array of soda and snack machines.

Ashlynne finally coaxed them into going to the beach, first stopping along the boardwalk to buy the essential sunscreen, beach towels, sandpails, and shovels. She only winced a little at the jacked-up tourist prices.

The girls loved the sand and the ocean and they stayed all day, until the lifeguards departed at six. They made numerous trips to the boardwalk for snacks and drinks, feasting on a variety of junk food, all of it delicious.

They were strolling on the boardwalk later that evening when a vendor with a huge bunch of colorful helium-filled Mylar balloons of assorted shapes and sizes captured the children's attention.

"Can we get a balloon?" cried Maxie. "I want a blue fish balloon! Please, Mommy!"

"Just five dollars!" the vendor called encouragingly.

"Five dollars for a balloon?" Ashlynne swallowed. She was determined to enjoy their vacation to the fullest, cost be damned, but *five dollars for a balloon*?

"Okay," she said bravely. "We'll take the blue fish and— Which one do you want, Daisy?"

"Can we have two?" Daisy asked.

Ashlynne stared at her, shocked. That was a Maxie question that not even Maxie had asked.

" 'Cause there's Uncle Cord with two parrot balloons," Daisy explained. "Am I supposed to get one here too?"

Ashlynne whirled around to see Cord walking toward them, holding the strings of two bright green parrot-shaped balloons. She blinked, wondering for an irrational split second if they were mutually hallucinating.

But Cord was no apparition.

"Imagine running into you three down here!" Cord exclaimed. "Small world, huh?" He glanced at Ashlynne's stony expression, at the children's excited, happy faces.

"Are those balloons for us?" Maxie sang out.

"They sure are." Cord handed each child a balloon.

"Do you want a fish balloon, Daisy?" Ashlynne asked, without glancing at Cord.

"No, I just like this parrot," replied Daisy. She beamed at Cord.

The kids did not find it odd that Cord had turned up and instantly made him a part of their group. The four walked along the boardwalk, the children holding tight to the strings of their balloons, Ashlynne holding a child by each hand.

She ended up holding the balloons when they reached an amusement pavilion with kiddie rides. With Maxie and Daisy on the junior race cars, she and Cord were left to wait by the exit gate.

"You haven't said a word to me," Cord said.

Ashlynne watched the race cars go round and round the track. "I don't have anything to say to you."

"Aren't you even curious about how I got here?" he asked patiently.

"You drove, I presume."

He smiled slightly. "And you and the kids took the eight A.M. bus from Exton."

Ashlynne whirled to face him. "Were you spying on us or something?"

"Or something. I hired a detective to track you down. It didn't take him long."

"A detective!" Ashlynne was flabbergasted. And enraged. "Oh, how dare you! What was my crime? Absconding with a Way?"

"I had to find you, I couldn't wait." Cord drew a deep breath. "I spent the whole night lambasting myself as the world's biggest fool and I showed up at your door promptly at nine."

"That's why I made it a point not to be there," Ashlynne retorted.

Cord was undeterred by her coldness. "First I stopped by Thorpe's office to clean out your desk. He permitted me to take Maxie's and Daisy's school pictures, a couple of drawings in popsicle-stick frames, and a coffee mug. He claimed everything else was his."

Ashlynne nodded, feigning indifference.

"He proceeded to try to goad me by repeating yesterday's allegations."

"Which you believed." She couldn't even feign indifference about that.

"I didn't, not really. That is, I realized that it didn't matter to me if it happened or not. All I care about is being with you. Taking care of you and the children." He put his hands on her shoulders and gazed down at her. "Please let me have another chance with you, Ashlynne."

"You're asking me?" Ashlynne said shakily. "Not telling me, not ordering me?"

"I'm begging you, Ashlynne."

Maxie and Daisy raced up to them, jumping up and down with excitement. "Can we ride the cars again?"

"You sure can." Cord was quick to agree. "Here are some more tickets."

Daisy and Maxie squealed with joy and scurried back to the race cars. Cord took the balloons from Ashlynne's nerveless fingers and tied them to the metal fence.

"While the kids ride, I can plead my case with their mother. An ingenious ploy, hmm?" He cupped her chin with his fingers. "Will you at least listen to me, Ashlynne?"

His touch made her quiver. "This humble-penitent routine is a new one for you."

"Ashlynne, I know what Thorpe did to you. This morning at the office, I was taunting him about Holly and he just lost it. She really is his Achilles' heel. He was so agitated he ended up blurting out how he'd taken you to his place and locked you in his bedroom."

"Which I escaped from," Ashlynne said quickly. She hated herself in the role of hapless victim. She did not mention the karate chop and was quite certain that Ethan hadn't either. It seemed too ugly, too vile even to think about amidst the normality and innocence of bright lights and carnival sounds and laughing children. Maybe some other time she would tell Cord the whole story, but not now.

"Ashlynne, sweetheart, I am so sorry—"

"—for believing I jumped into bed with Ethan?" Some devil imp seized her. The urge to bait him was irresistible. "Yesterday you seemed almost glad. You pointed out the advantages of the two of us being on an even footing."

He stared at her thoughtfully. "I was going to say I'm sorry for not being there when you needed me. For not being around to protect you."

"I can take care of myself," she assured him.

"I know. That doesn't stop me from needing you to need me, at least a little. And that bumbling 'even footing' remark . . . I just meant that I was in no position to cast any stones, Ashlynne. Your sister had my child! I guess I realized at that moment how much I was asking you to forgive. I wanted you to know that nothing could change my feelings for you."

Ashlynne's heart was beginning to race and she tried to tamp down the excitement and the hope that was already churning inside her. She'd been disappointed too often to allow herself the luxury of too much optimism.

"I'm not quite sure what your feelings for me are." Ashlynne was cautious. "You've never actually said."

"The lead-in I've been praying for!" Cord grinned broadly. He cupped her face with his hands and said the words he'd been practicing for hours. "I love you, Ashlynne."

Exhilaration spun through her as she gazed into his dark, dark eyes. "You love me?" she echoed softly, wanting to hear it again. Needing to hear it.

"I love you, I love you, I love you." It was so easy, he wondered why it had taken him so long to say it.

"Oh, Cord, I love you too!" She launched herself into his arms right there in front of the junior race cars.

They hugged each other, laughing at their surroundings and their ridiculous sense of timing, laughing with joy and love and the sheer happiness of being alive and together at last.

Maxie and Daisy joined them, clamoring for a ride on the junior boats.

Cord handed them tickets and they dashed to the entrance of the ride.

"They're so enthralled with the rides they didn't even notice we were hugging," Ashlynne mused.

"Maybe it seems so natural for us to be together, they didn't feel the need to comment," suggested Cord. "And now." He pulled the engagement ring out of his pocket. "Ashlynne, my love, will you marry me? I'm asking, not ordering," he added, grinning.

"Yes, Cord, I'll marry you." Ashlynne's eyes filled with happy, emotional tears as he slipped the ring on her finger.

"Tonight? We can drive to that place in Virginia where Kendra and Wyatt got married."

"I want to," Ashlynne said softly, "but the kids have their heart set on staying in the motel room tonight. It's their very first time in one."

"Then they will stay there tonight. We'll get married tomorrow."

Ashlynne smiled at him gratefully, lovingly. He understood, he always would. Love surged through her, and she gazed at him, her heart in her eyes.

Cord took her hand, his thumb moving over her palm, stroking in a slow, suggestive rhythm.

"I wish we were alone," Ashlynne whispered breathlessly. "It seems so long since we've been—together." And she wanted him so much. Admitting her love for him and hearing him declare his for her had fueled her passion to an intense level.

"Tomorrow night," Cord promised.

She closed her eyes. It seemed like an eternity to wait.

Less than twenty-four hours later, Mr. and Mrs. Cord Way stood on the small balcony of their hotel room, gazing out at the rainy darkness. A big king-sized bed awaited them inside but they made no move to leave the balcony, enjoying the balmy breeze that occasionally sprayed them with droplets of rain.

"The kids are finally asleep," Cord said, smiling at the memory of the children's excitement.

"They were so wound up, I thought they'd be up all night." Ashlynne leaned back against her husband, resting her head against his chest. His arms were around her and she linked her fingers with his.

"They crashed as soon as their heads hit the pillow."

Maxie and Daisy had been the flower girls at the hasty little wedding, wearing brand-new dresses purchased that day at the mall connected to the hotel, and carrying small nosegays of flowers. Kendra and Wyatt had insisted on driving up to join them and relive the memories of their own marriage a few days before.

Now the children were in the adjoining bedroom of the suite, Kendra and Wyatt had their own suite on another floor, and Cord and Ashlynne were finally, blissfully alone.

"I thought it was a wonderful wedding," Ashlynne murmured happily.

"I'm glad Kendra and Wyatt were here with us. And the news they brought was more than a little interesting."

"It was amazing!" Ashlynne laughed. "Holly has decided to run for Congress and is in the process of getting herself appointed the party's candidate. And Cindy Clarkston has already approached her, offering to head up an area women's coalition to support Holly's candidacy."

"Politics makes strange bedfellows, so the saying goes. But in this case, I think it's a mutual grudge against Ethan Thorpe that's united Holly and Cindy. Unfortunately, this candidacy keeps Holly in Thorpe's orbit. Or vice versa." He shrugged. "Maybe that's the whole point. I'm thankful we'll be in Montana and far away from whatever war they're waging against each other."

"We'll be in Montana and Kendra and Wyatt are moving to New York." Ashlynne swallowed the sudden lump that rose in her throat. "I'm going to miss her so much, but I know Kendra has always wanted to go there. I remember her talking about how she'd like to take acting lessons. Of course that was when she was younger. She hasn't mentioned it in a long time."

"Whatever Kendra wants to do or be, Wyatt will help her achieve it. And she broke him out of the dull, colorless life he'd been trapped in. Surprisingly enough, those two are good for each other."

"Like we're good for each other." With one lithe movement, Ashlynne turned in his arms and slid her arms around her neck. "In and out of bed."

"We certainly are." Cord gazed down at her, his dark eyes amorous. "We proved how good we are *out* of bed yesterday and today by putting the kids first. Now it's time to put ourselves first and prove how good we are *in* bed."

Ashlynne felt him pulsing against her, hot and hard and fully aroused. He was the most exciting man she'd ever met and the kindest, most generous one too. He was her husband. The impossible had happened—she had actually married Cord Way.

The fire kindling in her belly streaked upward, spreading the sensual heat to her breasts, and lower to the warm softness between her thighs.

"I want to make love to you, Ashlynne," Cord murmured against her ear. He picked her up and carried her inside to the big bed.

"Yes." Ashlynne closed her eyes as a stunning wave of love and desire and need swept through her.

They quickly shed their clothes and tumbled onto the bed, laughing and breathless at their incredible urgency.

"I love you, Cord," Ashlynne told him, exulting in the words.

"I've been looking for you my whole life, Ashlynne. Waiting for you, and I never even knew it. You're the only woman I've ever loved, the only one I will ever love."

"I'm going to hold you to that," she promised, taking him into her.

He was full and strong and unyielding, and she instinctively drew him deeper, as they moved together, joined intrinsically, passion weaving a timeless spell around them.

Again and again during the night, they reached for each other, until finally exhausted and almost insensate with bliss, they fell into a deep sleep.

"Are you still sleeping in there?" Maxie's voice penetrated the stillness like a gunshot. "Wake up!"

Cord sat up in bed and glanced at the locked door separating the children's bedroom from this one. Ashlynne was still sound asleep and he touched his fingers to his mouth, then placed the proxy kiss on her lips.

He scrambled for a robe and quickly opened the door. Maxie and Daisy stood there, grinning.

"Hi, Daddy." Maxie giggled.

"Hi, Daddy," Daisy said, a little shyly.

"We're hungry," Maxie told him.

He glanced at the clock on the bedside stand. "It's practically seven o'clock," he said dryly. "No wonder you're hungry." Despite his lack of sleep, despite the early hour, he felt fantastic. Considering he'd spent the night making love to his wife, no wonder he felt fantastic.

Smiling, Cord herded the two little girls into their room and closed the connecting door.

"Let's let Mommy sleep in this morning," he suggested. "We can watch cartoons in here while we eat breakfast."

Daisy looked around the hotel room. "There is no food here," she said patiently.

Cord grinned. He knew that tone; she used it when she was explaining something to Maxie.

"But there is a telephone. We'll call the kitchen and order whatever we want. It's called room service. We have it at our lodge in Montana too. I don't think it'll take you two long to get the hang of it."

"Daddy, it doesn't take us long to get the hang of anything," Daisy said, suddenly flinging her arms around him in an impulsive hug.

Cord scooped her up in his arms and held her tight. His dark eyes, so like hers, grew misty. Daisy was his child, his own little girl. And she was the catalyst who'd brought him together with Ashlynne. He loved her all the more for that.

"Daddy, Daddy, pick me up too!" demanded Maxie.

Cord was glad to oblige. He planted a quick kiss on each child's cheek. "I'm a lucky guy to have two such beautiful daughters."

"Yes," Daisy agreed.

"And you're going to be even luckier when we get our kittens," Maxie promised.

Cord laughed. "Daughters, cats, and the woman I love. Who could ask for anything more?"

Epilogue

Two years later

MATTHEW Michael Way, nearly twenty-four hours old, gazed intently at his mother's face as Ashlynne cuddled him in her arms. He had a shock of black hair and big dark eyes that almost matched the color of his hair. Daisy's eyes, Cord's eyes. Matthew looked so much like Daisy as an infant; he was as adorable and alert as she had been. Ashlynne's heart swelled with love for him. It was hard to believe that this time yesterday, he'd still been inside her, that she had yet to see his face. Now, smiling down at him, she couldn't fathom not knowing him.

Cord arrived shortly afterward with an armful of magazines and the day's mail. He sat down on the edge of the bed and kissed Ashlynne with lingering tenderness, holding both her and the baby in his arms.

Matthew began to fuss and Ashlynne handed him to Cord. "I think he'd like to walk around with Daddy for a while."

Cord dutifully paced the floor of the room and the motion soothed little Matthew into silence.

"He's so tiny," Cord marveled, gazing raptly at the baby's face. He laid his finger in Matthew's palm and the infant grasped it and held on tight. "What a grip he has! This is a very strong boy, Ashlynne."

Ashlynne watched, enjoying the sight of the father and son bonding.

"Maxie and Daisy miss you terribly and can't wait for you and the baby to come home tomorrow," Cord told her. "They've been talking about their new brother nonstop to the neighbors, their teachers, and their friends. Everybody knows about Matt. They've even talked him up to the cats, who were singularly uninterested."

They both laughed. Ashlynne glanced down at the magazines he'd brought her and her eyes widened. There were four different soap-opera magazines and Kendra was on the covers of three of them. All featured articles on "daytime's hottest young star" and the four articles were quick to point out that "beautiful Kendra Way is nothing like the character she plays, a conniving holy terror who wreaks havoc in the lives of the citizens of her fictional town."

"Kendra, a soap star." Ashlynne stared at the pictures of her little sister. The young woman smiled back at her, a striking beauty projecting both innocence and guile, sophistication and sweetness. "I still can't believe she landed that role on her first audition, after only a few acting classes. The magazine quotes the show's executive producer as saying 'Kendra is a natural-born actress.' Who'd have imagined it?"

Cord smiled. "Oh, I can think of a few."

"Here are some pictures of Kendra and Wyatt in their apartment." Ashlynne showed Cord the color layout. "The article says that 'Kendra remains incredibly centered despite her meteoric rise to daytime stardom and credits her husband, activist attorney Wyatt Way, for providing her with a secure and stable base.' "

"Wyatt as an activist attorney is more surprising to me than Kendra as a TV vixen. I remember how painful it was for him to give a speech. Not anymore." Cord sat back down on the bed with Matthew, who was beginning to doze. "There is a letter from Mother with some newspaper clippings. I think you'll find them . . . *interesting*."

When he used that droll inflection, Ashlynne knew that the clippings would be interesting, indeed. She quickly fished them out of the envelope. There was a long interview in *The Waysboro Weekly* with Congresswoman Holly Way, who'd been in town for a meeting with the local chapter members of 9 to 5, a working women's political-action group. Cindy Clarkston, a realtor who'd recently opened her own agency, headed the group, which pledged support for Holly in her bid for reelection.

"Dan or little Scotty or baby Tiffany aren't mentioned,"

Ashlynne remarked. "I sure hope Dan isn't still in the basement with his guitar."

Cord sung a few bars of "If Dan Had a Hammer," and they both grinned.

"Read the end of the article," he urged.

Ashlynne's eyes jumped to the last paragraph, where the reporter asked Holly about the rumors of Ethan Thorpe's alleged six-figure donation to her reelection campaign. It seemed an unusual move considering her outspoken opposition to his pet project, a discount strip mall by the Seneca Creek River. Holly's reply? A cool "no comment."

"Unbelievable, isn't it?" Cord shook his head. "Now Thorpe is trying to get Holly reelected! I hope she threw the check back in his face."

"Whether she did or not, I'm sure Ethan's busy plotting his next move." Ashlynne thought of her ex-boss and grimaced. "I'm just glad we aren't there to get caught their crossfire." She smiled, reaching up to stroke Cord's hard, tanned cheek. "I'm just glad I'm here with you," she added softly.

"I was thinking exactly the same thing." Cord pulled her gently into his arms, settling their baby between them.

FREE
Romance
(a $4.50 value)

Send in the Coupon Below

To get your FREE historical romance and start saving, fill out the coupon below and mail it today. As soon as we receive it we'll send you your FREE Book along with your first month's selections.